I0763152

# A CRUISE TO DIE FOR

## Also by *New York Times* bestselling author Heather Graham

*THE SWORD OF LIGHT*
*THE MURDER MACHINE*

### The Blackbird Files

*LEGACY OF BLOOD*
*MARKET FOR MURDER*
*DEATH BEHIND EVERY DOOR*

### The Blackbird Trilogy

*CURSED AT DAWN*
*SECRETS IN THE DARK*
*WHISPERS AT DUSK*
*THE REAPER FOLLOWS*
*SHADOW OF DEATH*
*CRIMSON SUMMER*
*DANGER IN NUMBERS*

### New York Confidential

*THE FINAL DECEPTION*
*A LETHAL LEGACY*
*A DANGEROUS GAME*
*A PERFECT OBSESSION*
*FLAWLESS*

### Krewe of Hunters

*THE UNKNOWN*
*THE FORBIDDEN*
*THE UNFORGIVEN*
*DREAMING DEATH*
*DEADLY TOUCH*
*SEEING DARKNESS*
*THE STALKING*
*THE SEEKERS*
*THE SUMMONING*
*ECHOES OF EVIL*
*PALE AS DEATH*
*FADE TO BLACK*
*WICKED DEEDS*
*DARK RITES*
*DYING BREATH*
*DARKEST JOURNEY*
*DEADLY FATE*
*HAUNTED DESTINY*
*THE HIDDEN*
*THE FORGOTTEN*
*THE SILENCED*
*THE BETRAYED*
*THE HEXED*
*THE CURSED*
*THE NIGHT IS FOREVER*
*THE NIGHT IS ALIVE*
*THE NIGHT IS WATCHING*
*THE UNINVITED*
*THE UNSPOKEN*
*THE UNHOLY*
*THE UNSEEN*
*THE EVIL INSIDE*
*SACRED EVIL*
*HEART OF EVIL*
*PHANTOM EVIL*

### Cafferty & Quinn

*THE DEAD PLAY ON*
*WAKING THE DEAD*
*LET THE DEAD SLEEP*

### Harrison Investigations

*NIGHTWALKER*
*THE SÉANCE*
*THE PRESENCE*
*UNHALLOWED GROUND*
*THE DEATH DEALER*
*THE DEAD ROOM*
*THE VISION*
*GHOST WALK*
*HAUNTED*

### Bone Island

*GHOST MOON*
*GHOST NIGHT*
*GHOST SHADOW*

### The Flynn Brothers

*DEADLY GIFT*
*DEADLY HARVEST*
*DEADLY NIGHT*

Look for Heather Graham's next novel
available from MIRA October 2026!

# HEATHER GRAHAM

MIRA

MIRA™

Recycling programs for this product may not exist in your area.

ISBN-13: 978-0-7783-0580-4
ISBN-13: 978-0-7783-0616-0 (Large Print Edition)

A Cruise to Die For



MIRA
22 Adelaide St. West, 41st Floor
Toronto, Ontario M5H 4E3, Canada
MIRABooks.com

HarperCollins Publishers
Macken House, 39/40 Mayor Street Upper,
Dublin 1, D01 C9W8, Ireland
www.HarperCollins.com

Printed in U.S.A.
26 27 28 29 30 LBC 6 5 4 3 2

For Tina Owen,
Megan Owen, and Carol Marchese, with so many, many thanks for so many things!

And for Marisa Young,
with deepest thanks for the empathy and generosity within her spirit!

# PROLOGUE

*Now*

SHE COULD SEE everything that was happening.

She could hear every little bit of noise around her.

She could smell day-old food, the chemicals in the air-conditioning and almost taste every little nuance in the air.

She could even feel the floor beneath her.

Her senses were vibrantly alive.

What she couldn't do was *move.*

She didn't know if she did or didn't blink; she could only feel the heaviness of her own body, as if she was frozen in space and time.

But she knew everything that was going on, she could see the horror of what was happening around her.

Her only option was to watch.

Watch and wait.

Because now, the horror that had claimed others, the terror that haunted those on the ship, would eventually come to her.

All she could do was hope, pray and believe that she and Wesley had followed the right steps . . .

And that there just might be a miracle.

Step by step. Her mind was active; she had to think back, back to the very beginning and determine just how she had gotten to be where she was . . .

And how the hell was she going to get out of the situation.

She couldn't even open her mouth to scream . . .

*Or could she?*

# ONE

"FROM EVERY ANGLE, we're extremely concerned. But we're hoping that what we have is a lead. Something is going on, and we believe that your investigation on this ship can fathom what it is and perhaps, even more importantly, *why*. Dead people. Suicide. Murder and suicide. Ridiculous and extreme coincidences? No. Two cars at an intersection at the same time may be a coincidence. But things happening like this? No. It's gone too far. So, what is happening? Simple greed, and a perpetrator with a personal agenda? Or something far worse? We don't know. And we're hoping to God that the two of you can sneak in and find out. All we do know is that every victim of this rash of suicides and murder-suicides has been associated with computers and IT in a big way."

Chloe McMurray stood quietly, listening as Assistant Director Alonzo spoke.

She wasn't sure what she was doing there since Alonzo was federal and she was an agent with *state* law enforcement—and she'd received the message to pack for a cruise ship.

A cruise ship?

On the surface, it didn't sound like a bad gig!

But she was savvy when it came to cruise ships out of the Port of Miami; they usually sailed to other countries, ports in the Caribbean, perhaps Mexico and perhaps even South America. Maybe they were just heading a wee bit to the north and east, for the Bahamas, Bermuda—still foreign countries—or maybe Puerto Rico, an American territory?

So, why was she, an agent of the state, involved? And why had she been asked to subtly change her appearance, cut her chestnut hair and dye it black?

She was going undercover, of course. And she had so much more to learn about the case. Chloe was just beginning to understand how much was known and suspected—and just how much wasn't known. What about pictures? Everyone posted everything these days and she might be recognized by someone on social media, even at a distance, if she didn't shake up her looks a little.

Well, *she* might be local, but apparently, she was being joined by a federal agent who was with Central and South American bureau "legat" offices. He had a strangely *appropriate* name for his vocation in law enforcement—that being Wesley *Law.*

He wasn't any kind of gigantic bruiser, but decent and probably very well trained. The man was tall enough—six-two or three, she estimated—and yes, with what appeared to be a lean, wiry strength.

Having come into the federal office straight from work himself, she found him strangely dressed on a workday. He was wearing jeans and a T-shirt and a light blue windbreaker. His hair, a dirty blond or light brown, was barely brushed.

Then again, apparently, she was the one off-base in her pantsuit; they had said *cruise.* Well, she had enough in her go-bag for a cruise. Shorts, halter dresses, T-shirts. She just wished she had a slightly better bathing suit, but that could probably be obtained on the ship. She did love sitting high above the water at the pool of a cruise ship. Generally, she loved cruising.

But she would be "cruising" with a strange federal operative—on an even stranger case.

Coming here, she'd been given the briefest information from her own supervising agent, but she still knew so little. She had been told she'd been specifically requested for the case by the upper echelons at the federal and local level because of her knowledge of and affiliation with cruise ships in general. She'd done her own research on her would-be partner as well—he had been born with the surname and his ancestors went all the way back to the Revolutionary War. And as was often enough the case with those who entered into law enforcement, his father had been a cop.

She didn't know much more because many of the cases he had worked on were classified as confidential.

And so . . .

There they were, she and the man she had just met in person, in Assistant Director Glen Alonzo's office in Miami, learning about the strange and convoluted case they'd be working on.

Despite Alonzo's ramblings, she knew that at the heart of his words was the genuine belief that they were being tasked with something deeply important.

It was strange. Was it even really a case? Yes, in the minds of those above their pay grades, there was definitely a case, or they wouldn't be there. From what she was learning, when things that were *that strange* happened, something was going on.

And it all had to do with computer systems, the internet,

gaming and, of course, AI. But the world grew savvier day by day when it came to such tech, so if someone was trying to eliminate every brilliant techie they had a long, long way to go.

"The ever-human hunt for more and more," Alonzo said. "Greed. Power. I'm not seeing any kind of personal vendetta. I'm assuming, as our best minds seem to believe, that people are dying because of what they do, not who they are. But, when you put all the puzzle pieces together, they've all attended the same meetings, workshops or conventions around the country at one time or another."

"They might have met," Wesley said. "But from what I'm hearing so far, I agree with our *best minds*. This sounds like a power play—since it is unlikely that this kind of situation could simply occur in what appears to be exactly the same way in different places."

"There have been many ways to look at this. While there seems to be a consensus on a course of action, an opportunity to infiltrate the community, we certainly can't guarantee that we know what is going on. The first few episodes initially went unnoticed because they occurred in different jurisdictions—in three different states—and then we were notified by a survivor who read about another death, got frustrated at the local level, and asked us to come in, and thus our current involvement as part of a task force with many agencies involved. As we started piecing the events together, we noticed that there appeared to be a pattern in which people had suddenly started committing suicide or killing others before killing themselves. While it escaped national attention at first, it beats the odds of chance. Naturally, before I spoke to the two of you and your supervising directors—and the director himself—we did the necessary deep dives and research on those involved. It's crazy. We know why it took a while. When the suicides started, it appeared to be more than *possible* that some of those who died were in a state of depression or had a self-perceived reason, but . . ."

Assistant Director Glen Alonzo stared at Chloe and Wesley, shaking his head.

"Am I making any sense yet?" Alonzo asked.

"Of course. Sadly," Chloe said, "people do commit suicide. And I understand with the crime scenes they found, local law enforcement assumed that to be the case."

"Well, we're not sending you out blind—you've a few hours here to read everything that we've got. You must be on the ship by four thirty. It's just noon now," he added.

"Um, sir, pardon me," Chloe said. "I'm still a little blind. I don't know what cruise we're going on and why you're convinced that going on a cruise can help solve—"

He smiled at that. "And you're right to be curious, eh? Once you've studied the situation, I hope you'll understand—and that our suspicions are on the money. Though, honestly, in my younger days, I'd have jumped at the opportunity to visit a cruise ship instead of the back alley behind a crack den. And we've all had a few of those."

She smiled. "Trust me, sir, I've nothing against cruises—" Chloe began.

"Of course not!" Alonzo said. He managed to smile. "Special Agent McMurray, I've naturally read your service files frontward and backward. We're well aware you and your last partner, Agent Rodriguez, played it all out and captured the boatyard killer. You know this state and you know this city. You've also been on cruise ships since you were a kid."

The man who would be her partner on the upcoming voyage was studying her.

Had he investigated her background, as well? Of course. Who wouldn't have done so? When you were suddenly thrown on a case you knew nothing about with a partner who wasn't even from the same agency, you did your homework.

"Nothing against a cruise," she repeated.

"All right, then. We'll start with the bad," Alonzo said. He pointed across his desk to the large video screen in his office and hit keys on his computer, indicating to them that they needed to take the seats in front of his desk and watch.

They did so.

And Alonzo began, tapping keys on his computer to change the images onscreen as he spoke.

"Jesup, Georgia. Frank Adams, forty, husband and father, technician for Adler Displays. They claim to make the best screens for everything: movies, gaming, you name it. His wife found him with a shotgun between his knees and still in his mouth. No note. But the gun was between his knees. At first accepted as a suicide, case closed. A month later, Cassandra Little and her husband, Hank. Hank was shot dead. Cassandra was found with the Smith and Wesson that killed him—and her—in her hands. They were in Palatka, Florida. An obvious murder-suicide. Oh, they both worked for Brandon Solutions, another tech company, one that's huge in cybersecurity. Third instance. Randy Templeton, Montgomery, Alabama, found in his bathtub, electrocuted, his electric shaver in the water with him. He worked for the local city government, online data. No note, but neighbors heard him and his wife argue frequently, so they thought that his wife had threatened to walk out and his depression had caught up with him. The wife, Myra Templeton, denied she'd ever said that she was leaving. She said they had fought, yes. All married couples did. She didn't accept his death as a suicide. But the police became suspicious, through their friendly neighbors, that she might look to be as sweet as candy but have evil inside. Their suspicion—no solid clues, no proof—was that she had murdered him. Not possible. She can be seen on a security video all day at a symposium on mental health. The woman is a therapist. Now she's the first who came to the Feds when the local police ignored her—and suspected her. She'd found references to the other events in the news. Then we have what happened in Broward County last week. A meeting of enlisted personnel and civilians who worked for the military, a party of six. Five were shot and killed and, you guessed it—as I'm sure you already saw in the news—the sixth person, a young woman named Jane Sewell, was found with her gun—a six-shooter—in her mouth. All planned out so well! And every shot straight through the heart. Was she ever in the military? No, she was a civilian working with the others. Motive? Jealous of those higher up, or was she maybe a home-grown terrorist? Her parents denied it fervently, came to us, too, and we were ready since we'd already started looking into the other odd deaths. Now, we're pulling legal strategies and exhuming corpses, trying to determine if something had been missed in the autopsies on the deceased that might help us. As you are aware, only certain drugs are tested in such victims in a customary autopsy. Oh, yeah, one more interesting fact, the weapons involved were tested for fingerprints. None whatsoever were there except for those of the person left with the weapon. Our firearms experts say that—especially since a few of the prints appear to be backward—that the condition they were discovered in is, once again, more than 'questionable.'"

"I can easily see why these are suspicious occurrences, and yes, it does appear that there is, beyond a doubt, something going on. Though on what level, who knows at this point," Wesley Law said, speaking up. "But these were all on land," Wesley said, "So—"

"Milestones," Alonzo told them.

"Milestones?" Chloe murmured.

"Oh, come on. I know you're *field* agents, but you do know how to use computers! Milestones is a huge corporation. The company is the next massive step in user-friendly computing and in computers doing just about everything for you, including—according to one ad—brushing your teeth. At any rate, the company is having an employee gratitude trip to celebrate their tenth anniversary on the ship *Silver and Sapphire Seas*, the newest luxury offering from Surf of the Seven Seas."

"That's the company that has luxury restaurants in every state—all offering several different surf and turf options, right?" Wesley asked. "In the cruise business, they're young, only being around about a decade or so."

Alonzo smiled. "That is true. And if nothing else, you'll eat well."

"So, you believe this killer is specifically after those who are exceptionally talented with computing, or those who—"

"Those who have the money or the management skills to keep the right people working, yes," Alonzo said. "And why this ship, you ask? It's not just the fact that it will be hosting so many computer nerds, but then there was this."

He clicked a key on the computer.

On the screen, they saw two of the bodies from the multi-death incident again, more closely pictured than they had been before.

Near one was a briefcase.

And sticking out of the briefcase was a folder.

Chloe couldn't see the entire folder, but she could see enough.

It advertised the free computer sessions that would be held onboard, offering classes to other passengers for those who were newbies to more experienced nerds.

Proof. Proof was what they needed.

*How many people were supposed to die in this—and yes, the big question, why?*

"The conference room is empty. You may take your computers and read everything we have in the police reports, from witnesses and from Myra Templeton—we have her on video when she first came into the local field office. You have a couple of hours. There's a blue sedan out there for you to take to the cruise port—no official drop-offs or the like. You're on the cruise as Chloe and Wesley Douglas. You're on vacation from your specialized tutoring jobs in NYC—the bigger the city, the harder for anyone to discover you're not who you say you are."

"And two hours to remember our names and our histories," Wesley said.

"Sorry, this all came up quickly," Alonzo said. "And you'll be given ghost guns, no metal so that they'll pass through any metal-detecting security, though there are bureau members and offices where your purpose is known—as *you* know, Wes, there are sixty-two legal attaché offices around the world with another thirty-six sub offices. There are those in each port that you can contact, numbers are in your burner phones under assumed names, but the names won't matter—emergency only. Got it? Go study your identities—as always, info was kept as close to what's real so that you're natural in any conversation—and study up on what you're looking for."

*Study up?*

People were dead. They were all involved in computer and internet expertise in one way or another.

*But they had all been staged to look like suicide or murder-suicide.*

Chloe looked at her new partner whom she'd just met, Wesley Law. He looked at her in turn, grimacing and arching a brow in question.

She nodded. "Oh, hell. We should go study up."

"Well, once we know about ourselves and what has been discovered regarding the victims, we should be fine. I know how to make contact if needed, though it's easy. Then I'll follow you. You'll know what we should and shouldn't do as just folks out on a cruise having a good time, where we should hang out. You are the cruise expert," he reminded her.

She wasn't sure why she needed to defend the fact that she was as familiar as she was with cruising—she just did.

"I grew up here—there were always specials out of Miami or Fort Lauderdale. My parents loved the water, my dad was once a navy SEAL. He loved any place where one could go diving and he made sure that his kids could swim—in Florida there's water everywhere."

"And alligators."

"Yeah, well, he taught us not to swim in canals and to always watch out—waterways connect, and the creatures can run faster than most humans, too. But I don't think that the abilities of alligators are going to be our problem. The *creatures* we're looking for will be of the human variety. But! Cruises offer cool cities, history—and lots of great dives and snorkel trips—though whether we'll be following anyone suspicious around such places or events remains to be seen, I imagine. Then again," she said, and paused, looking at Alonzo, "I still don't even know where we're going. I've never been on this ship."

"Go find out about your ports of call—but don't forget that you're pleased as can be you've chosen a cruise with computer classes," Alonzo said, indicating that they should go to work with the few hours they had to get up to speed on the case.

As they headed out of Alonzo's office and into their workroom, Wesley murmured, "So, we're undercover but almost as ourselves. I've closed a number of cases as different people, but it's been a while now since I've worked undercover. I looked you up—I know you've done a lot of really good work."

She smiled. "Only undercover once, so I'll be in charge of cruising—and you can help me out with the undercover."

"Keep it easy and natural, and—"

"And just remember my background," Chloe finished. "I worked with our local experts, some who went under for a few years! Of course, we need to study all the events Alonzo has just told us about. The people—"

"Yeah, honestly, I wish we had been part of this investigation from the start, but it is what it is. You do know you're free to refuse this kind of case, right?" he asked her.

She nodded. "Doesn't do much for your career."

"Now, that's true, if you're worried that it may not do much for your life."

She shrugged. "I have been in a few back alleys that might not have done much for my chances of a life. It's just that . . ."

"On board the ship, backup isn't a few minutes away." He paused and looked away for a moment.

"You've been in a situation where a few minutes was a few too many?" she asked softly.

"We all have, right? That's the name of the game. Anyway, I promise, we will discuss every move we make, and one of us is never that many steps from the other."

"Gotcha."

"So, study time!"

They sat on opposite sides of the desk in the room, heads down at their separate computers.

"Three states, but border states," Chloe murmured, looking over her screen at Wesley. "And now, a major case, supposedly murder-suicide. Back in Florida, Broward County. Six dead including Jane Sewell, who supposedly killed the others and then herself. Perfect shots on a roomful of people!"

He nodded. "All related to computers, new technology—and big money."

"I don't see any problem at all associating these events—but besides what they all did, what could connect them when they're spread out like that?"

"The tech departments have been making deep dives into company records and victims' social media—they should be sending us everything they've discovered within the hour. Maybe we use the time until then to work on ourselves," Wesley suggested.

"Oh, yes, right!"

She switched screens, seeking her own new biography.

"Well, hm. I am from Florida, Broward County, instead of Miami-Dade, but no surprise that I might have gone to the University of Miami. Background Norwegian on my mom's side, confused Northern European on my dad's. And now . . ."

"Now, my dear, darling wife, you've just opened your own business, promoting artists and their work, and you desperately need to improve your computer skills," Wesley said.

"That's not a stretch at all!" she told him. "And you, my darling, just what is it that you do for a living?"

"Mine is cooler," he told her.

"Cooler than art?" she demanded.

He shrugged, grinning. "I have a dive boat. I take people out to the reefs off Islamorada, where, of course, we're living these days. You are familiar, I take it?" he asked.

She grinned. "Oh, yeah. Speaking of cool, I used to love to go to Tavernier and head out on Captain Slate's Creature Feature."

He nodded. "Diving down, having nurse sharks blowing bubbles with you atop your head, stroking rays as they swim by . . . Yeah, cool."

"So, you've done that, too?" she asked.

"Came from the opposite end. I'm one of those kids who grew up in Key West."

"Wait, of course, I know that!" she told him. "Your father was a cop! A cop in Key West!"

Wesley nodded. "Yep. And let's see, hm. I do my own research, too, when I'm being assigned a strange case with a . . . stranger. Your mom taught at Nova. Your dad had been career military, retired, but took on a job with a security company and received a special commendation from the company and the country when he foiled a bank robbery."

"He was a great guy," she said softly.

"I believe you," he assured her.

"Wow," she said dryly. "In real life, we're almost stereotypes."

He laughed. "Worse things to be. Anyway, fake life . . ."

"Fake life, as you said, similar. Great idea, because you don't mess up as much in any casual conversation."

Wes nodded. "Second honeymoon. We've been married for three years, but both got so involved with our careers that we haven't spent enough time together. We thought about an Alaskan cruise, but like the sun too much. Oh, and our families are all over the country, so it wasn't like we could visit folks in one shot, and we needed together time more than anything else, so . . ."

"So, here we are. Diving—even though we spend our *real* lives diving."

"Ah, but we're excited to be on the cruise. We're diving different places for fun and for me especially, a true escape. I'm not responsible for the health and safety of others on this trip! It's just exploring the wonders of the sea with my beloved who is usually too busy babysitting insecure artists to really enjoy the water with me."

He was grinning at her. The guy seemed to be okay.

Great. She could get along with him. And pray, of course, that he really did live up to his reputation and would have her back.

He frowned suddenly, staring down at his screen.

"*Succinylcholine*," he murmured.

"What?"

A total change in the conversation.

He looked at her. "We just got some info on a few of the follow-up autopsies. They dug up the dead and did more detailed tests. And our cases are beyond a doubt related—the victims were dosed with a paralytic before death, succinylcholine, not something generally sought and discovered in the usual autopsy of a shooting victim unless such a factor had been indicated. Also, by the time a person's remains get to an autopsy, it's had a chance to dissipate. But apparently, they are finding trace amounts."

"That would explain the perfection of the shots on that many people. Straight through the heart, which typically doesn't happen unless your victims are nonmoving targets. So, they are drugged with a substance that leaves them awake but paralyzes them. How are they getting it into the victims?" Chloe asked.

He shook his head. "No answers on that yet. But, hey, we're putting together a nice sheet on people who were related business-wise to the victims, a few very wealthy, a few not so wealthy . . . Your sheet is up! Read, see what you think. Also, they followed the movements of these people over the last year in which all of this has occurred. They all attended special meetings or conferences which put them in the same general area as those who died."

She studied her computer. They'd been sent a list of six names, plucked from the many by a combination of factors such as possible resentments or goals and assessments and proximities from a profiling team.

She quickly saw that yes, everyone on the list worked in the computer field in one way or another. Naturally. But closer looks showed that each of the six had been working with—or against—those who were dead. In a few cases, the names of those on the list worked for the same companies.

In some cases, they worked for rival companies.

A few had been a few rungs lower on the corporate ladder.

"Edward Thompson," she murmured.

"Saw it," he said. "A vice president with the hosting symposium, Milestones, a company which among other things is creating a special screen for gamers *and* an affordable system that will also allow for hours upon hours of computing. Edward Thompson makes a nice seven-figure income yearly. But the pressure is surely hard on him at all times."

"Then there's Abigail Swenson," Avery said, looking over at Wesley. "She was under the first man who, hm, *committed suicide*. Frank Adams. He received a promotion that she had been up for, too."

"Her income is not enormous," Wesley noted.

"But better than most these days."

"True. Except in the tech world—" he began to remind her.

"You have the possibility of becoming a multimillionaire."

Wesley nodded. "Next. Broward County last week. A party of six. Five were shot and killed, and as Alonzo told us, the sixth person, a young woman named Jane Sewell, was found with her gun in her mouth. Ballistics matched. Six shots, five through the heart with one remaining so that she could kill herself when she finished with the others."

"And they'll discover that she and the others have traces of the drug in their systems—which explains the perfect shots. Seriously, very few people just stand there when a gun is pointed at them and they've already seen their friends or associates shot," Chloe pointed out. "We knew there was something off about it."

"True. So, Edward Thompson, Abigail Swenson—four more names. Daniel and Broderick McClintock, brothers who started up a company called Bulwark Cybersecurity. Their emphasis is on firewalls and so on that can lock out any malware or any other similar dangers. Interesting . . ."

"What's interesting?" Chloe asked. "In particular?"

"I'm pretty sure I read an article on them. They claim to have tremendous ability in shutting down the dark web—they've reportedly worked for the San Francisco police," he said.

"I don't see that here—"

"Rumor—I had friends working on a trafficking site. I wasn't on the case, but I believe they mentioned the company in their work."

"Why would they have appeared on the suspect list? Surely, at the federal level, this sheet would include—" Chloe started to ask, frowning.

"Keep reading. They did help the San Francisco police—they were exceptional in their ability to trace a site that bounced around twenty different countries."

"They are suspects—for being too helpful?"

He shrugged, looking at her. "Retired Special Agent Matt Greenberg, a specialist who was at the forefront of profiling, apparently wrote in a 'need to know only' memo about them. They were helpful, yes. On that investigation. But Greenberg's memo warned that while helpful, they also needed to watch for godlike tendencies within the pair. By helping, they were also learning how to avoid detection should they move into criminal online activities themselves."

"Wow. I can't begin to imagine being that powerful online!"

Wes shook his head. "I can navigate the usual tasks, but tracing IPs, et cetera, is not in my scope of brilliance. Thankfully—or maybe not—that's why we're field agents with the true brains of it all behind us."

She smiled and nodded. "Last two on this list of six are a married couple. Both employees of something called Amarylis Solutions."

"Money," Wes said, reading. "So, Celia Henderson started the company and quickly enlisted her husband, Jeff. They handle payroll for corporations around the world. Now, why would such a pair want to murder those involved in other aspects of computing?"

"They want more paychecks coming to themselves?"

"What they could embezzle right now is humongous."

"Is that a word?" Chloe asked.

"Sure! Anyway . . ." He frowned, looking at her across the table. "You're getting on a cruise ship like that? I mean, not that you don't look fine! Just . . . you look like a cop."

"Ouch! Okay, I'll change now!" she told him.

He grinned. "My wife can't be better dressed than I am!"

She groaned and stood and headed out to grab her bag from the front office and change. She had planned well enough, just . . . Coming to this meeting, where state and federal agencies were combining, she'd wanted to start off with a more professional look.

Most of the time, it didn't matter if she looked like a "cop." In fact, it could help.

But she chose a short halter dress with a flared skirt, a "fun" outfit, she hoped. She let her hair free and grabbed a light sweater, a "Florida" sweater, enough to take on a breeze—or air-conditioning that could bring a room down to sixty in defiance of the high eighties or nineties outside.

She met him at the door. Alonzo was there, ready to send

them out. Their bags had been repacked with the weapons that could pass through any screening. Alonzo nodded gravely to them, and they headed out in the nondescript car that have been given a fake license plate, as well.

As they headed to the car, Wes stopped and looked at her.

"What?"

"Are you going to be insulted if I drive?" he asked her.

She groaned. "I don't give a damn who drives. I mean, I am making my own assumption. You are a decent driver, right?"

He laughed and slipped into the driver's seat.

And as he drove, she studied their lineup again and spoke aloud.

"Edward Thompson, VP with the hosting company, Milestones. Abigail Swenson, Daniel and Broderick McClintock, brothers, and married couple Celia and Jeff Henderson. And they are all people who know one another already—they've been at the same conferences or meetings, all near the sites of our so-called suicide or murder-suicides. They will all be speaking on the ship."

"And there she is! Time to park our car, darling, and get on board!" Wes said.

The ship was beautiful. They quickly discovered that two decks held pools, one that was adults only, and offered lounges right in the water as well as whirlpools, bars and plenty of friendly waiters.

There were five choices of restaurants for food, and since their cruise was on a luxury yacht, there were less than six-hundred people on board, including crew.

The rear deck offered an exceptionally scenic view of anything that the ship might pass.

"Really beautiful," Wes noted.

They stood on deck with other passengers as the ship left

the port, waving—as others did—and watching the shore shrink behind them as they headed out to sea.

They returned to their cabin.

In truth, Chloe thought dryly, it could have been one hell of an amazing voyage. They'd been given a balcony suite.

A small elegant parlor with a plush sofa and a spacious restroom were just inside from the hallway entry. Through a second doorway, one reached the bedroom, an extremely elegant place with a giant bed, television screen, stereo system, a dressing table and a closet larger than some of the cabins Chloe had enjoyed as a kid, cruising with her folks.

"This is really luxurious. Alonzo has set us up nicely. Maybe too nicely," Wesley said, looking around. "All right, the sofa out here is mine—"

"That's okay. I sleep well on a couch," Chloe told him.

"No, no—"

"Hey, come on, we're both agents! You don't need to play the gentleman around me. I'm your coworker, your—" She broke off, wincing inwardly.

*Equal.* That was the word she'd been about to say. Which indicated, of course, that she assumed him to be a misogynist.

He grinned at her. "I totally respect being *equals*," he assured her. He shrugged. "I just don't need a dressing table."

It was okay. He made her grin. She hadn't been that offensive.

"You're suggesting that I do?" she inquired.

"Whatever," he told her.

"We can switch back and forth," she suggested.

"Whatever!" he repeated. "Right now . . . Well, the main dinner tonight is the captain's welcome. And we're at a reserved table—along with a few of our suspects. Good thing I'm hungry. So, dearest, do you need any repair—"

"You're suggesting I need repair?" she teased.

"Just asking. Hey, come on. *I* don't wear any makeup!"

She laughed and headed along to the tour that was starting soon.

"Darling," she told him, "don't forget all the ads for the excursions we might take! We should definitely discuss those at dinner and find out what our fellow cruisers are doing!"

"Onward."

He paused at their cabin door, looking back into the room.

He shrugged. "Nice. Sure. I can take the bed. You do wake at the drop of a pin, right?"

"Pretty much so. Why?"

"Because if an armed invader arrived, the person on the sofa will be the first to go," he reminded her.

"And you?"

"Oh, you bet. I also wake at the drop of a pin."

She grinned as he locked their cabin door, leaning close to tell him, "I also know how to set a trap for anyone trying to open a door. Much better than counting on our *sleeping senses.* Yours or mine!"

A horn sounded. A voice came over the speaker to announce the lifeboat drills.

"Hey, an important part of cruising—how could I forget!" Chloe murmured.

"Life-saving skills on this cruise could become very important," Wes noted.

"And they may have nothing to do with the sea," she agreed.

# TWO

THE CABIN WAS GREAT.

Wes could truly appreciate their accommodations. He hadn't cruised nearly as much as Chloe, but his parents had longed for vacations, too. However, they'd usually had pretty tiny interior cabins. That hadn't mattered too much. His folks had used what they had on their shore excursions and some of them had been terrific.

Nope.

There was no denying that this would be a great time if . . . if he was only on the ship to have a great time.

But, of course, they weren't.

They'd determined that they'd spend the hour or so before their dinnertime in the cabin once again studying the information they had on their suspects.

It was difficult at times not to wonder if they weren't just chasing their tails. There was no definitive proof that any of the people they were following was guilty. And it was strange.

Brothers? Was one guilty and one not? A married couple? Again, one guilty, one not, or perhaps a conspiracy . . .

To what end?

Chloe emerged onto the balcony. He gave her a sheepish sigh and shook his head. "No answers here," he said.

"Wow. I wasn't exactly expecting any yet. But it's about that time, dinnertime, rise and shine and check out what our tech people have done from hundreds of miles away."

"What's that?"

"We're at the captain's table tonight. Captain Archibald Millbrook, known to his friends as 'Archie.' Apparently, a man respected and loved and experienced in sailing these seas. But, of course, Archie isn't our target."

"Who is at our table?" Wes asked her.

"Celia Henderson and her husband, Jeff. They're running a few of the classes that cruise director and the Milestones people have put together. Also, we have the big man himself, Mr. Edward Thompson."

"Vice president of Milestones and their rep on this cruise, giving lots of speeches, hosting parties along classes," Wes said.

"You should get up," she told him. "We don't want to be late. Hm, hold on. Let me assess this situation. You might want to change!"

"Into what? A gorgon?" he teased.

But yes, *she* had changed again. The halter dress she wore now fell sleekly to the floor; it was a soft velvetlike emerald-green, a color that matched her eyes. And, of course, naturally, the darkness of her hair seemed to emphasize the richness of the color as well.

Okay, so she did appear elegant.

"It's a cruise!" he protested.

"That's right. No stuffy business suit. And come on, it's the captain's dinner!"

"Yeah, yeah, yeah! Give me a minute," he begged.

"A minute! We have our table, but we need to choose the right seats!" she reminded him.

"There won't be any wrong seats," he assured her, heading in from the balcony.

She was probably right about that. They needed to observe everyone on board and their interactions with the tech event onboard.

He had brought a casual amber suit. With the vest, it gave him a bit of a dinner-attire look, and minus a tie, it remained proper for him to be casually elegant.

He stepped out of the suite's large bathroom and pirouetted for Chloe as if he was a model on the runway before pausing and arching a brow.

"You'll do," she told him.

"Wow, careful! Compliments like that will go to my head," he told her.

She just raised her eyebrows and shook her head. "I believe you're well aware that 'you'll do' under just about any circumstances. So, darling, let's head out, shall we?"

Their very nice cabin was on one of the upper decks, just down a hallway to the elegant—or higher priced—dining room. A meal here was extra, but could be part of one of the cruise's executive packages.

Such a package had been bought for them. *Taxpayer dollars at work*, he thought dryly, except that someone in a powerful position had probably spoken with someone else in a powerful position and it was unlikely that they had paid what those traveling for sheer pleasure—or artful murder—had paid.

Chloe slipped her arm through his as they entered the dining room. "Captain's table is up by the stage, and I think that he says a few words tonight," she murmured.

"I see the table," Wes murmured. "And I see the lovely people we're about to get to know!"

The table seated eight, he saw. There was himself and Chloe and the captain. He recognized Celia and Jeff Henderson from their case studies, just as he recognized the Milestones VP, Edward Thompson.

Thompson looked like an executive; he was dressed in a suit and tie, and his dignified air was being aided by the iron-gray hair that was neatly cropped atop his head. He stood as he saw them coming, as did the captain—and the Henderson couple. But even as they walked up and shook hands all around, the last twosome to join them at the table arrived. The first was a handsome young man with a lock of dark hair over his forehead. He had warm brown eyes and what appeared to be an eternal smile. The second was an older man, bald as a buzzard, as the saying went, with bright blue eyes and a smile that matched that of the young to a tee. They quickly learned that the younger man, Billy Cliffton, was one of the current cruise directors while the second man was his grandfather, Elijah, retired from the chain that owned the cruise lines and on board for the fun of it—and to learn more about navigating his computer.

"This is amazing!" Chloe said, wide-eyed and happy as they took their seats. "Wes and I just chose this ship a ways back—second honeymoon. And then we found out that Milestones was celebrating employees—and offering classes for everyone on board!"

"Hey," Captain Millbrook told them, smiling, "I may even be in a few of those classes! Thought it was great fun when I heard about it, too."

"I hope so!" Celia Henderson said. "I'm hoping that I'm a good speaker and I give several people the help they may need." She laughed softly, looking at her husband. "I've already heard from a few people who are looking forward to learning how to safely make use of dating apps!"

"And there's a class in dating?" Wes asked, grinning.

"Well, we're calling it Know your Social Media!" Celia told him.

Wes smiled, studying the woman. He knew she was thirty-eight and that she'd excelled in computing and data research since high school. She might be considered a genius as far as those skills went. She was an attractive woman wearing a mini dress well. She had a quick smile, but . . .

Something about her engaging energy seemed a bit off. And, at her side, her husband seemed much more like a listener, an obeyer, a lackey?

Chloe laughed softly. "Captain Millbrook! So, social media—"

"Please, at this table!" he said quietly, leaning toward her and interrupting her, but doing so politely with a sheepish grin on his face. "Please, call me Archie! Yes, yes, I know! A captain needs dignity. He's above it all! Out on the vast seas, a captain needs to instill confidence in his passengers and crew. But, hey, I'm at sea too much of the time. And my dear wife passed away five years ago now. Everyone wants a little company now and then!"

Chloe gave him a sweet grin in return before assuring him. "Oh, sir! Archie. I'm willing to bet that half the people in those classes would be delighted to give you some company."

"One can hope!" he said. "I'm also aware that there are scams aplenty out there today and that we all need to be careful on the internet."

"And that's where I come in!" Edward Thompson announced, throwing a nod toward Celia and smiling. "Celia gets to be fun and games. I get more serious stuff. But that's why this cruise celebration is so important to us. We should be able to use the internet for fun and games—and be safe on it, as well. The world has turned to business and banking online—we need to do it, too!"

"And my grandson has done an incredible job getting the right combo of fun and games for Milestones—and a true learning experience for the seafarers about this vessel, where they're old codgers like me and need all the help they can get—or those on the rise!" Elijah Cliffton said, nodding toward his grandson, Billy.

Billy moaned softly. "Gramps! Keeping the passengers happy and busy is the job and working with Edward, well, sir, it's been an honor!"

"Honor has been all mine," Edward assured him.

"So!" Celia said, looking from Chloe to Wes. "I'm thinking you two aren't looking for any help with your dating lives!"

Wes grinned, shaking his head. "No, but, hey, knowing how to use any of the apps out there is a good thing. We like to see our families online—"

"And cute dog pictures!" Chloe put in.

"Who doesn't love cute dog pictures?" Wes said. "I'm sure that we all need to know how to use the social media safely. We put pics up of kids, families . . . I think we're looking forward to crashing all kinds of classes. We came on this cruise just to get away together and we had no idea when we planned it what a great trip it was going to be!" he said enthusiastically.

Their waiter was at the table; he'd been patiently waiting for the conversation to take enough of a pause so that he could get their orders. There was already wine on the table, red and white, but he was happy to get them anything else and he gave a great presentation on the dinner options that were offered that evening.

They ordered; salads and bread appeared almost instantly, and polite conversation continued around the table.

It seemed like the nicest group. The captain, in Wes's mind, was the man he claimed he wanted to be. Friendly, approachable and yet knowledgeable regarding any question that was broached to him about the ship.

Edward seemed the perfect VP; again, dignified, but intelligent, eloquent and approachable.

Celia was eager and sweet, and her husband . . .

Well, it seemed that he knew his place.

When dessert and coffee were served, Wes felt that they'd gotten to know the group.

And still knew nothing at all.

But they had just begun. And when they were alone, he'd be eager to hear what Chloe felt they had gained from the meal. If nothing else, he was certain that they had presented themselves as a loving couple, happy to head out for fun, equally happy as a twosome to have discovered all the extras they might have on this cruise.

The captain seemed to be the real deal, a nice man, using his first night's dinner to welcome the Milestones rep who was on board along with one of his major instructors and honorees and her husband, as well as the cruise director and his cruise-retired grandfather. Wes figured that someone had gotten it into the passenger information that they were a power couple and therefore, they'd been included, too.

"So, a dive boat!" Celia said to him. "I guess you're an expert in the water?"

He shrugged. "I'm pretty good."

She laughed. "You use the internet underwater?"

"You would be surprised how intricate using a computer has become on any boat," Wes assured her. "That's why I want to know so much more—I want to make use of all the knowledge that's out there now when I'm conducting a dive tour. I do short trips and overnight tours. I have a nice new boat, and it's rigged to do just about everything, once I really understand what I'm doing."

"Ah! But you seem to be just as excited, Chloe," Edward said. "I'm thrilled, of course, that we'll do more of these if the other passengers are as enthusiastic about them as you seem to be. But . . . you aren't doing AI art, are you?"

Chloe shook her head. "No, art is created in the hearts, souls and minds by talented human beings, and I never want to change that—not in my business, anyway. But I want to promote shows and people, the incredible artists I want to get out there! I mean, from little things like calendars to amazing pieces for people's walls!"

"Well, hopefully, we'll fulfill all your needs!" Edward said. "Celia's class might prove to be helpful." He winked at her. "Even though you don't need to worry about security on any dating apps!"

"Dating and security, so sad!" the captain said. He groaned softly and excused himself, welcoming them all on the cruise again, but telling them it was time to get back to the bridge.

They all bid him good-night, and then, of course, everyone at the table began to break away, Elijah Cliffton informing them that he was a wee bit past the age when a night getting wild sounded more inviting than the comfort of one's bed. Billy groaned softly, but said, "I'll walk you to your cabin, Gramps. I've got an early morning—we're a day at sea with dozens of activities going on!"

Edward said good-night and Celia hurriedly rose followed by her husband, Jeff, who apologized, as well.

"Classes tomorrow!" Celia said.

"We'll split up so we can cover a bunch!" Chloe assured her. "And thank you, thank you for doing all this!"

"Of course!" Celia said.

"Milestones paid for us—that worked!" Jeff whispered.

Celia groaned, Wes and Chloe laughed, rising to leave the dining room themselves.

"I guess we should be glad this is considered a luxury line and that there are only about six hundred or so crew and passengers," Chloe murmured dryly, sliding ahead of Wes to start out of the dining room.

At her side, he softly replied, "Just six-hundred-something! We should figure this out in no time. Well, at least we were able to spend some time with three of our prime suspects: Milestones VP Edward and the lovely Celia and her husband, Jeff."

"And?"

"Let's get back to the cabin," he said.

People were pouring out of the dining room, chatting, smiling. A cruise tended to be a place where people could just be nice to others—they were out to enjoy themselves and strangers were seldom enemies.

No one was listening, still . . .

Their conversation was one that should definitely be kept private.

They were quickly back in the cabin. Their steward hadn't made up the bed in the little parlor area.

Why would he?

They were listed as a married couple.

He could sleep anywhere on anything; this was something he'd learned long ago on the job.

"I get it tonight," he said.

"You get what?" Chloe asked.

"Sofa."

"Hm, do I trust you to hear the door?" she asked.

He laughed. "If you can't trust me to hear the door, we're both in trouble here!"

"No, no, I trust you when you're awake—"

"You plan on a string, maybe you even brought a bell. Of course, that doesn't help if someone just opens the door with a gun which, of course, would wake us both immediately."

"Okay, true. But they can't *just* open the door if the inner lock is on, and with the string—"

"If they're trying to break the inner lock, we'd hear it anyway," Wes reminded her, grinning. "A bell, a string, whatever! That's a bolt. If someone slammed the door hard enough to break that bolt in, we'd definitely hear it!"

"Okay, fine, you get the couch tonight and I was kind of making up my own arguments, you know, the part about a string and a bell—because there is an inner lock, a bolt. Someone messing with that would definitely wake us both up," she told him.

He grinned and nodded. "Yeah, we're both good. So, okay, before we try to get some sleep, what did you think and or feel tonight?"

She shook her head. "A strange dynamic. The captain, nice guy. Lonely, maybe. I would imagine that it's difficult to lose one's spouse and spend endless hours at sea. Maybe a dating app would be great for him." She made a face. "I do know people who met their partners on dating apps, but I know people who wound up with a lot of creeps, too. I guess in this business . . ."

"You come to believe you need to see people up close and personal?" he asked.

She shrugged. "Okay, but the captain. Just plain good guy, but, of course, he's not on our list derived by our own team, anyway. Ditto with the grandfather who used to be a cruise director and the grandson following in his footsteps—I think Billy's excited about his job and grateful to be at the captain's table and recognized by all the Milestones people. Of course, not on our list, either. Down to Celia, there's something about her that . . ."

"I agree. Attractive woman, eager to please, but evidently made of steel and cunning," Wes said.

Chloe nodded. "I get the feeling that her husband is on this and into computers because she's ordered it. He barely speaks—just when she gives him a cue that he's supposed to be engaging. It's almost as if he's afraid to talk without her go-ahead," she said.

Wes nodded. "So far, seems like we're getting the same vibes. Do you think that she's capable of being a cold-blooded murderer? And if so, why? If her thing is really social media, these other guys aren't really her competition."

"Double-edged question!" Chloe told him. "But that's okay. I'm not sure! The only thing I'm sure about is the fact that she brow-beats her husband. And even that could be . . ."

"For public appearances?"

Chloe shrugged.

"What about our VP Edward, Milestones emissary on-board?"

"That's harder," she said. "You get anything?"

He shook his head. "Seems like the real deal. But . . . Well, these guys are all capable of tracking others. They'd know schedules, who goes where when . . . I mean, any of them slipping into a house, staging a suicide or murder-suicide . . ."

"I believe that our people will be getting us more," she said.

He nodded. "We've tossed our real phones and our computers have been wiped. Our fake identities are really well-established online. But we've still got to watch our own backs. Look at the things our people can discover."

She nodded. "We're going to need to split up to manage this, but we need to make sure that we do know what the other is doing at all times."

"Absolutely. And don't forget, the phones we have can ping the other at any time of the day."

She laughed. "So, if someone gets one of us, they can find the other, too?"

"Ouch! Wow, your glass is half-empty. No, it shouldn't work that way. Only we know the ping color each day—the one that will refer to our locations—and that color is something we'll discover each morning when we look at the phones. Other colors will be meals, classes. We're in good shape, we work with good people."

"And it's a cruise! What could go wrong?" Chloe said, smiling. "Okay, so, tomorrow morning, I'm taking Celia's social media thingy and you're—"

"I'll head to VP Edward's class on security," Wes told her. "And, of course, in the afternoon, we'll need to get to know our other suspects."

"Exactly. We still have Abigail Swenson and the brothers, Daniel and Broderick McClintock. Abigail had reason to get rid of Frank Adams because he was above her in a supervisory position—getting the position when it had been between the two of them," Chloe said, scrunching her face up a bit as she remembered everything they had learned about their suspects. "And the brothers . . . Hm, maybe just wanting to rule the market?" She shook her head. "I don't get it!" she said softly. "I mean, could all this be over greed?"

"Greed can do remarkable things to people. We've both seen that," he told her.

She nodded. "I'm just hoping that . . ."

"That we can figure it out? Hey, I read great things about

you. That was an amazing case that you and Alex Rodriguez managed working undercover."

She winced and nodded. "Yeah, but Alex's injuries at the last showdown still have him . . . Well, he may be in rehab the rest of his life. And, well, you'll need to meet Alex one day. He's a remarkable human being. He's not bitter. He's grateful for his life. And he told me that he'd never been capable of slowing down on his own and now he gets to spend more time with his kids, so . . ."

"Hey, yeah, I'm sorry. I heard he was injured and that he was on medical leave from FDLE. He sounds great. I do hope I get to meet him."

She forced a smile.

"Sure."

"You blame yourself."

"No, no, I . . . I was a few steps behind—I was caught up tangling with another two members of the cartel and . . ."

"You got there in time to save his life, from what I understand," Wes said.

"Maybe. I don't know. There was a SWAT team right behind me," she said with a shrug.

"You know," he reminded her, "that with what we do, we know what can happen to us," he said softly.

"Of course."

"Hey, I'm glad you're the one who has my back on this," he assured her.

"Yeah, maybe? Well, I hope," she murmured. "Okay! So, anyway, I'm off to sleep so that we can get to know all our charming computer people tomorrow!"

"Right. Oh! I'm going to get friendly with our cruise director, Billy. Because that way, we'll know what excursions our suspects have opted to be on. Because . . ."

"Diving might give someone a chance to kill someone else?"

"Possibly. And one of the offerings in Jamaica is a trip to the Dunn's River Falls—lots of places to push someone off of the rocks there," Wes reminded her.

She groaned.

"Good point! All right, good night!"

She disappeared into the bedroom area of their little suite.

Wes decided that he'd shower in the morning.

He found a pillow and blanket in the closet and determined that he had more than enough to make himself comfortable for the night.

Lying down, he stared at the door. It was bolted from the inside. But tonight, he was certain that no one could suspect that they were anything other than a happy young married couple, ready to enjoy one another and all the wonders that the cruise had to offer.

He lay there awake. It had been one hell of a day. When he had woken up that morning, he hadn't had the faintest idea that he'd be going to sleep on a cruise ship when night fell.

That he'd be partnered with an agent from the state rather than the federal government.

He hadn't heard about the first so-called suicide of Frank Adams before they'd been briefed and left to study what was known. The deaths of the six people had made national news immediately and he could also remember reading about the wife who had supposedly killed her husband before eating the gun herself.

And it did so often come down to *why.*

Killers had an agenda, or they were stone-cold psychopaths.

Or both.

What were they looking for? Someone like Celia Henderson?

Or were she and her husband just the kind of personalities who strangely worked together?

Celia being the one who was calling all the shots.

Him being her obedient second, a man happy to have a powerful leader to show him the way?

They hadn't even begun to fathom the personalities of the others who were on their suspect list.

He groaned and twisted and turned and found himself thinking about his new partner.

Chloe was picture-perfect for the role with her shoulder-length dark hair and bright green eyes, sleek form and energy. She had managed to be passionate yet inoffensive when she had stated that art needed to be created by human beings and not artificial intelligence—not that AI hadn't already been used over and over again in the field.

And he hoped that she was really okay. From what he had read, it appeared that her timely arrival had kept her partner, Alex Rodriguez, from being shot dead straight through the heart—one of the "boatyard killers" they had taken down had been standing right over the man.

But he knew, too, that anytime a partner was struck in a situation, the second man or woman couldn't help but blame themselves. Maybe it was part of being human.

He jerked up suddenly; the door between the bedroom and the parlor had opened.

Chloe stuck her head out.

She smiled.

"Sorry, couldn't help myself, just checking. Hm, but had you fallen asleep yet, anyway?" she asked him.

"You'll never know," he told her.

She laughed softly.

"No, honestly, the little refrigerator is out here and I just wanted to get some water," she told him.

"I think you were checking on me."

"I think I really wanted water."

"Then you should get some!"

"Yeah. I'll do that!"

She slept in an oversized T-shirt. He wasn't surprised. He hadn't expected her to be clad in anything frilly and he wasn't sure why.

"What?" she asked.

"Nothing."

"You're secretly laughing at me."

"No," he assured her. "I'm laughing at myself."

"Oh?"

He shook his head, lying back down as he spoke.

"We've all taken profiling classes. And I guess I was profiling you."

"Oh?" she said warily.

"I just surprised myself. I was pretty sure you slept in something like that. Something comfortable and easy."

"Hm. I guess I had you down right, too, then."

"Oh?"

"I knew you'd be out here with the bare minimum, pillow, blanket—and that you'd sleep with your clothes on."

"Hey! I'm trying to be professional here!" he countered.

She acquired her bottle of water and headed back to the door, grinning. "And, of course, I'm trying to be professional here, too."

"Hm," he murmured.

"What?"

"You could have tried a little harder. That cotton kind of hugs your form!"

She let out a soft groan.

"Well, you know, I am on my second honeymoon. Good night, darling!"

"Good night, my beloved. Sleep well."

With a last grin and a shake of her head, she disappeared and the door between them closed.

He liked her. She was serious, but she had a sense of humor.

And . . .

He couldn't help but wonder more about her past. It was one thing to get to know someone through a dossier. It was quite another once you were with that person.

Naturally, she had to be wondering about him. It was never easy to be thrown into a situation undercover.

And sure as hell never easy when you were just beginning to know one's partner.

But . . .

He smiled to himself.

Something told him that it was going to be all right.

He closed his eyes and felt the gentle movement of the ship as it moved through the sea in the night.

One thing was sure.

He'd been far worse places.

And still . . .

Someone was out there poisoning people, paralyzing them, killing them.

And the powers that be believed that the someone they were after was on the ship.

In the coming days, they were going to have to discover just who that person might be . . . without becoming poisoned, paralyzed and killed themselves.

# THREE

CHLOE HURRIED OUT to the parlor with her clothing for the day as soon as the sun broke through the curtain. It was early, not quite 7:00 a.m., but she could be all set for breakfast, roaming the decks and attending her social media session with Celia Henderson. And if she was early, she didn't need to be in the way when Wes wanted to shower and dress.

Except that when she stepped quietly into the parlor area, Wes was already up, reading the various brochures that had been left in the room on the coffee table. He was casually dressed in Bermuda shorts and a tailored short-sleeved cotton shirt, perfect for a day at sea.

"You're ready—already!" she said.

He nodded. "Woke up, figured I'd be out of the way," he told her. "Oh, and our steward—his name is Lucas, by the way—already brought us a lovely pot of coffee. Shall I pour you some?" he asked her.

"Um, sure, great! I'll take two minutes, promise!" she told him.

She might have taken more like five, but Chloe was quick; she could be ready to go just about anywhere in a very short amount of time, another skill learned on the job. When she came out, he was seated on the sofa. His pillow and blanket had been shoved back into the closet and there was plenty of room for her to join him.

She sat and picked up one of the brochures.

"Dunn's River Falls," she murmured.

"I signed us up," he told her. "And, by the way, we'll be joined by one of our own."

"Oh?"

"Taylor Braxton. He's been working a drug connection over there."

He handed her his phone so that she could read the message he'd received.

Hey, Wes! I heard that you and your lovely wife are heading my way! Know you love the falls, meet you there, maybe some lunch after!

"The more the merrier. Obviously, he's been read in. I mean, you don't have a real wife, right? That's not something I missed—"

"When you read everything that you could to check out your odd partner?" Wes inquired, grinning.

"And you didn't do the same?"

"You already know I did." He shrugged, taking a long sip of his coffee. "Nope. You're the only lovely wife I have at this moment," he told her.

"So," Chloe murmured, "today at sea, tomorrow Jamaica, Dunn's River Falls and lunch with Taylor Braxton. But for now . . ."

"Yeah. Let's see if we can find any of our suspects at breakfast."

"Buffet one deck below, quick and easy, and I'm assuming our instructors for all these computer classes will want to grab and go," Chloe said.

"Let's do it," he said. "Oh, we'll have a chance to study the brothers on our list after our morning social media and security classes. They're giving a lecture on finding the best computers and screens for your particular interests, be it work, gaming, whatever."

"Both of us?"

"We could, yes, it would appeal to us both in our chosen fields." He arched a brow to her. "You do know something about art, right?"

"You read up on me. I majored in criminology, minored in art," she reminded him. "Besides, we're going to be okay. I'm not selling any of the classics—my work is with today's artists!"

"Still—"

"Not to worry. I can hold my own."

"Wasn't really worried. Just checking."

"And you? Can you actually dive?"

"Oh, ouch. That hurt."

"That means yes," she said lightly. "So, onward!"

She unlatched the door so that they could head out. A flight of stairs brought them to the buffet where many of the ship's passengers were gathered, so many that finding a table might not be an easy task.

But it worked out perfectly.

"Over there!" Wes said softly.

Chloe turned in the direction he indicated. A table had just cleared—and two of their suspects were about to take a seat.

"Grab me a croissant or something, I'll save our seats!" Chloe told him.

She hurried over to the table, asking quickly, "May I grab

these? Seems like no one wanted a formal sit-down breakfast today! Everyone's preparing for classes!"

She gave the two men her best smile.

The brothers Daniel and Broderick McClintock were an impressive pair. Like most of the men on board, they were wearing knee-length shorts and polo shirts. Daniel was a bit taller at about six-two; his brother was maybe an inch shorter. From reading, she knew that Broderick was thirty-eight and Daniel was thirty-six. Their parents had died in an automobile crash when they'd been in college and, apparently, they'd leaned on one another since. Neither was married; their company, Bulwark Cybersecurity, had been a focus for them since they'd founded it six years ago.

Prior to that, Daniel had worked for a major gaming enterprise and Broderick had been a cyber security officer for a bank.

They were handsome men, dark-haired and dark-eyed, fit, blending dignity with quick solid smiles.

And they gave her a pair of those very pleasant smiles.

"Of course, please! Tables are for all to share. Can we get you something?" Daniel asked her.

"Oh, no, no, thank you! My husband is in the line—I was just making sure that we had somewhere to sit!" Chloe told them.

Broderick pulled out a chair for her and she sat. "I think I know who you are. I mean, you two do look quite a bit like one another! Daniel and Broderick McClintock, *Bulwark Cybersecurity*!"

"Yes, I'm Daniel, and my big brother here is Broderick. And you have us at a disadvantage—"

"Chloe," she said. "I'm Chloe Douglas, and my husband, Wes, is heading our way as we speak. We're both coming to the class you're giving today. Oh, and it was such a surprise for us! We planned this trip way back, and it couldn't have been more perfect! I can't believe that Milestones and all the people they've brought on are being so wonderful and generous with their time!"

"We love to pay it forward!" Broderick said.

"And, of course, create a lot of goodwill for Bulwark Cybersecurity!" Daniel added, grinning. His smile slipped. "We need good things these days in all online fields."

"Well, creating these classes for everyone does create goodwill," Chloe assured them. But she frowned as well, looking at Daniel. "Oh! I read in the paper about a woman killing five or her associates and then herself! I see where you might be worried, but then again, that was one person, and the world is moving on the internet!" she assured him.

"I know, I know, it's just so sad and so . . . unbelievable!" Daniel said.

"We knew them," Broderick added quietly.

"Oh, I am so very sorry," Chloe told him earnestly.

Wes was coming their way with a tray carrying two plates of food and two cups of coffee.

He glanced at the brothers and introduced himself. "Wes Douglas, and I see you've met my wife. I hope we're not interrupting—this seems to be the busiest place on the ship at the moment."

"Not interrupting at all," Broderick assured him. Wes smiled his thanks and took the fourth seat at the table.

"Everyone is all in on going to classes on our day at sea," Wes said. He laughed softly. "We were thinking about the pool, lounge chairs, drinks with little umbrellas in them—okay, Chloe was thinking about the little umbrellas. I was thinking more about a few beers. But you get the drift. Now we're all excited about the classes we're going to take."

"Go figure!" Chloe said. "Sun, sea, soft breezes—and we realized that we'd both rather get in on those classes!"

"And what classes in particular interest you?" Daniel asked her.

She smiled. "Well, mainly social media, I guess. I own an art gallery and I'm always trying to promote local talent. I need to learn what apps I should be using, how I should be using them . . . you know! That kind of thing."

Daiel looked at his brother. "I guess she's not going to need to learn about security on dating apps."

"I can only hope not!" Wes said lightly, brushing his fingers through her hair.

"Oh, trust me, no! I just want to showcase my artists!" Chloe assured him.

"So, even though I understand some of it *will* be on dating, I thought that I'd attend Celia Henderson's class tomorrow morning," Chloe said, smiling.

"And you're not going?" Broderick asked Wes.

"I'm going to Edward Thompson's class at the same time. We're trying to divide and conquer—except we're both coming to your mid-morning class!" Wes said. "Chloe thinks we should both attend."

"Well, we're delighted, of course, and thank you," Daniel said. He grinned and looked at Wes and said, "As she wishes it, right?"

"Pardon?" Wes said.

Daniel laughed. "Sorry. I mean, you're a 'Westley,' right?"

"I am," Wes said, nodding slightly.

"Sorry, movie fan here. I'm thinking of *The Princess Bride* and the Dread Pirate Roberts. Buttercup's beloved Westley always told her, 'As you wish!'"

Wes looked over at Chloe before glancing back at Daniel and saying, "Yeah! Right. Saw that as a kid! I've been missing the mark!" He turned back to Chloe, lifted one of her hands and kissed it lightly, and then grinned at her and said, "As you wish!"

She groaned softly, grinning and shaking her head.

"If only!" she told the other two.

Wes groaned playfully and teased his fingers through her hair again. "Someone told me once that's the key to a happy marriage—"

"Whatever one's spouse wants!" Chloe interrupted lightly.

"And you two seem to be doing it right," Daniel said. "The chemistry even bounces all the way over here. Wes, you seem to be 'as you wish-ing' it just right."

"Hey, maybe I am!" Chloe protested. "Neither of you is married?"

Daniel winced. "Not anymore. Now I just 'as you wish it' to my brother!"

"Well, from what I understand, you have one of the most amazing companies out there, seeing as how it's rising and rising!" Chloe told him earnestly.

Broderick nodded. "We're doing all right, but . . . well, you must stay on it, stay awake, all the time in this field."

"There are always hackers out there. And no matter what kind of security firewall you come up with, someone will come up with a way to hack it. That's why it's such a tough business," Daniel added.

Chloe sipped her coffee and looked at the two brothers. They seemed to be in sync with one another.

*A family murder affair?*

"Whoops, we've got to get going!" Broderick said, glancing at his watch. "Anyway, great to meet you and so glad we'll see you later!"

"Yep, great to meet you," Daniel said, rising to join his brother.

"Thanks, guys, and, yes, ditto! Great to meet you both as well," Wes said.

The two men left, and Chloe and Wes stood, as well.

"So, time for our classes," Chloe murmured. "Meet at class two—with the brothers."

He nodded. "Yep. See you there. Oh, and seriously, watch out for those dating apps!"

"I'm a married woman," she reminded him.

"Yeah, it should be interesting. I worked a few cases that weren't . . . Well, they sure as hell weren't happy-ever-after. For families, keeping in touch . . . the internet is great. But when it's used in the wrong way . . ."

"Um, that's what we're doing on the cruise," she reminded him.

"Sorry. Dating apps. Kidnapping, ransom . . . simply taking people for all that they're worth. Seriously, should be an interesting class. Off to learn about security!" he told her.

They headed out together, checked the spaces where the classes were being held, and pointed them out to each other.

"Wow. Way more people want to date than worry about security!" Wes said.

"Promotion, too!" Chloe reminded him.

"That's right. Of course. That's why all those young people are going!"

He gave her a salute and took off. Chloe followed the group into the meeting that Celia and Jeff would be heading, smiling, chatting with others as she did so.

She had a notebook in her bag and took it out as she found a seat with the others. They were in one of the large upper deck spaces reserved customarily for game nights or other such entertainment on the ship, including trivia, cards, karaoke and bingo. She knew where they were since she had read all the brochures.

Changes had been made to pieces of the customary itinerary to accommodate this special occasion. And, of course, cruisers had been given the option to change their reservations or receive a full refund if it wasn't to their liking.

It didn't appear that they'd lost any passengers because of the new format.

Chloe was surprised to see that Jeff was the first to walk up to the podium at the front of the class. A computer had been set on a table and a large screen set up behind that.

Jeff welcomed everyone to the class first, explaining that they were going to talk about community and friendship.

"Community, of course, because if we're looking for love or trying to promote the right people, ideas or products to like-minded individuals, we all need our communities!" he said.

The man could be charming, she saw. He was a good speaker, talented at welcoming and explaining. He won the crowd over easily before introducing his wife.

They started with dating and Chloe wondered what cases Wes had worked that had made him so leery of dating apps.

Celia was an equally good speaker. She talked about the busy lives that most of them led, busy lives with work and family that often made it difficult to meet a partner in the customary way: through church, socials—or even bowling! Her parents had met at a bowling alley, she explained. Something not so common these days.

"Let's face it, though. We are living in a brave new world!" Celia reminded them. "And I have friends who are now married who met on dating apps. Friendships are formed even when romances don't bloom. But bad things can happen, too! Very bad things. To start with, only give out so much personal information! If an app appears to be asking too much about your personal life, you may be divulging your whereabouts at a time when you might be vulnerable. Always be wary of money scams!" She sighed softly. "I also have a friend who lost her mom. Her father was devastated. He fell for a woman online who wasn't a woman at all—and managed to clean out his bank account. So, let's get started on being safe while also using dating apps for their purpose of finding love and connection!"

Chloe pretended to be attentive; the last thing she wanted was to be on a dating app. Not that friends of hers—even in law enforcement—didn't use dating apps. She just tended to be skeptical—and too aware of the bad incidents that Celia had mentioned.

And, of course, she shouldn't want to be on one. She was a married woman—well, on this cruise, anyway.

Celia walked around the room as she talked, indicating to her husband who ran the computer and what was seen on the screen. Different apps were shown. There was no warning against a particular app; this pair had no intention of being subject to a libel suit. But safety was pointed out.

If they weren't on the suspect list as possible murderers, they might have appeared to be a true, bright, giving couple, knowledgeable regarding all that they were saying.

Knowledgeable about the internet, and about everything that it could give.

And take.

"Take a good look at the screen!" Jeff advised. "We have some recommendations for you if anyone wants to take notes."

Celia was still walking around the room. She paused by Chloe, grinning.

"No notes on dating apps?"

"No, maybe I should have been taking a few for friends!" Chloe said pleasantly. "But I am ready to learn all about the best user and community-friendly ways to promote my artists!"

"Next up!" Celia said. She bent low by Chloe's ear to whisper, "Sorry! A lot of people on this thing seem to be in need of love!"

Chloe laughed. "Not a problem!"

In a few minutes, Jeff went to the podium and told the group it was time to learn about social media for promotion and, of course, just for fun.

He did much of the speaking on the subject, telling them what apps connected with one another, how to best make use of several apps when getting news out and, of course, how to manage comments.

"They can all be confusing!" he assured the crowd. "And, of course, they often offer AI as a means to respond automatically, though there is the option never to use them. Personally, I find the automatic answers annoying—I don't want AI answering for me!"

It was a good class. Once again, Chloe had to admit that the couple seemed to know their business and seek to share it with others.

*Pay it forward.*

Chloe believed it. Many in the field did want to pay it forward.

And some wanted to make sure that they were at the forefront, ready to lead, ready to be the best—and rake in the income such a position afforded.

At the end of the session, Jeff and Celia thanked everyone for attending. Celia had barely finished speaking when an announcement came over the loudspeaker.

It was the young cruise director Chloe and Wes had met at the captain's table the night before, Billy Cliffton.

"Billy Cliffton here, folks, hoping that everyone enjoyed

their morning's sessions and, of course, giving a shout-out here to Milestones, with gratitude for setting this all in motion, and our thanks, too, for all the great and brilliant computer folks helping us out here on the ship! Now, for those who have been lounging on deck, enjoying the pools and hot tubs, our cooking lessons, or anything else, you have seen the perfect beauty of today! Clear blue skies and a gorgeous ocean with just light waves! Take a peek on your break from activities—or just look around you if you're out there lounging! And once again, thank you for sailing with us!"

The next round of classes, with Chloe and Wes attending the session given by the McClintock brothers together, wouldn't start for another thirty minutes.

They might as well take a look at the day! It was always a good thing to remember that the world could be beautiful.

Chloe headed out. She had the decks figured out well; their cabin was on an upper deck that held sixty such larger type suites, or salons, as they were often called here. The bridge was just above them and the rest of their deck offered a pool, tons of lounging areas, a whirlpool and even a badminton court. Of course, her parents had once taken her on a cruise that even offered a roller coaster, so it wasn't surprising to find out just how many activities could be offered.

Heading out was timely; she ran right into Wes.

People were all around them, some she had spoken with casually, and she thought it was a great idea to keep up appearances. Therefore, she greeted him with a massive smile, sliding slightly into his arms, and accepting the quick kiss he planted on her lips with affection.

"So, how was your class?" she inquired.

"Brilliant!" he assured her.

"So, we do need to *see* the *sea*!" she told him.

"Of course! Let's head on out!" he agreed.

Arm in arm, they headed down the hall to great double doors that led out to the deck. They moved with others to the deck's great balcony area to look out over the water.

Billy Cliffton hadn't lied.

It was a beautiful day.

"This is . . . wow. Gorgeous," Wes murmured. "Too bad . . ."

She laughed and said softly, "Too bad we can't just climb into bathing suits and soak in the sun and sea?"

He shrugged. "Yeah, something like that."

"So, how was your class? Really," she murmured.

He slipped an arm around her, pulling her close and speaking very quietly. "The man is very good. He talks about the fact that whether we like it or not, computers, the internet and AI are taking over. He points out the fact that while people are the ones feeding data to AI, the whole thing with AI is that it's programmed to offer us the desired result, but . . . we still need to be incredibly careful because that result may not be entirely accurate or correct. He was a great speaker and, of course, he seems to be sincere."

"So . . ." Leaning against him in a way that made it appear they were just husband and wife, enjoying the view, she murmured, "So far, Edward seems to be the real deal, Celia and Jeff are both good, though she rules the roost. But just because she can be a bit condescending to her husband, doesn't mean she's a murderer."

"But we know that someone is. And I'm a little surprised that we haven't heard more people talking about what happened in Broward County. I mean, although the news isn't out everywhere that a number of incidents across three states are probably connected, the Broward incident was big news."

"It was," Chloe agreed.

She looked around, assessing the ship and the people near them.

A family with a daughter of about twelve and a son who was maybe nine or ten.

Several couples.

A group of five young women, probably early to mid-twenties, attractive, laughing, evidently out to have fun.

Two men with the haircuts and look—even in casual clothing—that implied they might have come specifically for the computer classes.

"None of our people," Chloe murmured.

"Suspects?" Wes replied lightly.

She shrugged. "There are others, of course, who have given classes—"

"Hey, don't ever forget that we have some of the finest techs in the world searching through whereabouts, expenditures, contacts . . . if there's someone else we need to be watching, they will let us know."

"I know, I know, of course. And yet . . ."

"We always need to be careful. If any of these people should become suspicious regarding us . . .

He smiled, pulling her closer, mussing her hair.

"We're not giving them any reason to become suspicious!"

"No," she murmured.

And, as the word left her mouth, the brilliant blue beauty of the day was suddenly shattered by a tremendous scream.

And from where they stood, they saw the body of a man plunging into the sea beneath them.

And a cry went out.

"Man overboard!"

There were, of course, ship's workers who could follow the man overboard.

There were lifeboats, and life preservers.

But Wes apparently didn't trust any of them.

He leaped onto the rail and quickly plunged into the sea in the wake of the man who had gone over.

There seemed to be no other recourse at that moment.

Chloe followed him.

Because she didn't know who they could trust.

And she was both an excellent diver and swimmer . . .

It was still one hell of a distance. She hit the water like an arrow, plunging down and down and down . . .

She broke her pattern and with a tremendous kick, propelled herself to the surface. She could see the rescue efforts, but a few of those took time. Two men from the ship were in the water, desperately seeking their man overboard.

Life preservers floated all around them.

But people were still looking desperately for the man who'd fallen.

She heard someone shouting to Wes, at first condemning him for having followed and then asking him if he saw the man anywhere.

Wes answered with the direction he was taking.

He saw that Chloe had followed him and arched a brow.

She shook her head. She couldn't see the man anywhere.

Wes seemed to have been surprised at first, but it didn't take him long to realize they were in it together. He pointed, indicating that he was continuing his route.

She nodded, moving out, tasting the salt in the water, grateful that the sea was relatively calm that day, that the sun was providing light . . .

She saw him.

The man who had pitched over. He was wearing khaki pants and a short-sleeved tailored shirt.

His hair was iron gray, even in the water.

He was about ten feet down, just floating . . . not moving. He might already be . . .

Dead.

*And, oh, God! No. It couldn't be, but it was . . .*

She kicked hard and swam fast, finally reaching him, kicking with all her might again to bring them both to the surface.

When she got there, Wes swam up, reaching out.

"I've got him," she said.

"Yeah, but college lifeguard here, the water is starting to get a little choppy and I know the hold to get him back. Oh, God, is he breathing?"

"Barely!" Chloe ascertained.

Wes slipped his arm around the man in a way that allowed his head to remain clear of the water, his body trailing along as Wes used his free hand and arm and feet to move.

And he could move.

Someone tossed out a life preserver, but Wes didn't need it. One of the lifeboats had reached them and two young men on the ship's crew helped get him into the boat. Wes caught the hull and hiked himself in while Chloe managed to get on a little more awkwardly.

By the time she did, Wes was giving the man CPR.

Thankfully, it seemed, he really had been a lifeguard and knew the necessary techniques.

"We have a great doctor on board! I'm getting us in," one of the young men with the ship's crew said. "How the hell did he fall?" the man asked, shaking his head. "I mean, it's . . . it's Edward Thompson! The whole cruise is . . . Man, we warn people! Don't get so carried away on deck, don't look over too far . . . How did someone as smart as him manage to fall?"

*How indeed?*

# FOUR

DOCTOR BRENDAN KILBRIDE was an impressive man.

The ship's hospital was equally impressive, offering four private rooms and even an operating room. Most of the major tests done at the hospital could be done right on the ship as could minor or life-saving surgeries.

The doctor had two highly efficient nurses at his side, and standing in the waiting room, Wes—still dripping with an equally wet Chloe at his side—learned that there was always a second doctor on board, as well. His name was Dr. George Lincoln and while he was much younger, just having finished his residency at Tisch Hospital in New York, according to the equally young Billy Cliffton, the doctor had been top of his class all throughout medical school and been offered jobs across the country and beyond.

Normally, of course, they'd have been asked to leave since they were sopping wet, but they were apparently celebrities now that they'd been part of the overboard rescue.

That they were noticed didn't thrill Wes in the least. They were supposed to blend in with the crowd!

"We saved a life," Chloe said quietly to him. "And it's no shock that a man who runs a dive boat might have been a lifeguard at some time in his life. And, Wes! Remember. Our first priority, always, is to save lives!"

He nodded; he knew that he wasn't pleased with being noted—not that she hadn't been, as well. Just the dive off the ship was impressive and she had been the one to draw Edward Thompson to the surface.

"I'm okay with this," she said softly. "You must be, too. We had no other choice."

*But what if the man was the killer they'd been seeking?*

They didn't know that.

And it was more than possible that he'd been helped in his "fall" overboard.

Dr. Kilbride emerged from the room where he'd been examining the patient and giving orders to his nurses.

"We got him out of his wet clothing quickly and he's receiving warm intravenous fluids," Kilbride informed. He was studying the two of them. "The man was lucky you knew what you were doing with CPR," he told Wes.

Wes shrugged. "Who knew that needing a job in college could really pay off for me," he said. "I'm just grateful—"

"I'm grateful that you're the one who reached him. Our people have had training, but we've never had a passenger go overboard before. I like to believe that he would have been fine, but . . ."

The doctor was a tall man with mid-length silver hair, dark brown eyes and a serious demeanor. "Young lady, you might well have found him before he floated back to the surface, deprived of oxygen too long. You're heroes!"

Chloe shook her head. "Just good swimmers, Doctor, and I thought at one time that I might want to head to the Olympics as a diver, so . . . As my husband said, we're just grateful that we were able to be useful and that Mr. Thompson is alive!"

"And you two now need to worry about your own health. I would say that showers are in order for you," he told them.

"Is it possible to speak with Mr. Thompson?" Wes asked.

"He's out right now. I'd like to let him stay out for a bit, time for his body to warm up completely," Doctor Kilbride said. "I know he'll want to speak with you." He grimaced. "I've only one case of seasickness in here now, so I can promise you, I won't leave him until he is awake and talking and well on the way to full recovery. He's got a few good scrapes on him, but luckily, he didn't break any bones. A few days in here under observation and I believe he'll be able to rejoin the cruise, though I'm going to suggest that he take it easy and enjoy the lounge chairs when I do release him. Return to your cabin. I'll call as soon as you can see him."

Wes and Chloe thanked him and left the infirmary. As they passed other passengers, they were applauded and congratulated by many of them, and he tried hard to accept all the words of praise with courtesy and the humility needed to try to remain just a regular someone among them all. Chloe was good at it, saying she had surprised herself, but that she just instinctively followed her husband. She and Wes spent their lives on boats and in the water and when her husband had jumped in . . . Well, once upon a time she had competed in diving and, surely, they were just lucky to reach the man first; the ship's crew would have been fine without them.

When they reached the room at last, Wes groaned aloud. He almost threw himself down on the couch, but remembered he was soaking wet.

"You can take the first shower," Chloe told him.

He shook his head. "You go ahead. I know you're fast. I'm still mentally kicking myself over what just happened."

"Well, stop that fight!" she said sternly. "Wes, he wasn't breathing when I dragged him up! If you hadn't known what you were doing—"

"The crew is trained."

"Trained, yes. Not tested in a real emergency. And not that they wouldn't have been okay, and there definitely could be an emergency they get to be the heroes for one day, but . . . I'm going to shut up and take my shower so that you can have it!"

She disappeared into the bedroom area of their salon for a brief minute, grabbing clean clothing.

Then she got into the shower.

Just as she left, another thought sprang into his mind.

*What if he had been pushed? What if someone on the ship was determined on finishing the job? Was he going to be safe in the ship's hospital?*

His burner phone had been in his pocket; he drew it out, amazed to see that it was still working. Then again, Alonzo wouldn't have sent them out without the best available equipment.

He called the contact in his phone listed as "Uncle Joe."

Alonzo answered. "Joe here."

Always prepared. Making sure that it was Wes calling him, that the phone hadn't been taken, and that he wouldn't be known as who he really was.

Wes quickly described what had happened—and his fear for Edward Thompson now.

"No problem. I'll take care of it," Alonzo promised. "It's already been picked up by the media—that a man fell from a cruise ship. Apparently, from chatter, there was a massive school of dolphins frolicking near the ship, too, and that caused people to lean over the rails and press into one another."

"Sir, how—"

"Like I said, news travels fast. No secrets—it's all over the internet. We're lucky that with everything going on, none of the passengers got good shots of you or Chloe. I asked you both to change it up a bit in case you did wind up in family photos and there was the odd chance you'd be recognized as who you really are and what you do, but . . . Anyway, I guess it was such a zoo at the time and the distance from the ship's decks to the water was enough to pretty much show nothing but the tops of your heads in anything that our tech crews have been able to find. My point—the world knows what happened. It will be easy to see to it that Milestones gets a nurse of their own out there to watch over Thompson."

"Okay, but—"

"It will be George Garcia, who is a registered nurse practitioner—but also with one of our legat offices."

"Ah. Okay, thanks. I don't think that I could have figured out a reason for Chloe and me to be in there at all times."

"You think he was pushed."

"I do."

"I'll get right on it."

Alonzo ended the call. Perfect timing.

Chloe emerged from the bathroom towel-drying her hair. He frowned, noting that the towel had dark stains on it.

"Ah, come on. Obviously, black dye. And no matter how good, it comes off a bit," she told him.

He grinned. "So, what color is your hair really?"

"Like a light reddish-brown," she told him.

"Well, the black does enhance your eyes. Man, they are green!" he told her.

She laughed. “Good! Glad it all matches.” She frowned, looking at him. “And what about you?”

“Alonzo told me to change it up, too. I’d had a beard—well-trimmed, of course, kind of, at least. Now I’m clean-shaven and the opposite—and *my* hair is usually very dark.”

“And with any luck, neither of us will have roots showing during the time we’re here,” Chloe said. She wrinkled her face. “Not a fan of beards, anyway.”

“So sorry!” he said dryly. “Anyway, what’s important. Alonzo is getting a nurse on board who will be arranged by Milestones—with direction from the assistant director himself. We won’t need to worry about keeping watch over Edward Thompson hour after hour.”

“Or worry that someone will stick something else into his IV,” Chloe murmured. “We agree that we think he was pushed?”

“I think it’s more than possible. But . . .”

The cabin phone was ringing. Wes answered it quickly, nodding to her. Doctor Kilbride had seen that one of his nurses had called to tell them that Edward Thompson was ready to speak with them, anxious to do so, wanting to thank them.

“Two minutes!” he told Chloe.

Grabbing clothing, he hurried into the shower, and as soon as he was out, they headed to the ship’s hospital.

Again, he somewhat marveled that a ship’s infirmary could be so complete, spacious—and ready for just about anything. Then again, he supposed that was the kind of thing that came along with a luxury cruise.

They were led in quickly to see Edward Thompson. The man was covered in a blanket and an IV was still sticking out of one arm.

“You two! My heroes, I understand. Thank you very

much. So much! I want you to know that anything that Milestones can do for you, we will do!" he vowed passionately.

"We're just so grateful to see you looking alive and well!" Chloe told him, standing by the bed and squeezing his hand.

"And I made you—and tons of people in all the fear and excitement—miss classes they want to attend. But the people onboard here are great—they'll just reschedule anything that was missed," Edward said.

"Again, nothing compared to you, sir," Wes said politely. "What happened?" he asked, as if perplexed. "Despite the decks, the railings are pretty high. It's not as easy as one might think to just fall off a ship."

"I guess it was the excitement, people all wanting to see," Edward replied. "I heard there were a bunch of dolphins near the ship!" He frowned and shook his head. "I had a great position and then . . ."

"Then the hustle and shove of everyone trying to see?" Chloe asked.

The man's frown remained. He stared at Wes, narrowing his eyes.

"I couldn't have . . . I couldn't have been pushed on purpose!" he said.

His words were passionate.

The expression on his face belied something more behind them. "I guess, I mean, sometimes, the wrong people do get hurt! And in this business . . . No, I couldn't have been pushed on purpose!"

"Oh, sir, you're such a good and giving man," Chloe murmured.

"Oh! I know, sir, you might be thinking of the people in Fort Lauderdale," Wes said, as if the idea had just occurred to him. "That girl who went crazy and shot all the people with her—and then herself!"

The man lowered his head and sighed. "I knew her. I knew her well. Jane Sewell. She was such a sweet and giving person—brilliant! She had amazing and innovative ideas. I'd offered her a job and I believed that she was going to come to work for me! I can't imagine what happened except . . ."

"Except, sir?" Chloe said.

"Just Edward. Please call me Edward," the man said. "Jane could be . . . fragile. She was humble. She was in love and . . . maybe he didn't love her back. I'm still wondering myself what could have caused her to do such a thing. Again, she was a beautiful human being, and . . . Oh, seriously, no! I couldn't be in any danger. What happened had to have been an accident."

As he spoke, Doctor Kilbride walked back into his room.

"Mr. Thompson, you are a beloved man! I just heard from Milestones. They're sending in one of their nurses, a young man, and he's going to be with you for the next several days."

"But I'm already feeling so much better—"

"Sir, you took quite a hit to your entire system. I like and admire what Milestones has done. You're a smart man, sir. You know that it will be good to have someone dedicated to looking out for you, ready to act and get you back out on deck. No need to let something trivial become something life-threatening," Kilbride said.

"I . . . I guess," Edward said. "I mean, yes, of course, you're right. I am a lucky man. These two beautiful young people diving in right after me, and a company that cares enough to send someone to look after me. Thank you, Dr. Kilbride."

Wes glanced at Chloe. Neither of them wanted to leave the man before the legat agent/nurse arrived, he knew.

"By the way, Edward, we're so sorry about your friend, Jane Sewell," Chloe said.

"My heart breaks for those she took with her!" Edward

said, shaking his head. "For Jane, of course, too, but all those innocent others . . . I never even knew that she was such an amazing shot. She killed five people before she killed herself. They had no defensive wounds, nothing!"

Chloe glanced over at Wes. He knew that she was curious as to how Edward Thompson knew so much about the investigation. The deaths were common knowledge; the media had shared that much with the public.

But the specifics had never reached the media.

"Of course, our hearts are heavy for the families involved, for everyone!" Chloe said.

"And we're sorry that . . . well, that it's come up," Wes said.

"Right. Well, I'm still very grateful to be here," Edward assured them.

"And we're grateful, too. So!" Wes said. "We won't speak of tragedies anymore. Sir—I mean Edward—I want you to know just how very much I learned from your class this morning." He smiled. "I run my own tight ship. But, as I said at dinner last night, even dive boats can be so dependent on computers these days. Learning about security—and knowing that just about anything in the world can be hacked by the right hacker—is tremendously important to me. But while all this happens, learning to be as safe as possible is invaluable!"

"Thank you," Edward said. "And Mrs. Douglas, what about you?" the Milestones vice president asked.

"Well," Chloe said, offering him a tremendous smile, "as you may ascertain, I'm not interested in being safe on a dating app since I won't ever be on a dating app. But what I leaned about security for my people—my artists—and my art shows, well, it was all just wonderful."

"Celia and Jeff were good instructors?"

"Very good. They know how to teach and keep everyone involved and interested," Chloe assured him.

"I'm so glad. And I thought that—"

He broke off. Someone was in the waiting room, speaking with one of the nurses. Edward Thompson stared at her, frowning.

He seemed to give himself a mental shake. "Sorry, that's Abigail Swenson. I thought that she was giving a class this afternoon in utilizing the internet for business . . ."

Wes recognized Abigail Swenson, naturally, from the intel they'd studied before heading to the ship.

She was in her mid-to-late thirties, about five-five, with curly brown hair cut close around her face. Wearing a flowered sundress and sandals, appropriate for the ship, she cut an attractive figure. Abigal appeared anxious as she spoke with the nurse.

"Bring her in, please bring her in!" Edward said.

Wes smiled. "Got it."

He was happy to meet her and escort her in. She was the one remaining of their six suspects that they'd hadn't had a chance to meet yet.

Well, she didn't look like a murderer.

But who among their suspects did? And just what did a murderer look like?

In his experience . . .

*It could be anyone. Absolutely anyone.*

He strode out of Edward Thompson's hospital room and walked over to Abigail and the nurse, nodding to the nurse and greeting their suspect.

"Miss Swenson! How do you do. I'm Wes Douglas and Mr. Thompson—"

"Oh, Mr. Douglas! What a pleasure!" the woman gushed. "I was on deck! I saw what you and your wife did. I'm here because I just adore Edward, and I need to see for myself that he's doing all right!"

"He's doing well, right in there," Wes said, indicating the door.

"Oh, thank you!"

She moved ahead of him and started as she saw that Chloe was sitting in a chair by Edward's bedside. She quicky gathered her smile again. "And Mrs. Douglas! You were wonderful. You two should receive medals!"

"We're just happy that everything has turned out okay! Edward needs to be careful for a few days, but he's going to be just fine," Chloe told her.

"Abigail, I'm fine, just fine!" Edward said. "Aren't you—"

"Yes, teaching this afternoon!" Abigail said. "There was a lot of commotion. We have things rescheduled. Don't you worry! We're all grateful to you and your company, Edward, and we'd never mess up, but I just had to see you!"

Edward smiled at her. "And you see me," he said. "Thank you, thank you for caring so much. Thanks to my guardian angels here, I'm doing exceptionally well!"

"Ah, well, that's such a relief. I mean, you fell! You could have gotten a terrible injury . . . You could have drowned! But such a fall!" Abigail went on.

"They have an amazing doctor on board, but one of my guardian angels dragged me up and the other was an expert at CPR!" Edward said.

"No, no, I just happened to have become certified as a lifeguard when I was in college—needed to pay my way through. Well, my parents helped, but I needed to work, too. Never knew it would prove to be so helpful. I mean, we're the grateful ones here. My wife and I have had this cruise planned . . . Never thought it would be so wonderful as to have so many computer geniuses aboard!" Wes assured her.

"Well, I'm glad we're all so lucky!" Abigail murmured.

She smiled brightly, looking from Wes to Chloe. "Um, I can keep Edward company, if you two young people had something you wanted to do onboard!"

"Oh, we're just waiting for the next set of classes to start," Chloe said.

*Yes, they were waiting. They weren't leaving anyone alone here with Edward Thompson.*

"I wonder if the doctor wants this many people in the room with you, Edward," Abigail said.

"I'm sure—" Edward began.

"Not to worry! I will go get ready for my class," Abigail said. She gave them another bright smile. "You two get to go to the classes—I get to give them! So, Edward, don't worry, we all adore you and you will get too many visitors, I fear."

"Oh, he'll be all right," Wes assured her. "Doc Kilbride said that a private nurse is coming from the company to make sure he doesn't have any later repercussions from this whatsoever."

"Oh!" Abigail said. "Well, wow, you are an important man, Edward!"

Edward laughed softly. "No, just a lucky man with lots of good friends."

Abigail nodded, smiling. "Okay, then, see you later, alligator!"

"In a while, crocodile!" Edward responded, and laughing, Abigail left the room.

"Seriously, you two don't need to babysit me," Edward said. "You saved my life, that's quite enough!"

"Oh, we're fine," Wes assured him. "Like Chloe said, we're just waiting for the new schedule."

"Daniel and Broderick are very good. The hackers out there must really hate them! They have created one of the most impressive cybersecurity firms known to man. Most of the major companies out there use Bulwark," Edward told them.

"So important!" Chloe murmured.

Looking to the waiting room, Wes saw that another man had arrived. He met with a nurse and then the doctor came out as well, greeting him and smiling.

Wes realized that somehow Alonzo—through Edward's Milestones company, of course—had managed to get their nurse/legat out to them already. It hadn't been a full two hours since the event had happened.

But, of course, that was Alonzo. He'd gotten to where he was by being amazingly good and efficient.

"I think the man sent from Milestones is here," he said.

"Man? They couldn't send me a pretty nurse, eh?" Edward said lightly. "Just teasing, I'm grateful that they care so much."

"I'll go and—" Wes started to say and head out, but he didn't need to do so. The doctor was already leading the newcomer into the room.

"Hello!"

Wes knew several of the Bureau's extension people working in the Caribbean and both Central and South America. He hadn't met George Garcia, but of course, Garcia knew who they really were, just as they knew that the man had double-duty on the ship.

"Mr. Thompson!" Doctor Kilbride said cheerfully. "I've just had the pleasure of meeting Mr. George Garcia, the nurse practitioner who just arrived to make sure that you do okay through the coming days. Mr. Garcia, your patient, Mr. Edward Thompson, and his friends, Mr. and Mrs. Douglas—our heroes of the hour."

"Nice to meet you all," George Garcia assured them, nodding to Wes and Chloe and giving his attention to his patient. "I'm here for you, sir. I will never be far!"

"You did an amazing job of getting here," Wes told him.

"They coptered me in! It was great. And yes, fast," Garcia told them, grinning. "Doc Kilbride has caught me up to speed, so here I am."

"I'm sure they'll get you a nice little cabin—" Edward began.

"Oh, no, sir! They're rolling in one of those nice comfy chairs that doubles as a bed. Mr. Thompson, you are extremely important to Milestones. I will be sleeping like a good and loyal hound, right at your feet! But don't worry—I won't be bothering you, I promise. I've brought some good books along with me, as well!"

"Well, I thank you for being here, though I hate to be a burden—"

"No burden to get a nice gig on a cruise ship, sir," Garcia said.

Edward Thompson laughed. "Okay, great. I'm not *sir*, please, just Edward."

"And I'm George."

"Chloe—and that's Wes," Chloe told him, rising. "And since you are here, we're going to leave Edward in your great hands and head out so that we can get to our next classes! Edward, you take care. We will be back to check on you."

"You're my guardian angels, and you are welcome anytime!" Edward assured them.

With a wave, Wes set a hand on Chloe's back as she rose and they left the room, waving to the doctor and nurses as they left the hospital area.

They didn't speak; they just smiled and nodded to others they spoke to. The ship's hospital was on the same deck as the indoor and outdoor spas and the gym, making it a busy area.

They headed to the elevator to reach the upper decks where their cabin was and where the classes were being held.

"Cabin first?" Chloe murmured.

He nodded, hit the button for their deck, and then they hurried down to the privacy of their own salon.

"Well, this is all great," he murmured when the door was closed. "First, was it possibly an accident?"

"No way," Chloe said. "Because something you said was absolutely correct! On every deck, the railings are high enough. The sea was quiet—"

"There were a lot of people pressing against each other to see the sea!" he reminded her. "And, so we hear, several frolicking dolphins."

"Still, the railing is too high! He was pushed. I don't know how much force it would take—"

"It would depend on whether he was bending over the railing or not. People do stretch out over the railing," Wes reminded her.

"I don't believe it."

"Neither do I, but I thought I should play devil's advocate," Wes agreed. "Okay, so, on to our visitor—"

"Abigail Swenson," Chloe said. "The one friend to come in and see him and, of course, one of the suspects on our list."

"And," Wes added, "the first so-called suicide was a man who received a promotion over her."

"But after what just happened, would anyone have taken the chance of coming into the hospital, into his room—and killing him then? Not the kind of place where you drug someone and shoot them!" Chloe said.

Wes shook his head. "As far as the killer knows, law enforcement isn't aware of the fact that the victims were drugged before they were shot."

"Well, it would have been obvious if she was in the room and the man was shot."

"But he has an IV. She could have planned to drug him. Computer specialists can certainly study the web to find out what poison wouldn't be obvious in an autopsy," Wes reminded her.

Chloe let out a long sigh.

"So far . . . we like Edward Thompson. As a person—not a suspect!" she said.

"You don't think that he jumped overboard to avoid suspicion?" Wes asked her dryly.

She shook her head. "Wes, you did save his life. I don't think that he was breathing when I dragged him to the surface."

"Oh, yeah, as to that! If I jump off a cliff, don't follow after me!"

She grinned. "I really did do competitive diving and I've done cliff diving and . . . You really were a lifeguard, right?"

He nodded. "Yep. Certified after my sophomore year of college."

She grinned. "Well, maybe they did pick the right people for a ship."

"Oh, great! Before that you didn't think I was the right person?"

She groaned. "Class! Let's get to class."

They started out of the cabin, and she said, "I did think it was going to be a good idea for us both to attend the class that Daniel and Broderick are giving. Now I'm thinking that maybe I should see what Abigail Swenson is going to be talking about—and just how she manages a class."

Wes hesitated. He stopped in the hallway, lightly, and

pinned her against the wall, smiling in a teasing way as he spoke affectionately.

"Strange. I know at times we will need to divide and conquer. Right now . . . after this morning, after Edward was sent over the brink already, I think we should hang together. Maybe we can look out for Abigail later, try to see where she's headed for dinner."

He thought that she was going to argue.

But she smiled, playing his game.

"Okay."

"Okay?"

She lifted her head up toward him, as if she was being a sweet and teasing wife.

"I'm feeling a bit of what you're feeling," she told him. "Right now, we'll have one another's backs. And . . . yes, tonight we'll get all social and see who is doing what!"

He smiled, drew away, took her hand and continued down the hallway.

People were gathering to take their seats for the brothers' lecture. He realized that they were coming to casually know several of the people who attended the classes; they all nodded or said hi to one another.

It was a cruise, after all.

Daniel, the younger brother, spoke first, though he and his brother, Broderick, stood side by side at the podium.

"Security! We all want to think that we don't need it. Sadly, we all do. *Sadly*, things as simple as social media posts are hacked all the time, emails are hacked . . . then you get into hospital arrests, police records, business records and so much more! Unfortunately, there is nothing out there that can't be hacked—including many important records and reports within the government. Now, hopefully, none of us is hiding any state secrets, but . . . we want whatever our work is to be safe! Onward to security!"

"Bulwark Cybersecurity!" Broderick announced. "And so, we begin! Let's talk about when and where certain information can go out and then we'll move on to firewalls!"

Wes glanced at Chloe. She listened. She took notes.

And he did the same.

They were good speakers; they were good teachers.

Wes learned things he didn't know.

But sadly . . .

There was nothing about the brothers or their lessons that indicated in any way the possibility that they might be psychopathic killers.

# FIVE

CHLOE PACKED UP her notebook and looked over at Wes. She was surprised that she could read him so well.

They'd come, they'd seen . . . they had yet to conquer, but watching the brothers give their lecture and class had, at the least, given them deeper insight into the pair.

It was easy enough in their environment to play an undercover role, she thought. Wesley Law was no stranger to taking on a different persona. He knew how to play the game, as did she, of course. Then again, when the powers that be were as concerned as they were, it was natural that they had chosen who they saw as the best agents for the case even if they were from different agencies, or perhaps, even because they were from different agencies.

"Sweetheart, it's almost dinnertime. I think we should maybe allow ourselves a little break, a drink out at a pool bar . . . then we can stop in quick and make sure that Edward is all right and head to dinner!" he told her. He'd been sitting next to her and pocketed his small notebook. He turned toward her, taking her hands in his. "Sound good?"

Any of the passengers milling around them would have seen the exchange between them and heard Wes's words.

"Hm, sounds delightful!" she said in turn.

As they rose, he slipped an arm around her shoulder as he led them out of the classwork salon and down the hallway to the elegant double doors that stood open, welcoming passengers out to the adult pool, the bar and the lounges.

Wes glanced at her. She realized that he wanted her to distract anyone standing closer around the bar or taking up the seats.

She smiled at a young couple who were close, a man and woman in their early thirties, she thought, him dark and handsome in nothing but his bathing briefs, she a pretty brunette in a bikini.

"Hey!" Chloe said, speaking loudly enough to cover whatever Wes might be saying. "Wow! Did we get lucky with this. Not only the perks given to everyone by Milestones, but somehow, we've gotten the most incredible weather known to man. Clear skies, calm waters—just the right amount of warmth for the breeze!

"Oh, it is, it's amazing, we're so, so happy!" the young woman said. She offered Chloe a hand. "I'm Patty Easton, this is my husband, Ned."

"Chloe. Chloe Douglas and that's my husband, Wes, ordering for us. So nice to meet you both!" Chloe said.

"Chloe and Wes!" Ned Easton said, turning on his barstool to appraise her. "You and your husband . . . wow! You two just dove straight down, what, hundreds of feet, after that Milestones exec. You really are something!"

Chloe shook her head. "It's really not that big a deal. It's stupid, really. I'm sure the ship's crew would have been fine. Wes owns dive boats, he's been in the water all his life. I don't even know what all his certificates are . . . And, once upon a time, I thought I might be a major league diver, but then, you know, once upon a time, I wanted to be a mermaid, or a princess, or . . . well, you know. What we did was just kind of natural for us."

"Still, wow," Patty told her.

Chloe winced. "Honestly, it's a little uncomfortable now. I mean, we're all excited that Milestones offered all this amazing info for all the passengers, but we planned this trip months ago because . . . well, you know. Life! We needed some time to get away together, sun, sky, water—"

"Beer!"

Wes had gotten their drinks and handed an icy cold glass filled with amber liquid to her. She accepted the glass while he stood behind her, smiling at the couple she had just met. She wondered just what he'd been saying to the bartender that had needed her to keep others from hearing him, but as she took a sip, she knew.

He'd ordered alcohol-free drinks and while it might not have mattered, blending in on a cruise, they might look as if they were enjoying a bit of hard refreshment.

Introductions went around again as Wes met the couple. He winced as he was applauded again for his actions regarding Edward Thompson's "fall."

"Hey, sorry, cool, we won't mention it again!" Ned assured him. "You guys are nice and humble and just want to chill. But hey, Chloe was just saying that the classes were something cool you hadn't expected. Patty and I were lucky—we wanted this cruise and managed to get on because another couple canceled due to illness at the last moment. We really, really wanted to take a bunch of these classes."

"We did the morning stints, then decided that we needed a little downtime," Patty explained.

"What do you do? For work, or—"

"I'm a cop in Detroit," Ned said. "Beat cop, but I'm always fascinated by what our people behind their desks can discover—and the way they explain it all to us. But that's not why we're here, really," he added, looking at his wife.

She sighed. "I got hacked and it was bad. Just social media! Someone . . ."

"Someone Photoshopped a bunch of pictures of Patty and got them out on the web. She just had your typical casual social media, pics of our dogs, family members, our nights out with friends . . . But you would be amazed, absolutely amazed, how pics like that can be changed into something demeaning and horrible and totally reprehensible."

"And I don't want to be cut out of social media for the rest of my life—I love seeing pics of my friends and their kids and so much more . . . But, oh, man! They're still trying to track whoever did it. I wasn't the only one who fell prey to that monster!" Patty said. She looked at her husband with affection. "I, at least, am married to a man who shared my outrage and keeps up with the police and others who want to catch the horrible human being who is doing this to others!"

"That's the thing," Ned told them gravely. "First, some of the pictures are pictures I was in before they were twisted, secondly, I love my wife. I'm no profiler, but whoever does things like this must be a miserable, lonely human being who can only feel better by trying to destroy the lives of others."

"Wow! There was no attempt at extortion on these?" Wes asked. "They weren't doing it to try to blackmail money out of people?"

"No one ever asked for money—they just showed up. And

our cybercrime division is still trying to get to the bottom of it!" Ned told them.

"Wow. Well, I can see how this is important to you," Chloe said. "It's frightening that people can do that."

"Hey, they've done it to all kinds of celebrities, too. Different people doing it, I imagine, which makes it all scarier," Patty said. "I'm into Bulwark Cybersecurity! They're honest. Nothing is foolproof, but you can make things harder for hackers!"

"We went to their class. It was very good," Chloe said gravely. As she spoke, she noticed that one of their suspects was standing by the railing farther aft, sipping wine and looking out over the water. It was Abigail Swenson.

Nothing strange there. It was a beautiful time of day; classes were over.

But she smiled suddenly, waving and calling out.

Chloe saw that she was looking at Celia Henderson and that the woman was hurrying over to her, ready to greet her with a friendly hug.

The two knew each other.

Nothing surprising there.

But they knew one another very well. As friends, long-time friends?

As she tried to casually keep an eye on them and respond to the conversation going on with Patty and Ned, she saw that Jeff Henderson was joining the pair, too, greeting Abigail like a good friend, as well.

Chloe knew that she couldn't take it to mean too much—they had known that all their suspects were connected in one way or another, whether it was simply through conventions or meetings or because they had formed real friendships.

"Oh, did you attend anything with Celia Henderson and her husband, Jeff?" Chloe asked Patty and Ned, smiling and indicating that the threesome was near them. "I mean, they all talk about security, but I attended specifically because I want to keep my artists safe when I'm advertising a show. I want attention for them, of course, but with what you're telling me . . . wow. It's scary what people can do!"

"Very. We haven't had a chance yet," Patty said. "Tomorrow, we're in Jamaica and we've signed up to go to Dunn's River Falls. Did you? We've been before. It's so very beautiful!"

"I think so, yes. We did sign up, didn't we, Wes? It was one of the things that we had talked about!"

He nodded. Of course, they'd talked about the falls.

And about the dangers that could be found there. Part of the beauty of the place was walking up the falls. Of course they were going. And still, even going . . .

How could they keep an eye on everyone on that cruise who might be in danger?

There were guides; there were others.

Right. Dozens of people. Hundreds. And somehow, Edward Thompson had still gone over the rail.

"Of course we're going!" he said, and looking at Chloe he teased, "As you wish!"

She groaned aloud. Patty and Ned laughed. "So, it's Westley and Buttercup!" Patty said.

"Oh, yeah! I think of her as a princess all the time!" Wes said.

She smiled at him over her gritted teeth.

"Oh, yeah. And he's just like a dread pirate!" she agreed.

Wes just grinned and shrugged.

Patty laughed softly and said, "And we're at sea! But that's so nice that you're going to the falls, too. I guess we're going to go in and shower before dinner. We're doing sushi night!" Patty told her. "Ooh, and a little secret! We heard that the computer experts giving most of the classes are going to be there, too. I mean, food is great and there will be a band and all, but . . . maybe we get a little extra!"

"And it sounds like a great plan—and great food," Wes said.

"See you there!" Patty said, rising. She took her husband's hand and waved; Chloe and Wes waved in turn.

Chloe looked at Wes. "Buttercup?"

"Sorry, couldn't help it. Hey, the whole world loved that movie!" Wes said.

"You love it?"

"I did. I identified with the kid in the bed," Wes told her.

She laughed. "Not the Dread Pirate Roberts?"

Wes grinned at her and reminded her, "The move came out in the '80s!"

He moved close to her, affectionately whispering in her ear, "Okay, dilemma. Do we stay here and make sure that one of that trio isn't ready to push one of the others into the sea? Or check on Edward Thompson?"

"Check on Edward Thompson. Nobody is going to pull that one again so quickly. But I'm glad our new friends mentioned the sushi dinner. I'm going to love a word with our nurse practitioner, George Garcia."

"Right, great. Lovely beer, by the way."

"The only nonalcoholic option they had."

"I don't think one beer would have killed us."

"And we may want one later. I don't want to advertise the fact that we're avoiding alcohol. I mean, we're a young couple on a second honeymoon and we need to look like we're trying to enjoy ourselves to the fullest!"

"All right! Fun, fun, fun!" Chloe said. "But, of course, we've already proven that we're super cool. Anyway, let's go see that man we saved!"

They broke apart and headed in, taking the elaborate elevator to the deck where the hospital, spa and gyms could be found.

They didn't see Doctor Kilbride, but one of his nurses was at the desk. She waved to them and said, "He's awake. They're going to bring down some dinner for him soon but I'm sure he'd love to see you!"

"Thanks!" Wes called, and they walked into Edward Thompson's room together.

George Garcia was there, as he said he would be. A hospital chair—the kind that stretched out into a bed—had been brought in for him. He had a book out and it appeared that he and Edward had been discussing the merits of the book.

George nodded to them. Edward shook his head. "You two! Please, don't let my clumsiness destroy your whole trip!"

"Oh, no, sir—Edward!" Chloe said. "We're having a wonderful time, and part of it is because of you."

"Sorry, not falling off the boat again!" Edward said lightly.

"No, no!" Chloe said, laughing. "Because of these amazing classes you set up! We're totally enjoying them!"

"Well, that's great. You know, I've talked to the doc and to my nurse, my man Garcia here, and I'm going to go into Montego Bay for lunch tomorrow. They don't believe that I should head over to Ocho Rios for the Falls, but it will be super to get to be a little social again."

"I told him a *little* social!" George Garcia said. "And that, whatever kind of a companion I may be, he doesn't get to ditch me for a minute!"

Edward groaned softly. "Most people who survived a drowning would just be running around again now! And I'm stuck with this dude. Just kidding. George is great. And we're both fond of the classics! He brought me a bunch of audiobooks and I'm loving it!"

"Wow. That's wonderful. Maybe you're getting a bit of a break that you really needed!" Wes told him.

"I'll be up to my classes—with Mr. George Garcia watching over me—for our next day at sea. Tomorrow . . . I've always loved Jamaica. Montego Bay, the mountains and, of course, Ocho Rios." He made a face. "Kingston? Well, you know, that's any big city. But this ship takes us to Montego Bay and offers excursions to the right places. So . . ." He looked expectantly at Chloe and Wes.

"Dunn's River Falls," Chloe told him.

"So beautiful!" Wes said.

"Oh, you've both been before, right?"

"We have," Chloe told him. "And it's beautiful, but you do need to take of yourself, Edward!"

"Lunch. We're getting off the ship, finding a cool place, and having lunch!" George assured them. "I will be at his side."

"It's so good that you're here and dedicated to Edward," Chloe told him.

"Of course. And I'm lucky the company sent me. I'm excited about lunch in Montego Bay myself!"

Wes was glad when the man nodded subtly, assuring him that Edward, at least, would be all right.

And that if the whole thing had been an act and he was still among the suspects . . .

No. It couldn't have been an act. Unless the man had pitched himself into the sea and was suicidal, which Wes didn't believe for a minute. Edward Thompson had nearly drowned; he had stopped breathing.

"So, you children off to enjoy a good dinner tonight?" Edward asked. "A little dancing before heading to your cabin for the evening?"

"Something like that," Chloe said, grinning at Wes. "The

restaurants on this ship are amazing, all of them, from casual to elegant!"

"Food. Right. That's what I'm thinking about," Wes said, arching a brow to Chloe with a smile.

That afforded Edward a great deal of amusement, but he said, "Hey, this cruise line is owned by one of the most excellent restaurant chains in the business. Of course, the food is going to be good. But you two run along now and have fun! You don't need to spend your time babysitting me. I have Mr. George Garcia. And lately, we've been dissecting *Pride and Prejudice* and we're having a great time comparing literary classics to books being written for the contemporary commercial field."

"Books! That's great to hear," Wes told him. "I mean, you're all about computers and—"

Thompson interrupted him with a laugh. "Computers! Don't you know, you can read books on computers these days, too!"

"Right, of course," Wes murmured. "Well, I guess we should be getting on with dinner, my love. What say you?" he asked Chloe.

George let out a loud sigh. "I'm here, people, go have fun!"

"Wait!" Edward said suddenly.

"Yes?" Wes asked.

"You—you're afraid for me!" Edward said, as if he'd truly just made such a realization. "You think that someone . . ." His voice trailed.

"Edward!" Wes assured him. "Yeah, of course, we're worried about you. You're an incredible human being who is offering so much to so many people!"

"It's because of Jane. Jane Sewell," Edward murmured.

"Jane Sewell is dead, Edward—"

"But I cared about her. I still can't believe what happened.

I mean, you know, there had been a bigger meeting down in South Florida right before it happened and maybe there's someone out there who . . . You think someone may try to kill me, too!" Edward said with great alarm.

"Edward, whatever these two think is irrelevant," George announced quietly. "They're just a nice couple checking up on you because they're grateful for what you've done for everyone. And, sir, if you've any fears yourself—"

"Oh, yeah! I've got fears!" Edward said. "Now . . . now when I think back! There were so many people on deck, but there was a strange pressure against my back. I leaned forward to let people by behind me and suddenly . . . suddenly I was sailing overboard! And if it hadn't been for the two of you . . ."

"I'm here. Always!" George assured him. "You are my sole concern while we're on this ship. No matter what people think, no matter what is true and what isn't, I will let nothing happen to you, I swear it!"

"You're an amazing nurse, an amazing man!" Chloe said softly.

"George is the best," Edward assured them. "I feel badly that he doesn't get to have any fun. I mean, come on, this is a cruise ship! Never met a guy so dedicated."

"And I'm here for you," George reminded him.

"But you should get a chance to get some air, out on the deck—" Wes began.

"Tomorrow we will be going to lunch in Montego Bay. We'll get him off the ship for that, but . . . Hey, George! You should take a walk, a quick one, go with these young people for a minute—"

"Not leaving you, sir. The sick bay isn't full, but Dr. Kilbride is off having lunch. Yes, his nurses are here—"

"Hey! I'm here. George, take a walk with Wes," Chloe said, beaming. "I'm not a doctor, no, but we do think that

Edward is doing fine and you two should take a little walk! It will make your book discussions a little fresher—just like the fresh air!"

Wes glanced at her, managing a grin. It was the right response. But Chloe knew that he was gratified.

Because she knew. She wasn't sure how she knew, but she did. Wes really wanted to talk to George alone, to find out if anyone else had been in, if George had a new take on anything . . .

The man was a registered nurse practitioner. But he was also with the Bureau and he might have insight on something that Wes, in his undercover situation on the cruise, just might not.

"We'll be five minutes!" Wes said.

"No!" she protested. "Make it ten!"

The two men left.

"Let's do it!" he said. "Just walk out to the outer spa area on this deck. Chloe was willing to jump into the brine for Edward—she's not going to let anything happen to him!"

Chloe smiled and took the seat next to Edward where he lay in the bed as Wes and George headed out for a minute.

She was sure that none of them wanted to look ridiculous or overprotective in any way, so they stopped to chat with Dr. Kilbride's nurse for a moment before walking out.

"That really is one great guy," Edward said, indicating George. "Then again, so is your husband."

"Thanks! I certainly think so," Chloe said, smiling.

"But I get the feeling . . ." Edward mused.

"Yes?"

"Well, let's see, a private nurse from Milestones. Now, I am a vice president, head of continuing education, which is why I'm the rep on this cruise. But we have four VPs other than me and I'm not the CEO in any way, shape or form. Which makes me think . . ."

"Think what, Edward?" Chloe asked innocently.

"That Milestones is seriously concerned about my welfare. That someone there thinks that I may be in danger. Lots of people knew Jane Sewell well. She was a nice person, Chloe. She was bright and sweet and . . . I have a hard time believing that she could do something so awful. Maybe because I'm lying here, but it's bothering me more and more. Now I know that the cops didn't find anything but everyone dead and Jane with the gun, but there had to be something more!"

"I'm sure that your thoughts have occurred to others, sir. Including law enforcement."

"Chloe . . ."

"Seriously!"

He laughed. "I meant that you're not to call me sir!"

"Oh!" She laughed softly. "Edward. I'll try to remember that!"

"You had parents who taught you respect, I'm certain."

She nodded. "My mother was a big believer in the simple courtesy of manners," she assured him. "But, Edward, whatever the company thinks—"

"I'm grateful. But if someone came at me with a gun, what is a nurse—even a great nurse—going to do?" Edward asked.

"We're on a ship. No one can be carrying a gun around."

"You know that's not true. Where there's a will, there's a way."

*Beyond a doubt, his words were true.*

"I get the feeling that George is a very adaptive and clever man. And if the company has any suspicions, I'm sure he's been warned."

"You're a clever young lady—for a gallery owner and art lover," he told her.

"Well, I like to think so, anyway!" she said lightly.

She sat back in her chair, smiling. And then she frowned. Celia and Jeff Henderson had walked into the waiting room.

And they were followed by a man of about forty she'd seen in their class, the class on dating and promotion.

And he was angry.

"All this you're doing . . . You know that something awful just happened. You didn't even mention your friend! Didn't warn people to be careful of who they choose to be around because someone in this field is out to hurt others! You shouldn't go anywhere near Mr. Thompson!" the man was saying angrily.

Well, it was natural, of course. Word of Jane Sewell, who killed five people and then herself, had hit the news everywhere.

Maybe the real oddity was that it hadn't come up from anyone until now!

"Sir!" Jeff said indignantly. "We were as stunned and horrified as anyone else who might have heard about what happened. But that . . . that was a tragic event that had nothing to do with us, nothing to do with this cruise. The sad fact is that horrible things happen all the time. Sad, tragic and horrible, but still, that's not part of our day-to-day lives! For you to assault us—"

"I haven't touched you!" the man snapped.

The hospital nurse was on her feet, asking the unknown man and Jeff and Celia to please tone it down, to remember that they were in the ship's hospital and that she was hoping she didn't need to call security to have them removed.

"I knew it would come up!" Edward said quietly.

"Young woman," Celia said. "My husband and I were doing nothing but coming to see to the welfare of our good friend Mr. Thompson when this man ran in after us and attacked us!"

Chloe stood, ready to move fast, if necessary, but thankfully Wes and George chose that moment to return.

"What's going on here?" Wes asked politely as George hurried on past the visitors to enter Edward's room.

Naturally, since a window covered the upper portion of the hospital room so that a patient could be seen from the nurse's station, he could still watch what was going on.

"Do you know who that is?" George asked Chloe.

Edward answered quickly. "Celia and Jeff Henderson, two of the computer folks giving the lectures on the ship. And the man . . ."

"I don't know him, though I did see him in their class," Chloe said.

Wes was handling it, defusing the situation. He'd gotten the man to introduce himself; he was Howard Markowitz, an executive with a clothing chain, and while he had wanted to learn more about promotion from them, he had the ship's Wi-Fi package and had just seen another article on how all the people killed in Broward County had been in the tech industry.

"And I realized, that's what we all are!" Markowitz said.

"Sir, I can see your concern, but to suddenly attack these people for giving classes to those who want to go . . . Well, please. Strange and horrible things do happen every day and I'm afraid you can't go around accosting the people on this ship who happen to be in the same business," Wes said gently. "You being troubled is natural, sir, but everyone here was horribly upset by what happened."

Markowitz was a man of about forty; tall, with brown hair and a neatly trimmed beard and mustache. Chloe could imagine that in a suit he made an impressive-looking businessman.

"My wife is on this cruise with me! I just . . ." He paused and let out a long breath. "I'm sorry. I just . . . I'm leaving now. No need to call the ship's security."

He turned and left the waiting room.

Celia turned to Wes.

"Boy, you are a lifesaver!" she said. "In many ways."

"Well, naturally," Wes murmured to Jeff, his tone a little sheepish. "My wife and I have grown fond of Edward, and . . ."

Jeff laughed. "Oh, so it was cool that he attacked us, just not in front of Edward?"

"No, no, it's just why we were down here, to see him," Wes explained. "And it's true, of course. I mean, pretty much anyone with a phone saw the news about that poor woman who allegedly killed all those people . . . So very tragic and sad, but she took her own life, as well . . ."

"We all knew Jane," Jeff said. "And she was lovely. It's heartbreaking what happened, but we understood that she was . . . well, heartbroken herself. And maybe she felt that the world was taking away her chance to be really loved or . . . I don't know. None of us understands what goes on in the hearts and minds of others, right?"

"Too true," Wes told him. "Anyway . . ."

"Anyway! Onward! We're going to step in to see Edward! No classes tomorrow—we're in Jamaica!" Celia said.

"Absolutely. Jamaica!" Wes agreed.

"And the Dunn's River Falls!" Jeff said.

"Yeah. We're intending on going on the tour ourselves," Wes said.

"Nice! No computers, just lots of water. Yeah, we are on the water now. Crystal clear water, beautiful sun, but it is different," Jeff said.

Celia headed on into the room, smiling at Chloe and then George and Edward, of course.

"We came to see—" she began.

"Celia! I'm great!" Edward told her. "You've met this young man, George Garcia. With him at my side, I couldn't be anything but great! Now, all of you! I'm fine. Go to dinner. Go dancing. Go have fun—it's a cruise!"

"Okay, okay! We had a minute, so we thought that we'd drop by!" Celia told him.

She walked closer to him, giving him a kiss on the top of his head. Chloe wondered how easy it would be for someone to try to do something to him with so simple a gesture.

But George was standing right at Edward's side, watching every second.

Nothing would go unnoticed.

But then again . . .

Celia couldn't be their only suspect, not when they also had her husband, Jeff, brothers Daniel and Broderick, and Amelia Swenson.

And still . . .

Celia really could be nasty when she chose, even if she seemed to choose to aim that behavior toward her husband more than others. It wasn't that she was overt—it was in the tone she used when speaking with him, the way that something simmered just beneath the surface, as if she was the one who was always in charge.

"Shall we?" Celia asked, looking around the little room at her husband, Wes and Chloe.

"Yep, dinner! We shall!" Celia said. "Later, Edward. George, make him behave!" she added, heading out of the room with the others in her wake.

She glanced back at Wes.

He was playing the part, looking like nothing other than a man about to have a nice dinner with his wife and friends.

Except . . .

He'd learned something from George. She wondered how long she was going to need to wait to discover just what that was.

# SIX

BEYOND A DOUBT, Wes felt like he was a passenger aboard a luxury liner. Then again, most cruise ships were nice, but this . . .

Even the deck furniture was elegant; deep, rich carved wooden chairs and lounges with plush upholstery. Barstools were comfortable; the bar itself was handsomely carved mahogany, he thought.

What wind and rain must do! But then again, he assumed the crew was ready to protect the extravagance of the furniture when the weather threatened.

And now, of course, he was curious about the areas George had described.

As a crew member coming aboard, George had been privy to some of the different areas of the ship.

A lower deck that carried ballast.

One for the immense piles of garbage a ship at sea accumulated.

One for all the mechanics needed to oversee the power for the giant vessel.

Another for the crew, which was, George had explained, kind of like a massive dormitory, and which also had stowage compartments for those larger items that had come aboard, and passengers couldn't keep in their cabins.

George had painted a good picture for him with words; he'd also explained the different passages that led to the unseen parts of the ship.

And, of course, he knew that Chloe was anxious to learn what they had discussed, but she would stay patient and allow things to play out for the time being.

As she was doing now . . .

"What was it that you said everyone was feeling like tonight?" she asked Celia. "There are choices, choices! One of these nights, we want to do the elegant seafood restaurant—"

"Ah, you don't think that sushi is elegant?" Jeff teased.

"No, I do love sushi!" Chloe assured him.

The sushi restaurant was one that included both an inside and an outside area. Celia suddenly turned to wave at someone.

"Oh, look! There's Abigail Swenson—she has plenty of room at her table. Let's head that way!" Celia said.

"Sure, sounds great," Wes said, heading through the tables and passengers to reach the table.

He noted that the man who had accosted Celia and Jeff, Howard Markowitz, had also opted for sushi that night. He was several tables away, seated close to a woman with long dark hair Wes assumed to be his wife.

There were others at the table.

Howard looked up, glancing over at Wes. He simply nodded gravely.

Wes gave him a nod in return.

He hadn't come to have sushi in order to attack Celia and

Jeff again; he had gotten there first and Wes was pretty sure that the nod meant he didn't intend to cause any trouble.

And yet it was interesting; they either knew or had met and become friendly with the others at their table as there seemed to be a lively conversation going on around them.

And he wondered how many people on the ship—while appearing to be so delighted and intrigued by the classes—weren't wondering as well how all these people weren't more concerned about what had happened.

The other deaths hadn't been connected to the incident in Broward, not in the press.

And, of course, it was sad, but people did lose their minds and do horrible things.

"The menu is wonderful, everything you can think of! Sashimi, sushi, rolls, bowls, salads . . . There's even seaweed, rice paper, lobster rolls, you name it!" Celia said happily.

"And it's mostly all stuff that's good for you, too!" Jeff announced, looking over at his wife. "Celia likes to limit red meat, make sure she has lots of vegetables, you know, the body is a temple and all that!"

"Hey, he'd have a bacon cheeseburger for breakfast, lunch and dinner!" Celia told them. She smiled at him, but it was, Wes thought, a warning smile. It was just another little below-the-surface type thing that she said or did that cemented her as the alpha dog in the duo.

"Well, we're in the right place, then!" he said, nodding to Abigail as they all took seats at her table.

"Hey, guys, welcome!" Abigail said, looking up from her menu.

"Thanks, cool that we're joining you all?" Chloe asked.

"Of course! Table seats ten. I can't take up all this room on my own," Abigail said.

"And it's good when we get to talk to people—you know, besides taking different classes," Celia said. She leaned forward and said quietly, "You wouldn't believe what just happened!"

"What?" Abigail asked. "I mean, not—"

"No, no, just some idiot followed Jeff and I down to the hospital area, wanting to know how we're all acting so casual and not worried because of . . . of what happened with Jane. It made me so mad! They didn't know her. Oh, I'm sorry. Yes, we all knew her. You know, through the years, software events—just getting together. She had to have been in the deepest, most horrible bowels of depression!" Celia told her in a whisper. "I mean . . . there's no way not to think about it and get a little worried now and then!"

Abigail glanced at Wes and Chloe.

"And then—" she began, frowning slightly, as if this was something they shouldn't have been discussing in front of others.

"Well, then Wes swept in and politely calmed the idiot down," Jeff said.

"Truly the hero of the hour!" Abigail noted, staring at Wes.

He grimaced. "Hey, we've come to really like Edward and it wasn't right for someone to follow you into the hospital area like that!"

"Edward was okay?" Abigail asked.

"Edward was good. Chloe was in with him," Celia said.

"The guy was just—I think he just had a panic attack because he saw the news on his computer or something. Gee. Computers are so great! Every once in a while, though, the way they can give and give and give can be a pain," Wesley added.

"It's not the computer's fault if someone chooses to watch the news," Chloe pointed out.

"We're on a ship! A cruise ship! No one should be watching the news on a cruise ship," Abigail advised.

An older woman with beautiful silver-white hair and a friendly face came to the table, pulling out a chair and asking, "May I? Sally Brookins, all way down from Toronto to take a trip out of Miami."

"Please, please, of course!" Chloe said. She introduced the group around the table.

"And you three are with the folks helping out Milestones," Sally said, nodding toward Celia, Jeff and Abigail. "And you!" She beamed at Wes and Chloe. "You are the miraculous swimmers, divers! Who went down into the deep blue sea for Mr. Thompson!"

"Nice to meet you, Ms. Brookins," Chloe said.

"Please, we're on a cruise! I'm Sally. And I'm not going to talk your ears off during dinner about your classes, but I will tell you this! I booked this cruise the moment I heard about these classes, sessions, lectures—or whatever one may call them. Okay, I'm going to start by kissing your feet just a tad here! Sad to admit, but obvious, I'm afraid, I didn't grow up in anything that resembled the computer age, and I am going to be so glad to put my grandchildren in their places because I am learning so, so much! Now, I don't need to advertise any business because I retired seven years ago, but I am going to know how to post on social media, answer people on social media and torture my entire family with my absolute savvy! I am so grateful!"

"Sally, that's wonderful and so much fun!" Celia told her.

"That is very fun!" Jeff told her. "You'll know what's going on with the younger crowd!"

She nodded, smiling. "That I will. When my kids were young and cell phones first came about, I thought that they were a ridiculous extravagance. Then I discovered that you could find people that way when you were worried about them. I am all for moving into the future full speed! I just wish . . ." Her voice trailed.

"What is it?" Chloe murmured softly.

"Oh, that nice man, Mr. Thompson. I wish that he hadn't fallen, that he was going to be out among us more! He really put this all together, didn't he?" she asked.

"Well, there are a few of us he asked for help. But, yes, his company execs had the idea. He worked with the cruise line and then the captain and had a cruise director especially assigned to him," Jeff explained.

"Edward is an invaluable human being!" Celia said enthusiastically. "Not just to his company but to all of us. He's just ahead of the curve in so many things and, well, he does have one great job. When anything like this comes up, Edward is the man to call!"

The restaurant was getting busy. They all welcomed two other couples to the table, their orders were taken, and they were left to enjoy casual conversation as the waiter marched away. The talk turned to Jamaica, Sally telling them about a trip she had taken from Montego Bay to Ocho Rios and then over the Blue Mountains to Kingston when she had been young. "Back in those days, the mountains were just amazing! All the farmers up there had discovered what profit could be made in growing grass for tourists, and, well, you know, at that time of my life . . . Jamie and I were good kids, really. Young adults, I should say, just turned twenty-one and it was our last year in college when we made that trip, but the stuff was good—none of this fentanyl stuff that's going around these days!" she assured him.

"We're all going up the waterfall," Jeff told her.

"Oh, how nice!" Sally told them.

It turned out the other couples at the table were only doing tours of Montego Bay and Sally said that she was just going to find a great place for lunch.

"I wonder if we should stay in Montego Bay," Celia told Jeff. "I mean, if Edward is going to stay and have lunch, maybe we should keep him company."

"Oh, I'll be in Montego Bay!" Abigail reminded her.

"And I would love to keep that man company!" their new friend, Sally, assured them all.

"I don't think that anyone needs to worry about Edward," Wes said.

"He has George and the two of them have become fast friends!" Chloe added.

"That's right. His nurse will be with him," Celia said, looking at her husband.

"And that's great! Milestones really cares about George. I mean, this is possibly the most luxurious cruise ship in the luxury cruise ship space, and the company still sent him a personal caregiver—even though the ship has more than an infirmary, it has an actual hospital!" Jeff said. He laughed softly. "Wow! I would sure love to have his job!"

"We have our own company!" Celia protested.

Jeff laughed again. "Still, better that George fell overboard than me!"

Sushi arrived at the table and casual conversation continued, the group talking about their favorite ports, their own personal experiences with cruise ships. It was polite, easy conversation, and yet Wes found himself watching Celia and the way she looked at her husband every now and then.

Had she wanted to go after Edward Thompson in Montego Bay?

And was George's presence making that difficult for her?

To be where he was, Wes knew, the man had to be an extremely capable agent. George had told him that in situations where coworkers wound up injured, he was able to help. Medicine had always fascinated him, and he was one of those weird people who enjoyed classes and school and always wanted to go back.

And still . . .

Well, he'd already done his best to impress on the man the danger he could be in, trying to keep Edward Thompson safe. Maybe it wasn't so hard in the hospital situation. There was a doctor—or two doctors, at times—in the hospital along with two nurses. He could see anyone who was coming; anyone who came close to Thompson.

But in Montego Bay?

"Dancing?" Celia suggested, looking at Jeff as the meal ended.

"Um, hm. Casino?" he asked in turn.

She frowned. He groaned. "Dancing and then casino?"

"What do you feel like?" Celia asked Chloe.

Chloe smiled and stretched. "Bed! I'm excited about tomorrow. I want to make sure I get enough sleep."

"Oh, sure, yeah, they're going to sleep!" Jeff said in a whisper before smiling and looking at Wes and adding, "I think that's going to be an 'as you wish!'"

"It's as I wish, too!" Wes told the man. "Maybe tomorrow night, back on the ship, we'll dance—and even gamble a little!"

They rose and left the area, heading for the elevators with many of the people who had been dining and who were now going in different directions.

The ship did offer just about everything in the world.

But Wes knew that Chloe did want to get to the room

because she wanted to know what his discussion with George had been about.

In the elevator, he saw that Howard Markowitz was behind him.

"Hey, man," Markowitz said quietly, stepping out with him and Chloe when they reached their deck. "I wanted to thank you. I . . . My wife told me I was an idiot to be watching any news shows, but they were doing a report on that computer lady killing everyone and it got to me, I guess. I mean, it's all being avoided on this cruise, which makes sense, of course, but . . . I kind of flipped out. And you probably kept me from a night in the brig."

"Is there a brig on a luxury cruise?" Chloe asked, offering the man a small smile. "We understand, it is upsetting to think about those poor people and even the troubled woman who did it."

"Uh, first, yes, there is a brig on a luxury liner—you must have a place to keep someone, passenger or crew, who poses a threat to others or who needs to be held for illegal deeds. But, Mr. Markowitz, please, whatever your fears—" Wes started to say.

"Oh, don't worry. I won't be attacking anyone else. My wife and I are leaving the ship—we're going to fly home from Jamaica. I just can't stay on this thing right now. I don't know how to explain it, but I've been picking up the creepiest vibe. I mean, Mr. Thompson going overboard? Come on! Of all the people to be pushed over the rails? Right or wrong, I'm not comfortable. We're leaving tomorrow. But I wanted to thank you for stepping in and keeping me from winding up in the brig!"

"Think nothing of it, sir. No problem," Wes assured him.

"You know. You and your wife should get off this thing,

too. I mean . . . there's something just not right. I can feel it. I can really feel it!"

"Well, we can promise that we'll be really careful. Chloe and I have planned this trip for a long, long time," Wes lied, smiling over at Chloe.

"But we do thank you sincerely for the warning, Mr. Markowitz," Chloe assured him.

"Well, keep thinking about it! There's a way to go. And when you're in Jamaica, well, you be careful there. Who knows what can happen on foreign soil!" Markowitz warned.

"Thank you. And I'm sorry that you and your wife had your vacation upset by what happened in Broward County," Chloe told him.

"I'm sorrier for those people! I'll be able to take a vacation again. They won't," Markowitz reminded them.

"Of course," Chloe said softly.

Markowitz turned to get back on the elevator.

Wes and Chloe continued down to their cabin.

Chloe didn't speak until they were inside with the door closed.

Then she looked at him immediately and said, "So?"

"George is privy—as crew—to areas of the ship that we don't see. He drew them out for me," Wes explained. He sighed. "And I told him that I was worried about it being just him and Edward at lunch in Montego Bay."

"And?"

Wes smiled grimly. "I think he thought that I was questioning his abilities. I wasn't. I guess this whole thing . . . people shot without protest, drugs in their systems . . . I worry about anyone alone."

Chloe nodded. "Do you feel that you have any new insights from tonight?"

"I wish. Right now, the same as we've been thinking. But I got to considering Howard Markowitz," he said.

"He was very upset," Chloe said. "And from watching a program that the rest of the world had to be privy to?"

"And I think that Edward Thompson is becoming more and more convinced himself that he was pushed."

"Do you think . . ." she began thoughtfully.

"Do I think that he's faking? No, we've been on this route. He would have died, Chloe, if you hadn't found him—"

"If you hadn't performed CPR," Chloe murmured. "Okay, so we think that Edward is innocent. That leaves Celia and Jeff, Daniel and Broderick McClintock, and Amelia Swenson. Are you leaning toward anyone in particular?"

"Hm," Wes said thoughtfully. "I feel tomorrow is going to be important. I believe that Jeff and Celia and the McClintock brothers will be going on the tour to the falls. That leaves Amelia in Montego Bay. George Garcia is aware and prepared for anyone trying anything—he's probably the best bodyguard possible. In fact, the accident might have been a good thing because Edward Thompson will be just fine. He has a pit bull at his side for the rest of the cruise."

"Okay, so, we watch the others and their give and take with everyone else. But here is one thing that's strange . . ." Chloe murmured.

"What's that?"

"Well, our dinner companions were talking about his job, how they would love to have a position like his. Jeff joked, of course, that Edward received much better treatment from his company than Jeff would from his own wife. Do you think that Edward Thompson was the target on this trip? And that he naively asked the very people who were after him to speak for his program?"

"Possibly," Wes agreed. "But I think that it's something

bigger than that. Edward wasn't the focus of any of the other attacks. But he is in a position where he could just about take over the company from his bosses. Milestones is about the biggest thing in the business right now. Business, gaming, security, you name it. Milestones is huge and the promise of the future, so it seems. I think that someone wants the whole kit and kaboodle and getting rid of others who might be potential candidates for the company along with Edward Thompson might be the way to get in there for a less-than-hostile takeover."

"And you could be right. Which would mean that one—or two—of the suspects we're chasing may be guilty. And the others might be targets?"

He nodded grimly.

"They needed more than the two of us on this ship!" Chloe murmured.

He smiled. "Remember, I'm pretty sure you even wondered if it was a wild-goose chase, that we didn't have enough to go on. But let's focus on the good. Edward Thompson will be well guarded. And at Dunn's River Falls . . .

"Though there are wet dangerous rocks, there are also local guides, of course, as well as dozens of people around to see anything that might happen," Chloe interrupted. "But, you know, someone could have an accident there. As in a real accident."

"Like a soaring overboard?" he inquired.

"No one saw anything!" she reminded him.

Wes paused, picking up one of the brochures at the table. "Early morning! Off the ship at eight, on the bus by nine . . . an hour and a half to the site where we'll get to climb up the falls starting at about ten thirty or so. Three hours to climb, an hour and a half at a lunch spot that's preplanned. Then we're back here and out to sea again by seven."

"So," Chloe murmured. "We really should get some sleep. Edward is safe with George, but . . ."

"But the others are dancing or in the casino," Wes said dryly. He shook his head. "I think we're safe to get some sleep tonight."

"Because you think that something is going to happen tomorrow," Chloe said.

He shrugged. "And how would we stop it? Call it in with absolutely nothing conclusive? We have no leads except what the tech departments—our own—already discovered for us as far as suspects, no way to just say that hey, something is way off in big tech, stop the world?"

Chloe sighed softly. "Yeah, you've got a point. And . . . I don't know why. I don't think that anything is going to happen tonight, either. Whatever they're doing now . . . Well, whoever it is might have figured out that law enforcement just might decide that something wasn't right about several people shot dead without seeming to have protested or fought back in any way. And if so, whatever they do now is going to need to appear as an accident."

"Are you doing all right?" he asked her.

She frowned. "Of course. Hey! Okay, state law enforcement, not as big and bright as that going around the country, but we're incredibly well-trained, we work—"

"Stop! Please!" he begged her, grinning. "I didn't mean in that way. I just meant, well, you know, this takes an emotional toll. I mean, I'm not bugging you when I play with your hair or—"

"You stop! Yes, you're cute enough, but not to worry—I'm not going to turn around and attack you or throw myself into your arms!" she told him, grinning.

He shook his head, laughing, as well. "I'm just asking because it's natural to become frustrated!"

"Well, in this field, we spend most of our lives frustrated." She winced. "Now I didn't mean—"

"And I didn't mean to imply!"

Chloe laughed again softly. "Okay, so I say that we get to Ocho Rios and do the Dunn's River Falls. Have a lovely lunch—and another hour and a half bus trip back to the ship. Then, we shower and change, grab dinner—and hit the dance floor and then the casino. You a gambler?"

"Not really, though the powers that be have allowed us a little bit of a budget. And, yeah, I can play poker, craps, or . . . Well, anyone can play roulette," he said with a shrug. "And you?"

"I can play a mean slot machine if I must," she told him, before frowning. "Hm, not. I'm not taking taxpayer money into any big games!"

"Fine, you can play the cheapest slots, and I'll see what's there when we go in. And, more importantly, who's there," he said.

"That works for me!" Chloe agreed. "I can take the couch—"

"Take it tomorrow night," he told her. "We'll be a great deal more tired!"

Chloe, grinning, shook her head and retired into the cabin's bedroom.

She peeked out for a minute. "Such a gentleman!" she told him.

"I told you when we boarded—"

"Just kidding! I don't mind my nights on the bed at all!" Chloe disappeared into the bedroom.

Wes sat on the sofa, smiling for a minute. Playing husband and wife on this was no hardship. The longer they worked together . . .

The more he liked her.

The more he respected her, too.

But, of course, he was human. And no matter what the color of her hair, Chloe was a truly beautiful young woman. She could be quick to smile . . .

She could play a part incredibly.

And he was one hell of a liar. Frustrated? Oh, hell yeah! He could get frustrated.

But he could stop emotions and physical responses, too. He could, did and would. And most of the time, he was too busy reading people to give much thought to his emotions or reactions to any stimuli.

He grabbed his pillow and his blanket and was just getting ready to throw them on the sofa when there was a tap on his door.

He hadn't carried his weapon—the gun which had been created from plastic with a 3D printer—out on deck and while hanging out in groups, because Chloe had easily been able to carry hers in her bag. At the tap, he hurried to his small suitcase to dig around his clothing and find it, holding it to his back as he went to the door.

He looked through the peephole and frowned.

It was Markowitz.

Sliding the gun into the front of his pants, covered by his shirt, he quietly opened the door.

"I'm so sorry to bother you!" Markowitz said.

"It's all right. What is it?"

"I just . . . well, I wanted to warn you. I mean, you and your wife, you seem like really nice, good people. That guy . . . the big guy, Thompson, he wouldn't be alive if it weren't for you two."

"I know that you're getting off the ship and I respect you doing so, but—"

"No, I know you two don't want to leave your cruise. But

be careful. I don't like that lady. I wanted you to know that she was having a big fight with her husband in the casino. He pretended it was over money. But I heard them. And she just told him to shut up, that she was the breadwinner, he was lucky that she let him hang around. I think that you need to be very careful around her, and I know that I sound like a paranoid kook, but . . ."

"No, no, I can understand your feelings. She can be very rude to him, but some people are just like that and—"

"Why does anyone stay? Unless she is promising something big!" Markowitz said.

Wes shook his head. "Who knows? All kinds make the world go around. But thank you. And the best to you and your wife. I hope you're able to have a good vacation sometime soon!"

Markowitz nodded. "I hope I'm just being paranoid. Well, please, do be careful. You have a brave and beautiful wife, sir. Take care of her!"

"Not to worry, I intend to," Wes assured him.

"Well, good night, then," Markowitz told him. "The best to you, too."

Markowitz turned to leave. Wes watched as he walked down the long hallway to the elevator.

He closed and locked the door.

He swung around, almost drawing his plastic weapon, but he smiled because he expected what he saw.

Chloe was there. She had changed into a long nightdress, but he knew that she stood by the door to the bedroom, half opened, because she had her plastic gun out and she'd been standing there, quietly listening.

"You had my back," he said.

"Always," she promised him."Did I miss anything?" she asked.

He shook his head. "Nothing we didn't know. Celia Henderson is a narcistic ballbuster and when people hear what she says to her husband, they don't like her very much."

"But it is possible that she's much more. Possible that she's been responsible for these deaths and that he's scared, too, doesn't want to go to jail or wind up dead himself, and falls right into line so that something like that doesn't happen."

"He could go to the police," Wes said.

"He could be too scared. Then again, maybe somewhere along the line, if she is the mastermind behind some imagined takeover, he has plans to turn against her."

Wes nodded. "Possibly," he said softly.

"My fault. We should have gone dancing with them tonight."

"How could you have known?"

"And, of course, we will be with them on an hour and a half bus ride!"

"Plenty of time to listen to the lovely couple argue."

Chloe smiled and nodded. "Okay, well . . ."

"You were armed, right?" he asked her.

"Always. You know I carry one of our little plastic pieces at all times, just in case. And, of course, when I saw you open the door, you had already dug your weapon out, too, right?" she asked him.

"I did. Which makes me think . . ."

"What's that?"

"Tomorrow, bathing suits, almost nothing on . . ."

"Wes! Of course, I'll have a bag. We need towels and our wallets, right?"

He laughed. "Yeah, of course. What was I thinking?"

She grinned. "That you're frustrated?" she teased.

He groaned softly. "Okay, then. Good night. With any luck, we can just go to sleep now."

"With any luck. Good night."

She disappeared behind the door again.

Wes picked his pillow and blanket back up and stretched out on the sofa. He still lay awake. Lying down, he smiled for a minute. Yeah, he was frustrated.

In many ways! But . . .

If Celia was guilty and she was planning something on this cruise . . .

Where and when did she intend to strike?

# SEVEN

NATURALLY, THEY WERE up bright and early.

And, as seemed to be the norm when Chloe emerged from the bedroom, Wes was already up, dressed in swimming trunks and a short-sleeved cotton shirt, ready to hit the road.

"Five minutes!" she told him.

"No rush, we're okay. Not quite seven. Time to grab a delicious breakfast before heading out for an hour and half on the bus," he told her.

She laughed. "I think that the bus trip is bugging you more than anything," she told him.

"Okay, I admit it—I don't like buses. But hey! From what I've gathered, we'll have four of our suspects with us, the McClintock brothers and Jeff and Celia Henderson. What a wonderful way to get to know them!" he said.

"There will be about thirty of us on that bus, you know," she reminded him.

"In truth, it's been interesting talking to others. Howard Markowitz and his wife are going to fly home from Jamaica, so it's not just the powers that be who are so worried about what's going on," he reminded her.

"Well, we'll just be a pair of social butterflies!" she said.

He smiled at that. "I know you'll do great!" he told her.

"So will you. And I wonder sometimes if it's a bad thing, as you thought, that we both responded on instinct and went after Edward Thompson . . . People do want to talk to us," she said, grimacing.

"They do. So let's go have fun on that bus!"

Chloe laughed at his feigned enthusiasm and hurried into the bathroom, showered and stepped into her old bathing suit, wishing she'd spent the time to get a new one, covering up with a pair of shorts and a tunic top, and heading on out, bearing towels to stick into her bag.

"Cute!" he assured her.

"Trying, anyway," she said.

"More than that, you're succeeding."

"If you say so . . ."

"Am I hunky enough?" he inquired, arching a brow.

She groaned. "Let's go to breakfast!"

They headed up to the Sea and Sand dining room, the most casual restaurant on the ship, where they discovered that most of the passengers had gathered. But while it was extremely busy, it wasn't difficult to grab a couple of breakfast sandwiches and cups of coffee—the restaurant was always working to get people in and out, especially on days when the passengers were headed off on tours.

Heading out to join the throng to leave the ship, they saw George Garcia and Edward Thompson.

Poor Edward was being hailed and addressed by just about everyone near him; he seemed to be a truly loved character.

George was at his side every step of the way, ever watchful. He saw Wes and Chloe and gave them a nod of assurance.

Disembarking was ridiculously quick. Cruise ships had it down to a science, with passengers having a quick picture taken as they stepped off the ship, which were compared to the ones they took when first boarding when they returned to the vessel. Airports were using eye and facial scans, so this seemed to be something similar.

In line, they found themselves next to the woman who had been at their table the night before, Sally Brookins. She was cheerful and excited, a fountain of energy. An attractive older woman with her curiously beautiful silver hair, straight demeanor and quick smile.

"Hello, honeymooners!" she said, greeting them. "So, you two are off to the Falls!"

"We are. And you're going to head off and explore Montego Bay?" Wes asked.

"Yes!" She lowered her voice and murmured. "I may run around and . . . Well, you know! Keep an eye out for others on the cruise. See what they're up to!"

"Oh?" Chloe said.

Sally laughed. "As if none of this has occurred to you two!"

"None of this—?" Wes asked her.

For a moment, all the humor left Sally's eyes. She was deadly serious and, in truth, appeared shrewd and knowing.

And she spoke quietly, determined that no one near them would hear her words. "Come on! I heard that man the other day, spouting off! That so-called murder-suicide that occurred in Broward Country, six people dead and all of it blamed on one woman who was probably as innocent as a newborn baby!" Sally told them gravely.

Wes frowned. "Sally, if you're that concerned, you should do what Howard Markowitz is doing—leave the ship!"

"Oh, hell no, young man!" she told him.

"But Sally—" Chloe began.

Sally waved a hand in the air, cutting her off. "Not to worry. I'm a member of a group called the Wednesday Sherlockians. We love to read, of course, Sir Arthur Conan Doyle, first and foremost. But Randy Mann in a retired cop and Sheila was CIA for a decade! There's no way that we don't study current crime and put our heads together," she said.

Wes shook his head. "Sally, if there is something going on—"

"You don't fool an old broad like me! You know there is," Sally said.

"They're dangerous! You need to stay away from them! Don't follow people, take great care, don't let anyone suspect that you're suspicious—" Wes said, concern deep in his voice.

"Young man! Not to worry. I'm just a sweet old bird! And I never act like anything but!" she assured him.

"Oh, Sally!" Wes murmured.

"Really!" Chloe added, looking at Wes. She was very afraid that the woman might get herself hurt.

Or worse, killed.

As they were speaking, Chloe noticed that George and Edward were just a few people down the line behind them.

"Hey!" she said, waving to the pair.

"So, we're just off to a lovely lunch and you people are climbing a waterfall today, eh?" Edward called.

"We're going to go get wet," Wes called. "Sally is going out for lunch. Maybe . . ."

Chloe knew that somehow—she wasn't sure how—but that Wes's simple words had alerted George to the fact that they were worried about the woman.

But it wasn't George who answered.

It was Edward.

"Sally! We're just going to lunch and then back aboard the ship, all at a leisurely gait! You're welcome to join us!" he said.

"How lovely!" Sally said. "Thank you so very much. I'd be delighted to join you!"

"Wonderful. Then we'll meet—" Edward began.

"I'll just slide back there right now—the people between us will be happy to have one less person in line ahead of them!" she said.

With a brilliant smile, she thanked Chloe and Wes for being so friendly and headed on back to join Edward and George.

George gave them a wave.

Wes nodded.

Chloe looked at Wes. She moved closer, keeping her voice low as before. "Great, Markowitz leaving the ship, Sally convinced something is up—" she began.

"Chloe, I'm sure that many people are suspicious," Wes said.

"But it didn't come up at all before. Now . . ."

"Now, most people probably believe that sad and tragic as it may have been, one woman went a little crazy. The only way the other deaths have been connected is through federal investigations, so . . ."

"You have people who may also be part of something like a Sally's Wednesday Sherlockians—and others who were in law enforcement of some kind at some time," Chloe said.

He nodded. "It just makes what we're doing all the more important."

"You think that Edward and Sally will really be all right with George?" she asked.

"I do. A, the man is an experienced agent. B, he's also a nurse—suspicious of any dangers that those not in the health profession might skip over entirely. Yeah, I think they're okay with George," Wes assured her.

Off the ship, they had a chance to bid goodbye to Edward and George and head for their bus.

And they got lucky. While Celia and Jeff Henderson were seated at the front of the bus several rows ahead of them, they wound up with Daniel and Broderick McClintock in the seats directly behind them.

They had a bus driver and a tour guide. At first, the guide spoke, welcoming them to Jamaica, describing the country's history and how it, like so many places, had its first European visitor be Christopher Columbus, on his second trip to the New World in 1494.

But there was, of course, a history before that.

People known as the Redware People because of their pottery were the first known inhabitants of the island, circa 300 to 600 AD. Next up, the Arawak arrived, followed by the Spanish and the English; the native peoples fled to the mountains along with many of those who had been enslaved. Spanish rule became English rule.

Their guide went through the centuries quickly, giving them a general overview of the island, ending with Jamaica's Independence in 1962 and talking about the beauty and the many splendors of the island.

"They're forgetting the crime rate!"

Chloe turned. It was Broderick who had spoken. He looked at her and grimaced. "Well, it's true. They don't have a great crime rate. That's why it's always important to me that we go with the flow—you know, trips arranged by the ship. There was a story once—I forget where, not Jamaica, but some port—and some people figured it was cheaper and best just to go with some friendly guy at the port. Husband and wife. They were never seen again," he told them.

Chloe smiled. "Well, we are on a trip planned by the

cruise and last I read, Jamaica was doing a good job at getting a handle on their crime. Hey, I was here as a college kid—we went over the mountains with just a few friends. The biggest danger we experienced was someone getting higher than a kite, there was so much marijuana being planted, harvested—and sold to dumb tourists!" she said cheerfully.

"So, you were a bit of a stoner, then?" Broderick teased.

"Oh, not me! Even in college, I had far too much respect for my parents!" Chloe said.

"You mean you were afraid of them?" Daniel asked.

"No, I just didn't want them to be disappointed in me," Chloe said.

"Wow. You were a good kid," Broderick told her.

She shrugged. "I guess they were good parents."

Daniel laughed softly. "So, she makes a good wife, too, eh, Wes?"

"That she does!" Wes assured him with passion.

"As you wish, as you wish!" Daniel said, laughing.

"Hey! I think we told you all, we just learned how to be . . . hm, successful, I guess? We both try to do the 'as you wish' thing," Chloe reiterated, rolling her eyes. "Sometimes, something matters more to him, sometimes it matters more to me. We do a pretty good job of making it all work that way!"

"Nice," Broderick murmured, looking out the window. "And, yeah! Nice new friends, and nice views we're getting here along the way!"

As if on cue, their guide began to speak.

They passed through Falmouth with its charming Georgian-style architecture. Their guide pointed out the park that celebrated Christopher Columbus's first landing on the island. The bus driver slowed so that everyone could get a good look out the windows.

From there they moved on, with the Falls within easy reach.

It was an interesting ride, Chloe thought. Wonderful, like any friendly excursion away from a cruise ship.

People chatted, as they had been doing. But the passengers were respectful, tending to stay dutifully silent when their tour guide was speaking, only chatting as they drove along the road.

She was startled when Daniel McClintock, seated behind them, leaned forward. "It's cool, we've got a little bar in this area, some wet rocks to climb, lounge chairs in the shallow pool area. But I wish that they'd offered us the Fall and Dolphins tour!" he said.

"Oh, I know, I love that one! I absolutely love dolphins," Chloe assured him.

"Maybe we'll find a few when we're diving at the next stop!" Wes offered.

"Yeah, but the ones who are accustomed to playing around with people are so much better! There's a place in Marathon in the Florida Keys, the Dolphin Research Center, and, oh, man, is it cool. They've saved all kinds of creatures. I'm not sure if they still have it, but they gave a loving home to a blind sea lion . . . It's a really cool place. But, hey, this will be cool, too!" he said.

Broderick had leaned forward, too. "You can tell which of us does more real work! I'm just grateful to sit in a lawn chair by the beautiful sparkling water and chill!"

"Hey, I like wildlife," Daniel protested.

"He does. The house was filled with *wildlife* when we were growing up. Daniel never saw a stray that he didn't bring home," Broderick told them.

"Not a bad thing!" Chloe assured him.

"My mom will tell you that our grocery bill for pets was

bigger than the one we had for people," Broderick said, chuckling.

"It's nice that your parents were into rescues," Wes said. He twisted in his chair, too, looking back at the brothers. "Mine let me bring home a one-eyed terrier and a cat, and then I was told we had enough pets."

"Hey, they let you have a rescue!" Daniel said. "That's better than some."

"I know! So many people want *designer* pets these days! Any rescue is a good rescue," Chloe assured him. "Dogs and cats worth thousands of dollars, when so many animals need help!"

"Animals," Broderick said, nodding. He shrugged. "I almost opted for a different tour—horseback riding on the beach, right in the water."

"That was a great choice, too," Daniel said. "And they have ATVs that go out from Montego Bay. There's too much to choose from!"

"Horseback riding on the beach!" Chloe said to Wes. "That would have been fun, too!"

"Ah, yes, but here's the thing. Only one day in this port and this was what we chose. It's going to be great!" Wes said.

"And you know it, because you've been before," Daniel said.

Their guide stood as the bus rolled into its parking space.

"All right, here we are!" he told them. "The waterfall is about one-hundred-and-eighty-feet high and about six-hundred feet long and tiered just like stairs! Now, we'll be parked out by one of the gorgeous bar areas, right by a ground-level pool that looks toward the wonder of the steps! Some of you may just want to chill, to sit in the rush of the fresh, wonderful water, watch it dance and fall, drops like glitter in the air! Others are more adventurous—and more coordinated, we always hope—and will look forward to climbing the steps. Whatever your choice, my friends, you will seldom find such natural, untainted beauty! Enjoy!"

"Hey, I didn't come to just sit on my butt," Daniel said, rising from his seat on the bus and looking at his brother.

"Hey, we're not attached at the hip or anything," Broderick told his brother. "You go climb. I am going to sit my butt down in the water and just enjoy the sun!" He glanced at Chloe. "Whoops, sorry for the anatomical reference—I'm sure my brother is, too!"

"And I'm sure our Princess Buttercup has heard the word before!" Daniel groaned. "Take your time, guys! I'm off!"

Daniel did seem to be in a hurry. Broderick just shook his head as his brother made his way past those who were taking bags from the overhead bins.

"I guess we're going to do some stair climbing, too," Wes said, looking at Chloe.

She shrugged. "As you wish!"

Broderick seemed to sincerely enjoy their banter. He laughed softly, waiting for them to rise and head out before them.

Chloe rose, smiled at him and headed off with Wes right behind her.

There was no doubt that the landscape in Jamaica was spectacular.

Chloe knew that the island was known and loved by residents and world travelers alike for its diverse geography; while the Dunn's River Falls were probably the most popular, the island was filled with spectacular falls and the island offered rich forests, mountains, fresh water and incredibly beautiful beaches.

Many, many cruise ships offered ports on the island for their passengers. And, speaking to the McClintock brothers, she hadn't been lying.

She'd been to the falls with her parents.

And she had traveled the mountains as a college student. But that, she knew, was a great part of this particular undercover gig—the truth was useful, it helped keep their conversations natural, made it so that they could keep their mission a secret while still sharing real facts about their personal lives and upbringing.

"So!"

Their guide announced the single word as they gathered at their starting point.

Some of the guests intended to just chill in the lagoon pool where they were gathered.

Some intended to walk up the dryer rock on the side of the falls.

And some intended to take the steps that put them in water that was ankle deep to waist deep.

Broderick intended to chill.

But since Celia, Jeff and Daniel were going to do the falls the "wet" way, that was the track that Chloe and Wes would take, as well.

It was no great hardship.

While approximately fifteen members of their group were going to be following another young guide up the falls' rocky wet slopes, they managed to get positions near Celia and Jeff in the lineup, just a few people back from Daniel McClintock. Of course, their group was friendly—they'd all been cruising together, running into one another in the restaurants and casinos . . .

And relaxed people tended to be nice.

"Wow! The water is so cool, clear and refreshing!" one young woman claimed, taking her first step up the rocks, laughing as the water startled her as a spray burst out at them from above.

"Glad you're having fun—at last!" an older man behind her approved.

The young woman, perhaps about nineteen or twenty, glanced at Chloe, rolling her eyes. "Hey! I'm just not a big fan of the casino—I was out of the money I had in ten minutes!"

"That can happen!" Wes said, nodding.

"Now, the computer classes are cool, really cool! Thank you, guys!" the young woman said, tapping Daniel McClintock on the shoulder. "And you guys, Celia, Jeff! We can't thank you enough!"

"Are you kidding?" Jeff said. "We love what we're doing. Hey, careful, the rocks are getting a little more slippery here!"

He reached out to offer a hand to his wife.

Too late.

Celia hadn't gotten good footing, but . . .

"Jeff!"

She started to slide back, her body skimming the rocks to the side, enough to slow her down, but . . .

Chloe knew that Wes could move fast; she'd just never seen him move *that* fast. He was behind Celia in two seconds.

He caught her before she could slip and crash down into the foot of water covering the rocks where they were stepping.

"Oh!" she cried. "Oh, my!"

"Celia, Celia, oh, my love, are you all right?" Jeff demanded, hopping down by her side.

"I'm . . . my arm. My arm is a little cut up. I . . ."

"Come on, we're going to take the dry path!" Jeff said.

"No, no, I—"

"Celia, dry path or we can chill with Broderick down in the lagoon area," Jeff told her.

The young woman who had just been speaking with them was staring at them in dismay. "Sweetie," her father said, "come on, now, let them make their own decisions!"

The young local guide they had for the climb came down to them, trying to ascertain if Celia had really been injured.

She'd scratched her arm.

That was it.

And she and Jeff made the decision just to head down and enjoy the pool with Broderick.

"Hey, do you need me?" Daniel asked them.

"Hell, no! I mean, sorry, thanks. No, we're fine!" Celia told him. "Please, Daniel, you go ahead and enjoy!"

Chloe glanced at Wes.

Now, three of their suspects were down in the lagoon pool.

But they might be too obvious following them at this point and, in truth, she wanted to talk to Wes about what had happened.

Apparently, he'd been seeing what she'd been seeing.

Something a wee bit different.

"I think she'd intended to fall," he murmured quietly in Chloe's ear.

And it was what she had been thinking. Jeff hadn't really missed his wife's hand.

She had meant to fall.

Insurance? Had she wanted to sue someone, either the cruise ship owners, their bus guide or the young man guiding them at the falls?

*They had all signed waivers, acknowledging what they were doing and that the falls could be dangerous.*

Or . . .

Did she want to hang around a nurse. Get closer to George. And through George . . .

Get closer to Edward Thompson?

"Poor thing!" the young woman said. "Oh, and she's so great! I loved taking her classes on the apps, how to be safe . . . But then I heard . . . Oh, sorry!" she murmured.

"No, no, please!" Chloe said. "What were you about to say? Oh, and I don't think that we've met formally. I'm Chloe Douglas and this is my husband, Wes!"

"Darlene Jordan and my dad, Bryan," the young woman told them quickly.

"Darlene!" the girl's father warned.

"Dad—"

"Wait!" Bryan said softly.

Chloe frowned. She realized that Bryan Jordan was watching Daniel McClintock.

But Daniel was already moving on, chatting with a few young women, obviously in "flirt" mode.

"Dad, I need—"

"Darlene!" he said again, firmly.

He seemed to be making sure that Daniel McClintock was far ahead of them.

Bryan Jordan didn't let his daughter answer. He interrupted her with a loud groan, shaking his head. First, he murmured to her, "You don't want to be offending people you want to teach you things, young lady." He turned to Chloe and Wes then, explaining, "Darlene loves her computer, and she already makes a decent income—helping herself through college—as an influencer. She was beyond excited to be on this cruise. I just told her that she had to keep me out of her *influencing* thing. No camera while we're at the falls, phone camera or otherwise. She can look up just about anything and she wants to ask all the teachers on this thing what they think, like why in the world would that other young woman become so murderous and why did all those people just sit there and get shot. I'm sorry—I'm sure you heard about it, but I don't want my girl asking questions and making anyone nervous!"

Chloe glanced at Wes.

Human nature, maybe. Or the circumstances of the crime.

Maybe anyone who knew about what had happened in Broward County was suspicious!

"I believe that law enforcement is looking into the incident," Wes said. "But here's the thing, Darlene. None of the people on this ship were there so none of them is going to know what happened. And your dad is right . . ."

"Just pretend that nothing happened? Is that fair to the people who died?" Darlene demanded.

"No, doing nothing isn't fair to them. But leaving it up to law enforcement is fair because those people are trained to investigate," Wes said.

"He's right," Chloe said. "I mean, you're loving the classes. You don't want the people teaching them, lecturing or whatever, to think that you suspect they might be awful people, even killers!" she said.

"They won't want you in their classes," Wes told her gravely.

Darlene sighed. "Well, you know, I've talked about it all over social media. And I'm not the only one!"

"Of course not. It was bizarre. But while I don't know for sure, I'd bet big-time that many agencies are working on discovering just what the truth of the situation might be," Wes told her.

Darlene grinned. "Can I interview you for my TikTok?" she asked.

Chloe groaned. "We're on a second honeymoon, Darlene. And, seriously, we don't know anything!"

Darlene laughed. "Yeah, I guess you two are a bit too old for my followers, though, hm, who knows?"

"Trust me. We're too old," Wes said, wincing. "And trust your dad. Just go to the classes and enjoy and keep your mind off the bad stuff."

"Ah, come on! We're not too old, we're too much in love, and we just want to . . ." Chloe began.

"Oh! I know what you want to do!" Darlene said, laughing.

"Darlene!" her father moaned.

"It's okay, Dad. I know the facts of life. And, hey, it's cool, they're almost *young* lovers. Okay, I'll keep my curiosity to myself and hope that someone is out there seeking some kind of justice!" Darlene said.

"Good choice!" Wes said.

"Hey!"

They were all startled back to the here and now when their tour guide called to them, looking concerned.

"Um, we're moving on. Did you want to keep climbing, or do you want to head back down to the pool—"

"Oh, no! We're sorry!" Darlene said quickly. "We're coming!"

"And you?" the guide asked Chloe and Wes.

"On our way," Wes said firmly. He turned to Chloe, arching a brow. "Sweetheart, do you need a hand up to the next rock?"

She grinned at him. "Oh, hell no! I'm glad to have you at my back, sweetheart!"

And so, they continued.

If they had just been out for a day of fun, it would have been just that. Darlene, as they discovered, was a student in journalism at Florida State. Her father, Bryan, was a contractor in the Orlando area.

Yes, of course, they loved Disney World. And Universal Studios, LEGOLAND and all the wonders to be found in the area. Bryan had grown up there as had his parents. They hadn't moved to the attractions; the attractions had arisen around them.

And still . . .

There was nothing like a cruise.

"Hey, and you're on the dive tour in the Bahamas, too, I think. I remember seeing your names when we signed up for it," Bryan told them. He made a face. "Sorry. The whole ship knows you, you know. I mean, you two did dive into the water for a rescue mission!"

Chloe grinned. "Not so heroic—we're just both experienced divers. Once we're in the water, you know, it's just instinct to dive and dive!"

"Right. Well, it will be fun to be with people so experienced!" Bryan said.

Darlene sighed. "He just never really has faith in the two of us!"

"I do! Hey, I'm pretty good, I was diving before you were born, kid," Bryan told Darlene. "But in Belize once I went on a tour that had a pack of navy divers. It was incredible because, with them, I really wasn't worried about a thing!"

"Well, heck yeah, we'll be looking forward to it!" Wes assured them.

They were nearing the top—or the top that they could reach on their walk. Their guide asked them all to pause and enjoy the incredible vista of the landscape around them.

They did so.

And then it was time to climb back down, join the others in the lagoon pool or at the nearby bar, all arranged for their vacation pleasure.

In the bar, they all ran back into Celia and Jeff—who had joined Daniel McClintock who was now back with his brother, telling him everything he had missed.

Chloe interrupted him as they joined the group, her attention on Celia Henderson.

"Celia! Are you all right? Really?" she asked with concern.

Celia showed Chloe her upper arm; she had just a scratch on it.

"I'm fine. Really fine. Thanks to your husband—if not my own!" Celia said.

Jeff Henderson groaned. "Celia, I was trying to take your hand—"

"And I just happened to be behind you," Wes said.

"But you had fun anyway, right? Did they want to get you back to the infirmary or to a doctor on the island or—" Darlene began.

"No, no, no! You can see! It's just a scratch," Celia said.

"But maybe you should have had some kind of cleaning, something antibacterial," Darlene suggested.

Celia laughed. "I hate to say it. I am not the most coordinated person in the world. If I needed medical help for every scratch, I'd be in trouble. Thank you all for caring. I'm fine. Really fine! And besides—" she said. But she broke off, shrugging. "We stayed in the cool water, in the sun . . . It's all good," she finished at last.

"Well, I guess the water is all good," Wes said, looking at Jeff.

Jeff shrugged. "She says she's fine. Besides, we'll get back on the ship. And once we're on the ship, well, they don't majorly advertise their ship's hospital, but it's supposed to be one of the biggest and best in the business. The doc has a pedigree a mile long."

Celia was looking at him oddly, Chloe thought.

But the woman just shrugged, shaking her head.

"And not only that!" Darlene said brightly. "That man, George Garcia, the man looking after Edward Thompson! He'll know before we even get back on the ship if you should be worried about anything!"

Celia smiled at the girl.

Chloe thought that it was a forced smile.

"Right," Celia said. "There's always Nurse Practitioner

George Garcia! Anyway!" She stood up from where they were seated at barstools around a little oval table. "We've time! One last bourbon. Can I buy anyone a drink?" she asked.

"Me!" her husband said.

She groaned dramatically and headed toward the bar.

Their bus tour guide arrived to announce that they all needed to reboard in ten minutes; it was time to head back to the ship.

"We missed lunch!" Darlene murmured.

"I guess so. Well, it's time to start worrying. There's never any food on that ship!" her dad said, his voice dripping with sarcasm.

They had missed lunch, spending too much time on the rocks.

And now . . .

Now it was time to head back.

And once again, Chloe realized, they had more questions than answers.

*Had Celia been trying to get hurt? Had Jeff let her hand slip a little bit too easily? Was she trying to get just hurt enough . . .*

*To spend time at the ship's hospital? To get closer to George Garcia and therefore . . .*

*Closer to Edward Thompson?*

*Close enough to give him a little jab, a little mosquito bite . . . with a good shot of a paralyzing drug?*

# EIGHT

CHLOE WAS, BEYOND any shadow of a doubt, one of the most professional partners with whom he'd ever worked, Wes thought.

Because, once they returned to the ship, she was truly in and out of the shower in ten minutes, hair washed and all. Not that showering fast was really on any agency graph regarding professionalism; it was more a representation of her entire being, swiftly ready to move and act in any direction.

He emerged quickly himself, though that day he could have stood under the hot water for a long, long time. The questions in his mind raced, seeking logic in it all was like trekking through a mire . . .

But he wasn't going to be outdone and so he emerged casually but nearly attired for whatever they determined the evening would hold for them.

Chloe was on the sofa, sipping coffee, staring into space.

"Same questions, right?" he said.

She shrugged. "What else? But . . . I think about those rocks. Celia could have been pretty seriously hurt. Would anyone really do that to themselves? Of course, you saved her, so we don't have to wonder—"

"Chloe! What was I supposed to do? I had no choice there!" he said, frowning.

She shook her head, smiling. "Of course you had to save her! No, no, no, I know that you had no choice, but I'm still wondering if . . ."

"If she meant to get hurt. Then again, hm. If she'd been really hurt, they might have wanted to send her to a Jamaican hospital or even air-lifted her somewhere. As good as the hospital on the ship is, it's not everything that a hospital can be."

"A dilemma!" Chloe said.

Wes nodded, walking over to the coffee pod machine in the room and brewing a cup for himself.

Chloe already had one, so he didn't need to worry about choosing between the gentleman his mother had tried to raise or the hardcore partner Chloe expected him to be. Then again, maybe the two things didn't need to be mutually exclusive!

"So, tonight, what do we do?" Chloe asked. "Did anyone we're hunting say anything about where they're going for dinner?"

"I'm in contact with George Garcia on this burner," Wes told her, indicating his phone. "Though that shouldn't surprise anyone if they somehow steal this phone and realize who I've been talking to. After all, we're so concerned about Edward, the man we dove in to save! Our dear Celia has already been to see him. He made sure he kept his own body between her and Edward and prescribed an antibacterial cream for her little scratch. She wasn't really hurt at all—barely a scratch on the outer flesh. Anyway, Edward had talked about his excitement over being able to move about. George will be escorting him to the ship's restaurant called The Beautiful Sea tonight. I don't know, so far," he said dryly, arching a brow to her, "I was feeling a craving for crab or lobster or maybe even their specialty, New England–style scrod. Best buttered breadcrumbs in the seven seas, so I've heard," he told her.

"Seafood it is!" Chloe said. "We've got about thirty minutes before first seatings. Oh! Did we need a reservation for that?"

"We have one."

"Hey! You didn't ask me—"

"George added us in on his reservations," Wes told her, grinning.

"Oh!" Chloe winced and gave him a smile. "Sorry. I mean, I was teasing, and it would have been fine. We seem to be on the same wavelength most of the time."

"We do. Good partnership," he said.

She laughed. "And great marriage! We fight less than anyone I know," she told him, still in her light and teasing frame of mind. But then she was suddenly deadly serious. "I am so frustrated! How do we really determine the truth about any of these people?"

"We just keep getting to know them," he told her quietly. "And, of course . . ."

"Of course, what?"

"I hope that we're right about Edward."

"You mean, we both think that he's innocent and remains in danger?" she asked.

He nodded.

"Instinct?" she asked him. "I don't know. But we've seen people trying to get near him. It would be interesting to know how lunch went today. And thank God they sent George because I don't know just how far we could have pushed it, watching over Edward and trying to see what the others were up to, too."

"We do have George," Wes agreed. "And if we head out, have a few of those amazing nonalcoholic beers, head into dinner . . . we'll find out more."

"Yes, right. Of course. I'm ready!" she told him.

They really hadn't taken much time since their return to the ship, but then again, when the captain said a time to leave the port, he meant it.

When they headed up to have their mocktails, the ship was already at sea again; Jamaica was a memory disappearing into the dusk.

"A day at sea," Chloe murmured as they headed out.

"And more computer and internet classes, should we choose. We haven't attended anything by the lovely Abigail Swenson yet," he reminded her.

She nodded. "Then again, I wonder what our people are doing when they're not speaking to the crowds."

"Let's find out."

"Maybe we'll be the only ones having dinner with Edward and George—"

"Oh, I guarantee you, the lovely Abigail will be there."

She laughed softly. "And maybe our new friend. The wonderful silver-haired Sally Brookins!"

"I do think she has a crush on the man."

"And why not? She's lively, fun, attractive . . ."

"Edward seems to like her!"

Chloe nodded, grinning. "Well, we head on and . . . wow."

"Wow?"

"I'm tired tonight! All that climbing, sun, sea and water."

"Ah, we'll need to get some vitamin B—we need to go dancing, maybe try a few slots in the casino . . ."

She made a face, and he laughed, and then sobered quickly.

"All right, well, it won't do us any good if you pass out on the dance floor. If you want to go and get some sleep early—"

"And make my beloved husband play by himself on our second honeymoon cruise?" she asked with horror. "Never!"

"Oh, okay, gotcha! But seriously—"

"Seriously. I'll make it!" she snapped playfully.

He almost chose to remain silent.

"Our first fight, my love. Okay, whatever. Oh, yeah, I remember. 'As you wish!'" he told her, a smile in his voice.

They'd reached the restaurant that they'd chosen for the night—where George had automatically added them to his reservation—and he opened the door quickly.

Chloe stepped in ahead of him and he followed.

He shouldn't have been surprised.

George must have determined that Sally Brookins was an unexpected asset; he had her positioned at the bar by Edward while he was seated on the stool to the left side of the man.

George was good. Damned good.

He saw Wes and Chloe and lifted a hand to wave. "Hey, you two. We are so happy that you've chosen to join us! We're going to have a great party going on at our table—we're stuffed with computer geniuses!" he said lightly.

Wes arched a brow.

"Well, at lunch, Abigail asked if she could come and then Broderick gave Edward a call once passengers were back on the ship and he'd barely finished that conversation before we heard from Celia and Jeff!"

"That's fantastic!" Chloe told him.

"Hail, hail, the gang's all here," Wes murmured. "Chloe, seriously, how cool! We were so excited about meeting all these computer or web or whatever people . . . computer scientists? Is there a name for all that brilliance?" Wes asked.

Edward swung around on his barstool, grinning.

"Genius!" he said. "I'll go with that title. I really like it. Though . . ."

He looked around and lowered his voice. "I'm more of a genius at supervising, at organizational tools . . . at being a boss!" he told them. "Some of these people . . . they can hack into anything, traverse the dark web as if it came with a street map! Don't ever tell anyone. I'm not that . . ."

"Criminal?" Wes asked, laughing.

Edward grinned in turn but quickly dropped their angle of conversation. Wes saw that Celia and Jeff were arriving.

"Hey, we were early, so we stopped at the bar, but I think that our table is about ready. I like it that they have the round tables—round tables, you all get to talk together. Those long ones, you can only hear and respond to the people by you or across from you. And this! This is becoming quite the family we have here!"

*Quite the family?* Wes thought dryly. *Hm.*

Edward rose and Sally and George did the same. Wes and Chloe stepped back, leaving room for George and Edward to head to the restaurant's host and to create a bit of a wall between them and the new arrivals.

But then again . . .

*What could they do here, in the crowded restaurant? If they were to hit Edward with any kind of a drug—a quick needle like a tiny insect bite—what would happen? George was there; Edward would be immediately rushed back to the hospital and there would most likely be no way to just pull out a gun and pretend he was going to shoot himself or others and then himself.*

Of course, these killers were learning.

Because Edward Thompson had been helped in his overboard dive, Wes was certain of it.

Chloe was greeting Celia and Jeff with enthusiasm, joking and laughing about how long it had been since they'd seen them, but then Chloe grew serious, asking Celia if she was really, truly okay.

"Of course! Hey, your strong man there caught me, I didn't knock my head—I barely got a scratch! Ask Medicine Man George here, I'm fine!" Celia said.

"Not so fine," Jeff said bleakly. "She thinks I dropped her!"

"No, I know that I just slipped, trying to move . . . You know, people were ahead of us, on all sides . . . I think someone brushed by me. Probably trying not to fall themselves!" Celia said. "Anyway, that is not going to be the topic of conversation for dinner. I'm fine!"

"And I'm fine!" Edward said. "We're going to think happy thoughts and have happy conversations!"

"Of course! Although!" Sally put in. "I guess it's terrible to be a bit glad we needed to worry about Edward for a bit. Maybe I wouldn't have had the wonderful chances to talk with him that I've had!"

"And we have had some great chats!" Edward said. "Okay, table, surround and sit! Oh, yeah, the last seats are for the McClintock brothers. They should be here any minute!"

"Not to worry," Wes said lightly. "We'll be, um, ten, I think—George, Edward, Celia, Jeff, Daniel, Broderick, Sally, Amelia, Chloe and me! And it's a table for ten. We'll all be good and only take a seat per person!"

"Oh, he's a funny guy!" Jeff groaned, his tone teasing.

Laughter followed his words; then they saw the last members of their group, Daniel, Broderick and Amelia heading in, and they all waved, showing them where they were.

Coming to the table early had been good; Sally and George had taken the chairs that were on either side of Edward.

Greetings went around and next up was choosing from the gourmet seafood entrées that were available.

"Lobster!" Edward announced.

"The cockroach of the sea!" Celia warned him.

"I'll take my chances."

"New England scrod—with the best buttery crumb topping known to man? I must try that!" Chloe announced.

"Hey, did you know that they're having a cooking class tomorrow?" Celia asked. "Don't worry, Edward, it's not during my class time. And Abigail and I are in. Chloe, you should come and take that class with us! Oh, um, you, too, Sally!" she added politely.

Sally smiled, but Wes thought she knew that Celia didn't really care if she opted in or not—she wasn't young and up and coming.

"Oh, I've done my share of cooking," Sally said. "I'm thinking about lying around the adults-only pool, maybe hopping in and out of the whirlpool. What do you think you'll be up to, Edward?" she asked.

"Lounging around!" Edward said, smiling at her.

Sally might have had him by a few years, but it was evident he returned her feelings. They had something. Maybe just friendship. He didn't know.

And who the hell was he to judge?

*So long as she isn't a killer—the only thing that really matters on this cruise!*

"So, how was lunch in Montego Bay?" Wes asked, looking from Edward and George to Abigail and Sally. "Good, I'm assuming."

"Charming! We had the sweetest waitress ever!" Sally said. "Jamaicans are truly nice people!"

Edward laughed. "Well, for the most part, Jamaicans are nice people! No matter where you go, people are human beings and we're all a bit different, right? Still, a truly charming lunch was had by all. Right, George?"

"I enjoyed it very much," George said.

"Abigail?" Chloe asked lightly.

"Um, yeah. It was fine. I guess I'd been hoping to get a little more done with Edward on the business side of things—" Abigail began.

"Business!" Edward groaned. "Abigail, I'm—we, all of us at Milestones—are so grateful to all of you for being on the cruise, for talking to people, helping, giving so much! But, come on, sometimes, we need to let it go. And I told you, I'm not the one in charge of the promo media department. You need to speak with Jonathan Martin about that."

"Right, right, I'm sorry, so sorry!" Abigail said. "Lobster! Cockroach of the sea! Sounds delicious to me. I'm rhyming here, but, seriously, lobster? It's delicious!"

Abigail was good, quick to joke and join in the flow. But Wes couldn't help but feel a sense of frustration again.

It seemed that they had cleared only one of their six suspects—and had they really cleared him?

All of their questions just led to more questions rather than answers.

"So, how was the day at Dunn's River Falls?" Edward asked. "Well, of course, other than Celia getting her little boo-boo!"

"The falls are absolutely beautiful. It was a great day!" Chloe assured him. "Well, we managed to miss lunch, which, in my mind, is going to make dinner all the more delicious!"

His partner leaned close to him, smiling, her face just inches from his own.

"That's what we've decided. Right, my love?" she asked.

He looked around at the others, grinning. "As she wishes. Always!"

"Ouch! We share in the same wishes! Always," Chloe protested.

Jeff groaned. "No, no, no, the answer to a happy marriage

is always making sure that the Buttercup bride gets what she wishes! Isn't that right, dear?" he asked Celia.

Celia made a face and grinned. "As you wish, dear," she told her husband.

"If only!" Jeff said.

And once again, laughter went around the table.

They ordered their food and drinks and spoke about the island, the ship and then how the classes were going.

"They're amazing!" Chloe said. "I mean, I'm independent, a small business, but I love what I do. I'm an art fanatic, and I especially love to promote my artists, so this has been wonderful for me. Promote them, of course, without putting them into danger!" she added, nodding sagely to Daniel and Broderick.

"Safety is key," Broderick said. "Many of our great—and even not so great—American politicians, military advisors and more have stated now—and years ago as well—that the internet would be our undoing. That's why I love the way we've entered into the field. Security is everything."

"Ah, yes! Security is important, extremely important!" Celia agreed. "But social media is here to stay. And, as you were saying, it's important to be *secure*, but for many people, it's the best way to put themselves out there. All kinds of people have found jobs—their livelihoods—as influencers. And many, many people have found the love of their lives! So, yes, security is important. But so is learning how to manage the zillions of apps that are out there, how not to put oneself in harm's way—and still enjoy all there is to offer. Hey. We never know if another pandemic will hit. And at its best, the internet kept us all connected when it wasn't possible to be social in a physical way!"

"True," Wes murmured. "Different apps helped us all through a difficult time." He shrugged. "It's like everything in this world. The internet offers the very, very good—and it offers some severe difficulties, as well."

"Aha! But not so much when you know all about security!" Daniel announced.

They all laughed.

Their food was served; Wes had decided on the scrod with Chloe, and it was excellent; one thing about the cruise, it did offer wonderful food. Couldn't complain about that.

When the meal ended, Broderick announced that he was heading to the casino and Celia turned to Jeff and said, "Ah, come on, I know you're tired! But . . . a wee bit of dancing!"

Wes leaned forward jokingly. "Ah, come on, as she wishes!" he teased.

"Hey, I may even hit the casino!" Edward said. "George—"

"Not a gambler, but I'll happily watch you throw your money away!" George told him.

Wes slipped his arm around Chloe's shoulders as they headed out of the dining room.

"Dancing first!" Celia said.

Chloe laughed softly. "I'm pretty beat from today, too, but a dance or two and . . ."

"Casino!" Wes said.

"As you wish!" she told him.

They headed to the large lounge where a band was playing and couples were already whisking around on the floor or chatting at more of the circle tables.

The band was good.

They were playing a swing number as they entered, and Chloe looked at him with an arched brow.

He smiled and took her by the hand.

Thanks to his mother's obsession with ballroom dancing, he'd been dragged to a studio since he'd been about ten years old.

He could arch a brow at her in turn.

And it worked! Apparently, someone had dragged Chloe to a dance studio, too. They fell into step easily; he led, and she followed, perfectly, to a tee.

He swept her into an impressive dip as the song came to an end, grinning down into her face as he held her.

There were others on the floor, of course, but he was glad when he saw that Jeff and Celia had been dancing near them and were then staring at them.

"Wow, that was impressive!" Jeff said.

"Very," Celia agreed.

"Well, you know," Chloe said, smiling as she looked over at Wes, "practice makes perfect. Except, oh, we're far from perfect."

Celia laughed. "Well, practice makes you two look pretty damned good! But, hey, listen! Isn't that a tango coming up?"

"A tango!" Chloe said.

Wes shrugged. He'd never thought he'd have been quite so grateful for his mother's obsession.

But he could tango.

And so, they stepped out on the floor again. Once more, he knew that he could lead, and once more, he was certain Chloe had also been dragged into taking dance lessons herself. Maybe she hadn't been dragged.

But it was rather incredible, and certainly convenient. They could appear to be a couple who had known one another, learned about one another, and just what they could do together as a couple.

The tango ended with them alone on the floor and actually receiving applause along with the band.

"I'll bet you two can rumba, samba, Viennese waltz . . . I lose Jeff when it gets too complicated," Celia said.

"Hey, I was a great lineman in high school and college! I

didn't have time to dig into the local Fred Astaire or Arthur Murray studios!"

"And now we play football every day!" Celia said dryly. "Hm, and they're coming up next with a foxtrot!"

Jeff groaned.

"Hey! Wes will take you out on the floor," Chloe said. "I'll sit this one out with Jeff for a minute or two. I'm a little muscle weary, anyway."

"Sure!" Wes said. "Happy to oblige."

He swept Celia out on the floor.

She wasn't the partner Chloe had been, but she did know the dance and they moved along easily enough.

He wasn't sure what conversation Chloe would have with Jeff, but since he had Celia, he decided to press her on the day.

"You really got nothing but a scrape, right?" he asked her.

She groaned as she moved about. "I keep telling everyone that I'm fine!"

"I know, I know. I was just hoping you didn't get a twisted muscle that you're barely feeling now, but that might hurt tomorrow."

"No twisted muscles, thanks to you, my savior!"

"Well, it is slippery up there. And we were kind of bunched together."

"I know," Celia said. "I think that I was trying to let Daniel by me, but there were others around, too."

"I'm sure he would have never pushed you on purpose. But despite our really good guide, we did wind up almost on top of one another now and then."

"And I don't think that Daniel would have minded if I'd fallen," Chloe murmured.

"Pardon?"

"Oh, no, no, I didn't mean anything bad, really. It's just sometimes . . ."

"Sometimes?"

"Oh," she said, twirling out of his arms and then returning, "you know, Broderick is the brains behind that company. Maybe Daniel is trying to prove himself too much sometimes, I mean, maybe, you know."

He laughed and swung her out and back in.

"Well, you're the brains in your company, right?"

She laughed. "Jeff is great. He's a follower. It's not his fault that I happen to know a lot more than he does. But! He can be really charming when it comes to social media—and on how to show others enthusiasm when they're working on self-promotion. Everyone has their place, right? Ah! Except maybe that's why you and Chloe get along so well—you both have your own businesses, you're not doing the same thing."

Wes smiled at that, clutching Celia when she almost made a misstep.

"Who knows? We're all separate personalities, right? Some of us are tougher, some of us are driven and some of us are more tender," Wes said.

"That's it! Jeff is a tender soul," Celia exclaimed.

The music was coming to an end.

"One of those cool finales you were doing with your wife!" Celia begged.

"Sure," Wes told her, allowing them to end with a sweeping turn and a dip.

As the song ended, he looked around the room, as did Celia.

"There they are!" Celia said, pointing over to the bar where their two "spouses" sat on stools.

Wes wondered if Chloe had learned anything from or about the man in their private chat, but he was also still wondering if he'd learned anything from Celia.

Other than reinforcing their certainty that Celia found her husband to be weak.

If something was going on, she was the one pulling the strings. How to prove it? Prove that she might have slipped into a meeting, managed to get a drug into half a dozen people.

And shoot them at just about point-blank range.

In his mind, looking at the logistics, it had to have taken more than one person to pull it all off. Maybe not the earlier deaths, but getting a paralyzing drug into a party of six in order to have them sit nicely to be shot?

He and Celia reached the bar as the band moved on with a waltz.

Wes didn't wait for any suggestions. "Casino!" he said.

"Just for a bit!" Chloe told him. "Come on, my love, it has been a long day!"

"And the casino isn't going anywhere," Jeff said, laughing. "Hey, we're at sea all day tomorrow. A time beloved by the casino—players are stuck with a place to play!"

"Casino, casino, casino!" Celia said. "Come on!"

"So, Celia, happy? You got a great dance in with Mr. Fred Astaire Junior here," Jeff said to his wife.

"You need to take lessons!" Celia told her husband.

Jeff groaned.

"Hey, there are no football teams for has-been high school cool boys!" Celia said.

"I was good!" Jeff protested.

"But you're an adult man now," Celia told him.

"So, that means I have to dance?" Jeff demanded, groaning. "Wait! I am one hell of a poker player. I'll go redeem myself!"

They all laughed as they reached the casino. Wes saw that

Broderick McClintock was at the craps table along with Edward, his new friend, the silver-haired Sally and Abigail Swenson.

Daniel was at the roulette table.

"Ah, I shall get some chips and join the craps players!" Wes announced.

"Penny slots?" Chloe asked.

Wes laughed along with Jeff and Celia.

"Oh, honey, there hasn't really been such a thing as a penny slot in forever. But, hey, sometimes you may get away with forty cents a bet, or something like that!"

"Then I'll take some chips, too, Wes!" Chloe said. "I'll try roulette. I like those odds—a number or color will or will not come out!"

"Let's hope there are no loaded dice!" Jeff said.

They split up. Wes watched as Chloe slid in by Daniel McClintock at the roulette wheel. She smiled at him, and the cybersecurity expert returned the smile.

Wes was surprised to feel a strange tug on his emotions and he almost laughed aloud at himself.

Jealousy.

Chloe had given the man a beautiful smile. The smile that Daniel had returned was that of a man who appreciated the charm and beauty of the woman.

His wife.

Not really his wife. They were professionals undercover!

"Hey!"

Edward and the others they were coming to know greeted him at the craps table. He asked how it was all going and George, ever watchful, shook his head but answered for the others, "These guys are doing okay. 'Cause I'm willing to bet they'll all come back and return their winnings tomorrow!"

"Place your bets! Place your bets!" the dealer called.

Those around the table gave their attention to the game. But this time, Broderick didn't put any money down. He collected his chips and shrugged. "Yeah, I'll probably come back and return it all tomorrow!"

He walked away. While playing and chatting, Wes noted that Broderick exchanged a few words with his brother, who then went on to head toward a giant Buffalo machine.

Except Daniel didn't stop at the machine. He walked past it—and was hidden by dazzling art of a raging buffalo that rose high on the giant machine.

Someone was joining him. It was Jeff Henderson.

Wes had money on the table; he had been joking with the others. Running over to see what was going on would have been extremely telling.

But he didn't need to worry.

Chloe was on her way over to the Buffalo, looking as if she was fascinated by the size of the machine and the graphics.

"Snake eyes!" the dealer called after the roll.

"Ouch!" Wes said, collecting his chips from the tables. "Too rich for my blood!" he announced, leaving the table and heading over toward Chloe, the Buffalo machine and the two men who had disappeared behind it.

But he could hear them. Just as he was sure that Chloe could hear them and had heard whatever had gone on before he had come close.

He only came in on the tail end of the conversation.

Just in time to hear Daniel say, "It was messed up, man. It was so messed up."

He couldn't see it, but he heard something of a whacking sound, as if one of the men had given the other a good slap against the shoulder.

Then Daniel walked around the machine.

Wes pretended his interest was in his wife.

"Hey, sweetheart, buffalo, eh?" he murmured, sliding into the chair meant for two in front of the machine.

"Hey, yourself. It's a cool machine!" Chloe said, her attention on him.

Wes looked up. "Oh, hey, Daniel. Have you played this one yet?"

"Sure, it's cool—you get to feel like a herd of buffalo is going to come crashing over you!" Daniel said.

*Is he studying us a little too intently?* Wes wondered.

*Play it out.*

"Oh, hey! Jeff, you're back there, too? More machines?" Wes asked.

"Naw, though I thought there might be. Just a door and I'm guessing it's leading to the bank or the vault or whatever they call the place where they keep chips and money. Oh! Yeah, and probably cameras to make sure no one is ripping them off!" Jeff said. "Chloe, you hit the jackpot, and you can get—"

He broke off.

Chloe had hit the jackpot, and the graphics were spinning and spinning.

"Ah, man, you really did hit it!" Daniel said.

"A hundred and twenty-three free spins. Hey, man, Wes, you should get out of here and let this lovely lady do the gambling!"

Chloe looked at Wes. Well, they couldn't leave. Like everything else, they were going to need to play it out.

Chloe was going to make thousands.

He wondered how that worked with the brass. His undercover work hadn't led him into a casino before.

Chloe looked a little distressed and he felt the undeniable need to comfort her and assure her everything would be okay.

Wes stood and said, "Wow! Cool! We can pay for another trip now! Cruising!"

And, of course, as the free turns spun and spun, he pulled his "wife" to her feet, encompassed her in a loving hold, and kissed her.

And kissed her again. Hey, it was the natural thing to do.

And just a little bit too good, but, of course . . .

Chloe was the ultimate professional. She played along.

When he broke the kiss at last, Edward and George and half the people who had been in the casino were behind them.

"Karma!" Edward said. "You saved my life and the fates are rewarding you! Wow, well-deserved, beautiful people, well-deserved!"

Once again, they were awarded a massive round of applause by those in the casino.

Finally, the game came to an end and a casino employee came out. You didn't make that much money without filing it. On this ship, though, they just filled out a claim form.

And, of course, thankfully, the powers-that-be who had set them up had taken care of their identities.

But they were going to get all kinds of advice.

"IRS will still be after you!" one man warned.

"But we are in international waters," someone else advised. "Harder for them to catch you!"

They laughed and accepted everyone's congratulations.

Then Chloe looked at him and he knew that she was beginning to feel the effects of exhaustion from the length of the day, the physical and the mental pressure.

"On to our room! 'After all,'" he quoted, "'tomorrow is another day!'"

They managed to escape. To reach their cabin.

And there, Chloe almost threw herself down on the sofa, before she looked up at him.

"I know you're exhausted. I am, too—"

"He said something, Wes," Chloe said. "Something I don't think you heard."

"And—"

"Daniel said it, Wes. Daniel said it to Jeff, before that comment about things being messed up," Chloe told him.

"And—"

"He said six people. Six people, supposedly just sitting there. Six people dead. Too much, way too much!"

Wes stared at her.

The comments weren't enough.

Not to arrest someone.

But that they had been said by one of the men to the other was . . .

That fact, if not damning, at the very least intriguing.

And whether it was one of the two men who was guilty—or if it was both of them—it suddenly seemed to solidly reinforce a theory they'd been working with.

Something *was* planned for the cruise.

Something big.

# NINE

CHLOE DID WAKE easily, at the least sound.

Therefore, of course, she heard the door click. It was just about 3:00 a.m. when it did so and she flew out of bed, swiftly grabbing her 3D-printed gun and heading out to the parlor area.

Wes had his hand on the doorknob, hesitating, wincing at the sound he had created that had awakened her.

"What is going on?" she demanded.

"I'm not sure. I heard someone out in the hallway and I'm pretty sure that they paused at our door before moving on. Tonight . . . well, something about the exchange I heard bothered me. Something is going to happen on this ship and I just want to take a little walk out on deck and see . . ."

"See if you can find whoever was in the hallway? Wes, there's no way in hell you can walk this entire ship!"

"I'm just going to take a quick walk, see . . ."

"Wes—"

"I'm all right—there's security at night. Just a quick stroll, I promise!"

He was gone, giving her no more chance to argue. But he didn't lie; he was back quickly.

She was waiting for him, standing in the center of the parlor area, arms crossed over her chest and a serious frown on her face.

"Well?" she demanded.

He shook his head. "Well, I said hello to one of the security guards."

"So, nothing?"

He had a curious look on his face and Chloe pressed the point. "Wes, what? You look as if something is bothering you!"

"I'm not sure—"

"I don't care if you're *sure* or not, what is bothering you?"

"Wow. You're beautiful when you're mad," he told her, glancing away for a moment.

"Wes! You're trying to get out of just talking to me!"

"No, it's true, but you know that you're an attractive woman. I mean, you must, and . . . All right, all right. I headed out on our deck, and I was talking with one of the security officers who works for the cruise lines. I just told him I was restless, couldn't sleep. And he laughed and said that I'd be surprised, that's one of the reasons their night crew was as big as their day crews—lots of people loved to come out in the middle of the night and just look at the stars. Anyway, I thought . . . I thought I heard a splash in the water, but he didn't seem to hear anything. I thought the sound came from the adult pool, but I hurried to it and . . . nothing. So, I guess, I'm letting frustration take control a bit. And . . ."

"Hey!" Chloe told him. "I know!"

She wasn't sure what compelled her, but she walked over

to him, placing a hand gently on his arm. "Trust me, I know. I feel like . . . I don't know. Frustrated, too. We're on a wild-goose chase on the one hand—and possibly in the middle of a mass murder or the like. I understand. Seriously, I understand!"

She shouldn't have touched him. She shouldn't have felt his warmth. She'd thought too many times that if they were really married, they'd have forgotten the frustrations of the day, come back to the room, shed whatever they were wearing and . . .

She stepped back quickly. He thought that she was beautiful? That was nice, so nice, especially when she thought that . . .

She'd like to screw the mission, professionalism, and everything else and feel the warmth of his naked skin, when they were curled together, when she could touch that flesh with her lips, feel his touch in return . . .

"Back to bed! I'm going back to the room. But! You do not even think about taking off without talking to me first!"

He laughed and nodded. "You've been hanging around Celia too long! Turning into a bossy shrew!"

"Wes!"

"I'm teasing, I'm teasing! We do need to get some sleep. I promise. I will be professional in every way."

And she would be, too.

She gave him a nod and quickly escaped. It was time to get some sleep.

But at first, she couldn't sleep at all. She stared at the ceiling. When she finally began to drift, her half sleep was tormented by dreams. Wrong, wrong, wrong. They were working a case. They were both so professional! But nothing could change the fact that they weren't any kind of AI—they were people.

And people . . .

She smiled slightly to herself, trying to turn off her thoughts. Her imagination.

Somewhere in it all, she finally fell into a deep sleep. And for the first time since they boarded the ship, she woke up because she kept a morning alarm on her phone—just in case she should oversleep.

And it was morning. Time to get serious, clear out her mind, concentrate on what they were doing and what they needed to do.

And this morning . . .

A cooking class. Well, Chloe determined, a cooking class certainly couldn't hurt her. She could boil water just fine, create a few things she was fine eating, but she'd never been known as an "Iron Chef."

As always, Wes was dressed and ready when she emerged from the bedroom. She showered quickly, dressed for their day at sea in a bathing suit—the old one she wasn't so fond of!—beneath a halter dress.

"Prepared for anything, my love?" he asked her teasingly.

"Breakfast, and the cooking class. And so far, neither of us has taken one of Abigail Swenson's classes, so . . ."

"Should I cook, too?" he asked her.

"Hm." She shrugged. "I don't see why not. But while we're at breakfast, we can also see what everyone else is doing!"

He laughed. "I can go to the casino!" he told her. "Play with your winnings. Oh, wait, I was sitting with you when the bonus came in. And we're such a delightful and perfect married couple—half of it must be mine!"

She grimaced. "Um, seriously, we're undercover, and we made money, and . . . Okay, I have never had anything like that happen to me before, working as myself as an agent or undercover!"

He laughed. "I'm sure we could hang around with our new friends and pay some of it back. Still, I was joking. The casino stuff seems to happen at night. I'm hoping desperately that we get something solid soon and, after last night, I'm thinking that we might have been looking at the wrong duos."

"Meaning?"

"Okay, Celia and Jeff are a couple—she holds the reins. Daniel and Broderick are brothers but Broderick is the older one and it seems that he calls the shots. Amelia . . . hm. Have no idea yet on Amelia, other than that she wanted something from Edward that he claims he can't answer for her. Edward—seems like the nicest guy in the world and while George is watching him, I believe that whether he's innocent of not, he won't be able to kill anyone."

"George is still a human being. One human being," Chloe reminded him.

"And that is true. And here's something that is true, too. Despite all the best work possible in our tech and forensic teams, we could be on a cruise that's just a cruise," he said. "But—"

"You don't believe that and neither do I," Chloe said.

"No, I don't. But our situation makes it difficult to have all the information we should have at hand, though our burner phones lead to burner phones and we can ask questions if we need to. But if anyone had more answers for us, they'd be calling us," Wes said. "Anyway! Hey, my love, it's breakfast time. I'm hungry."

"Right, okay, so . . ."

He grinned as he headed to the cabin door. "Maybe we should have a little spat. I think we're too perfect as a married couple."

"That's because we're not really a married couple," Chloe reminded him.

"That's my point!" he said. He grinned and shrugged at her. "Although, honestly, you don't make a bad wife!"

Chloe groaned, but he'd made her laugh. He could do that, even under the tension of their current situation. And, of course, she was human.

Wes was not an unattractive guy and there had been moments when he'd been holding her, touching her that . . .

*There have been moments when I almost believe that it's real, when I've wished that it's real . . .*

"Breakfast!" she announced, nor wanting to linger in the room with her thoughts. She tried to remind herself that they'd just met.

But, of course, that was a wee bit different when you were thrown together as closely as they were and when . . .

When it surprisingly seemed to go so well, at least between the two of them. The case, their mission, was frustrating.

But they could share their thoughts and frustrations.

"Where shall we wander this morning?" he asked her.

"The open deck—that's where our usual crowd seems to gather!" she told him.

"Open deck buffet it is!"

They headed out of their room and toward the inside/outside open deck buffet breakfast where, as Wes had noted, it seemed their growing group of friends appeared to be congregating.

Their six murder suspects.

With a few additions. Sally, always eager to find Edward, and, of course, George Garcia, ever vigilant for another attack on Edward.

"Think Edward might be in danger from a sweet silver-haired lady?" Chloe asked Wes.

He looked at her, grinning.

"We've both learned that any number of threats might

come from the least dangerous-looking people in the world," he reminded her.

"A member of the Sherlockians, or whatever!" Chloe murmured.

It seemed that Edward, who appeared to be the head of their strange new group, had held seats for them. He waved, indicating chairs at the table, as they stood in the buffet line.

"Well, at least getting close is easy!" Wes murmured.

"Too true!" Chloe whispered back. "And, wow, nice-looking veggie omelets with cheese! Eating on this mission is not a problem."

"Waffles! Too much sugar, but I'm going for them anyway!" Wes told her. "Another day at sea. And, of course, I'll need the energy to sit in a session or hang around on a lounge chair." He hesitated, always talking close as if they were sharing intimate thoughts. "But, of course, you never know. Still, tomorrow, diving on a private island . . . that just seems a likelier possibility of something going wrong."

"But you never know," Chloe said.

"You never know," he agreed.

In a few minutes, they had their food and joined the others at the table. They were the last to arrive that day; Sally was again seated at Edward's side while George Garcia was to his left. Jeff and Celia were across the table flanked by Amelia Swenson on the one side and Daniel and Broderick on the other.

As they joined the table, Sally was busy telling the others about the group she belonged to, the "Sherlockians," people who were in love with the work of Sir Arthur Conan Doyle and eager to enjoy his work while studying the changes and advances in police science and investigation since the man had lived. Hers wasn't the only group—many such groups across the country met using the same guidelines and they even had huge Zoom meetings every now and then. "But, of course, there are many kinds of 'Sherlockians!'" Sally said. "There are game-playing Sherlockians, reading Sherlockians, you name it! Sherlock Holmes is in the public domain, although I'm wondering if we should have been the Sir Arthur Conan Doyle-ians!"

"The man was a writer, a storyteller," Edward reminded her. "To the best of my knowledge, the writer was never a detective himself."

"Right. But what an incredible character he created! So, the name. Sherlockians. I mean, people make fun of us, of course!" Sally was saying. "But we've helped the police on occasion. We have a great social media site going—which is, of course, one of the reasons I'm so thrilled to learn more and more from these wonderful, giving people!"

"Doesn't it ever make you nervous?" Daniel asked her.

"Pardon? What?" Sally asked.

"Well, you said that you and your friends investigate and help the police," Daniel explained. "But if criminals knew what you were up to, you and friends could be in danger," he added, shaking his head.

"Oh, no, because no one would ever know who sussed out the information!" Sally assured him. "Everything we provide goes through one detective—I guess we're kind of considered confidential informants!" Sally said happily.

"Sally!" Celia said. "You've just told all of us that you investigate cases! So, what if one of us was a horrid criminal?" she asked.

"But you're not! You're lovely people who teach us great classes!" Sally said happily.

Edward groaned, patting her hand where it lay on the table. "Sally, yes, at this table, we're all gainfully employed people who would never commit a crime or hurt anyone. But what if in conversation with someone else, one of these guys slipped and it just happened that they were in a group with a real criminal?"

"I'm okay on the ship! All you wonderful people and security around. And when I'm home, well. I live in a gated community with a guard on at all times and honestly, I don't share with people usually. It's just that this group is so giving!" Sally said.

Edward laughed. "Pay it forward, eh? Well, let's be honest. We all get something out of this. In truth, it's one big advertisement for our companies. And, of course, Milestones is incredibly lucky that we have such amazing teachers and givers who have signed on to help with this project!"

Chloe glanced over at Wes casually, hoped that neither of them visibly reacted to Sally's words, and whatever responses might have been going on in the minds of those at the table.

She sipped her coffee, thinking that it was a very good thing Sally was so attached to Edward. That meant she was usually with George. But when she wasn't . . .

Well, she was a new worry for her and Wes now, too!

"So!" Jeff Henderson whispered, leaning low and grinning conspiratorially, "Sally! What great puzzles have you and your Sir Arthur Conan Doyle–reading friends solved?"

"Well, most of the time, we look into cold cases and come up with answers that we have no way of proving. Last year, a man was killed in the city and it was through our sleuthing into video files and the like that we were able to prove the wife was a liar, that she had killed her husband because she was planning to escape with her lover to a country without an extradition treaty with us. Oh, and guess what? She did escape, but she made the mistake of thinking that she was perfectly safe coming back—and the police were able to arrest her!"

"Wow. That is impressive!" Celia said.

"Wow is right!" Amelia said. "So, you guys have your own detective on call, too—a real life one!"

"And you didn't catch a petty thief, you caught a murderer!" Broderick pointed out.

That was enough for Chloe, enough to instill fear in her for Sally. She was blithely talking to people who might already have killed several times over.

Sally was beginning to look like she could be in danger, as bizarre as that might appear, seeing the way she was on the ship, her tiny frame, her trusting nature.

"Okay, okay, too much for me!" Chloe said, faking a fierce shiver. "What are we going to be cooking? Do you know, Celia?"

"I think we get a few choices. There's the head chef and two of his assistants giving the classes. One is on main courses, one is on desserts and bakery items and, oh, there's even a specialized class for vegetarians," Celia said.

"I'm afraid I'm going to be opting for desserts!" Amelia said, grinning.

"And I'm going to be giving a question-and-answer session while you all cook up a storm," Edward said.

"Oh, nice," Wes offered, glancing at Chloe. "I was just thinking that I still have a few questions—"

She interrupted him, laughing. "We're sitting with some of the finest teachers and knowledgeable web people on the ship!"

"Right! But, hey, they're on a cruise, too. I don't want them to work because of me when they're *not supposed* to be working! And . . ."

"You don't want to go to a cooking class!" Chloe said, laughing. She leaned toward him as the others laughed, being charming, the perfect loving wife, as she added, "My love! My turn. 'As you wish.' You are perfectly welcome to attend one class while I head off to another!"

"Aw, you guys are too cute!" Celia said.

"If I weren't so jealous, it would be sickening!" Daniel moaned. "No, no! Don't take offense. I am jealous."

"What? We're not as sickeningly sweet?" Celia demanded.

"Oh, no, you guys are just . . . um, adorable, too?" Daniel suggested dryly.

"You're all lovely people, and that's that!" Sally said. "And, oh, I do think I need another cup of coffee! Excuse me."

"Sally, please, sit, I'll get you another cup!" Edward told her.

"I want another cup myself. I'll get it!" Wes said, rising quickly. "Anyone else?"

"How many can you carry?" Broderick asked him.

"For however many we need—I was a waiter once upon a time, too," Wes told them.

"A true jack of all trades!" Amelia noted.

"Coffee all around—seriously, I'll just grab one of those trays they have up there, no problem!" Wes said.

As he headed off, he almost walked into Billy, their enthusiastic young cruise director.

"Hey! Wes, you need something?" Billy asked him.

"It's all good. I'm on a mission!" Wes told him. "Did you need anything, Billy?"

Billy laughed. "I'm just *cruising* around to make sure that everyone is doing all right. My main computer people are here and, of course, passengers who I hope are enjoying all that they're learning!"

"I think they are!" Edward offered. "Except a few of them are going to learn to cook today!"

"Maybe one of us should learn to cook," Broderick said dryly.

Daniel laughed. "We don't live together and I'm perfectly happy ordering my meals by delivery when I am home!"

"Okay, computer classes, cooking classes, whichever!" Billy said. "I'm really just checking out the room, checking in on everyone, hoping all are having a good time!"

"We're having a wonderful time," Chloe assured him.

"Brilliant!" Sally said.

Nods went around.

"Well, then, I'll let you go on your mission, Wesley. And thanks, all!" Billy said.

He was indeed cruising the room. He headed to the next table, cheerfully greeting the passengers, and Wes moved on over to the coffee buffet.

"Hey, there are some more folks who are giving classes," Sally noted, nodding to indicate the table where Billy was talking to the group seated there.

"Yes! The older gentleman is from a company that develops software specifically for an older crowd—"

"Go figure on that!" Sally said, laughing. "But there is a difference now that we're not spring chickens—kids go to school with their computers and tablets now." She looked at Edward and grinned. "Remember when the remote control meant one of your parents telling you to walk to the television and change the channel?"

"How many more people on board are giving the classes?" Chloe asked. "I should have been paying more attention, except I was focusing on a few of the classes that I knew I wanted—"

"You're with my main people," Edward said. "We have eight others, but they're only doing a few classes each, though they are welcomed, of course, by Milestones. You, my dear Chloe, are with . . ."

He lowered his voice and looked around conspiratorially. "You're with the cream of the crop! Quote me on that and I'll call you a horrible liar—even if you did save my life!"

He was teasing her, of course, and it seemed that everyone was amused and their table was having the best time ever.

Wes returned with coffee and after a minute or two, their group rose, ready to head to their various projects for the morning.

Edward, George, Sally and Wes started to head out together for the session Edward was giving but Wes stopped suddenly, looking back at Daniel and Broderick.

"You guys cooking or coming this way?" he asked.

"We're giving a speech—a repeat, really—for those who couldn't come to our original class on cybersecurity," Broderick said.

"We could cook for a minute, but . . . no, not me! I like my food delivered!" Daniel reminded them.

Grinning, Wes went on and followed Edward out.

Chloe turned to Celia and said, "Where is this cooking class? Jeff, are you going to it?"

"I'm taking a nap!" he said. "And this afternoon, all I have planned is lying on a lounge chair!"

"I have to run to the room for a minute," Celia said.

"Room? It's a ship, remember? You're headed to our cabin!" Jeff told her.

Celia just groaned.

"I'm also heading to my cabin-slash-room!" Amelia told them. "And what to do with all my free time! Ah, decisions, decisions!"

"Cooking class is in the big galley, Leisure Deck!" Celia told Chloe. "See you there!"

Chloe made her way out of the dining area, heading for the elevators. As she did so, she smiled at those she passed, said hello to those here and there she had met casually aboard the ship or when they'd been at the falls in Jamaica.

She wondered again how they were ever going to catch a killer on the cruise. A killer? Killers?

And did they need to worry about everyone on the ship who had anything to do with the classes?

*What the hell is the motive for it all? Simple greed? Simple greed could cost so many lives!*

She'd had a class once on serial killers. It was estimated that twenty-five to fifty were active in the United States at any time. But that was a different animal than the killer or killers they were seeking. The deaths were targeted.

"Hey!"

When she entered the galley area where the classes would take place, Chloe was greeted by Darlene Jordan, the young student she had met on the bus trip to the falls.

"Hey, so . . . you're learning to cook, too?" Chloe asked her, grinning.

"Yeah," Darlene told her. "I'm not in a dorm. My friends and I have an apartment with two bedrooms, two of us per bedroom." She grimaced and smiled. "Keeps us on the straight and narrow as far as getting too close to the wrong boys, but sometimes . . . Anyway! Even state schools can be expensive, and we all try to take a night creating some kind of dinner. Maybe I can get good!"

Chloe laughed. "Yeah, I remember. My folks helped, but, yeah, if you want any spending money while you're in school, you need to be careful. Unless you're born filthy rich. I wasn't."

"But I guess you do all right now?" Darlene asked her.

"I'm happy. I love art. And Wes has his business . . . We get along."

"But no kids yet?"

"Not yet. But since we are both established in what we do, they might be on the horizon!"

Darlene nodded. "I'm still trying to figure out what I want to do when I graduate. Mass communication! Once upon a time, I wanted a job with the best newspaper out there. Now, social media is huge! I'm trying to figure out if I can get off the ground as an influencer who tells the news—just the news. Not my opinion of the news, but what has actually happened. I feel like everything is skewed these days. I don't want to do that!"

"I will be very impressed, and wherever you are, I'll be keeping an eye out for you!" Chloe assured her.

"I'd love to get out there with one big story. I mean, I've got different channels now on various apps, I've done video—I'm really good with my phone—to get a lot of what goes on during one of these trips and I have a following . . ." She broke off, shrugging. "And, of course," she added softly, "I don't know if you've noticed or not—most people haven't, they're just here for the classes—they have signs up asking that no pictures or video be taken. And I had wanted to get a lot of what was going on in these classes! I mean, you heard about what happened to those computer folk in Broward County, right?"

Chloe felt an instant pang of unease.

Darlene was such a bright, attractive and eager young woman.

And if they were right and a killer was on the ship, just like Sally with her "Sherlockians," Darlene could be putting herself in danger.

"What happened was absolutely horrible, but we must let the police and other law enforcement deal with it," Chloe said. "Darlene, seriously—"

"You made it!"

The call from halfway across the room alerted Chloe to the fact that Celia Henderson had arrived.

"I made it!" Chloe said, laughing. "I was here first! You were the one who had to return to her cabin!"

"She's so cool!" Darlene, still close to Chloe, murmured.

"She knows her stuff!" Chloe agreed, and she spoke quickly, hoping to end it all before Celia reached them. "Please, kid, be careful. Whoever was behind it all, that person—or those persons—are dangerous!"

She did speak quickly enough; she had finished her warning while Celia was still several feet away.

But Darlene wasn't done.

She greeted Celia enthusiastically, complimenting her on her classes, on all that she had learned from her and Jeff.

"And it's so important for me!" Darlene said. "I'm going to be a journalist, maybe live, maybe on paper, maybe both! But I was just telling Chloe how I wanted to get the news out there, news, not skewed news, about what's happening, what's fun, dog shows, you name it—and what's deadly serious, like those murders in Broward County!"

"Right! Using trustworthy apps, seeing what information you disclose about yourself will be very important. You're not going to want people to know where to find you if you're doing hard-hitting reporting!" Celia said.

"I was just warning her to be careful!" Chloe said sweetly.

Amelia was behind Celia then and she looked around the woman.

"Hey! They just told us to pick our places! If we're going to get good spots in the center of the room, we need to move!" she said.

"Amelia's favorite—we're heading to the bakery part of

this deal," Celia said. "Why not? I can actually kind of cook! But desserts are fun, and I'm supposed to be having fun when we're not giving classes."

"Desserts sound good to me!" Chloe assured her.

As Amelia had advised, they were already moving.

But Chloe was thoughtful, trying to appear as if nothing more than dessert was filling her mind.

There was something different about Celia since she'd seen her last, but Chloe couldn't figure out what it was.

And since both Amelia and Darlene wound up between her and Celia when they moved up their tables to start their lesson, she didn't get a chance to figure it out.

The bakery chef welcomed them all, thanking them for being there, assuring them that their reward was getting to eat what they cooked.

They were creating bananas Foster!

"Ingredients!" he announced. "Always using the freshest ingredients in any creation is of the utmost importance! Now, on a ship that isn't easy, but thankfully, we have a demanding master chef aboard, so will be working with the finest ingredients possible! And now, a creation from a city where delicious food is a given, our recipe is straight from the finest chefs in the incredible city of New Orleans!

The lesson began. They worked, they listened and each and every one of them created bananas Foster.

Nothing in the least bit dangerous was said during the work. Darlene did note that she wasn't sure that bananas Foster passed for dinner, but she was sure going to impress her roommates.

It was an intensive workshop, flambéing their bananas, creating the look of their plates, arranging the rum sauce and bananas over the ice cream.

It was a great idea for such a class since there was no oven time when everyone just sat around.

Instead, they were soon eating their creations and enjoying coffee, sodas, cocktails, beer or wine provided to go along with their culinary delicacies.

And it was finally, when they were sitting, eating and chatting, that Chloe realized what was bothering her.

Celia was wearing more makeup. A lot more makeup.

And despite that, Chloe could see that she was wearing it to cover the bruising on her face. She didn't quite have a black eye, but there was some dark bruising around her right eye, almost invisible beneath the foundation.

Chloe waited until Amelia and Darlene had risen, offering to refill their coffee cups since the four of them had determined that coffee went best with the dessert and if they wanted to have a full day of fun at sea, they should leave the alcohol for later.

But when they were gone, Chloe leaned forward, looking at Celia just as any concerned friend might.

"Celia! What happened?" she asked in a low whisper.

"With what? I did nothing wrong. My dessert is delicious!" Celia said.

Chloe shook her head. "Celia! I can see it. You have a bruise on your face. Oh, no, no—Jeff didn't freak out at something and slug you in the eye, did he?"

"No!" Celia said, horrified at the idea. "No, no, of course not. Never. I—I'm a klutz! I was hurrying up—I'd forgotten to get my premier pass. You know that thing that says we're cleared for all the classes and upgrades—and I was hurrying and . . . Well, of course, that was dumb because I slipped and fell against the door and . . . and, oh, no, of course not! Jeff would never!"

"Should you see the doctor?" Chloe asked.

"No, no, I'm fine, really. I promise."

"And you tripped?" Chloe asked. She was purposely letting Celia know that she didn't believe her.

"I tripped! That's it!" Celia said.

Darlene and Amelia returned to the table with coffee. They talked and laughed a few minutes more, and then it was time for the experience to be over—to give the galley back to the real chefs.

When they exited the galley, Edward's class had ended as well and Edward, Wes, George, Sally and both McClintock brothers were standing outside the doorway, talking and waiting.

Chloe determined that it was time to shake things up.

She greeted them with a friendly smile, as did the others. But she managed to get close to Jeff and say, "You know, I may look skinny and all, but I must say, if I ever knew of a man taking his fist to a woman, I'd knock his socks off!"

Jeff stared at her and then Celia with dismay.

And Wes came up to her, taking her arm. "Cabin!" There was a growl in his voice. "Cabin, now!" He gave himself a visible shake and smile and told the others. "We're going to go slip into something more comfortable and find some lounge chairs!" he announced.

It was obvious, however, that his hold on her was strong as they started to move away.

Chloe bowed her head and secretly smiled.

Because as they walked away, she heard Daniel McClintock tell the others. "Oh, boy! They are a married couple, for real! Troubled waters at last!"

Edward told him, "Oh, yeah, but they'll solve it fast. That couple is real, of course, but so lovey-dovey, too! A great married couple!"

# TEN

THE EXCHANGE HAD been interesting, Wes thought. Just as watching the group in Edward's question and answer session had been. Most questions were centered on the best uses and security for individual businesses. Some had been more specific regarding the kinds of money that could be made on major websites and management.

Billy Cliffton and his grandfather, Elijah, had been there, with the young cruise director welcoming those who came into the classroom and Elijah appearing to be somewhat bored, but springing into old-cruise-director mode when someone needed help with something.

Jeff, Daniel and Broderick were all in attendance.

*Strangely quiet*, Wes thought. And, as they hurried along the hallway, his hand firmly on Chloe's arm, he lowered his head and smiled. Chloe had surely shown Jeff!

If, of course, Jeff had been the one to give his wife a black eye.

"I'll admit, I thought you were crazy at first, accosting

Jeff—" Wes began, once they were in the privacy of their cabin.

"I didn't accost him. Seriously. That was an if-the-shoe-fits-wear-it kind of a comment. I happened to be close to him when I said it," Chloe explained.

"Right. But where I thought you were crazy, I think it came off rather perfectly," he told her.

She smiled. "Thanks."

"But we do need to watch it," he warned. "We want to be friends with these people, watch what's going on. And still . . ."

"Have a spat here and there so we look like we're really married!" she said. "True. But I don't think that newlyweds need to fight that much."

"We're not real newlyweds. We're on something of a second honeymoon," he reminded her.

"But! If we're on a second honeymoon, that suggests we more or less still like each other, right?" she teased.

He groaned. "Right!"

"And?" she said. "Did you learn anything?"

"Not really," he said with a sigh. "Lots of people had lots of questions, but then tended to refer to their own businesses, none of which would be in any position to rival Milestones."

"And what about the guys—"

"They all arrived later than me—Jeff and Daniel and Broderick."

"Which . . ." Chloe said thoughtfully.

"Which," Wes suggested softly, "means that you think that one of them decked Celia. You don't really think that henpecked Jeff was the one who gave his wife her black eye?"

"Yeah, and I'm not even suggesting one of them. Both Amelia and Celia went to their cabins before coming to the class and the so-called fairer sex is not averse to a bit of violence now and then. And, oh, Darlene gave me a scare, too! You know, the young journalism major we met. She started talking about investigative work. So now, whoever this person—or these people—are, they may be afraid of not just Sally, but Darlene, as well," Chloe told him earnestly.

"Okay, so we're almost positive that one of these guys—or more—is pure evil. We just need to keep an eye on them—" he began, trying to be assuring.

"Easier said than done," she said flatly.

"George is always with Edward. Sally has a thing for Edward, so she's always around him and George," Wes reminded her. He shook his head. "Whatever is going on, it's changed up. I mean, maybe Edward was supposed to die when he went into the water—that would leave a major power vacuum at Milestones. Did they plan on more? Who knows? But now I'm still curious about the fact that Jeff was talking to Daniel last night—behind that massive Buffalo machine. And that they were talking about what happened in Broward County."

"I'm willing to bet that many people are talking about it," Chloe said. "We just haven't heard them. And that's what's worrying me. What if something major is being planned?"

"Well, there's this. I doubt if there's a bomb on the ship. That could take the killer out, too, and this killer isn't suicidal. This killer, I believe, wants to rule the world through the internet, taking over every major company that handles anything that has to do with communications, business and pleasure, records, security, gaming, you name it. And if you're going to rule supreme, you need to stay alive."

"But if you're the alpha dog in charge of your mission, you may not mind sacrificing a few of your obedient pups," Chloe said.

"Or mind giving them a black eye for being too uppity?" Wes asked. "So, either Jeff did freak out and deck Celia—

which seems strange to me since he is so obsequious around her! But if it wasn't him, then he must be in on whatever is going on—otherwise, even little chicken that he is, I think he'd have a problem with someone decking his wife."

Chloe smiled at him. "Wes, that's because you would never let anyone hurt your wife!"

"Of course not! I've got your back."

"I mean, your real wife. If you had one or I imagine when you have one."

"If I ever have a real one," he told her. "I can't imagine she'd be any more wonderful than you."

The words were out of his mouth before he realized two things—they were spoken honestly, and because they were on a case, they were way too personal!

"Sorry!" he added quickly.

But Chloe was smiling. "That's really nice. And you know what? When the time comes, I could do far worse!"

"Not quite as flowery," he told her, grinning. "But nice! So, beloved, shall we get ourselves out on deck to watch the wildlife?"

"We need to get ready and head out," Chloe said.

"Exactly. Let's do it."

"All right! I'll act especially married. I get to run into the bathroom first to get changed for our delightful day of hanging out on lounge chairs."

"Wow, painful," Wes said. He lifted a hand quickly. "I know! I'm frustrated, too."

"And you know what, darling? I really need a new bathing suit! The one I have with me is all frayed," she told him, shaking her head.

"I wouldn't begin to choose an article of clothing for you," Wes said.

"But you know me so well," she teased.

He laughed. "Okay, I'll act really married, darling. Get your own freaking bathing suit!"

Shaking her head, she disappeared first into the cabin and then headed into the bathroom to change for their day in lounge chairs.

But as usual, she was quick and professional, appearing a moment later with a little lightweight pool dress over her bathing suit.

He managed to get in and get out just as quickly.

Wes was grinning as they headed to the aft deck area with the adults-only pool. He had a feeling that both he and Chloe might have enjoyed the kids' pool with its two winding slides and "spray and splash" zones.

"Don't worry," Chloe said, pointing out a pair of lounge chairs with several empty near them. "We'll get on the slide one day."

"Ouch!" he told her.

"Ouch?"

"What are you? A mind reader? I'm going to need to be careful regarding not just what I say around you, but what I'm thinking as well?"

"Oh yeah?" she arched a brow to him. "What evil thoughts are you thinking?" she demanded.

"Ah, you don't know!" he teased.

Chloe grimaced and walked over to the towel rack, procuring those fitted for the chairs and for use once they were wet.

"I'm going to the bar before anyone else can get here," he told her when she returned.

"More of those—"

"Nonalcoholic beers, yes, they're not that bad!"

"Everyone else seems to be having tropical drinks, you know, like margaritas or piña coladas or . . . Hm, you're right. At least I can almost pretend that I'm having an iced tea!" Chloe told him.

Wes walked over to the bar, showed his premiere badge and ordered their drinks. The nonalcoholic beers had just been poured into glasses when he saw that Jeff and Celia were heading to the bar. They seemed to be deep in conversation.

"Hey!" Jeff said, seeing Wes.

"Hey. We found some loungers right over there," he said, pointing. "Chloe is putting towels down on several. Right by the pool and the hot tub!" Wes said.

"Great. Hey, honey, why don't you go lay claim to two of those chairs and I'll get our drinks!" Jeff told his wife.

"That's a decent plan!" she told him, waving to them and heading over toward Chloe.

Wes set his hands around his beer glasses, ready to head back over, too, but Jeff moved to block his way.

"You need to know something!" he told Wes earnestly.

"I do?"

"I know that you dragged your wife away this morning before she could take it any further. But you need to tell her! I didn't hit my wife, and I would never hit my wife!"

Wes grinned. "Not to worry. I didn't think that you'd hit her."

"Because you think that I'm too much of a wuss, right?" Jeff asked dryly.

"What?" Wes protested.

"I didn't hit her because I just wouldn't. She's always saying something that aggravates the hell out of me. But I don't hit people because I'm angry," Jeff told him, determined that Wes understand.

*You don't hit them. But if they have something you want, if they're standing in your way, do you drug them and shoot them point-blank?*

He sure as hell couldn't give away that thought.

"Look, Jeff, first of all, your married life is your business and no one else's. Secondly, yeah, I figured I'm getting to know you a little bit. You grew up in the same kind of household where I grew up. Men don't get violent with women. You don't hit girls. Of course, we're all trained not to talk the way we do sometimes, but we all know that hitting people isn't right—no matter how good it might feel!" he told Jeff.

And Jeff grinned at that.

"Unless they're bigger than you are," he said. "'Cause then they can hit you back and it can really hurt. Or, you know, if they're trained in martial arts or something like that," Jeff said. "Yeah, I'm sorry. Celia said that she fell and I know that's the truth because I didn't hit her."

"I gotcha, Jeff, I gotcha."

"How do you guys do it? You never fight," Jeff said.

"Yeah, we do. Little things. We're just pretty good at keeping it private. I, um, need to admit that we had a bit of a thing . . . I told her that we couldn't just assume that you'd hit Celia because Celia had a black eye."

"Did she believe you?"

Wes laughed softly. "After we talked, or let me say, after I talked, for about then minutes. I mean, you can't really blame her because most people who get close to the two of you . . . um . . ."

"Probably think that I have the right to deck her?" Jeff suggested, grinning.

"Maybe. If it makes you feel any better, Chloe doesn't like the way that she talks to you. She told me once that she'd never be like that with me because she knows that I'd be out of the house in a flash."

"You think I should leave her?" Jeff asked.

"I told you. I don't think anything. Your marriage is your business."

"Yeah. And the internet and social media and promotion and cybersecurity and all that . . . Well, that's our business, too, and Celia knows what she's doing with it," Jeff said.

Wes grinned. "Hey, you didn't order your drinks."

"Oh, yeah. She wants something frilly. You know, something fruity with a little umbrella in it."

"They're doing blackberry margaritas that look good."

"But you ordered beer."

"I don't need a frilly umbrella," Wes said, grinning.

Jeff groaned, showed his premiere badge, and ordered the blackberry margaritas Wes had suggested.

Luckily, the drinks were met by Celia with an expression of pleasure. She thanked Jeff and looked at Chloe and said, "These are so pretty!"

"They are pretty," Chloe agreed.

"And you don't want to try—"

"I learned years ago that I'm fine on beer!" Chloe told her. "Too much hard alcohol and I get the worst headaches! I can admire from afar!"

"Oh, look, there are Edward, George and, of course," Celia said, giggling, "Sally! She does have a serious crush on our man."

"Hey, Edward doesn't seem to mind," Wes pointed out.

"True. I guess I was just thinking . . ." Celia broke off and started laughing. "I guess with a man of Edward's power and position, I thought he'd have a pretty young thing, table-dressing on his arm."

"Hey, we all like what we like," Jeff said.

Celia turned and smiled at her husband. "And very lucky for me, you like strong women who stand up for themselves!" she declared. "And, okay, so perhaps just a little bit waspish!"

she added while making a face and drawing laughter from Wes, Jeff and Chloe.

"And what's going on here?" Edward asked as he walked up on their group, George and Sally behind him.

"We're explaining love, what makes the world go round!" Chloe told him.

"Oh, nice. I didn't know it could be explained, even by the most advanced internet searches out there!" Edward said. "Um, I'm seeing towels on these chairs. I was hoping—"

"I put them there, especially for you!" Chloe assured him. "I'm not sure I'm supposed to save that many chairs, but I considered our entire dinner group so yes, of course, Edward, three are for you! And those right there are for Amelia if she comes out, and I see Daniel and Broderick over at the bar, so . . ."

"And there's Broderick, looking over at us!" Edward said. He waved at Broderick and pointed to a few of the chairs. "Chloe, thank you! How nice that you thought to do this for all of us!"

"Well, I lied a little!" Chloe told him. "I told the towel guy that you'd specifically asked for these chairs and Edward, you're kind of a big deal on this cruise!"

"Aw, that's not using someone, my dear, that's playing it smart!" Edward announced. He looked at George and Sally and asked, "What can I get you? These folks have their drinks—frilly and not—and I believe I will have something myself. George, I know you're on duty—"

"Sir, you are as kind as can be, but I'll take a soda!" George said.

"There's Amelia!" Celia said, waving wildly so that she'd be seen. "Here she comes! We can see what she'd like to have before you head to the bar!"

Amelia was on deck; she'd been looking around but saw their group, waved in return and made her way toward them.

"This is so cool! Perfect seating!" Amelia said, joining them. She had a terry throw on over her bathing suit, but quickly tossed it aside, opening her arms to the sky. "What a day, what a beautiful day! Perfect to be out here—in this *perfect* seating!"

"Well, we can thank our *perfect* married couple for that!" Edward said, grinning. "Chloe and Wes got here first and found these seats for us. Just in time! The place is beginning to fill up! So, Amelia, I'm making the bar trip. What can I get you?"

Amelia and Sally opted for the pretty blackberry drinks. "I'll head over with you and help you!" Amelia told Edward.

"Great! I can't stand it a minute longer. I'm hopping in the water—and look! The pool is almost empty. I can get in a few unhampered laps if I get in right away," Sally said.

The woman evidently did exercise. Out of her cover-up, she was still attractive and even younger-looking for her age than usual. Wes figured that she was a determined person—determined to keep up with her physical activity for her health as well as for her looks.

She headed to the water.

"I'm going to hop in, too, I think," Chloe murmured. "The water does look wonderful."

"That it does!" Wes agreed.

He lowered his head for a moment, remembering his quick stroll out on the deck in the middle of the night.

He could still swear that he'd heard a strange splash. But if so, so what?

What the hell could the splash have meant?

Maybe someone had gone in when the pools were officially

closed for the night, a teenager determined on doing their own thing.

A drunk adult or someone who just didn't care about the rules?

He wasn't sure why it still bothered him so much and he knew he needed to appear chill with the rest of the group. He spread his towel out on the lounger by Chloe, smiled as he stretched out on it beside her, reaching out to run his fingers along her arm, just like a loving husband might do.

He found himself smiling. It was odd . . . he could imagine spending all his time with her.

More intimate time . . .

But as his thoughts veered where they shouldn't go, he realized that Chloe was suddenly sitting up.

"Hm, I just watched Sally do one of her laps and now . . . now I don't see her," Chloe murmured.

"There is the possibility that she hopped out to use the ladies' room," Daniel said, shaking his head at her worry.

But Chloe stood, looking out over the water.

Then she stood, frowning, and headed slowly toward the water, looking around.

Wes jumped up, as well.

"My lord, you people are worrywarts!" Broderick commented.

"Yeah, dumb, I know, but . . ." Chloe murmured.

Then she was gone. Looking at the others and lifting his hands, Wes stood and headed after her.

When he reached the side of the pool, she was already in the water.

And then he saw why.

Sally had not hopped out to go to the ladies' room. She was at the bottom of the pool by the drain, and it appeared that . . .

The drain was sucking water inward, when and where it shouldn't have been. And Sally was fighting to free herself from the suction.

Chloe was headed to her, grasping the woman around the waist, trying to drag her away from the suction.

Wes dimly heard a whistle blowing from outside the water; the lifeguard had seen what was happening. He would be in the water in seconds . . .

*But how long has Sally been without air?*

None of it mattered because he had already headed down himself. And grasping Chloe in a life-saving hold, he managed to wrench both women away from the drain and spring to the surface even as the lifeguard appeared, ready to take Sally from his hold and get her quickly to the side of the pool.

At first, Wes feared she wasn't breathing.

But even as the young lifeguard moved to begin his lifesaving techniques, Sally coughed and sputtered, sending a spray of water over all of them.

She sucked in a deep gasp of air, opening her eyes, staring at them all incredulously.

"What the hell?"

By then, of course, the lifeguard had been joined by others belonging to the ship's crew; the pool had already been cleared and now they were asking the guests to please leave this area until the problem could be solved; the other pool remained open and they were beset now with a mechanical problem that had to be investigated and cleared as quickly as possible.

Always on board, the safety of the passengers was the most important element of any cruise!

George Garcia had momentarily left his charge, hurrying over to make sure Sally was all right, but Sally was a trouper.

She was already reaching for Wes's hand to rise, thanking

him, thanking Chloe effusively, then turning to assure George that she was fine.

"Sally, you came close to drowning—" George told her.

"I sure know how to hang around the right people!" Sally said lightly, looking at the young lifeguard and assuring him. "I know, young sir, that you would have been there in seconds, too, and I'm just fine and I don't want to ruin the cruise—"

"Ma'am," the lifeguard told her solemnly, "I can't begin to tell you how grateful we are that you're fine, but now you surely understand that such a thing should have never happened, and we must investigate and make sure we're not going to put any other passengers in danger! And thank you for being so amazing. We'll file an incident report, of course, and due compensation will be made—"

Edward had made his way to them by then, apparently pushing his way through the crew personnel emptying the deck area by insisting that he was "family."

"You can sue, that's what the young man means!" Edward told her. "Sally, Sally, are you really all right? You poor thing! It was all so fast, we barely saw what was happening and . . ." He paused, looking at Wes and then Chloe. "These guys! They do see everything, they seem to be . . . Wow! You two should be sainted! That's the second life you've saved!"

"Others would have done the same. We just happened to see that there was a problem with the drain and the suction!" Chloe told him quickly. "And you know—"

"Right. College lifeguard," Edward said, looking at Wes.

Wes shrugged. "As long as 'all's well that ends well!'" he quoted.

"I still want my frilly drink!" Sally said, grinning. "Um, maybe not at the pool. I was thinking of heading to my cabin and then maybe to that lovely little deck bar just below us! So, I do think I'll shower quickly—"

"I'll head there, too," Edward told her, smiling. "Though—"

"We'll still need to file an incident report," the lifeguard told him.

"Naturally," Wes said, feeling sorry for the young lifeguard, a man who couldn't have been more than mid-twenties. He'd probably never expected he'd be doing more than cleaning cocktail glasses out of the pool or clearing his throat and telling adults that intimacy was for the cabins, not by the water.

Chloe looked at Wes.

And he knew that she was thinking about the night before.

About the fact that he'd thought he'd heard something in the water.

"So, let's do it, huh? Get that incident report going so that we have something of the afternoon and evening left!" Wes said. "Okay, so a few of us are a bit wet, but plenty of towels around here! Let's do it."

"And," Sally said, smiling and setting a hand gently on the young lifeguard's arm, "I don't sue people. Something wacky happened here, but I'm fine! Everything is fine!"

"Sally! At the very least, let them get you on another of their great cruises for free!" Edward said.

Sally laughed.

Wes saw that they had emptied the area; the only other people visible were crew members. The pool, the bar and the deck area had been quickly cleared and closed.

Edward and Sally and George were with them.

But the others . . .

Amelia, Daniel, Broderick, Celia and Jeff . . .

All gone. Naturally. They didn't have Edward's power or

determination to get close to Sally and make sure that she was really all right.

If that was what they had wanted?

*But how the hell can we tell who might have been in the pool, who might have gotten caught up in the suction of the faulty drain?*

*Does it matter who it had been?*

*Or was Sally jumping into the pool so quickly something they hadn't counted on?*

*Had the intended victim been someone else?*

One thing appeared to be true.

No matter where you were when something happened, there was always going to be paperwork.

# ELEVEN

"THAT WAS SCARY as hell!" Chloe said when they returned to their cabin at last. "And, of course, more confusing than ever! Was that random? Was someone else supposed to be in the water? I mean, why in God's name would anyone want to kill Sally? And yet, I had a few minutes to talk to the lifeguard who was on duty," she told Wes. "And, according to him, Sally loves the water and heads into it any chance that she gets!"

"We need to know more about her," Wes said. "Maybe there is a reason. Maybe it was all just to cause some kind of an incident?"

"She could have died."

"But you remembered what I told you and you were looking for her, Chloe. Thank God you did," Wes said.

"Wes! What would have happened if she had? I mean, would we head right to a port, would they helicopter the body somewhere?" Chloe asked.

"She would have been taken to the ship's morgue and while

cruise lines don't have actual grief counselors, they have people trained to deal with grieving relatives and to help a family with repatriation, getting the body home, to a funeral home, back to their loved ones. Depending on the ports next visited, a body may be brought inland, but many of the smaller islands don't have facilities and won't make arrangements for repatriation. But you'd be surprised. Especially because there are cruises that appeal specifically to retirees and older people, there are many deaths that take place every year on cruise ships," Wes told her.

"You just happen to know all this?" Chloe said.

He laughed. "And you don't? All those cruises your family took you on for years and years? We didn't go on half as many, but my mom was always careful about insurance just in case something happened. Not only would such a situation be devastating in the grief department if a loved one died on a ship, but the repatriation of the body and all the legalities involved can be staggeringly expensive." He winced. "Then, of course, there was the COVID-19 pandemic. Across the world, millions of people wound up sick, and again, across the world, millions died. Now, I'm not sure how they managed that as cruise ship morgues don't tend to be very big."

"Okay, we're getting really depressing here!" Chloe said. "Thankfully, Sally is really and truly fine." She winced. "Then again, we are on this cruise looking for a murderer, so it's pretty . . ."

Wes walked over to her, set his hands on her shoulders, and told her, "And we're both good at what we do, no matter how frustrating this case is. We're going to find out what is going on, who is causing the deaths—and stop them and bring justice to those who were taken far too soon. Seeking the truth. Finding justice. Those things are important, it's why we do what we do."

She smiled at him, then quickly lowered her head, remembering her strange dreams.

If only . . .

"Well, everything done, incident report filed, crew working on whatever went wrong with the pool . . . Bar?" she asked.

He nodded, but didn't seem to be in any hurry as he turned away.

"Wes?" Chloe asked softly.

"I don't know," he admitted. "I can't begin to figure why drowning someone—and there could be no guarantee on who might be drowned—would further anyone's agenda. Sally was the one caught. She had nothing to do with the programs being taught on the ship. She has no business interest in computers, the internet or cybersecurity companies . . . I just don't get it. But," he added, "that could mean we'll have a quiet decent night!"

Chloe laughed softly. "All right, then, darling, it is time for another lovely nonalcoholic beer and then dinner."

"I may drink a six-pack of the real stuff once we're out of this!" he told her dryly. "Anyway, sorry, can't help it, haunted by my mother, please go on in and take the first shower."

Chloe laughed. "I just realized how much we don't know about each other. Where is Mom? Whoops, I'm sorry, first—"

"Is she still living? Yes, she and my father are alive and well and looking forward to their imminent retirement," Wes told her.

"Good, happy to hear it. Siblings?" she asked. "I read your file, of course, but it concentrates on you—"

"One younger sister. She fell in love with a navy SEAL and is living in Hawaii. Your turn."

"Parents also alive and well. One older brother, teaches history, geography and government at the university in

Tallahassee," Chloe told him. "They leave me alone because I got into this because my dad was a cop—and because my brother has already given them five grandchildren."

"Ah, so the heat is off!" Wes said. "So, at least, in this romantic marriage of ours, we don't need to worry about procreating too quickly! Please, if you will—"

"I'm going, I'm going!" Chloe assured him.

She chose a somewhat alluring and festive dress for the evening, a halter dress in an emerald-green chiffon.

Wes whistled when she emerged.

"Gee, I sure have had much worse undercover assignments!" he assured. "What a hardship! You could be walking down a runway in Paris."

She grinned. "Flattery! Clean up so we can at least pretend we're having a great time on a gorgeous cruise!"

He gathered his clothing and disappeared into the bathroom. When he emerged, she was checking her hair.

One thing about even the best dye job, she had to hope she hadn't lost any of its color. Luckily, the ship's pools were salt water and treated differently; there wasn't a ton of chlorine to remove all the darkness with which it had been dyed.

"Well?"

She turned. Wes was out, decked in dark blue jeans, a light blue shirt and a casual jacket. She grinned because he managed to look something like a college-aged beach boy with just enough maturity in him to suggest he might be a decent businessman or, better still, a truly competent dive master.

"Am I, um, equally gorgeous?" he asked her lightly.

"You'll do," she said, grinning.

He groaned. "You and your compliments! They'll go right to my head. Anyway, it's been a long day, I'm ready for my nonalcoholic beer!" he said.

"Eventually," she told him, "someone is going to notice that you're only ordering nonalcoholic beer."

"I'm going to blame it on the amount of alcoholism in my family," he told her.

"Oh?"

"I've a cousin who has done great in a program. And when the family is together, we respect his sobriety. He doesn't expect others not to drink. But we're family. We support him."

She nodded. "And that's great! Okay, so . . ."

He bowed politely to her with a sweeping gesture and opened the door so that she could head out of the cabin.

"No," he murmured suddenly, closing the door he'd just opened.

"No?"

"Phone vibrating!" he told her.

He pulled it from his pocket. "I got a message out earlier. I wanted to see if someone could crack the surveillance cameras on the ship."

"But, if there was someone out there, wouldn't the ship's security guards have been on it already?" Chloe asked.

He shrugged, shaking his head, studying his phone. "Our cyber guys will make sure that this can't be tracked. Come over and look with me," he told her.

She walked to where he stood and came close to study his phone with him. Naturally, as asked, they were shown the footage from the pool area in the middle of the night.

Surely the ship's security was on this, as well. And, of course, having seen it, their people on land were working with those at sea.

Chloe wondered if the cruise company's CEOs might not decide to end the trip themselves.

Then again, they might feel themselves perfectly capable of dealing with any threats.

But there in the footage was a dark figure. The person was dressed in a black wet suit that covered them from head to toe; their eyes were barely visible. There was absolutely no way to discern who the person might be.

*I don't think that this is Amelia—Amelia is too small to be the dark figure moving across the darkened rear deck.*

And, of course, it might have looked as if a determined cruiser just wanted to go for a dip when the pool was officially closed.

But there was the splash. The sound that Wes had heard from a deck below.

The black figure disappeared and reappeared about five minutes later.

"So," Wes murmured, "someone was down there, messing with the drain."

"But still," Chloe said, "we have no idea who—or even if that was just some jerk who wanted to go swimming in the middle of the night."

"We know," Wes said. "What I can't figure out yet is why? I mean, a death would just throw the cruise all out of whack, especially since it would have been a death caused by the ship. As I was saying before, especially on retiree cruises, there are deaths and the cruise goes on, but something like this . . . But there couldn't have been a target."

"Maybe something was supposed to happen when we were forced to return to our port of origination?" Chloe suggested.

"Maybe. But then again, why?"

"Well, hm. Let's see how our people are doing. Feel free to open the door for me again," she told him, grinning.

"Of course, of course!" Wes said, once again making a sweeping gesture out of opening the door for her.

"Thank you," she told him as he joined her in the hallway.

"But, you know, you should get the bed tonight. It's finally my turn to take the couch."

"That sofa and I have gotten to be pretty good friends," he assured her.

"And you think that you can slip out into the night from there without waking me, but I think I've proven you wrong on that!" she told him.

"Hey, I was just acting on a hunch."

"And you still need to share your actions with me!"

He was silent, halfway smiling as they moved down the hall. He slipped an arm around and brought his head low to whisper in her ear, "'As you wish!'"

Her groan was loud, and they both laughed.

Their group seemed to gather at the same deck bar every night and they naturally headed in that direction.

And they were right. That night was proving to be no different.

As they emerged from the hallway, they saw that Daniel McClintock was talking to a pretty blonde woman at the bar.

Broderick was there, deep in conversation at one of the tables with a man, probably discussing something about cybersecurity since the man he was speaking with had the appearance of an older dignified businessman.

*Then again, he could work at a grocery store!* Chloe thought. You couldn't always judge people by first sight—in fact, it was a mistake to do so. Sometimes, she had learned, in conversation and after watching someone function when they weren't noticing that they were being observed, you could learn a lot and make some educated assumptions.

And still . . .

All this time. All this interaction.

And they still didn't know who among their suspects might be a calculating killer.

"The McClintock brothers are here," Wes noted softly, leaning to whisper in her ear. "Jeff and Celia Henderson duly noted, at the railing, looking out over the water. Darkness is falling and they appear to just be enjoying the view. Amelia . . . hm. No Amelia Swenson yet."

"And no Edward, George or Sally, either," Chloe commented.

"They're probably together," Wes said. "I'll go and order our predinner nonalcoholic drinks," he said dryly.

"Oh, and look! Daniel is trying to pick up a pretty girl. I'll come with you and ruin his night for him!" Chloe suggested.

Daniel looked up and saw the two of them coming. It was impossible to tell if he feared his night being ruined or not, but there was little choice for him other than to greet the two of them with smiles.

"Hey, good to see you. Gina!" he said, addressing the blonde, "I'd like you to meet the ship's superheroes, Mr. and Mrs. Wesley and Chloe Douglas," Daniel said, creating a flourishing gesture as he spoke. "Douglas duo! Meet Gina Holden of Atlanta, Georgia. She's a model with dozens of fans and we're doing everything we can to help her learn how to stay in the fields of demand and popularity while keeping all the creepy guys who are after her all the time at bay!"

"Ah, security, security!" Wes said.

Gina Holden gave them a beautiful smile and seemed to be truly glad to meet them. "You two are something else!" she told them. "First, bringing Edward Thompson out of the deep and then that lady last night! Hey, you've kept this incredible cruise and event on track! We're all very grateful."

"We just managed to move first," Wes said. He shrugged. "Things you do when you're really young that pay later. And my business is running a dive boat, being a dive captain. And Chloe did a different kind of diving, so . . . We were just lucky. But, seriously, this ship has an amazing crew. That young lifeguard last night would have gotten to Sally, and, again, thankfully, she's a swimmer, so she was okay! In fact, we usually see her out here," he added, looking around.

Daniel laughed. "She's wherever Edward is, I'm willing to bet!"

"Probably," Chloe agreed, grinning. "And Edward seems to be very happy with her company, so it's all good."

"And he still has that nurse hanging around him," Daniel noted. "Hey, that works out, too. A nurse watching out for Edward—and now he can make sure that Sally doesn't have any aftereffects from her own brush with death. And I heard that the situation has already been fixed! Some little broken screw caused that drain to suddenly turn into a vacuum."

"Did you go back to the pool?" Wes asked him.

"No, they've fixed it, but they're not reopening it until tomorrow," Daniel said.

"Ah. I guess they want to make sure that it's all really solved," Wes said. "Good idea on their part."

"Oh, yeah. If Sally had a mean bone in her body, she could sue big-time. In fact, most people would probably do so," Daniel said.

"I guess she's just not a litigious person," Chloe offered.

"They do make just honestly nice people!" Gina chimed in.

"So, hey. We've gotten our drinks. We were just about to head over to the table where my brother is sitting over there," Daniel said. "As always, you superheroes are welcome to join us."

"Thanks. I'll just get our drinks," Wes told him.

"We can wait—" Daniel began.

"No, no, you all go ahead!" Wes said. "I'll be right there."

Daniel shrugged and indicated that Gina and Chloe should go ahead of him. Chloe did so, but Gina turned back to talk to her as they walked.

"You guys really are amazing, you know! Almost as if you were trained to save lives!" she said.

"Right place at the right time or wrong place at the wrong time or something like that!" Chloe said with a shrug.

"I just wish sometimes . . ." Gina began softly.

"Wish?" Chloe asked.

"I wish that I was—useful. I mean, I make a great living so I'm grateful. But I'm . . . ornamental. Sometimes I wish . . ."

"You know," Chloe told her, "I'm sure you are useful in ways you don't even know about! I mean, it probably makes people happy just to see pictures of you. When they're depressed, need a smile! I'm sure you're very useful and more—it sounds to me as if you're just a really nice and decent person and that's incredibly important these days—well, and always!"

"I do try to give to important causes, too," Gina told her.

"And that's being incredibly useful!" Chloe said.

"Well, it's one way!"

"An important way. Not everyone has the resources to help others and you do and that's wonderful!"

"Thanks. And now we're here and I'm learning more and more about how to provide for my own safety! You wouldn't believe how many jerks are out there in the world!" Gina told her seriously, shaking her head in wonder.

"I can only imagine," Chloe told her.

Oh, yeah, she could imagine. She'd met enough "jerks." Hers just tended to be criminal and homicidal.

But she imagined that someone as lovely and popular as Gina might have problems—and need all the cybersecurity she might learn about on the voyage.

"Hey, Broderick, brought you a bourbon!" Daniel said, walking toward the table ahead of them.

"Thanks," Broderick said, rising, as did the man with whom he'd been speaking. "Jonas Milton, you've met Gina, this young lady—" he began, indicating Chloe.

"I know who this is! The incredible Chloe Douglas!" the man introduced to her as Milton said. "I think everyone aboard this ship knows who you are—and your husband, of course!" he added, nodding toward Wes as he came to join them at the table.

"Hello, sir!" Wes said, setting the beers down and shaking the man's hand.

"Enough business!" Broderick murmured. "You know where to find me at all times, Jonas. I think we should get on to the menu tonight! What's everyone in the mood for? Casual, hamburgers and hot dogs? Fish! With their incredible lobster servings. Then again, there's some delicious steaks to be had, as well!"

As he spoke, Chloe noted that Edward and George were heading toward the bay; they were out for the predinner social drink, as well.

There was no sign of Sally, which seemed odd to Chloe. The woman was always wherever Edward was now.

Edward was looking around, frowning. Was he looking for Sally?

"Hm. There's Edward, and he's solo," Daniel commented.

"Not exactly solo!" Broderick noted. "As ever, George is with him. He's a good guy. He was telling me about all the uses the hospitals have for the internet these days, how much security is needed. He worked at a hospital where the records were hacked and there were some real problems because of it!"

Edward didn't stop at the bar; he had seen them and was walking straight for the table where they were sitting.

"Hey, all," he said. Chloe thought that Edward already knew Jonas Milton; they greeted one another with a smile.

He'd also met Gina. He gave her a smile and a quick wave before looking at Daniel and saying, "Beauty and the Beast, eh? Gina, great to see you, and Milton, always. And there, by the rail, Jeff and Celia. Still, we seem to be missing a few of the crew who seem to have become dinner buds. Amelia and Sally. Anybody seen either of them?"

"Amelia," Chloe noted, because Amelia Swenson was just emerging out on deck, looking around, taking in a deep breath of air before opening her eyes, seeing the group and waving to them all.

"But no Sally," Edward murmured unhappily. "We were together until an hour ago. She wanted to get dressed for dinner. Well, maybe—"

"Ah, sometimes, it can take a lady a while to dress for dinner!" Daniel said lightly.

"We hadn't decided on a place to go this evening," Edward said. "But we all know that we meet out here first!"

"Speaking of—I just remembered that there is a special Italian Night at the steakhouse this evening. That's where we need to go," Broderick said. "I mean, if everyone agrees," he added, looking around at the group.

"Italian sounds lovely," Edward agreed, looking around. Everyone in the group either nodded or shrugged.

Italian it was to be.

"You people go on. Stake out a great table for us. I'll wait here for Sally," Edward told them.

"Why don't we just give her a call and tell her where we're going to be?" Daniel suggested. He was waving to Celia and Jeff as he spoke, and the couple moved on over to join them.

Greetings went around again.

And Edward repeated his determination to wait for Sally.

Chloe felt that George was looking at her. There was no way that he was going to tell Edward to move on, that he'd wait for Sally.

George wasn't going to leave Edward. The man was his assignment.

"Let's go with Daniel's suggestion!" Chloe said. "Let's call her and tell her and she can head straight to the restaurant."

"Great idea!" Edward said, pulling out his phone. He speed-dialed Sally's number, then frowned.

He obviously got her answering machine. "Hey, call me, please! We're all out on our usual bar-slash-deck area, but the natives are restless. And hungry. They want to head into the steakhouse for Italian Night. But call me when you get this, please! Let me know that you've gotten this message!"

He tapped a button on his phone screen to end the call.

"You guys go—" he said again.

"Hey, no! Please," Wes told him. "You go be with your people and Chloe and I will enjoy some of this beautiful ocean air and the sight of the sea with the sun setting over it all! We're the odd ones out here, really, and—"

"I hardly think of the two of you as the odds one out!" Edward told him.

Chloe laughed softly. "It just means that compared to you all, we're computer and cybersecurity illiterate! You guys go! Please. We'll wait, and if she calls you, Edward, just give us a call."

"Gotta get your number," Edward said.

"Of course!" Wes gave it to him.

There was nothing that anyone could ever draw off the number he'd given; cyber techs who were absolutely amazing were seeing to it that nothing could be culled off their phones, whether someone had the number or even the phone itself.

"Come on, oh, great chief!" Jeff Henderson told him. "We'll get a great table and we'll be able to describe all the specialties to our latecomers when they get there!"

The group, now including Gina and Jonas, moved on. When they were gone, Wes looking at Chloe.

"Do you think that something is wrong?" he asked her. "With Sally? You know that she's not on our list—"

"But she might be on someone else's list!" Chloe told him. "Wes, I'm even thinking that maybe we should look for her."

He frowned, but nodded slowly. "If you think so."

"Not 'as I wish?'" she asked.

He shrugged and smiled. "That, too. But she might be on her way out here."

"I'm having one of those feelings—"

"Then by all means, we'll look!" he said.

"You don't think that she'll look at her phone and call Edward if she's all right?" Chloe asked. "It doesn't matter. One of us can stay here. Oh, I don't know what cabin she's in. We'll need to call and get someone on a list—"

"Aha! I can help there. I know what cabin she's in," Wes said.

"How?"

"I saw her coming out behind us one morning when we were heading to breakfast. She's just two doors down from us, two doors toward the aft, starboard side, same as us. Should we head to her cabin?"

Chloe nodded. "Wes, she has such a thing for Edward! She just wouldn't let him go anywhere without her, knowing that he does want her to be with him."

"Let's go, then."

Wes rose. They left their almost untouched nonalcoholic

beers on the table and headed back into the hallway, hurried to the elevator, and then to their deck.

Wes moved on ahead, reaching Sally's door and nodding to Chloe. He started to knock at the cabin door.

It hadn't been fully closed.

His knock caused it to open, and he looked back quickly at Chloe, frowning, before pushing the door open the rest of the way and hurrying in.

She followed him.

Sally was there; she was dressed and ready for dinner, but lying on her bed, hands folded over her chest, as if . . .

As if she had been prepared for a viewing at a funeral parlor.

Chloe rushed over to stand behind him; he was checking her breathing, checking her pulse.

"Wes!"

"She's alive—we're going to need help!" Wes said. "It looks like anaphylactic shock. She's allergic to something—she must have an EpiPen somewhere!"

Chloe instantly looked around for the woman's purse. It was on a little table by the door; Sally had been heading out when whatever had hit her had occurred. Chloe didn't suffer from allergies herself and certainly not severe allergies, but . . ."

"EpiPen!" she exclaimed. Because, thankfully, it was there in the woman's purse.

Wes apparently knew what he was doing; he gave Sally the shot while telling Chloe that she still needed to get the doctor to the room as quickly as possible.

She picked up the cabin phone, said it was an emergency, and she was quickly connected.

Dr. Brendan Kilbride was there mere minutes after she dialed.

He was quickly by Sally's side. He asked what she'd eaten recently, if they knew what her allergies were . . .

They didn't. But Sally was already breathing more easily. Her color was returning.

Kilbride had been kneeling by Sally's side. He rose and looked at Wes. "She should have known to grab that pen herself. She must have gotten hold of something that contained nuts—at least, I'm thinking it was probably nuts because they're one of the biggest known allergens for a large, large number of people. She's smart, she knows . . . She had an EpiPen but she hadn't used it?" he asked.

"There's a group of us who tend to have dinner together," Wes began to explain.

"Ah, yes, Edward's group. I keep an eye on all my patients, even when they have someone as incredible as George, a most unusual circumstance!" Kilbride said.

"Anyway, when she didn't show up, Chloe thought we should check on her."

Kilbride stared at Chloe. "You saved her from drowning yesterday, so I heard."

Chloe shrugged. "I happened to see that she was stuck before the lifeguard did," she explained.

Kilbride smiled and nodded. "Wow. You people are pretty humble about being lifesavers. I mean, it's a nice thing, and I know that Edward is very grateful to you both. Now, I'm sure Sally is, too. You've saved her. Twice."

"I can't figure out why she didn't save herself!" Chloe murmured.

"She probably had no clue until it was too late for her to still be thinking in any way that was coherent. Anaphylaxis doesn't always result in blotchiness or a blocked airway. Sometimes it can result in a dizzy spell or even fainting! Maybe she thought that she just needed to rest for a minute.

One way or another, you've saved her life. Again. But I'd like to keep her down in my little hospital for the night and keep an eye on her. I'm going to get a few of my nurses up here and we'll take her down. Come and see her whenever you like. She should be conscious soon and she may fight the idea of being watched, so . . ."

"You don't need to worry. I know who to talk to who will come down and convince her that she must stay," Wes said.

Kilbride laughed. "Edward?"

We nodded.

"Great. That means she'll have a nurse with her, as well," Kilbride said.

"Wow. Seems like a rough trip—" Chloe began.

But Kilbride laughed. "No, trust me, I've had trips with serious accidents, serious illnesses . . . A ship becomes a floating village. People are human—and sometimes, more daring than they should be. So far we're not doing all that badly this trip. The EpiPen did its work. I'm just a cautious man who likes my patients to stay well. But, for now . . . I think she'll be out a bit longer if you want to tell Mr. Thompson what has happened."

"Thank you!" Chloe told him.

She glanced at Wes. It was time for the two of them to head to Italian Night.

She waited until they had left Sally's cabin behind to speak softly to Wes.

"I don't get it! I'm sorry, I can't believe that this was an accident. Edward said that they'd been together and, of course, no one knows what makes anyone else tick, but I could swear that he really cares about her. Oh, and if she was with Edward, she was with George. George wouldn't have let someone sneak anything into anyone's food or drink. But, Wes, this couldn't have been an accident. Definitely not after yesterday! Was she meant to be a drowning victim? And if so, why? I mean, now this is getting really crazy. Sally doesn't own or even work for a computer company!"

"No," Wes said thoughtfully.

"What are you thinking?" Chloe demanded.

He paused, turning to look at her. "I think we need to be very observant when we give our friends the news about what has happened. I agree with you. Two accidents in about twenty-four hours? And you're right. Why would anyone target her? We need to figure out who did and why."

Chloe nodded and they hurried onto the elevator and then to the steakhouse where Italian Night was taking place.

Edward was looking upset. His phone was in his hand.

When they arrived, he stood immediately, looking at them with hope and then confusion.

"Where is she? Did you two just leave? I've dialed Sally again and again—"

"She can't answer the phone," Wes said evenly.

"Oh, no! Oh, no! What happened?" Broderick asked.

"She's not—not—not—" Celia stuttered.

"Dead?" Jeff asked, his voice sounding sick.

"No, she's not dead," Chloe assured them, watching the group. "She did eat something that she's allergic to. But she's going to be all right! She's being taken down to the hospital. The doctor wants to watch her overnight, but she had an EpiPen and she's going to be fine."

Edward sank back into his chair and then bolted out of it again. "I have to see her! I have to see her right away. I'm, uh, sorry, I won't be staying for dinner." He started to walk away, but turned back and looked at Wes and Chloe. "Thanks, thanks so much. How did you know, how—"

"Oh, when she didn't come, we decided to try and find her. Her cabin is just down from ours," Wes explained.

"Right, right, thank you, thank you!"

Edward rushed out. George was instantly up on his feet. He nodded to Wes and Chloe and quickly followed Edward out.

"Wow," Broderick murmured.

"Well," Daniel said, "that's a damper on our dinner party. But, hey! She's going to be all right! So, I say, let's eat!"

# TWELVE

NONE OF IT made any sense.

Then again, Wes thought, from the beginning, none of it had made any sense.

Except that it did, of course, if the deaths they were investigating had to do with greed. It had been amazing to him to see through the years what people were willing to do to satisfy their greed.

Sometimes, bad things happened because of desperation. In his early days working in law enforcement, he'd let a thief slip away. The thief had been a boy of about twelve and he had literally stolen a loaf of bread. There had been something about the kid, something in his eyes that spoke of his absolute sorrow over doing what he was doing—it turned out that he'd been trying to get away with the bread because his mom was sick, his dad was dead and his little brother was starving.

That episode had, amazingly, turned out well. Wes had paid for the loaf of bread himself, explaining why to the shopkeeper.

In turn, the shopkeeper had given the kid a job for a few hours a week so that he could earn the money to buy a few groceries. And Wes's assistant director had gone to see the mom who was on a regimen of cancer treatments to get her into the right program.

Of course, he had checked on the kid through the years. And he was exceptionally happy to see that the boy was now working his way through college—still a kid with an amazing work ethic and a determination to pay it all back.

Sometimes . . . things could turn out okay.

This wasn't one of those times.

Okay, so greed. If someone was trying to take over a massive company, or several companies, to make a fortune in the current world where the internet was king, then greed was most likely the motive.

*But what the hell would killing Sally have to do with any of that?*

"Wes?"

He looked up. Chloe was smiling at him, the others were looking at him and their young waiter was standing behind him.

"Um, hm, the pecan pie!" he said, hoping that the young man was there to take his dessert order.

He was.

"Thanks!" the young man said. "Okay, four pecan pies, four key lime pies. Thank you and they'll be right up. Oh, and I have two Irish coffees, two espressos and three cappuccinos—"

"Please make that four on the cappuccinos!" Wes said. He made a face at Chloe, noted by everyone around the table, he was sure. "I think I almost dozed off! Want to stay awake a bit longer," he told her.

"Yes, sir," the young waiter said before disappearing.

"Maybe we should all just call it a night and head to sleep!" Broderick said. "Tomorrow we're at the private island and there are all kinds of excursions. Oh, hey, I'm willing to bet that I'm on the same excursion you're going on, Wesley. Although maybe you're not! If you run a dive boat and take people down into the briny depths all the time, you might have opted for the dune buggy tour!"

Wes shrugged. "No, I opted to dive. New place, new reefs, new fish, maybe. Oh, and there's a wreck down there. I never miss a wreck," he said.

Strange, maybe, that they were just starting to talk about the plans for tomorrow. At first, everyone had been talking about poor Sally and, of course, speculating on just what the relationship might prove to be between her and Edward. They'd ordered—and Italian Night had been terrific with Chloe and him determining that she'd go with the chicken rotini Alfredo and he'd get the lasagna.

A pair of strolling musicians had played and sang Italian love songs, which had limited conversation, as well.

He'd wondered if anyone else would want to leave the meal, to run to see how Sally was doing.

If she had been poisoned and was supposed to be dead . . .

That person might wonder if she was awake and aware—and able to point out who might have been attempting to murder her.

*And why!*

"And you, Chloe? What's your plan on the island?" Celia asked.

"Wait, wait, I can answer that! They are the perfect married couple, remember? If Wes is diving, Chloe is diving. Am I right?" Jeff asked.

"I am going diving," Chloe said.

"You guys are teasing her!" Gina reprimanded. "And that's the most amazing thing in the world—a couple who just really get along and are the perfect married couple!"

"Thanks, Gina," Chloe murmured.

"Hey!" Jeff protested, looking at Celia. "We're a perfect married couple, too, right?"

Daniel laughed and answered that. "Indeed! Celia says jump! And you say, how high, my love?"

Jeff groaned and Celia protested. "I'm just more savvy when it comes to our business."

"That's just it," Jeff said. "I know that I'm a lucky guy. So, yeah, I ask just how high I'm supposed to jump!"

"All marriages are different," Broderick supplied. "And different doesn't even mean good or bad. People are just different."

"Now isn't that the truth!" Daniel said.

Pies and coffee went around as did compliments on the dessert, the different coffees and the food in general.

And then Daniel posed the question.

"Shouldn't we be checking up on Sally? Making sure that she's really all right?" he asked.

"Maybe we could call Edward and see what he's learned," Celia suggested.

Broderick had his phone out. He dialed. After a minute, he shook his head. "Straight to voicemail," he said.

"Well, you know, Daniel, she is a super sweet lady. I don't know . . . I mean, I guess the infirmary is small and we don't need to flood it, but . . ." Gina murmured, looking at them all with a troubled grimace.

"On this ship, it's like a real hospital," Chloe provided. "There's plenty of room in the little waiting area. We can all take a walk, check on Sally and maybe enjoy the rest of the night doing something."

Daniel laughed. "For me? Enjoyment is going to be sleeping! I'm a decent diver, but not the best ever and I want my beauty sleep before heading out for that kind of physical activity."

Daniel looked at Gina, arching a brow.

"One or two dances!" she said. "I'm going to need my sleep, too."

Jeff laughed. "Notice Gina didn't say *beauty* sleep. The kid doesn't need any more beauty!"

"Thanks, Jeff, But, yeah, I'm like Broderick. I love to dive, but I want to be rested to head out on that excursion," Gina told them.

"Okay, then!" Wes said, rising and looking at Chloe before addressing the group. "I think that if we're going to visit, we should stop chatting and actually head down!"

The group gave assent with various mumbles, and they rose and left the dining room, heading for the elevators to take them down to the ship's hospital.

Sally was in the room right off the waiting area where Edward had been after his fall into the ocean. The drapes over the windows were open and they could see that George was perched in a corner of the room while Edward was seated in a chair at Sally's side. He held her hand and watched her sleep.

Doctor Kilbride came out from the doorway right behind the reception area that led to his office.

"I'm afraid I can't allow her more visitors. Sally is sleeping peacefully, and she should be fine by morning. I can tell her that you all came to see to her welfare, but I'm afraid that I can't let anyone else in," Kilbride told them.

"Well, unless Edward wanted to come out!" Jeff said lightly. "Ooh. That's not going to happen. Anyway, Dr. Kilbride, would you be good enough to tell her that we were here, that we wanted to check on her and let her know that we were all thinking about her."

"Of course, and thank you, I'm sure that will mean a lot," Kilbride said.

"Well, I'm off to bed!" Broderick said. "Good night, all."

"Dance floor, briefly," Gina told Daniel.

He groaned but waved to the others and followed her out.

"I guess all of us are going on that dive tomorrow," Jeff said. "Celia—"

"Bed," she said firmly. "Good night!"

Wes and Chloe were left with Amelia, who was still looking through the windows.

"Well, I'm not going on that dive tomorrow," she said. "But . . ." She paused and looked at Wes and Chloe. "I guess I'll call it a night. I hear the island is beautiful, so . . . I'm off to my beauty sleep! Good night, all!"

"Good night, Amelia!" Chloe told her.

But Amelia still hesitated. "Oh! Edward has looked up at last. He sees us, maybe he'll come out."

Edward waved to them, rose and came out as expected.

"How's she doing?" Wes asked.

"Sleeping like a babe," Edward said. "I haven't had a chance to talk to her yet, but she may wake up at any time, so . . . I'll be here," Edward said.

"May I run in while you're out?" Amelia asked. "They say that sometimes, when people are sleeping or even in a coma, they can hear you. I just want her to know that we all really care. And, Edward! We care about you, too!"

Edward smiled. "Thanks, Amelia. Thanks so much. Um, sure, I'll chat with these guys for a minute," he told her, indicating Wes and Chloe.

Amelia headed toward the door to the room. But as she did, Wes lowered his head and smiled.

George had already taken up a new position by Sally's bedside. Amelia couldn't touch her or get close without George right there to stop her if she attempted anything even remotely harmful.

"Well, I still don't get it. I mean, I even knew about Sally's allergies. She's so careful. I don't know how she got hold of anything that had nuts in it in anyway," Edward said. He sighed. "I called the ship's main chef. He assured me that they're very careful these days. An allergy to nuts is apparently far more common than anyone might imagine. And deadly for far too many people." He looked at Wes. "Someone had something . . . but not in our group, I don't think. She mentioned her allergy when several of us were together."

"Several as in those teaching and speaking for the tech industry?" Wes asked him.

Edward nodded. "I don't remember exactly who was around, but . . . I don't know. From the time I met Sally, there was just something about her. I enjoy her company so much. She's just nice, I mean, not an evil or mean bone in her body. I've spent a lot of my life fighting to get to the top. And I'm around people all the time still fighting to get to the top. Sally has no ulterior motive. She isn't trying to get anywhere, she just honestly likes me for me!"

"Edward, you're a nice man. That's not so shocking," Chloe told him.

Wes realized that while they were carrying on a serious conversation, none of them looked at one another.

They were all watching through the windows.

Amelia was sitting by the bed with George not even a foot away.

At last, she stood and came out. "Still sleeping! Well, maybe she'll be okay and up and cheerful in a bit!" she said. "I'm heading on out for the night!"

They bid her good-night.

George was looking through the window at them. He gave Wes a solid nod and Wes knew that George suspected something had been done to the woman.

He probably had the same question.

*Why?*

But George's job was to keep watch over her and Edward.

And it was their job to find out just what the hell was going on.

"I think I may turn into a pumpkin soon myself," Chloe said. "Let's head on up and get some sleep. Edward, if you need us for anything—"

"I know where to find you. And thank you."

They left the room and headed for the elevators. Amelia and the others had already disappeared.

"We could go watch Gina and Daniel dance," Chloe said. "But—"

"But I think we've done all that we can for the day. And tomorrow . . . Well, a dive can be dangerous."

"Do you really think—"

"Doesn't matter what I think. Only that we're completely vigilant!" Wes said, shaking his head.

Stepping out of the elevator, they almost ran into Celia and Jeff.

Wes quickly slipped his arm around Chloe's shoulders. He realized that yes, it was the gesture of a "married" man.

And more. He was feeling protective of her! And, of course, he knew that she was a trained agent, a well-trained one, and that she could take care of herself.

But no way out of it.

Instinct kicked in. He'd never tell her that, of course. She was far too proudly determined that an agent was an agent, whether state or federal.

"Hey!" Wes said to the two. "Thought you were heading in—"

"To sleep," Celia said. "We decided on one dance!"

"Want to join us?" Jeff asked.

Thoughts flashed through Wes's mind.

*Were they really heading to the dance floor? Should we follow them? Maybe they were heading back to the hospital, maybe they really wanted to see Sally before she woke up!*

But even if they tried, they wouldn't get past George and Edward.

Chloe must have been thinking the same.

"I'm beat!" she said. "I think we're just going to call it a night!" She yawned expressively and leaned against Wes, smiling into his chest.

"Okay, see you on the excursion—or, wait, knowing all of us a bit, see you at breakfast before the excursion!" Jeff told them.

"Yep, besides, not just knowing us, it's a good idea to start a physical day with a good meal," Wes agreed.

They stepped out of the elevator. Celia and Jeff stepped in and it closed behind them.

"Do you think . . ."

"I think George has the situation in hand."

"Yeah, I agree!" Chloe told him.

They headed on down the hallway to their cabin. Wes opened the door and Chloe stepped in ahead of him.

He carefully locked the door behind them.

She was looking at him, nodding sagely.

"What a gentleman! But it's your turn for the bed!"

She kicked her shoes off and headed for the couch.

"Ah, come on! Let me be the gentleman! I'm accustomed to the couch. I probably couldn't sleep in a bed now!"

To stress his argument, he kicked his shoes off and plopped down next to her. She looked at him, grinning, and he meant to reach over and help her up. But she smiled and surprised him by whispering, "We do make a good married couple."

"In many ways . . ." he began. But they were touching. Their faces were close. "I guess I just need to be sure . . ."

It was almost as if he heard himself murmuring the words with no intention of really saying them.

But he ended his words when his mouth touched down on hers, barely, yes, barely a touch at first, but . . .

She didn't draw away. Her lips pressed to his, and his pressed then with greater need, and before he knew it, his arms were around her and they were falling into a half-prone position with one another and his tongue was playing with hers as hers played with his.

So very unprofessional.

And yet . . .

So amazing, so very amazing.

The kiss deepened into something incredibly passionate, urgent, hungry. And their hands began to move. There were moments of abandoned awkwardness that became moments of laughter that broke between the touch of their mouths as they struggled to remove their own clothing and help one another at the same time.

For a few blissful minutes, Wes decided they were going to forget all about being perfectly professional.

And maybe they were necessary minutes. Time to remember that the world really was beautiful, that incredible people existed, that beauty could outweigh ugliness.

Because they had both made this crazy decision. And once made, it was all out.

Clothing was strewn everywhere.

Touching hands went everywhere.

His kisses touched upon the silken soft beauty of her flesh, and hers aroused him to levels he wasn't sure he'd ever known.

And being together, coming together completely, hard and urgent and yet each movement like something of a sleek and stunning ballet . . .

And then . . .

Breathing, just breathing, hearts thumping, and still . . . her face against the dampness of his chest, yet when she looked up, she was smiling.

"We did that really well," she said lightly. "Just like a real couple!"

"Yeah," he agreed lightly. "It was pretty real!"

She smiled and stretched and murmured, "If there had been a problem, George would have called you. So, we're good. And you know what I was thinking?"

He laughed. "No, not at all right now."

"That there is a beautiful king bed in that little room. I mean, at this point . . ."

"We should both just sleep in the bed?"

"Exactly!" She rested her chin on her hands on his chest, grinning at him.

"I don't know," he said lightly. "A bed . . . hm. I might be tempted to really try it out!"

"And if you weren't, I'd throw you out!" she assured him.

Laughing, he lifted her to her feet and joined her, caught her hand and led her into the bedroom.

A real bed. It was going to be fun to sleep on one when they finally got to the part of the evening where they were really going to go to sleep!

When the alarm rang, he was up like a bolt of lightning. Waking, being together as they were, might have been far too tempting.

And the morning, of course, was important.

And so he was showered and dressed when Chloe brought her clothing through the little parlor area, grinning at him as she headed into the shower.

And as usual, she was showered, dressed, hair brushed, everything done to make her ready for the day in a matter of minutes. Of course, he'd expected to see her in her bathing suit; they had both planned on the diving excursion.

But he was surprised that she was in a wet suit—a lightweight one, not the heavier kind that were created for cold water, but just an encompassing suit that protected the body.

"Nice!" he told her.

"Hey, I'm from Florida. I've been diving when we've run into jellyfish, other stuff—I don't like weird things touching me."

"Other than me?"

She laughed. "Well, at least you're not wet and slimy. At first!" she corrected herself lightly.

He groaned.

*Should we talk about it?*

No.

"I definitely like it," he said, giving her his approval. "And I usually wear a rash guard for the same reason, lots of things in the water. Though, supposedly, by the private island the nasty creatures know not to come."

"You think?"

"Not for a minute," he chuckled. "The ocean is the ocean. Ocean creatures swim where they can lay their eggs, where there's food . . . And a wreck can provide shelter and more!"

"I've a terry cover-up, too. About to throw that on. Makes it all really easy, too. Wear the cover-up to the dive, take it off for the dive, get to put it back on if I'm wet and the air-conditioning in the bus is too chilly!"

"Perfect, so—we're ready?"

She nodded gravely and then frowned. "Did you hear anything from George or Edward?"

"No. And I think that no news is good news on this."

Chloe nodded. "Well, great. I'm starving."

"Even for food!" Wes said lightly. He already had the door

open. And, as they came out in the hallway, they ran into Celia and Jeff.

"Hey!" Celia said happily. "You guys are in time for breakfast, too. The usual?"

"A buffet this morning will work!" Chloe said. "They start getting people off the ship and to their various destinations and excursions right at nine, so . . . we've got an hour!"

"Plenty time to wolf down a good breakfast—and hopefully digest it on the way to the dive!" Jeff said. "But, hey, you know what's cool? I have never felt more comfortable about a dive before, knowing that a real dive master is among our group!"

"Well, I'm not the dive master on this—" Wes began.

"But you'll be there. And you two lovebirds have already proven your lifesaving abilities!" Jeff said.

"It does make for a nice feeling of confidence," Celia said.

"Well, good!" Wes told her. "It should be great. A lot of the wrecks that I've been to are deep, way deep, and most recreational divers don't get to see them. This one is on a reef, just thirty feet down."

"I know! I'm excited. It will be my first wreck!" Celia said.

They chatted casually as they made their way to the elevator and then out to the deck where they'd dined before, lining up for the buffet and looking about for tables.

"Busy this morning," Chloe noted. "I guess those who just kind of enjoy the ship when we're at sea like to get up and going when they have a plan!"

"And that's natural," Wes said.

"I hope we get to sit together!" Celia said. "I'm looking for a table—oh! There! Broderick, Daniel and Daniel's new obsession, the young Gina, are at a table already and it looks like . . . yep! They're holding seats for us!"

They were.

Once they had filled their plates, they made their way to the table where the brothers were waiting for them.

Wes thanked them as they brought their food and took their seats. Then Daniel murmured, "Hey! I guess she really is okay! We need the rest of the table, too. Edward and Sally are out on deck and, of course, George!"

Sally was up, on Edward's arm, smiling at him and then waving at their group. They soon joined them, with Sally apologizing as she sat. "I'm so sorry. I mean, first off, thanks for saving places for us! We weren't hurrying because Edward and I have decided that we're not getting off the ship. I told him we could, no problem, but—"

"But we can get massages right in the ship's salon!" Edward interrupted. "I told Sally, I don't care. We both had our moments. We're just going to enjoy time."

"That's lovely," Chloe said. "Sally, you really feel all right now?"

"I do, and of course, I am so sorry to have frightened everyone and to have been such a bother!" Sally said.

Wes smiled at her. "Sally, you were absolutely not a bother. We're just grateful that you're all right. But how—"

"Oh! Thank you, thank you! I heard that it was the two of you who found my EpiPen and got me the care I needed. I can't thank you enough!" Sally told him.

Wes shook his head. "Sally, I understand that you know about your allergy. How did you happen to—"

"Well, you see, I don't really know!" Sally told him. "I'm so careful about what I eat. But there was a little welcome packet at my door, bars wrapped in a ribbon with a note, and I thought that it was plain chocolate, and it tasted like plain chocolate . . . It was only a little bit and I ate it all but, oh, silly me! I should have known better. I mean, the whole world doesn't need to avoid nuts and I wouldn't want others to not have something that they enjoyed because of me . . . But, anyway, thanks to you and Chloe, I'm here and well. Again! You both pulled me up and out of that swimming pool! And now, well, I'm starting to think that you're more than the perfect couple—you're guardian angels!"

"Just in the right place at the right—or wrong—time," Chloe said, glancing at Wes. "But I thought that the ship's crew had been made aware—"

"Oh, I've mentioned my allergy—it's on some paperwork somewhere. But not everyone reads everything and . . ." She broke off, shrugging. "Go eat! You people eat. You don't have that much time!"

"I guess we should hurry a bit," Gina said. Wes lowered his head, smiling. The young woman was stunning and did belong on a runway or magazine cover. And yet, he thought, she had nothing on Chloe, whether Chloe's hair was dyed, short, long or . . . whatever!

She was probably good at what she did. And he'd overheard her talking to Chloe the day before; she wanted to be useful.

Giving to the right causes was extremely useful.

But she was with Daniel and . . .

Daniel just might be a greedy murderer.

"Interesting," Broderick noted.

"What's that?" Edward asked.

"Hail, hail, the gang's all here, including you and George!" Broderick said. "But no Amelia!"

"Well, she said that she wasn't going diving," Celia told them with a shrug. "Maybe she's sleeping in."

"She was by this morning," Sally said cheerfully.

"Edward stepped out for a minute so that she could step in. They're very strict about no more than two people being in a room with a patient," George told them.

"Well, that's sweet and nice of her. Curious that she isn't having breakfast with us," Broderick said, and he laughed softly. "She is very serious about business!"

Chloe suddenly rose, excusing herself. "I'll be right back! I left my brush in the room. I'll look like a hedgehog if I don't have it when I get out of the water!"

"Honey—" Wes began.

But he knew that something was bothering her; really bothering her.

"Well, I guess I'm done!" he said to the table. "Edward, Sally, George—see you later. Broderick, Celia, Jeff, Daniel—see you on the bus!"

They were due to exit the ship soon to make that bus to the diving station.

What was Chloe doing?

He followed after her and found that she was speaking with one of the gentlemen with security.

He hurried up in silence to find out what she was up to.

"I have the head cruise director on the line, Mrs. Douglas," the officer was saying. "One second, he's checking everything for me . . . Sir!"

He spoke into the phone and listened.

"Thank you, sir, a concerned cruiser is asking and there's a good reason. I'll have her—" he paused, looking at Wes. "I'll have them speak with you directly."

Chloe took the phone and identified them both as Mr. and Mrs. Douglas; Wes realized that she had come to the man asking about any welcome gifts that might have been left outside the rooms.

"I can assure you that there were no such gifts. And, of course, I'll be speaking with all my crew, finding out if any of them know of any such gifts from Milestones or the like. We can also check our hallway cameras. And we'll let you know as soon as we know something, but it's going to be difficult. Families travel together, um, romantic situations arise, and people like to give each other little gifts under those circumstances. Still, hopefully, the cameras will give us all that we need."

Chloe thanked the man.

Wes spoke up. "It would be good to know anything as soon as possible. Before we all leave the ship."

"Stay where you are," the man told him. "Give me five."

"We're right here," Chloe said, looking at Wes. "I know who did it," she said softly. "What I don't know is why."

Time had gone by quickly. As they stood, waiting, a voice came over the ship's speakers, telling those who were departing for excursions to please have their papers ready as it was time to exit the ship.

From where they stood, they could see that a line was forming on the deck below.

"We need to stop her!" Chloe said.

He quickly scanned the crowd leaving the ship.

And, of course, the clues had been there all along.

Amelia Swenson was almost the first in line. And she was carrying a large bag.

*Amelia doesn't intend to get back on the ship! Because somewhere out there, probably in the video, was the truth. She had given Sally the chocolates.*

"Wes! We need to get her!" Chloe cried, shoving the phone back into the hands of the security guard and racing for the stairs into the hallway.

She didn't go for the elevator; she was racing for the stairs.

He followed because, yes, of course, the clues were all there.

But why would Amelia Swenson, lesser nobility among

the tech crowd, be out to kill Sally Brookins, who wasn't in tech at all?

Then again, she had talked about belonging to her group, the people with whom she studied Sir Arthur Conan Doyle, Sherlock Holmes . . .

And had helped police catch a killer.

# THIRTEEN

CHLOE HAD TO ADMIT, security on the ship was good. Most of the time, they were police, they behaved as if they were there to greet passengers, give them directions aboard the ship.

But they were on the ball, so it seemed.

It took Chloe and Wes almost no time to reach the deck where passengers would be disembarking.

But despite their speed, security had been alerted and one of the officers had reached Amelia.

That meant, Chloe knew, that the security footage had shown them all that Amelia Swenson had made a delivery to Sally Brookins's door. And, of course, having listened to Sally, Chloe knew what it was. A little packet of chocolate bars in pretty little wrappers with an attached note that welcomed her aboard.

Chocolates tainted with nuts.

"Miss, stop, I'm afraid you must. It's not a request. We have some questions for you before you can disembark for the day," an officer was saying.

"Questions? About what?" Amelia demanded. But she looked flushed, uncomfortable and scared.

She hardly had the look of a hardened, clever or calculating criminal.

And yet . . .

"Ma'am, I'm afraid you were caught on our security footage delivering a package," the security officer told her. "You must come along with me. The captain wants to speak with you."

Wes caught hold of Chloe's shoulder; she knew why. Amelia was guilty of something, yes. But he didn't want the two of them giving themselves away to the ship.

Amelia would be questioned. They needed to behave like ordinary passengers.

That meant, of course, that they needed to give George a call.

Because Edward Thompson had taken Sally on as a new best friend, it would be easy for George and Edward to insist on knowing what was going on. The captain would take grave care. First, of course, he'd be appalled by an attempted poisoning on his ship and secondly, Edward was, on this particular cruise, his most important passenger, and the captain would see to it that Amelia was not just questioned but held.

"They've got it," Wes whispered into Chloe's ear. "Security is on it. We need to maintain our cover."

"I know. But obviously—" she began.

"Yes. Obviously, she attempted to poison Sally. And trust me, the captain isn't just going to tell her to behave—she'll be held. I imagine she'll face charges when we return to home port. But we don't know if she's completely involved, if she's a low-level flunky or if others are involved. Or if it's all even part of one conspiracy."

"You're right. This is . . ."

"Different. We need to see where it will lead us. And today, we just need to be two people out on a dive," Wes reminded her. "Chloe, major players are going to be on the dive."

"Right. Okay. But—"

"We have faith in George and even in Edward," Wes told her.

She nodded again and turned to look at him. Of course, people were staring at Amelia and the security officer.

Amelia had lowered her voice; they couldn't hear her words from the position they had taken up in the line.

She was still objecting.

But the security officer wasn't taking it. "Ma'am, you can walk with me or I can take you forcibly for the discussion the captain wishes to have."

The officer had Amelia by the arm. She was visibly shaken and upset, probably worried and scared, and she barely noticed Wes and Chloe as she was dragged back through the line and into a main hallway.

Wes took out his phone, stepping back so that he wouldn't be heard. Chloe knew that he was telling George of what was going on—and making sure that Amelia was going to be held somewhere until they returned.

Of course, since they were just a loving couple out for a romantic vacation together, it might be tricky managing to talk to Amelia themselves.

But, Chloe determined, between her, Wes, George and the powers that be at home, someone would figure out something.

For now . . .

They needed to watch those who were going to be with them on the dive. Four suspects who seemed more capable of manipulation than Amelia.

Daniel and Broderick McClintock and the not-so-charming married couple, Celia and Jeff Henderson, along with Daniel's new crush, Gina.

Close to her, he whispered softly in her ear, "Praying that both our gut instincts are correct and that Edward Thompson is entirely innocent."

"And I really do believe that he's innocent. I still think he's a target and that thankfully, George is as good as he is," she said softly in reply.

Despite the ruckus over Amelia being taken away, the line began to move. They were given eye scans as they disembarked and looked for the signs for the bus to take them to the dive station.

The others in their group of friends caught up with them as they reached the bus.

"Oh, my God!" Celia said, "did you hear what happened? I guess the captain was worried about the cruise line being sued and he had his people look at all the security footage! Did you see? Did you hear?" she demanded.

"I think there was some commotion in the line—" Chloe began.

"It was Amelia!" Daniel supplied. "Edward is so upset. He's the one who asked her to be on the cruise, to speak to people and all."

"And, of course . . . wow!" Broderick said. "Why? Why on earth would she put stuff in someone's chocolate like that? Why give her the chocolate—"

"Silly boy!" Daniel said. "Jealousy. Amelia was horrendously jealous of Sally! That was evident. I think Amelia believed that she was going to get to be Edward's plus-one. And then, go figure, Edward falls for a slightly older woman and there's Amelia . . . Poor Amelia! Just out of the running."

"Daniel, don't be mean!" Gina murmured.

"Mean?" he demanded. "Amelia almost killed Sally! She probably meant to kill her, get her out of the way so she could go after Edward again. And I'm being mean?"

"I can't believe that Amelia meant to kill her," Gina argued. "She probably thought that she could make her sick or maybe give her an ugly rash . . . I don't imagine that she realized how smitten poor Edward is and that he'd sit by her side no matter what. Because that's what real caring is!"

"Exactly. Edward cares for the woman, and cares deeply," Wes murmured.

Chloe realized that she liked Gina more and more. The girl had a real heart beating in her body. Beautiful inside and outside, as the saying went.

But . . .

While the morning had kept her from thinking about the night in which she and Wes has so *unprofessionally* indulged, Gina's words made her think about the world on a more personal level, about herself, about that night, their incredible intimacy . . .

And Wes.

She couldn't blame it on alcohol since they'd indulged in nothing but nonalcoholic beer since they'd been on the trip. But she didn't want to blame it on anything. She couldn't remember when she'd met anyone like Wes. Yes, they were pretending. They were undercover; they had taken on different identities for the cruise. There was always discussion about the real role of undercover work, especially when some agents lived a double identity for months or even years when they were trying to break into cartels or other criminal enterprises.

Last night, she had made choices as herself, realizing they'd both been oh-so-professionally fighting a mutual attraction. And that could mean . . .

She realized that if she'd thought of it as a one-night stand, it never would have happened. Just as she enjoyed seeing the genuine person behind Gina's beautiful face, every day she was with Wes made her both respect and admire him more.

And now . . .

She couldn't help it, though she knew that what they were doing was the right thing. Unless they uncovered the clue that would solve the many homicides that had taken place, they had to keep playing the game. And, as suggested, Amelia might just be an incompetent and jealous woman. She hadn't handled the concept of being questioned with the irritation and feigned innocence of a hardened criminal. And still . . .

She might be in on whatever was going on. A pawn in a game being played by clever minds.

Maybe it wasn't just jealousy that had caused her to take such actions. Maybe whoever was running the conspiracy feared Sally—because of her armchair crime-fighting friends. That was possible—far-fetched, but possible.

"She'll be in the brig!" Daniel said.

"Does our ship have a brig?" Celia asked. "I mean—"

"It has a brig," Daniel assured her. "She'll be processed back at the Port of Miami. Attempted murder!"

"Maybe it's just attempted *sickness*," Chloe said.

"Ah! Another bleeding heart among us!" Daniel told her. He quickly glanced at Wes. "And I mean that as a nice thing!"

"Well, anyway!" Broderick said. "Here we are, on a bus again!"

"Yeah, but just for a few minutes," Celia told him. "The place is close!"

And it was.

As they left the bus, they were escorted into something that resembled a classroom—or was a classroom, dive-style. They filed in with other passengers, all excited about the little dive boats they were about to get on. It wasn't a training dive, sometimes done from the beaches of certain ports, but a dive for those who were certified to various depths and degrees, as only certified and experienced divers were allowed to sign up.

There were others from the ship that Chloe of course recognized by then, including Darlene Jordan, her father, Bryan, and a few others they had met on board. Twelve passengers in all had signed up for the diving excursion. It was a limited choice; first come, first serve.

A man in his forties—wearing a light wet suit much like Chloe's own—headed to the front of the class. He appeared fit and able and a little bit weathered. But then, such a man probably spent his life in the sun and the elements.

"Hello and welcome to the Dive the Santa Teresa Excursion!" he told them. "I'm Percy Williams, your guide today. We'll also have Sammy Beck with us. I'll be leading and he'll be following up behind us, making sure no one gets lost. Now! I know for many of you, the shipwreck is the prime piece of this dive. Yes, she is amazing and how she came to be here, so close to our reef, is equally amazing. So! The ship left a port that you cruisers might know, the Port of Lisbon, Portugal. Portugal was a major seafaring nation with Henry the Navigator starting a determined effort sailing around Africa, circa 1419, and making their way by voyages to India. Then, of course, came the discovery that the world wasn't at all flat, that there was a New World to be discovered. And it was in 1500 that a Portuguese nobleman, Pedro Álvares Cabral found Brazil! Fast forward to the year 1545 and Santa Teresa left the Port of Lisbon. A beautiful ship, just a decade old and she'd been at sea several years. As usual, she crossed the Atlantic easily, heading for several ports in the Caribbean when behold! Something happened, something known to explorers, pirates and anyone who traveled to these parts. A storm arose, a massive storm, the kind we know of today with the power to almost level cities! And so, she tossed, she turned . . . she sank! Neither she nor any of her crew or cargo made it to any port. Not even she, brave valiant ship that she was, could survive the onslaught of that storm. And so, she went down. Down, down, down to the bottom of the sea."

"Was she a treasure ship! Did they find gold years later?" a man, waving his hand wildly, asked.

"Divers went down in the late 1800s. A difficult feat! Remember, scuba tanks were invented in 1943 by Jacques Yves Cousteau and a colleague, Émile Gagnan. But in 1823, a man named John Deane patented a device he called the Smoke Helmet. This allowed for surface air to run through a hose to a diver. This type of device was used by many salvagers and, of course, there were others, but diving was not made easy until the scuba tank came along. But when divers did reach the ship, there wasn't much truly classified as treasure to be found. Historic pottery, silverware and a few such items were discovered, but she hadn't been carrying any New World gold—she hadn't reached the ports she was to visit. And that deep and that long in the water . . . Well, belts, buckles, some jewelry was discovered, but nothing of the kind of value that salvage divers dream about. She was deep, even by modern standards, but some divers could reach her and explore her, and they did. For most people, for recreational divers, she wasn't easy and wasn't happening. But! Years later, just about a decade and half ago now, there was another storm. A storm, one of our massive hurricanes, lifted her from the deep seabed and smashed her against our reefs here just beyond the isle! She was thrown into the rocks, and went down and now she is there, a magnificent piece of history that can be enjoyed by even those divers who are not certified to study those wrecks down a hundred feet or so. She rests just twenty-five to thirty feet down and we are going to explore her today!"

A round of applause greeted his words.

"Next!" he told them all. "It's most unlikely that we'll run into any great white sharks, but we have lemons, makos, Caribbean reef sharks and hammerheads out there, to name a few. We've never had an attack, but I'm assuming that you are all aware not to thrash and attract such creatures, should we see any. Jellies—yeah, they can be out there, too. Avoid them—if you're stung, or if you wind up in distress in any way, signal your partner or one of us and we'll see that you get up safely and onto the boat. Now, what you will see are beautiful tangs, all kinds of angelfish, rock beauties in all colors . . . don't disturb the wildlife, look and enjoy! Got it?"

"Got it!" his audience echoed.

"And at the ship! Be careful. Rotting timber, ancient metal . . . Don't catch any body parts on broken wood or the like, right?"

"Right!" someone echoed.

"Now, then! Safety!" He nodded very solemnly. "Safety is always our priority. Our equipment is checked and double-checked, but you're responsible for making sure that your flippers, buoyancy control vests and mask and snorkel gear fit and aren't going to fail you along the way. So! Enough of me talking. We'll head to the equipment barn!

Chloe loved diving and still headed down to the Keys and out on a dive boat when she had the time. She doubted that she was as experienced as Wes—even though he didn't really run a dive boat or act as a dive master off that boat.

That she knew of, anyway!

But at the equipment barn, she knew that he was studying the snorkels, flippers and everything else that they were handed by a friendly young woman working behind the counter, taking foot sizes and making judgments on the proper BCVs to hand out.

Whether people owned their own equipment or not, on this dive, they were required to use that provided by the island dive shop, all part of the excursion. The equipment, guide and dive boat were all part of the package.

"Seems to be top-notch stuff," Wes noted quietly.

"Always good. And the oxygen tanks—"

"They'll be set for everyone on the dive boat itself. I believe we're a group of twelve, if my counting skills are still applicable. And it sounds about right for a decent-sized dive boat. I mean, they come in small and much larger . . ."

"But this is an excursion and that sounds good to me," Chloe told him. "Easier to watch those I'm worried about."

"You're a good diver?" Wes asked her.

"Well, hm, over time? I've been out at least thirty or forty times."

"Maybe we should split," he told her.

"Okay?" she murmured.

"Darlene. I know you're worried about Darlene. Let me go with her, you go with her dad."

"All right, but—"

"We trail each other."

When everyone had been outfitted with equipment, it was time to head to the boat. Chloe managed to sit next to Darlene with Wes on her right side.

It was a well-fitted motorboat, and Chloe saw that it was planned for the exact number of people on the tour. Air cylinders were provided at the seats that ran along the starboard and port sides, ready to be attached for each diver.

Their guide, Percy, introduced them all to Captain Ken Larkin and his mate, a young man who grinned when he was introduced as 'Buddy.' The four islanders—Percy, his fellow guide, Sammy Beck, and Captain Larkin and Buddy—would help everyone prepare to get into the water. The number of people on the dive was always even—everyone had a dive buddy, as well.

"I can't wait!" Darlene told Chloe. "A wreck! I have my basic certificate, but I haven't ever trained for a hundred feet or anything like that and one of the main wrecks down in the Keys that I've seen from a distance is down nearly a hundred or so. I mean, I got my license because my dad has always loved diving—and ships and boats, as you might have noticed—but I've had other interests, too, of course, and now college . . . Anyway! I'm very excited."

"So, your dad is a really experienced diver," Chloe said.

She smiled. It was easy to do so. The wind was blowing beautifully around them. The sky was clear, an exquisite shade of blue. It was truly an amazing day for such an activity.

"Dad has spent years diving. He's good. But I'll bet he's not as good as your husband! I mean, he runs a dive boat! He's a dive captain," Darlene said.

"Well, since this is your first wreck, you should buddy up with Wes and I'll buddy up with your dad. How's that sound?" Chloe asked her.

"Really? But isn't this like a second honeymoon for you guys? I don't want to split you up," Darlene told her.

Chloe smiled. "It is like a second honeymoon, but you won't be splitting us up. We're still all on the same dive, just switching partners for a few minutes. I mean, if your dad won't mind."

"What about Wes?"

"Wes loves showing newer divers the ropes. And it's a wreck. I'm sure we go right along the side and through something like a main highway, but still, I've had friends get lost in wrecks and panic for a minute or two, so . . ."

"So, if anyone wants me to go off in a different direction—"

"Wes will deck them," Chloe said, grinning.

"Can you deck someone in the water?" Darlene asked, laughing. "Deck him on a deck. I guess that works. That's sweet."

"Make sure your dad doesn't mind."

Darlene turned to talk to her father. Bryan leaned forward and looked around his daughter and grinned at Chloe. "A lovely new lady for a partner—even if she is married. Sure. Seriously, it will be great for Darlene to have someone as incredibly experienced as Wes!"

Eventually, the motor stopped. The anchor was tossed, and everyone was assigned and fit into their air tanks and only when he saw that all twelve of his people were ready did Percy head to the little rear platform. "One by one, when you're all in the water, we go down! Down, down, down!"

Percy was good at what he did. He had a sense of humor and could tell a good story, but he was also deadly serious when checking his divers out before heading to the platform himself. He was, in fact, far more determined to check on each individual, each piece of equipment than Chloe had seen a dive master manage to do before. Of course, this was all part of the luxury yacht experience, and she had no doubt that while she believed with her whole heart that the company did think of their passengers' enjoyment and safety above all, they might have been smart enough to be aware of liability, as well.

Percy fit the bill well, as did Sammy, the captain and even young Buddy, who had helped people meticulously.

They were soon all in the water, and the water was as

beautiful as the day. Sometimes, in Chloe's mind, the water—especially water that led to deep water—could be chilly, even on a warm day. But this water seemed to be in sync with everything else that had gone on so far.

"Tallyho!" Percy called. "Stick with your buddy! Any problems, I'm right in front and Sammy will be behind. No wandering off, my friends. This isn't a mobster movie—we're not leaving anyone to sleep with the fishes!"

With a grin, he set his mouthpiece in place and went under.

They had ended up treading water near Percy while everyone entered, and Wes gave Chloe a nod.

It wouldn't hurt to have the girl they worried about be right behind their diving guide.

"Darlene, let's follow the guy who knows the place!" Wes said.

She nodded.

The two went down; Chloe and Bryan followed.

And it was beautiful, truly beautiful. They were led first by some of the spectacular coral reefs, places where colorful tropical fish darted in and out of the little holes in the rocks. They didn't encounter anything remotely dangerous as they started out.

Chloe had always loved diving, loved the soothing sound of her own breath through the tubes, the feel of the water, the easy glide she made through it with the slightest movement of her flippers, the strange, peaceful quiet. And for a few moments, she let herself feel the enchantment of their movements and the aquatic world around them.

But she didn't forget that things had happened on this cruise, and being in the water—even a mere thirty feet down—could be dangerous.

Their party seemed to stop in unison as the great hull of the medieval ship came into view. It was something to see:

surreal, a little bit magical, very much like something out of a storybook.

At the head of his crowd, Percy made a movement with his hands, indicating that the party should follow him along the hull. People fell in line and did so.

Chloe noted that Celia and Jeff were right behind her and Bryan, and that while Daniel was diving with Gina, his brother, his usual partner, was doubled up with another younger woman who had apparently been on her own for the excursion. Both sets of partners were behind another married couple they had briefly met and seen about the ship. Another couple, who appeared to be father and son, brought up the rear, followed by the ever-vigilant Sammy.

It was fascinating to see the giant hull of the medieval wreck—albeit with a massive gash along the side—in the water. It naturally made her wonder about the people who had gone down with it in the storm. She could only imagine the fear of such a situation, trapped with no recourse by the mercilessness that could be nature.

And so strange to think about on a day such as this one! Not a worrisome creature in sight, just all kinds of quick-moving and beautifully colored tropical fish, rushing in and out of the coral rock and all around them.

The first part of the dive was about twenty minutes; it ended with the tour around and through the wreck.

They came around the hull with no difficulty. Toward the aft of the old ship, Percy paused again, making another expansive hand gesture in the water that they could all easily understand.

This one indicated that they go straight. Straight through the ship. They didn't wander into the old cabins, seek the old cannons or any other such thing.

They stayed together.

They entered the ship.

There had been no arrangements made for lights, but on such a day, lights weren't necessary. In fact, they might have detracted from the surreal feel within the wreck. The sunlight tore through the ancient timbers and created fascinating shadows and a murky gray darkness that still allowed—or perhaps more so allowed—them to see the interior of the old ship.

They didn't need to seek out the galley; they went through it. Some shelving still stood; remnants of tables, secured to the floor when the ship was built, still remained. They passed through the old galley and past cabins that no longer had doors; they saw what remained of the wooden structures for bunks. It was eerie, fascinating . . .

Darlene was moving along easily with Percy in front of her and Wes following right behind, her ever-watchful dive buddy.

Behind her, Chloe heard a bit of commotion, thuds against the wood.

She turned and saw that Celia had gotten hung up . . . on something. An ancient nail protruding through a doorway?

Chloe turned back to help, but, of course, Percy had heard the strange and unusual clumping sound that carried through the water, as well.

He turned back, coming through, determined to detach Celia from whatever it was that she'd become stuck to.

Naturally, that stopped all the movement, and they wound up gathered close with first Jeff trying to free his wife, then Wes and Percy, who managed to disentangle her almost immediately from the strip of wood she'd gotten caught on.

Percy indicated that they move on through the ship.

As they started out again, Chloe saw that Darlene had gripped Wes's arm. She was indicating her tank and hose and looking distressed.

Something was off.

But their determination on positioning had been good.

Wes took out his own mouthpiece, giving it to Darlene. He glanced at Chloe and she knew that he was going to bring Darlene immediately to the surface, something he indicated to Percy, as well.

*How? How the hell had anything happened? They had all been there together, clumped up a bit, albeit everyone concerned about Celia!*

This time, however, there was never a danger of death. Not when Darlene was with Wes. He would have no problem carefully rising the thirty-something feet to the surface while holding his breath.

But, of course, Bryan nodded at Chloe; he was naturally going after his daughter, assuring that she would be all right, with everyone curious about what had caused the problem.

Chloe and Bryan surfaced soon after Wes and Darlene. He'd been asking her if she was all right, but of course, she was since she'd had his air supply on the way up. The boat was near and the captain and Buddy were right there, calling out, throwing a float and helping their foursome out of the water.

The others, of course, were just minutes behind them.

They had been at the end of the dive when Celia had been in distress and then Darlene.

Chloe couldn't help but wonder if Celia getting caught up had been part of a plan. Cause confusion, leave a gap in there where someone could easily put a little pinprick in an air hose, enough to cause a problem.

The way everything was done so meticulously . . .

It just seemed unlikely that she'd suddenly have a problem with a piece of equipment that had been so carefully checked.

The captain and Buddy were extremely helpful, asking, as did Chloe and Bryan, about what had happened.

"I don't know!" Darlene said. "There was just suddenly no air coming through!"

Percy, when he'd helped the rest of the divers out of their tanks, hurried over to Darlene, anxious to ask the same question.

"I'm really fine, maybe I just panicked!" Darlene said. "And I'm so sorry! I didn't mean to ruin the tour—"

"We were at the end!" Percy assured her. "And have no fear. We'll check out every single piece down to the atoms to find out what failed you!"

"Hey, it's good to have a dive captain for your dive partner!" Darlene said.

Percy looked at Wes. Wes shrugged.

"Any of us down there could have shared our air—we didn't need to surface from being too deep. It's all good, Percy," Wes told him.

"All good!" Darlene said.

"Hey, young lady, you had a real problem," Celia said, looking over at Percy apologetically. "I did exactly what you said not to do!"

"People get excited—they get too close to ancient rotting things," Percy said. "It's happened before, and . . . well, you see why I run a tight ship! Buddy system all the way."

"Hear, hear!" the captain's mate, Buddy, said, causing everyone to laugh.

"Seriously! We had an amazing time, thank you!" Broderick said. "And, hey, what's a good time without a little drama?"

*A little drama. We seem to be having a lot of it lately!* Chloe thought.

She looked at Wes. She knew that they were due back at the dive station where all equipment would be returned, they would gather whatever they had left there, and board the bus for their return to the ship.

But she knew, too, that before they left, Wes would be talking to someone.

And that he'd be damned if he'd leave before he knew just what had caused the problem with Darlene's equipment.

# FOURTEEN

OTHERS HAD ALREADY headed for the bus, Chloe among them, Wes knew. He had watched as they started out. Chloe was walking along with Darlene and her father, and Wes knew that Darlene was still trying to apologize, telling them that she had been trained, she knew she could have asked to share air, and that she could have gotten to the surface on her own without causing such a problem.

And, of course, everyone was assuring her that they'd been at the end of the dive anyway, they'd seen the wreck! Everything was well.

And, of course again, he assumed Celia was telling her that it was probably her fault, not Darlene's, because she'd managed to get them close together in the ship's broken hallway where protruding metal and wood might have caused some kind of puncture in her air hose.

Right.

"I swear to you, sir, we thoroughly test our equipment and

we're vigilant about it, about measures to make sure that all mouthpieces are purified and . . ."

Wes looked at the young technician working on Darlene's air hose as he spoke.

Percy walked up. "You know, I warn people about getting hung up on something when we're in the wreck, but this might have been my fault. I didn't think to remind them that they had to watch out for their equipment, as well. You know, we have never had a single incident before and today we had two. Well, you live and learn. And thanks, man, you were so fast, but I hear that you're a dive master—"

"I was just there. Anyone who has been diving anytime would know to share air," Wes told him.

"But you did it without blinking, without causing a big disturbance," Percy said. "Thank you!"

"Hey, don't worry. They stress that divers are supposed to be experienced," Wes told him. "It's all good."

"I wasn't worried about being sued," Percy said, grimacing. "I, um, actually care about people. And that lady . . . well, she did exactly what I said not to do. But that poor kid! It's a scary thing when you're suddenly inhaling water with your air."

"It all turned out fine—"

"And there it is!" the tech suddenly said. "Well, I guess you're right about the old rotten wood and all. There's the scratch against the hose and the hole that it caused is so small! But big enough so that the air pressure wasn't enough to keep out the water. Kid must have brushed against something."

"That couldn't have been there before she went in," Wes said.

"We test—"

"No, sorry, that wasn't a question. It was a statement—

she would have been choking long before we were in the wreck," Wes told him.

"Your bus is about to leave," Percy said. He frowned. "Um, if you're still worried about these events or have any other questions—"

Wes grinned and shook his head. "Percy, we do not think that you or anyone at this dive station are culpable in any way. I was just hoping to understand what happened and, yes, of course, I assumed that she passed by something protruding and sharp without knowing it. That happens. You know, dive master—like to check things out so that I know what to watch out for myself!" he told them.

"Sure, well, thanks again!" Percy told him.

"No, thank you, guys," Wes said. He nodded to Percy and the tech and headed on out. He wasn't surprised to know that the two events were the first incidents they'd had of any kind during the dive trip—far more care was taken here than on most dive trips he'd been on. Not that most places were shoddy—people who loved to dive often had their own equipment and the dive boat captain and crew weren't responsible for problems with it. And, again, divers were usually expected to know what they were doing and held to a greater amount of self-responsibility.

He was the last to climb on the bus. The seat next to Chloe was empty, awaiting him. Broderick was in a seat across from the empty place intended for him and Daniel and Gina were behind her. She had evidently been chatting with them and with Darlene and Bryan, who had seats in front of Chloe.

"Hey!" Broderick said. "Once again, the conquering hero!"

Wes groaned as he took his seat. "C'mon, you're a diver. If it had been your partner, you'd have done exactly what I did."

"I don't know. My dive partner is usually my brother. I'd have to think about it!" Broderick said, teasing Daniel.

"I'll remember that!" Daniel warned him, grinning in turn. "Gina, thank goodness I was with you today!" he told her before turning to Wes and saying, "Still, man! You are good at what you do. All the water stuff."

"I'm sure grateful!" Darlene said, twisting around. "Hey, did you find out—"

"Well, it's the wreck, apparently," Wes said. "And, yes, Percy was great. He warned everyone. But water itself moves, so . . . I don't think anyone meant to do anything outside the rules, but in the water, it's easy to brush up against things and in a wreck, some of the things that we might brush up against are sharp."

"Yeah, but the hoses are thick," Bryan said, turning around as well.

"Right. And, under normal circumstances," Wes said, "I think it might take a lot to cause a breach, but . . ." He lowered his voice and looked swiftly back to where Celia and Jeff were sitting. "If we hadn't all gotten concerned trying to free Celia, this probably wouldn't have happened. We kind of got into a clump when she was stuck."

Bryan sniffed. "She was trying to look into what had been some kind of cabin or stowage unit," he said. "Doing what we were told not to do."

"Dad," Darlene murmured.

"Well, I call it like I see it!" Bryan said.

Chloe shrugged. "Bryan, really, it's easy to forget things. Celia was probably just curious." She offered a smile. "But, here's the thing! Celia is fine, Darlene is fine and we all had a great day! I say that we leave it at that!"

"Yeah, until we get back to the ship and find out what

Amelia Swenson has been up to!" Broderick offered quietly, shaking his head. "I still can't see her as a murderer!"

"Hey, I said before she might have just been trying to make her sick!" Chloe said. "I mean, in Amelia's mind, she figured that if Sally was covered in hives or something like that, or if she had a fever and was sick, well, she wouldn't be hanging around Edward."

Darlene was frowning. "What are you guys talking about? I heard a guest had been really sick, but that she had an EpiPen and was all right."

"She is. She's fine," Wes assured her.

"And lucky as a cat with nine lives!" Daniel said, nodding his head. "First, she gets caught when the drain went berserk, then she gets a gift that's filled with nuts. What might happen to the poor thing next?"

"Nothing, if Amelia is . . . hm. Where will she be?" Gina murmured.

"She'll be held until we return to port," Wes said. "Then the district attorney will determine what charges should be filed, if anything."

"There's a jail on the ship?" Darlene asked, her brows hiked.

"See! Not everyone knows all about the bowels of a ship!" Daniel said, grinning and turning to look at Darlene. "We had this conversation on the way here. Of course, we're all stunned about Amelia. Why, Edward invited her on the cruise and, naturally, many of us have known her for years and . . . well, we sure didn't expect this!"

"Jail on a ship!" Darlene murmured.

"It's called a brig," her father told her. "And, yes, even on a luxury liner like this one, there's a brig. Not used all that often . . . Well, I was on a cruise once where some drunks had to be held overnight. But . . . anyway, you need to have a place to hold people if they do get rowdy or out of hand or—"

"Try to poison someone?" Daniel suggested.

"Oh, wow, how horrible!" Darlene said. "But . . . wait. Amelia caused Sally to get sick? But wouldn't Sally know what to eat and what not to eat?"

"You didn't see the commotion when we were getting off the ship?" Broderick asked her.

"We were at the tail end of the line," Bryan told them ruefully. "I was afraid that we might miss the bus!"

"So how—" Darlene began again.

And, of course, the full explanation went around again. They knew that Amelia had given Sally bad chocolate.

"Then they must charge her with something!" Darlene said. "Assault at the very least. I think I told you that I wanted to be an influencer, maybe even sharing real news! I took a lot of classes, because being an investigative reporter was something I'd been thinking about and my trying to decide just which way to go meant lots of journalism and media classes but also forensics and criminology!" she told them proudly.

"She could be an attorney! She'd be great," Bryan said proudly. "But she's also great on camera!"

"I'll bet you're great at what you do!" Gina said.

"Thank you, and coming from you . . . Well, thank you! It's quite a compliment!" Darlene said.

Gina laughed. "I just try to look good. Investigative reporting? That's *doing* good!" she said. "Ah, we're back!" she noted, indicating the fact that they had returned to the bus's spot at the parking lot by the docks. Strange that they didn't drop us in their little town, let's head out to lunch there."

"I think they did at one time, but from what I heard through a crew member, people didn't like it because they were all wet and salty and needed showers. Anyway, the buffet is open all afternoon—I read those pamphlets they gave us all!" Wesley said. "And you know what? I'm with that passenger who wanted to return to the ship. I need a shower!"

"I guess we could all use showers," Chloe said. "I'm beginning to feel like a salt lick, too."

Murmuring arose as agreement went all around that they should have showers. Whoever wanted to join the others could do so down at the casual restaurant where they'd met so often—and which was just about always open.

The bus parked and they all headed off, ready to have their eyes scanned and allowed back on the ship.

As soon as they reached the room, Wes pulled out his phone. He nodded to Chloe who knew that he was calling George.

"Four minutes while you talk this time!" she told him.

She headed into the shower, not stopping to get clean, dry clothing. He smiled to himself. They both knew they had no time.

But neither was she going to pretend that him seeing her in a towel was any kind of a problem now.

George answered Wes's call immediately.

"You can talk?" Wes asked.

"Yeah, cool, beautiful day. Edward and Sally are fine. In loungers, but talking about a late lunch or early dinner," George told him, and Wes knew that he was with Edward and Sally, smiling and pretending it was a casual conversation while moving away a bit so that he could speak.

"Amelia was indignant, insisted she was innocent, confronted with the ship's security footage, then swore she was just trying to be nice, and she didn't know that she had given Sally chocolate that had nuts in it. Claimed she bought the chocolate in Jamaica and had no idea what it contained, then pretended she didn't know that Sally was allergic to nuts. She started demanding a lawyer, claiming we had no proof she was trying to do anything to anyone except be nice. Okay, so the crime occurred at sea, but this ship's registry is in the USA, the company owns the island, but it's small, very few facilities, and the captain is going by the fact that there is a United Nations Convention on the Law of the Sea and because Sally might have died twice under suspicious circumstances, he's holding Amelia until they investigate further. She is being held in the brig, though she's threatened every lawsuit known to man, sworn that while the corporation may have billions, they'll be penniless by the time she's done with them. Good thing Captain Millbrook is no pushover. He's explained that for the safety of others he must investigate further before he can set her free on the ship with so many other passengers."

"I'd like to figure out a way to talk to her," Wes murmured. "Find out—"

"If she's an idiot or involved with other events, you know, like pushing Edward Thompson overboard?" George asked dryly.

"Yeah, though the two don't jive, unless . . ."

"I know. I've thought that myself."

"Unless, of course, Amelia needed to get rid of Sally so that she could get closer to Edward and cause another *accident*."

"Right."

"So . . ."

"You can talk to her," George told him. His voice lowered further as he said, "You're going to need to speak with Assistant Director Alonzo, Wes. You're in your cabin. Give him a call. As you know, this call and that one can't be traced." His voice suddenly went up again. "Glad to hear that despite your few difficulties, it was an amazing dive! Yeah, Edward," he said, indicating that the man was close enough to him to hear anything that was said. "Great! Edward and Sally are talking about casual dining again—late, late lunch or early dinner! Okay, see you soon."

George ended the call.

Wes immediately called Alonzo, who answered on the first ring as he'd been expecting Wes to call in.

"Talked to George—what do we need to know?" Wes asked.

"Well, I don't like this any more than you're going to, but it came from over my head. Apparently, Captain Millbrook is friends with a few of our senators and he hasn't been liking what's been going on during his cruise. In turn, they called in favors to a few people who knew that we were handling the rash of tech-related deaths. In the end, we had to inform him that we had investigators undercover on the ship. He's a good man and the information will go no further. I can't see and don't know the different personalities on board but I trust you and Chloe to use excellent judgment. You figure out how you want to play it. But if you want to speak to this woman, Amelia Swenson, he will see to it that you're able to do so. Act as a friend who has access to the best criminal attorneys in the world, perhaps. Your call. And keep me posted. Again, we're looking at a situation with twists and turns that could mean just about anything. Keep me posted."

"Will do."

As he ended the call, Chloe emerged from the shower wrapped in a clean towel.

He looked at her unhappily.

"Good news or bad news?" he asked her.

She frowned. "Bad first, I guess."

"The captain knows who we are. Alonzo was instructed by those higher up in the chain to let him know because he reported to very powerful friends that he's extremely unhappy about things going on during his cruise."

"Oh. All right, from what I've seen—"

"He's a good man who would never intentionally give anything away. But secrets stay secret only when they're secrets that aren't shared, so we'll now need to be triply vigilant. The good news: he'll get us—or one of us, at least—in to speak with Amelia," he told her. "And uh, on the lighter side, you are quite fetching in a towel. But George informed me that Edward and Sally are ready to have a lovely late lunch or early dinner—"

"I'm getting dressed. So, we go and have a meal. Then Amelia?"

He nodded. "We need a little time to figure out how to play it. Alonzo suggested that we pretend we know some great lawyers. I'm trying to figure out if there's a way where we come across as just trying to help her because we believe that she did it, but that she wasn't really trying to do anything truly evil to anyone and we're trying to make the captain understand that so he'll get her out of the brig."

"I think I like that idea," Chloe said. "Oh, and we can pull the string that we were the ones to get Edward out of the water and even save Sally's life."

"Great. Okay, I'm going in. Get some clothes on!"

"Aye, aye, sir!"

Chloe disappeared in the bedroom. He headed into the shower.

"Don't look so anxious!" she told him when he emerged.

He smiled. "I won't, I promise. I'm going to be intrigued to discover just what more Edward is going to have to say now. See, I'm intrigued for what we're doing."

She smiled at that, but it faded quickly. "She may be good, as in really good. Pretending that she's all innocent, but she's screwed up, if so. From what I've gathered so far, she's completely guilt-free as in she just wanted to do something nice for Sally, or she knew there were nuts in the chocolate, but she just wanted to make Sally sick."

"I am anxious to talk to her myself, but . . . I won't look anxious. I promise. No big pile of anxiety!"

"Shall we?" Chloe asked, indicating the door.

He made his usual gallant gesture in opening it and she headed out into the hall. But as they walked, she took his arm and said, "I'm worried about Darlene."

"I know. I am, too."

"Someone tampered with her air hose."

"Almost certainly."

"Well, it couldn't have been Celia. She was attached to the wreck!"

"But she could have planned to be attached to the ship so that someone could get by Darlene with no one noticing."

"Yep."

"Ah, time to turn back into a charming social couple," Wes warned her.

Celia and Jeff were heading along the hallway, too, showered and ready to join the others in the little group they had formed.

"Hey, hungry?" Jeff asked, reaching them as the elevator arrived. "I know I'm starving!"

"I must admit, yes, starving," Wes agreed.

"Men are pathetic!" Celia said. "We've barely missed a single meal! And, may I remind you that the brochure about the excursions warned that the dive trip was straight there after breakfast, but back a little late for lunch."

"A little late!" Wes groaned.

"It's almost dinner," Jeff said.

"I think it is dinner, except maybe later we can have a late-night snack. But not too late. I think this is going to be another early night for me. I mean tomorrow, we're at sea all day. We can sleep late, eat breakfast late, lie around all day—and dance and explore the casino again at night!" Celia said. "And, wow, Chloe, you did so great at that Buffalo game the other night! You could play all night if you wanted!"

Chloe laughed. "Well, as you said, that will be tomorrow night! Being in the water the way we were . . ." She shrugged. "It tires me out!"

"Physical activity. It will do it every time," Jeff said. "Hey! Have you heard anything more about Amelia Swenson?"

"No," Wes lied. "But I did talk to George briefly. Can't help it, I feel the need to check on Edward and Sally, so . . . I gave him a call. He just said that they were heading to the restaurant and hung up quickly, so I figured we'll find out more when we see them."

"I can't imagine what Edward is going through. I mean, on the one hand, he's so crazy about Sally so he must be furious. But he's also the one who arranged for Amelia to be one of the instructors, speakers, teachers, or whatever we are on this, so . . ." Jeff murmured, looking at Celia and breaking off.

"He's got to be upset all around," Celia said.

"So, the captain questioned her," Jeff murmured. "Well, I guess we'll find out!"

They were about to find out, as Jeff said, because when they arrived at the casual restaurant, Edward, George and Sally were already at a table along with Daniel and Broderick and Gina—and Darlene and her father, Bryan, as well. While the tables usually seated ten, Edward had apparently asked for an extra chair so that there was space for them all.

"And I thought we were fast!" Wes said.

They headed over to the table where four seats waited for them.

"Thought you'd never get here!" Broderick said.

"And we thought we were faster than rockets!" Wes told him.

"Don't let him give you any grief—they've been seated for about all of thirty seconds!" Edward told them. He smiled. "But it's nice, really nice! We're back together here. Okay, in my mind, the hot dogs are just hot dogs, but the pizza is pretty good."

"Pizza will work for me," Chloe offered.

"We can get a bunch of them for the table!" Sally suggested. "Try a few, like the vegetable pizza, the pepperoni pizza . . . or whatever anyone wants!"

"Sally, you're doing well?" Celia asked.

"Good as gold, thank you!" Sally assured her. "Though we heard that there was excitement on the dive trip."

"My fault!" Celia said. "I mean, I meant to be good! But it's a wreck, it's fascinating and I don't get that kind of excitement often! Anyway, I'm pretty sure that Darlene's hose got compromised while everyone was trying to help me!"

"But it's all good," Daniel said. "And . . . okay, there's an elephant in this room, or at this table, anyway. Edward—"

"She's in the brig," Edward said. "If you're asking about Amelia, she's in the brig. She's screaming and ranting and threatening all kinds of lawsuits—against the ship, the captain, me, you name it! On the one hand, she could be totally innocent, just a nice person trying to do a nice thing. Of course, she claims that she had no idea the chocolate had nuts in it and that she didn't think she could hurt anyone with a goodwill gesture to a new friend. But! Thankfully, our captain is no fool!"

"True, but . . . wow. I am stunned, still," Celia said. "I mean, not really well, but I've known Amelia for years. I find it so hard to think that . . . to think that she would really want to hurt someone!"

"Possibly kill them!" Edward said angrily.

"Eddie!" Sally murmured.

He shook his head. "I could swear she knew that Sally was allergic. And I'm willing to bet she knew that the chocolate had been made with ground nuts."

"Well, she's in the brig. But hm, I wonder what they will charge her with," Jeff said. "It will be hard for prosecutors to prove that she wasn't just trying to be nice and that she didn't know there were nuts in the chocolate and Sally was deathly allergic to them."

Bryan cleared his throat. "Well, one way or the other, the woman is in the brig! And we need to decide on pizza and drinks!"

"And the day did turn out great!" Darlene assured Edward and Sally. "Chloe made me partner with Wes and, man, when it comes to diving and the water, truly, he is the best!"

"You were fine. We weren't that deep," Wes said. "And you were calm—that's the most important thing."

"Thanks!" Darlene said. "And we were, thankfully, at the end of the dive and like Celia said, it was so cool! I'd never been to a wreck before. And, of course!" she said, smiling over at Celia, "we know for our next experience that when you're warned about ragged wood and metal, pay attention!"

"We learned!" Celia agreed, laughing. "And onward! To pizza—with absolutely no nuts!" she said.

Their waiter arrived. They ordered breadsticks with marinara dip, mozzarella sticks and four different extra-large pizzas.

And, finally, they got off the topic of Sally's allergies and the events that had taken place on the wreck.

The rest of the group at the table listened to the waiter for the best wines to accompany their different pizzas.

They didn't order their nonalcoholic beers.

When asked, Chloe said, "Hm, not for me. I would love to have iced tea. I hate to admit it, but after the dive I'm starving, and wine would hit my stomach like a splash of pure acid right now. I'm a lightweight."

"Wes?" Edward asked.

"I'll go iced tea, too," Wes said.

Broderick laughed. "You are a good husband!" he said.

"Yeah, yeah, always! As she wishes it!" he said lightly. "Naw, tonight I'm just really wiped out. A lightweight in my own way!"

Their drinks arrived almost immediately and soon after their appetizers, then the pizzas.

They talked about the next day.

Yes, there were going to be classes.

"And I will honestly explain about Amelia," Edward said, "and, of course, apologize about it being my invitation that brought her on the ship—"

"Wait! Should you?" Broderick asked him. "I can only imagine that some people are doubtful that anything was planned. I mean, well, she'll be tried in America. Innocent until proven guilty."

"True!"

The merits of the system along with possible detriments went around the table.

And yet . . .

Wes felt that he knew, knew for certain, that Amelia had meant to harm Sally—if not kill her.

And he knew that Edward felt exactly the same way.

Still, he listened.

Finally, cannoli desserts arrived along with various coffees. And as they finished dessert, he noted that Chloe excused herself after a well-executed yawn.

"Whoa, that's it for me! Thank you, everyone. That was

a great dinner with new friends!" she said, smiling broadly. "But . . .

"Time to head to the cabin for a bit," Wes said.

"You do realize it's dinnertime, right?" Daniel asked, grinning.

"No. I realize it's nap time!" Chloe said.

She rose and Wes rose, too, looking around the table. "Yeah, hm, the nap may turn into all night and then we'll be awake when the roosters crow, but . . ."

Darlene spoke up. "Thank you again! Thank you both so much."

"You're so welcome, but you owe us no thanks, really," Wes assured her. "You were a great partner."

"And I got a lovely lady for a partner, too," Bryan said, nodding to Chloe.

"And I just thank everyone—that I'm not still attached to a broken beam or whatever it was down in the wreck!" Celia said.

"Hey, guys, come on! It was just a great day after all, and . . . well, after everything!" Gina told the group.

"It was," Chloe said. "So, okay, it's not even really dark. But good night, all!"

"Good night, Chloe. Good night, Wes—you wuss!" Jeff teased.

Wes just grimaced and shrugged. "Hey, you're the one who called it! It's all as she wishes!"

He and Chloe looked at one another, grinning. He took her arm so that they could leave the table.

Daniel laughed as they walked away.

"Sleep! Yeah, right!" he said, and though Wes could no longer see the group, he knew that they all smiled and stifled their laughter.

*Truer than they knew.*

And yet, good. Very good. It was more than necessary that everyone believed that they were just a loving couple wanting intimate alone time.

They were playing it all right.

And . . .

Maybe just a little bit too true.

# FIFTEEN

IT WAS EASY enough to get in to see Amelia, Chloe thought, though she was unhappy that anyone, including the captain, a man she considered to be honest and respectable, knew who they were and why they were on the ship. Obviously, he knew about George, too, but was probably grateful to the man.

And to them, of course. But the only secret that remained a secret was one that was never shared—yes, they knew that.

Still, they returned to their cabin first, just as they had said. Then Wes had George connect them with Captain Millbrook.

The man came to the cabin himself, serious and grim, thanking them first for their service. "Although," he said, "I should have known, with the way you've saved us from many situations that might have caused chaos!"

"Just doing our jobs, sir, but—"

"I swear, under pain of death, I will not give you away!" he promised.

"Hopefully, it will never come to that!" Wes murmured.

"But, Captain, you've questioned Amelia Swenson. What do you feel the truth to be?"

Captain Millbrook shook his head. "I don't know. I just don't know. She claims she just meant to be nice. That they—Edward's group of internet speakers and teachers—were one big family and that Edward evidently cared about Sally, and she wanted her to feel welcome. But she's also slipped up a few times in her story to various people. She didn't know that there were nuts in the chocolate or she knew, and she just wanted Sally to get sick enough to get away from Edward. A number of people seem to believe that she has a thing for Edward and that Sally got in her way."

"But what do you think?" Wes asked.

Millbrook shrugged. "Okay, I think that she did willingly try to make the woman sick. Whether she wanted her to die or not, I don't know. And, of course, it was a risky action because Sally does carry her EpiPen. She might have used it right away, except, of course, she didn't know what she was eating. So, was it an attempt at murder? Or just an attempt to get a rival out of the way? I don't know. Either way, what she did was criminal and she'll wait it out in the brig."

"Thank you," Chloe told him.

"And I figured if I came for you myself and we were stopped or seen, I'd just pretend that I was giving you a tour of the ship. You have behaved in an amazing manner, so no one might doubt the fact that I'd want to give you a bit of special treatment."

"Good plan, Captain," Wes assured him. "Thank you. Shall we?"

"The brig is one deck below the hospital, spa and loungers," Millbrook told them. "Next to the waste collection. Not the prettiest part of the ship."

He was right. They hit the elevators, running into no one

at first, but then seeing Darlene and her father with a small group of college-aged kids.

"Captain! And, of course, our new dear friends!" Bryan Jordan said. "Nice to run into you. I thought you two were out for the night!" he added, addressing Chloe and Wes.

"I'm just giving them a bit of a walkabout," Captain Millbrook explained. "Figured they should see the ship and enjoy a bit of special treatment."

"Oh, they deserve it!" Darlene said.

"You know the cool kids!" one of Darlene's friends teased.

"Okay, okay, I'll introduce you all!" Darlene said. She pointed out the two girls and the young man who accompanied them. "Marla, Nancy and Lennie!"

"So, I'm being a good dad!" Bryan said. "Taking these guys for facials. Something a dad can do for a girl."

"Hey, a facial is good for guys—even guys who play football!" Lennie explained.

"I hope you're getting a group discount!" Captain Millbrook told Bryan lightly.

"I'll need to ask!" Bryan said.

The elevator reached the spa floor and Bryan looked back, holding the door.

"So, you all are heading to stowage?" he asked. "Or the mechanical deck—"

"The parts of the ship no one sees!" Millbrook explained dramatically with a smile.

"Yeah, believe it or not, I wanted to know what you did with all the garbage for this many people on a ship," Chloe told him.

Bryan laughed. "Enjoy!" he told them.

He followed his group on down the hallway and the elevator doors closed behind him, bringing them down below.

It was impressive to see that, even in the so-called bowels

of the ship, everything was neat and tidy—as pristine as garbage could be. Millbrook described the different sections of recycling, of what was done on the ship and what was brought where to be recycled or become part of a landfill somewhere.

The security offices were down there, too, perhaps naturally. Just as in a police station, one went through the reception and offices to get to the brig.

By then, they'd casually met many of the security personnel on the ship and, of course, everyone in the place paid heed as Millbrook walked in.

Millbrook explained their purpose and said that he'd be waiting for Chloe and Wes to have their conversation.

"Can't say I'm giving you a tour if I'm not with you!" Millbrook explained.

Chloe and Wes thanked him and one of the officers, Doyle Stratton, looked at them ruefully. "We don't have much of an interrogation room. But Ms. Swenson's accommodations here just include a decent enough cot, sink and toilet, so I'll bring her to you in our little office area for such conversations."

They thanked him as he nodded, indicating they should follow him. He pointed out a door to the left as he moved forward.

Before entering the little room with the desk where they'd question—no, no, chat with—Amelia, Chloe noted that at the end of the hallway where Stratton was headed, there was a heavy metal door with a small barred window. They could see that there was an electronic keypad to lock and unlock the door. But it was an impressive two-tiered system. Stratton also had to use a key.

When they were holding someone on this ship, they intended to hold them.

She followed Wes into the room with the desk. It was small, as Stratton had told them, but not terrible. A very simple desk sat in the middle with two chairs on either side. There was no one-way mirror in the room, just bare walls.

She and Wes took chairs and Amelia, still looking like a pouting child, was brought in.

"You? You two? I'm not drowning and I didn't fall overboard! And you're not attorneys, so just what are you doing here?" she demanded, plopping down and staring at them before quickly adding, "Not that I mind. They won't let me have a computer in there, no internet connection . . . One of those guys found me some bad historical book to read, so I guess you're my entertainment for the day. I'll start right off. I am going to sue the butts off all these people!"

"Amelia, you're not drowning, no," Chloe said. "But we are trying to help you. We're trying to figure out the truth of what happened because . . . Amelia, I'm afraid that this can only go down so many ways!"

"What? Are you an attorney when you're not having some kind of bad artist showing at your gallery?" Amelia asked.

"Her dad's an attorney," Wes lied.

Tears suddenly sprang into Amelia's eyes. "I'm sorry. I'm horrible. It's just that this is so, so messed up! Okay, the truth. I was jealous of Sally, but I was trying to fight that feeling! I really just wanted to do something nice. Okay, I don't really read labels. The chocolate looked good. There might have been something in the display about ground nuts, but I was in a shop in Jamaica and I . . . I don't really know how they do their warnings or whatever—the ingredient list they had up could have been for several items. And it never occurred to me that any allergy could be so horribly severe!"

Chloe glanced at Wes, who was giving nothing way.

"I guess when we don't have allergies, we don't see how severe they can be," Wes said, shaking his head. "And, Amelia, I just wanted to say thank you, too, for talking to us about this. We figured if we could get a good feel for what really happened, we could explain it all to the captain."

"We were pretty sure you had no malicious intent!" Chloe told her.

"Well, thank you. And I'm sorry, but . . . I will have my attorneys go all over this! I came on this cruise to be helpful, because I do have such respect for Edward, but then he turns around over that ridiculous woman and believes that I could have done something to hurt her? I cared for Edward! And this is what I get. A beautiful cruise—spent locked in a tiny little miserable room!"

"Well, I guess it would have helped if you would had gone right to them and apologized, explained that you were just trying to do something nice," Chloe told her, grimacing.

"Are you kidding!" Amelia said. "You do know that news on a ship this size travels at the speed of sound! I would never have had a chance. I don't think they had the woman down to the hospital before the whole ship was abuzz with rumors that she had been poisoned! I couldn't have said a thing at that point that might have changed anything, I just . . ." She broke off, shaking her head. "I listened to everything. I quickly heard that Sally was going to be all right. And, stupidly, I forgot that there were security cameras all along the hallways and that . . . Well, I guess it's good to know that the ship has good security."

"That's always good," Chloe murmured.

"Except that . . . well, this is ridiculous! Nothing that I've supposedly done will stand up in a court of law and they will all be very, very sorry!" Amelia assured them.

That would depend on what was allowed in on a trial, exactly what she was charged with and whether a jury found her credible or not, Chloe thought.

"The whole thing is very unfortunate," Chloe said, shaking her head sadly.

"Can you get me out of here?" Amelia asked, looking from Chloe to Wes.

"We can talk to the Edward and the captain and see if we can get anywhere," Wes told her. "I'm so sorry, Amelia, we just don't have any guarantees. But again, thank you, because we were hoping that we could be helpful, so . . . we can try!"

"Edward really doesn't know just how liable he is!" Amelia announced. "I will make mincemeat out of him and his entire company!"

Chloe nodded gravely and unhappily, as did Wes.

But she couldn't help but wonder.

Was Edward in truth a very lucky man that he'd become so attached to Sally—and that George was on board, with him at every move? Amelia's venom might have masked something quite a bit deeper.

She was certain that the woman had knowingly found chocolate with nuts so finely ground in the mixture that Sally wouldn't notice.

Perhaps she had just meant to make her as sick as a dog—so sick that she couldn't attend classes, meals or anything else with Edward.

Or had she known the severity of the allergy and meant for Sally to die? To what end?

To leave Amelia free to be the shoulder that he leaned on, the person who gave him comfort . . .

Who managed to always be with him.

"All right, well, we'd best get going," Wes said. "Again, Amelia, thank you so very much for speaking with us. And, I promise, we'll do everything in our power to get to the bottom of this."

His words were real and passionate. They would do everything to get to the bottom of this, but Chloe noted that he didn't add that they would do everything in their power to get Amelia out of the brig.

Because they didn't really intend to do that at all.

Chloe rose, thanking Amelia herself.

The woman blinked, as if tears were rising to her eyes.

Except that they weren't. Her anger was all truth. Her sorrow over anything was entirely feigned. She was just angry, angry, perhaps, even with herself. Because a cunning and manipulative mind surely should have known about the security cameras.

Wes rose, as well. One of the officers had been waiting at the door; they were barely on their feet before the door opened and the man nodded solemnly, letting them know that he was ready to take Amelia back to her room in the brig.

Amelia left with him, shaking off his hand when he placed it on her arm.

"I can walk just fine on my own!" she snapped.

Then she was gone. Chloe looked at Wes; they couldn't talk now, but they hurried on out, knowing that the captain was waiting for them.

"Well?" Captain Millbrook asked.

"I'm not an attorney, but I do think that she can get a good defense lawyer of her own to possibly convince others that it was an accident," Wes said. "Was it attempted murder? Possibly. But proving that might well prove difficult. Even an assault charge might prove difficult because she's adamant that she was just trying to be nice and welcome Sally into the group that started hanging around together."

"She did it, and she's going to get away with it!" Millbrook said, shaking his head. "I've been in touch with my superiors, of course. They must weigh every move. She'll sue, for sure. But they've agreed with us about holding her until we arrive at our home port—it would have been far worse if she proved to be guilty and someone was murdered."

"I think she's where she should be until the absolute truth is discovered. I believe our law enforcement from both countries will work together to get into the shop where the chocolate was bought and find out just how it was advertised and sold. Montego Bay is a big tourist destination and they're not going to want this to cause any disturbances with their many, many tourist shops, so . . ."

"I did the right thing in your mind, too," Millbrook said.

Wes smiled. "As you said earlier, the alternative could have been far worse."

"All this going on! And I just had to be the captain on a cruise with a pack of computer experts!" Millbrook said. "Well, I'll let you get some sleep or dance or have a nightcap or . . ."

"I'll be honest! This was fascinating," Chloe told him. "Seeing what passengers don't see on a cruise ship. I'm amazed, too, that this deck, with all that it holds, doesn't smell bad at all! What's below us?"

"Mechanics and whatever items need to be stowed. Oh, all our supplies for the pools, the kitchens . . . She is, in comparison, a smaller ship, a yacht, so we're very compact in all that we do! Oh, and ventilation! The key to maintaining decent working conditions for all involved."

She thanked him and they headed back to the elevators.

And up.

This time, they didn't run into anyone. People were at meals, in the casino, listening to music or dancing the night away. They headed back to the room, and once the door was closed, Chloe quickly turned to Wes.

"Well? Really?"

He shook his head. "I believe that she's a strange kind of narcissist, enraged that she's not being seen for her entire worth. Does she have the kind of case that will probably get her off—what proof does anyone have that she intended murder? Maybe it was just supposed to be a welcoming gesture."

"Won't that depend on how many people can testify that she knew darned well that Sally had an allergy?"

"That could give credence to the charge that Amelia knew what she was doing to Sally, but it doesn't prove that she knew anything about nuts in the chocolate," Wes said. "However, law enforcement will be checking out the shops, finding out when she bought the chocolate and if there were warnings anywhere about there being nuts in the chocolate. But as far as the end of this cruise goes . . ."

"None of that means anything. But what we think may mean everything," Chloe said softly.

"And I think that I'll think better after a good night's—"

"Sleep!" Chloe finished for him.

He laughed, smiling at her. "Um, sure, if that's what you'd like. It's all 'as you wish,' my love."

She smiled and walked slowly to him.

Their case was as great an enigma as it had ever been. But neither of them forgot it for an instant. And the plan that night . . .

Well, it was for Mr. and Mrs. Douglas to spend time in their cabin, resting after a long day of physical activity.

Physical activity.

Chloe gently placed a hand on his face. "Well, I am . . . tired."

"Of course," Wes began, and she smiled, because whatever he was feeling, he would always respect the desires of the other person.

"Mentally tired. You know how physical activity can help you get a really good deep sleep? And maybe a really good deep sleep can stimulate my mind!"

"I have been thinking about stimulation," he told her with a straight face.

Then he grinned.

And she paused, wincing slightly, and he took her shoulders and said softly, "Chloe, please don't worry, we can just go back to—"

"I don't want to go back!" she told him, meeting his gaze and shaking her head. "I don't know . . . Did we just play a married couple so well we need to take it all the way? Should I have known you all my life? Does any of it matter right now? I don't know—"

"We can't know right now," he whispered, gently moving a stray lock of hair from her forehead. "But we are here, playing a married couple and in real life, we're adults with, I like to think, a modicum of intelligence and human decency—"

"Decency?" she inquired, causing him to grin again.

"Okay, I can try to be very indecent, but the point is—"

"So tonight you'll be indecent," she said lightly.

"By morning's light we'll be decent human beings, always, no matter where we go, where this leads, how it ends," he said. He cocked his head to the side slightly. "From the beginning, my love. 'As you wish!'"

"Ah, but 'as you wish,' as well!" she assured him. And she smiled. "Because that's how you make things work, right?"

"Could we not bring Celia into the room?" he inquired lightly.

"Hey! You just said her name!" she told him.

"Hm. I've got to fix that. Oh, okay!"

With a sudden strong gesture, he swooped low and swept

her into his arms. "The couch isn't nearly as comfortable as the bed, though when I'm touching you . . . hm, I barely notice anything else!"

She curled her arms around his neck. "Smooth talker!"

"I try!"

They were both laughing when they crashed down on the bed.

Then they weren't laughing. They were urgent again. And she loved the fiery heat and the vibrant play of his muscles under the touch of her fingers, her lips . . .

Loved the way they could be so intense, so hungry, so urgent . . .

And laugh together in a tangle of their clothing before they could discard it all.

And even in the end . . .

She loved lying next to him, feeling his arm around her as she curled against him.

Loved drifting to sleep . . . waking at his touch . . . grinning . . . finally, drifting into a deep and real sleep that lasted them the night.

When she woke, he was still lying next to her, his head on the pillow next to hers. He was awake, eyes gentle as he smiled at her and she realized that he had watched her sleep for several minutes.

"Hey," she murmured.

"Hey," he said, giving her a pained look. "And it's morning. Wow. Another morning of the beautiful sea, of the blue sky above and a gentle wind blowing! And, of course, still not knowing what the hell is really going on!"

"Well, it is the job," she reminded him. She smiled. "We're called agents, but state or federal, our job is that of investigators."

"Right. Well, so far, at least, we've kept two people alive!"

"Well, there you go. Life is the one thing you can never get back, so . . . okay, yeah, yeah, it's morning. Up and at 'em!"

He rose quickly and headed out of the bedroom for the shower. She smiled, watching him depart in all his naked glory.

But then again, everything happening was so complex. But she did respect, admire and care for the man—as well as find him extremely amazing in every intimate way. Not just in the culmination of that intimacy, but in the tenderness he was capable of with every movement, no matter how wild, hard, exciting and . . .

The ship would dock. And then . . .

The ship would dock, but not yet. And, she realized, whether Amellia was guilty of attempted murder or not, she still believed that something was still planned on the ship. Either the death of a major player, like Edward, or . . .

*Many deaths, as had occurred in Broward County.*

"It's all yours!" Wes called.

She was good at getting ready, but damn, he was fast!

She forced herself to rise quickly and streaked into the bathroom, noting only that Wes, hair still damp from the shower, was nevertheless dressed for the day at sea. He was wearing swim shorts and a casual knit shirt.

She'd throw on her suit beneath a terry cover-up, she thought, and they'd be ready for anything they chose to do without having to return to the cabin.

A few minutes later, she was ready as well.

"People did go off to bed early last night," Chloe reminded him.

"We don't really know if that was true for everyone," Wes reminded her. "Remember, Buffalo Queen, others might have gone dancing or gambling." He smiled "*We* went to bed early, remember?"

She laughed and teased, “Did we?”

He just shook his head and opened the door. “Whatever, I did work up an appetite. We’ll head out to the usual.”

When they arrived at the breakfast buffet, only Edward, George and Sally were there. But Edward, looking very serious, waved to them, indicating that they should come and join them. Wes nodded to the man and he and Chloe went through the line.

“You are hungry,” Chloe laughed, seeing that he chose an omelet, a waffle, a stack of bacon and an extra plate of fruit.

“Hey, come on, you didn’t work up any kind of appetite?” he teased.

“I ordered an omelet,” she said sagely. “Only so much will fit in the stomach no matter what!”

He grinned. “Well, at least you have toast and breakfast potatoes with your little plate of eggs!”

“Gee,” she teased. “I guess it just wasn’t that exhausting for me!”

“I didn’t think I was doing all the work,” he returned.

Grinning, she headed for the table with Wes right behind her.

When they had taken their seats, they realized that Edward was staring at them speculatively.

“Is everything all right?” Chloe asked him.

“I heard you got a tour of our beautiful yacht!” Edward told her.

“We did. Captain Millbrook . . . Well, he was very nice. He said that we deserved the ‘works,’ but since we got the tickets with the ‘works,’ he thought that a real tour of the ship would be great. And it was!” Chloe assured him.

“And, yeah, well, this is way bigger than what I’m accustomed to!” Wes assured him. “I thought I had a nice dive boat. Then again, mine is kind of like the one we went out in to dive to the wreck. Except that I have a pretty decent cabin and a galley, things that many dive boats don't, since they're set up for trips that last maybe four or five hours. Still, nothing that compares to a mega yacht!"

"I wasn't thinking so much about the ship," Edward said. "I was wondering if he brought you in to see where they're keeping Amelia."

Sally set a hand on his arm. "Edward, dear, please, please, you need to let this go! Maybe the woman was really, truly, just trying to be nice!"

George cleared his throat. "Well, Sally, even I heard you talking about being careful because of your allergy to nuts."

"But you honestly couldn't tell that there were ground nuts in the chocolate!" Sally said. "I mean, it was delicious chocolate! Normally, you can see a piece of an almond or peanut. So, I understand. Maybe she just didn't know. And now, of course, she's furious, and I'm so afraid that she'll really cause trouble for you and the others and the captain and the company that owns the line! And this . . . this really is such a wonderful cruise! So luxurious and a casino, too! Not many of the luxury vessels like this one have casinos! And of course, the private island! So much that's so very nice! Our captain is amazing, the security people are top-notch—I just hate that I'm the one causing trouble!"

"Sally," Chloe assured her, "none of this is your fault."

"Of course not. And Amelia is right where she should be. I went with the captain." He arched a brow to Wes. "I, too, was privileged to see the waste containers! But I . . . I needed to see where they were keeping her. And it's not horrible at all—I didn't think she should be locked up with only a bare floor. But I wanted to make sure that she was really, truly locked up and that she wouldn't be trying to kill Sally a third time!"

"Edward, we don't know that—" Sally began.

"You're nice, you're way too nice, Sally." He lowered his voice, although only the five of them were at the table. "There's more security footage, you know. Someone came out to twist some valve or something that caused the drain in the pool to turn into a vacuum! And while you sure can't see who it was all covered in a black suit and mask and all, I'm willing to bet that it was Amelia Swenson!"

Chloe kept from glancing at Wes, but she knew that neither of them had known Edward had seen that footage.

"Anyone could have gotten caught in that drain," Sally said.

"But everyone knows how you love the water, how you're the first to hop in, swim to the deep end, head underwater!" Edward said.

"But no guarantee," George reminded him, "no guarantee that someone else might have been first."

"But that woman! I don't think she would have cared if someone else had gotten caught—it was a gamble on her part," Edward said.

"Edward, there's just no way to be sure about this, or any of the things that have been happening. There was strange trouble on the dive," Wes reminded him, "and Amelia wasn't even there!"

"Thankfully, my friend, you were!" Edward said.

"Hey, so, what are you planning for today?" Chloe asked.

"I have a lecture at one. Right now, of course, we're enjoying breakfast!" Edward said. "Then . . . hm," he said, smiling at Sally, "Whatever this lovely lady would like!"

"I like just being with you!" Sally said. "But I do love the pool. And don't worry—I will wait until tons of people are in it before I go in."

"I truly wish that I thought what happened was purely

accidental!" Edward said. "But I'm not worried today. Amelia is locked up!"

George excused himself; his phone was ringing. He stepped away from the table for a moment.

"We were thinking of lounging around the pool, too," Wes said. "I guess—if they're not giving lectures—our usual crowd will be around."

"Daniel and Broderick—and their new ladies!" Edward said. "Well, as I said. It will be a lovely, relaxing day! Amelia will not be out. There's a security office in front of that cell—and a good metal door on it! We'll be fine, and we will have a great day, and she can try to sue from here to eternity, but once we're in court . . . she underestimates the talent of many of the fine prosecutors out there!"

George walked back to the table, looking troubled.

"What is it?" Chloe asked him.

"Um, well, Amelia isn't locked up anymore," George told them.

"What?" Edward almost shouted the word. "She couldn't have escaped—"

"She didn't," George said quickly. "But she's not in the brig—she's in the hospital. She was vomiting so violently that they had to get her to the infirmary. And she's burning up. They've, uh, asked if I mind coming down. Edward—"

"Go," Edward said. "I'm fine and I've been fine, but I do enjoy your company, sir!"

"And we'll stick to him like glue!" Chloe promised sweetly.

"But, George!" Edward said.

"Yes?" George asked, getting ready to leave them.

"If she's dying, well . . ." Edward paused, shaking his head, and then speaking very softly but with distress and passion, "After all this . . . maybe just let the murderous woman die!"

# SIXTEEN

THEY WEREN'T AT the table long before they were joined by first Celia and Jeff, and then Daniel and the beautiful Gina and his brother Broderick.

Naturally, the conversation went around again about Amelia being in the hospital now instead of prison, with everyone tactfully avoiding Edward's somewhat sinister suggestion.

"It's pretty serious. They've called George down there," Edward said gravely.

"Well, must be the prison grub!" Daniel said lightly. He shrugged. "Maybe she should be sick, after everything that she did."

"Okay, guys," Gina put in. "We don't know the truth! Therefore, I think that we need to use a little caution when we're talking about her."

"Gina!" Celia said, laughing. "I don't think that you need to worry. You're not part of the group that may find themselves sued!"

Gina shook her head. "We just don't really know!" she said.

"I mean . . . Edward! You're an amazing man. What you and your company tried to do for this cruise—yes, yes, promotion for yourself, too—is amazing. But please! Let's have a nice day, let's not think about Amelia anymore, or let any speculation ruin a beautiful day at sea!"

"Hear, hear! I like this lovely woman!" Sally said.

"Right, okay, yes, of course," Edward murmured. He looked around the table, forcing a smile. "A day at sea! Who is loving the wind and the water, lazing it out on a deck chair, and who is heading to some music, some dancing . . . the casino?"

"Hey, who is to say that you can't do a little of both?" Daniel asked lightly. "Though this lovely lady has mentioned dancing, but that will be a bit later. Oh, but we're doing something incredibly important today, too!" he said.

"What's that?" Edward asked.

"Coming to see you speak, offer any further explanation, keep our mouths shut, whatever you'd like!" Broderick told him.

Edward laughed. "Trust me, I never thought that I knew it all!"

Wes listened, laughed and determined his next best move was getting to speak with George.

He wanted to know what the hell had gone on with Amelia.

Two things occurred to him . . .

Someone could have gotten to her. Poisoned her, as she had tried to poison Sally.

Or . . .

*She's managed it all herself in an attempt to get herself removed from the ship's brig. There really wasn't a way out down there. From the hospital . . .*

Well, there was no massive metal door for one.

He made a point of stretching and wincing. "Babe," he

said to Chloe, "you didn't happen to remember to bring any of my back medication, did you?"

"I brought it, sweetheart, but it's in the cabin," Chloe told him.

"Of course, thank you. Excuse me. I'll be right back!"

He left the table, hurrying toward the hallway and the elevator. But instead of heading to the cabin, he hurried to the hospital deck.

He found George in the waiting area, pacing.

"What the hell?" Wes asked him.

He shook his head. "Seems like the kind of sickness you might get from really bad fish or something similar. Food poisoning."

"I know damned well they didn't serve bad food on this ship," Wes said.

George shook his head. "I spoke with three of the security officers. You know, they do go through extensive training. The International Maritime Association keeps great tabs on people. The oceans go everywhere and I've gotten to know several of the officers, Wes, and they're good. They're honest, they're passionate about the law and people at sea. They didn't allow anyone in. They swear as well that they all ate the same dinner that Amelia ate. So, whatever is plaguing her . . ."

"She did it to herself," Wes said. "She did it to get out of the brig."

"I think you're right. But I'm keeping close tabs on her, I promise you," George said.

Wes nodded. "Call me if you need me. I don't care who thinks what on this. If anything, if you need help—"

"I will call you immediately. At this moment, the woman is no danger to anyone. The doctor is treating her, and he is one of the best. But it will be a while before she could begin to be dangerous to anyone."

"Right. Thanks. I'll be in touch."

George nodded gravely.

Beyond a doubt, they needed to keep in touch. The day at sea stretched before them, and anyone on board could be in danger.

And he couldn't begin to imagine just what someone might be planning.

Wes headed to the elevators and down the hallway and then back to the table, smiling as he rejoined them, nodding to Chloe as if assuring her that he'd found everything just fine.

"So, any plans?" he asked.

"Well, for me, since I get to my lectures and Q and A sessions early enough to welcome those who arrive, I figured I had just the right amount of time for a rollicking good game of bocce ball!"

"There's bocce ball on the ship?" Wes asked.

"Near the kids' pool," Gina assured him. "We're in! Ready for—what did you call it, Edward? A rollicking good game of bocce ball!"

"Very well, I believe we are all set," Wes agreed.

"The great game of bocce ball!" Edward told them all. "The ancient and great game of bocce ball! Historically, the game was first played in ancient Greece and then the Romans took over. Those Romans were known for taking over!"

"Roaming Romans, roaming all around!" Jeff said lightly.

"I'm going to beg out on this," Celia said. She nodded toward a woman Wes had seen in a few of the classes who was at a nearby table. "I promised a little bit of a private session with the lady over there. She's a young widow, just forty-eight, but she lost her husband to cancer a couple of years ago. She met him in high school and she's incredibly awkward when it comes to dating and, of course, naturally online dating, since it didn't exist back when she and her husband met one another."

"Aren't we all!" Chloe said, adding sagely, "I can't tell you how grateful I am to be married to the love of my life. Dating is . . . wow. I never did get into the whole online dating thing—I wanted to see people in the flesh! Well, anyway, I hope you can help her, Celia, because I wouldn't want to be back out there!"

"Probably not," Broderick said. "Trust me, it is still painful and awkward. You know, there was a video that went viral about a year ago. There was a woman who was going on and on about how it was impossible to make women happy. You open a door, you're too macho. You don't open the door, you're a rude, unmannered slob! It's impossible to find that middle ground that makes you the perfect gentleman. Dating can be a nightmare."

"And guys can be just as bad, if not worse," Celia assured them. "Seriously, I've heard plenty of nightmare stories about men, too."

"Hey, we're all part of humanity, right? Male and female. We come in nice and not nice. Some of us have manners, some don't. Anyone, male or female, can be great and anyone, male or female, can be a monster. Whoever this woman was doing the talking on the video, ranting on and on, I'm just sorry to hear about it. She must be an extremely unhappy person," Chloe said.

"Oh! Your 'Buttercup' is just too lovely a person!" Jeff told Wes, grinning.

"His lovely, lovely angel!" Edward said. "And if only there were more in the world. Especially the corporate world!"

Daniel laughed softly, looking at Gina. "And I guess I got lucky, too. I believe I found the perfect woman, definitely an angel!"

"It all depends on who I'm with!" Gina said in return, smiling.

"All right, then. I say break!" Wes stood. Jeff rose right after him, looking at the other table and then the group. "Hm. You want my help, Celia, or you want to talk to her alone?"

"You go. Play bocce ball!" Celia told him, rising as well and gently touching his cheek. "I'm fine. I can manage this one on my own. If I finish up, I'll join you guys. Then again, I can't really be an angel and still beat the pants off all of you with my incredible ability at bocce ball!"

"Ooh. Are you that good?" Daniel asked her.

Celia laughed. "No. But it sounded pretty tough, right?"

Everyone laughed and Celia gave them a wave.

They watched as she headed over to the other table. Wes noted that Bryan and Darlene were seated there, too, and he waved to the women. Darlene waved back enthusiastically.

"Now there's a kid who will probably never have a problem with anything social!" Gina said. "As sweet as can be!"

"She is sweet, and her dad seems to be a good guy, too," Chloe agreed.

With a huge smile, Darlene was waving to them all.

"Yeah," Jeff murmured, "but her dad wants her and himself to sit in with us on this—he's so afraid she's going to meet a predator online. Well, that's a fear for dads all over the world these days."

"For anyone any age," Edward said.

"Man, is it good to be off the market!" Chloe murmured, bringing another round of smiles to the group.

"Okay, onward to bocce ball, while I still have an hour or so to show you young people how it's done!" Edward told them.

"Young people?" Sally said lightly. "You're going to show me, too, right?"

"You have the youngest heart of all, my dear!" Edward assured her.

Chloe glanced at Wes, arching a brow. The little affair going on was charming and it seemed to be a safe affair for now.

Amelia might not be in the brig, but she was out of the picture.

Hopefully. But George was watching.

And George, he reminded himself, was good at what he did. George could keep his eye on Amelia.

He and Chloe would play bocce ball. And the only one in the list of suspects they wouldn't see at any given moment was Celia.

He didn't like that. He had to remind himself again that just because Celia could have an acidic personality, it didn't make her a murderer.

"So, Edward, you sure know a lot of trivia, even when it comes to this game!" Chloe was saying as they reached the elevators.

"Bocce! It comes from the Italian word for bowl, *boccia*! Now, the point of throwing your ball is to get it as close to the target ball, or the *pallino*. And one of the best things about the game is that you can play it alone and improve your own skill, play with one other person or play in teams, as we shall play today!"

"Hm, okay, but you're the king of bocce, so it seems. Who is on your team?" Daniel asked him.

"Sally, of course, and—"

"Me and Gina!" Daniel told him. "That leaves my charming hulk of a brother with Chloe and Wes and . . . Oh, man, Celia messed it all up by not coming! Jeff is going to be the odd man out!"

"I can supervise!" Jeff suggested. "Call it as I see it. I'll be the emcee. No, wait, you don't call it an emcee . . . I'll be the referee, the umpire, the game official!"

"Ooh. Maybe I'd rather be that and let you play, Daniel!" Sally said.

Wes knew how he could fix the problem. He pretended that his phone was ringing. "Excuse me a sec!" he told the others, stepping back to feign a conversation.

"Well, I'm afraid we've just had the perfect solution," he said apologetically, turning back to them.

"What's up?" Edward asked him.

"I'm afraid I've got to get back down to my computer. There's been a problem at the marina, and I've got to get the right people working on it." He wrinkled his nose. "That's the problem with being the sole proprietor in a small business. I mean, it's great to be your own boss but if anything happens, you're in charge!"

He paused for a moment. He had told George that he'd be the one looking out for Edward.

And Sally.

Two accidents on this ship where Sally was concerned were two too many.

He saw that Chloe was looking at him and she nodded gravely. He lowered his head, smiling.

She would stay with Edward and Sally, stick to them like glue.

And she was good, in so many ways, of course. She'd have never been paired with him on this mission if she wasn't amazing at her job. He needed to have real faith in her.

And he did.

"Go!" she told him. "I'll have to try to uphold the family bocce ball honor on my own! Do what you need to do, Wes, seriously. We have all day at sea."

"Right! So. Have lots of fun for me, okay? Chloe, I'll call you in a bit and let you know how it's going. Hopefully, I'll be out in time for Edward's lecture."

Wes had no idea why, but he couldn't shake the idea that something was up. Something was up with Amelia being in the hospital rather than the brig. He smiled as he headed back inside ahead of the crowd, anxious to get to an elevator alone.

As he left the group, he saw Celia in front of him, walking toward their group.

"Finished already?" he asked her.

She shrugged. "I asked them to come play bocce ball, too. They're just going to hang around the pool. Where are you going?"

"My cabin. Work—you know. When you're the sole owner . . ."

"Ah! Well, I'm so sorry! See you tonight!" Celia told him, hurrying on by.

Wes shook his head. She was an extremely unpleasant person, but . . .

Amelia had been different.

She had seemed decent at first, and he had to admit, just from the rudeness of her behavior, he'd assumed that Celia had to be the main culprit behind everything. And, maybe, she still was. Maybe Amelia was just a bitter woman who couldn't begin to figure out why a man like Edward Thompson had chosen a woman like Sally over her. Had she meant for Sally just to get sick—or had she wanted the woman to die? They might never know.

He headed off to the elevator on the hospital level. Since the spa and another of the beautiful lounging decks were accessible though the hallway as well, there were several people moving along the area, some headed off for facials, massages or other such treatments, some just looking out for cool and beautiful views of the sea as the ship traveled along.

He would never know why, never really understand "gut" or instinct, but he knew from the time he approached the door to the hospital area that something was wrong.

The curtains were closed in the little room where Edward and Sally had once been during their separate "accidents."

But the doctor was behind the reception desk, frowning and studying a book of notes.

He looked up and saw Wes and greeted him right away.

"Hello, of course, you're here. Always checking on the welfare of others! I know that you're concerned when George isn't with Edward, but he was incredibly helpful to me today. One of my nurses had a family emergency. We had to leave her in Jamaica so that she could hop on a flight home. And this Amelia thing . . . her symptoms suggested she'd eaten or consumed something that caused serious food poisoning, but I've worked on this ship a while and I guarantee you, the food is good. And safe! I mean, that's one thing—when a well-known chain of gourmet restaurants opens a cruise line, food is going to be one of the major assets on board!"

"I've been extremely curious about that myself," Wes told him. "I'm with you. I believe with my whole heart that the chefs on this ship are cautious to the extreme."

"Well, I don't have the answers. She hasn't been sick since she's been here and despite the incredible tools and services they've managed for the hospital on this ship, I have no way of testing vomit that has been compromised with cleaning fluids since, of course, the security officers were horrified by the mess and don't think like crime scene channels when they have a sick prisoner."

"Crime scene?" Wes said.

"I'm sorry! I mean, all those guys wanted to do was get the place cleaned up, which is too bad, just in case there was something bad in the food. Anyway, I believe that Amelia will soon be fine and that, according to the captain's wishes, she will be returned to the brig."

"Is it all right if I take a look and see how she and George are doing?" Wes asked.

"Of course. You, sir, are always welcome here!" the doctor assured him.

Kilbride smiled at him and set his hands firmly on the desk as the ship made a perceptible movement.

"We've got some waves today!" he said.

"Waves may be rocking us around a bit, but it's still so beautiful out!" Wes said reflectively.

"Right, beautiful." For a moment, Kilbride appeared to be confused. He frowned, looking at Wes.

"You needed something?" he said.

"Checking in on George and Amelia," Wes reminded him.

"Right. George and Amelia."

In a matter of seconds it seemed, Doctor Kilbride had gone from being perfectly lucid to a man on the edge of dementia.

"Doctor—" Wes began.

But before he could say anything further, Dr. Kilbride blinked once and fell to the floor.

"Doctor!"

Wes cried the word and hurried around the reception desk. Kilbride's eyes were closed; he was lying in a heap on the floor.

Wes fell to his knees, checking the man's breathing and pulse.

Pulse, weak, breathing shallow. But he was alive.

Wes hefted the man up in his arms and hurried quickly

to push open the door to the nearest hospital room and lay him out on the bed, checking his vitals again.

Thankfully, he was alive.

*Drugged.*

Wes left Kilbride to hurry into the room where Amelia had been earlier, where George should have been keeping watch over her.

There was no sign of Amelia Swenson. Or George.

Swearing softly to himself, he pulled out his phone. He called Chloe's number.

No answer.

He tried Edward. No answer.

As he started to head out, one of Kilbride's nurses came into the waiting room, speaking as she arrived. "Got it, Doc, just as you ordered! Giant black coffee with exactly two teaspoons of sugar!"

She froze, seeing Wes.

"Get in there and take care of Dr. Kilbride. How long have you been gone? Were Amanda and George here when you left?" he demanded.

The poor young woman looked distressed and confused. "Yes, of course, and there was a security officer right outside . . . I thought that maybe he'd come in here. But—"

"They're gone, Amanda, George and the security officer. And whoever did this dosed Dr. Kilbride with something! I'm going after them. Get in there, and please, please, please take good care of Kilbride. Pulse is weak, breathing is shallow—but he's alive. Keep him that way! I'll send an officer but if you can lock yourself in here—"

"Oh, I can, and I will!" she swore. "I just don't know why the officer would have left, why George would have allowed Amelia out," the young woman told him, her fear apparent in her eyes.

"Lock the door behind me!"

Wes hurried out of the hospital cabin on the ship, waiting just seconds to hear the click of a lock and the slide of a bolt behind him.

He tried Chloe again as he raced for the elevator. Hurrying up to the kids' pool area with the other games, he found the little bocce ball court at the open deck toward the back.

There was no sign of Edward, Sally, Gina, Celia, Jeff, Daniel or Broderick.

This time he called the captain, and he was grateful when the call went through. He searched through the people on the deck.

"Amelia and George and one of your officers have disappeared and worse," he explained quickly. "Chloe had eyes on Edward at the bocce ball court, but that whole crew has disappeared, too, except . . ."

As he spoke, he saw that Daniel McClintock was stretched out on one of the loungers. He hurried toward him, still speaking with the captain, telling him to get on the security footage from the decks and the hallways, to find out where the group had gone.

"I found one! Back to you, please get on that, immediately!"

Captain Millbrook was evidently upset, but he was a strong man who had weathered many rough seas in the literary sense, and in life as well, Wes imagined.

He ended the call to hunker down by Daniel McClintock.

"Daniel!"

No response.

"Daniel, damn it, Daniel!"

No response.

He shook the man. His eyes rolled in their sockets, and

he tried to focus on Wes. "I . . . I didn't know . . . I . . . He means to kill me. I . . . I tried . . . the needle . . ."

Succinylcholine? Was that the drug that whoever was doing this was hitting people with? But how could he, she or they have moved people around once they'd struck them with a needle? Kilbride had fallen after a few words, apparently having no idea that he'd been hit with anything.

And now . . .

Here was Daniel, flat out. But there was no sign of Gina—or the others.

"Daniel, try, please try! Where did they go? Please, help me!"

Daniel's mouth moved. His eyes flickered.

"Down . . . down . . . down . . ."

The man's eyes closed. He was out. And no matter how hard he was shaken, Wes knew, there was no way that he would speak again.

*With any luck, he's only been drugged. He will live. Unless . . .*

Was the *he* his own brother? And did whoever had done this plan on coming back to kill him when he'd finished whatever he was doing? Who the hell was involved—and who, besides Edward, might the intended victims be?

"Hey!" Wes shouted. "Anyone medical? Please, if so, come help this man!"

He was gratified when a woman of perhaps thirty-five excused herself from her group and hurried over to him.

"Can't take him to the doctor right now, the hospital area is compromised. Please don't spread fear until we can rectify the situation, but he's been drugged if you can keep an eye on his vitals!"

"Oh, my God!"

So much for *don't spread fear.*

"Hold on, please."

His phone buzzed. He answered it quickly, praying first that it might be Chloe, but grateful to see that it was Captain Millbrook.

"Security cameras were compromised, but not before I saw your group heading to the elevators going down. And not before I saw Amelia leaving the infirmary with George weaving around all over the place, just like the man who had been at the door. I'm afraid to leave the helm right now—"

"You don't need to leave the helm. You do need to get a couple of security officers up to the kids' pool to help a woman look after a man who has been drugged. I'm going down. Send backup behind me, but tell them to stand down until they hear my order, we need to know who is doing this and who is victimized. Order them quickly, please!"

"You got it. Can we keep an open line—"

"Oh, you bet!"

"Help is coming," Wes told the woman.

She nodded, obviously getting a grip, though she was still nervous. "Melinda Dougherty, Doctor Dougherty, pediatrician, but I went to med school. I know who you are—the guy who saves everyone. I'm here, go stop this, whatever it is!" she told him.

*The guy who saves everyone.*

Wes realized he had never prayed so hard to be someone that others expected him to be.

He nodded to her and strode as quickly as he could back to the hallway and down to the elevator.

*Down, down, down, but to which deck?*

He thought he knew. The deck where the security offices were behind the rows and rows of recycling.

Cruise ships were allowed to dispose of certain rubbish at sea, and if that was where all the recycling and trash was kept, a disposal apparatus would be found there, as well.

*Was that the intention? Paralyze a group of people, and then dispose of them in the sea?*

As the thought raced through his mind, he heard Millbrook on the line, still there from the call they had never ended.

"I was thinking, I don't know, but while security offices are below there, there's also a clearing section beyond the bins, places where what can be disposed is sorted out from what must be recycled or—"

"My thought exactly, sir. I'm on my way!"

The elevator came to a halt.

Wes stepped off as silently as he could, reaching beneath the casual jacket he had worn, grateful that he had chosen to carry his 3D-printed weapon.

He inched along, heading away from the security office, following along a row of the giant green bins.

There was movement behind him. He spun.

It was his backup.

But he lifted a hand; the man in the lead nodded gravely. The five men followed slowly and silently.

Finally, Wes heard soft laughter from ahead.

"Well, we've gathered you all here for a lesson! One of the best lessons you'll ever learn, except, sadly, you'll never get to use it. You see, that's the thing. It's a dog-eat-dog world, my friends, and we're going to climb to the top of it! How, you ask? You see, those of us who should be in power, who should be at the top, well, we'll be found here . . . survivors. Because that's what you have to be in a dog-eat-dog world. Survivors! Now, we're just about ready, I have everyone I need, and of course, a few of you who are—sorry, guys—collateral damage!"

Wes recognized the voice, but the man had said *we* and used *survivors* in the plural, so . . .

He turned, nodded to his backup and indicated that they should come close, but still hang back.

Then, he went down to his knees and carefully crawled along the last of the green recycling bins until he could see the sorting area.

And . . .

Chloe.

Chloe, lying just inches from him, prone, flat on the deck.

*Of course, they've managed to drug her. To get her down here. But she knows what they are doing, she would have avoided a needle . . .*

*But she isn't moving!*

*She isn't moving at all. I can only pray . . .*

Chloe was good; she might well be pretending, or . . .

Only halfway paralyzed?

One way or the other, he needed to let her know that he was there, that others were behind him. First, however, he had to inch forward; he needed to see.

Who was creating this horror.

And who was a victim.

Still . . . Chloe had to know. Had to know that he was there.

And that someone might well die that day, but it sure as hell wasn't going to be her!

"As you wish!" he whispered softly. "As you wish!"

# SEVENTEEN

CHLOE COULD SEE everything that was happening.

She could hear every little bit of noise around her.

She could smell day-old food, the chemicals in the air-conditioning and almost taste every little nuance of the air.

She could even feel the floor beneath her.

Her senses were vibrantly alive.

What she couldn't do was *move*. Every step of the way, she had felt more and more as if she was turning to stone. She hadn't thought that she'd been hit hard enough for much of anything to get into her system!

And yet, she had come along. She had come along because of the blade of the knife that was positioned right between Edward Thompson's ribs by his heart. And she had come along because . . .

While there was breath, there was hope.

Of course, they had long suspected that more than one person had to be involved for the deaths to occur in more than one place, and in the end, to more than one or two people at a time.

But all the while they'd investigated, she hadn't seen this combo clearly. Perhaps she should have. She'd imagined things the other way, perhaps. Daniel McClintock and Jeff Henderson working together, the two men who were lower on their individual totem poles, resentful, determined to take control.

But no . . .

There they had been playing bocce ball when she had suddenly seen Daniel and Broderick get into an argument, then the two walk away and Daniel sink down into one of the lounges, looking away from his brother.

Meantime, she'd heard Gina let out an "Ouch!" The woman thought that she'd been bitten by a flying bug.

And as Daniel sank into the chair and Gina gasped, Chloe had heard Edward let out a strangled sound as well and she looked over to see that Sally was white as a sheet. Broderick was next to Edward, standing as if he just had an arm around the man, but . . .

His other hand was on the man's chest, the knife all but hidden by the fall of Edward's casual jacket.

She'd seen Jeff's look of stunned horror as he stared at his wife and heard her warning to him that he could die if he didn't shut the hell up as she jabbed something into his arm.

Her 3D-printed gun was in her bag, on one of the chairs. With the right manipulation, she might have gotten to it. And she had. Of course, Broderick had stared at her and warned that she'd be the one to kill Edward if she didn't go along with what they were doing. She'd felt Celia Henderson behind her and she thought that she'd twisted enough to avoid the full thrust of the needle into her arm.

She'd heard Broderick whispering to Celia, letting her

know that Amelia was ahead of them; she'd called. She'd taken care of the doctor and George and even the guard who had come in to help when she'd called out in distress.

Doctor Kilbride had been left behind, but she'd coerced George and the security guard down with her.

They were flat out on the ground, just as Gina, Sally, Edward and Jeff were—right along with her, right in the place where they separated waste before either recycling it or sending it out into the sea.

But Wes would know! He had gone to the hospital, she knew. He had gone to check on George and Amelia.

*He'll know! He'd known when Amelia had managed to get out of the brig that she was planning something. And, of course, one of them would have gotten into the ship's computers and made sure that the cameras were down.*

But Wes was out there, somewhere. Somewhere close.

And still . . .

Since she'd been a little kid, she'd always been taught to be independent. To take care of herself—and to help others when they couldn't take care of themselves.

But she had been hit with the needle.

Still, she'd known what it was, and she'd twisted; she couldn't have gotten the full dose intended for her. In fact, she could still feel the wetness where the liquid in Celia's syringe had failed to reach its target.

Wes was out there on the ship somewhere!

Was he close?

Did he know?

She listened to Broderick, who seemed to have gone into a full-throttle psychotic break. He wasn't going to shoot this group.

He was going to send them paralyzed into the water, let them drown.

She had to do something! She had grabbed her bag as she'd nodded, agreeing to go along with whatever they were doing. Because at first, of course, he'd made it sound like they'd live if they just obey.

"With Edward out of the way, along with my hanger-on brother and Celia's pathetic excuse for a husband, Celia, Amelia and I will reign, we'll reign supreme! We will eventually own the entire cloud!"

"Not just the cloud!" Amelia added, smiling. "We'll own the world, no, the universe!" She was as pleased with herself as could be. But then she grew serious. "Come on. Let's get to work. Find the disposal shaft. Don't forget, the security offices are just down the hall past all the bins up in the aft area! We've got to move! Oh, and trust me! This time I will take care of Sally."

"Let's hope!" Broderick said. "You messed it up pretty badly before."

"Two times!" Celia told her. "Let's hope—"

"I'm out here and I brought everything necessary, right?" Amelia snapped back.

Chloe didn't know if she did or didn't blink; she could only feel the heaviness of her own body, as if she was frozen in time and space.

But she knew everything that was going on; she could see the horror of what was happening around her.

She could watch. Yes, she could see clearly.

And . . . she discovered she could blink. And she had to do more. Much more.

The horror that had claimed others, the terror that haunted those on shipboard, would eventually come to her—and she'd be expelled to drown right along with those she was sworn to protect.

All she could do was hope, pray and believe that she and Wesley had followed the right steps . . .

And that there just might be a miracle.

Step by step. Her mind was active; she had to think back, back to the very beginning and determine just how she had gotten to be where she was . . .

And how the hell was she going to get out of the situation.

She couldn't even open her mouth to scream . . .

*Or can I?*

Then she heard it. The softest whisper.

"As you wish!"

She realized then that, miraculously, somehow, Wes was there; he was inching toward her, coming around the giant green recycling tank that sat just by her position. And she heard him whisper, "Oh, and another quote from my favorite movie: 'Your friend here is only mostly dead. There's a big difference between mostly dead and all dead!'"

She realized that she could smile. Wes had known that she would have avoided the full thrust of a needle—the full dosage needed to absolutely incapacitate her—if she could.

And he might have acted; she knew that he had his 3D-printed weapon. But he was watching as well for what weapons their captors were holding over them, preparing to use on them, Chloe imagined.

Wes . . .

Her smile grew. Even now, caught up in the deadly tail end of their investigation, he would ease her mind with jokes about *The Princess Bride*, since he'd been teased over the name "Westley" since they arrived on the ship. The second he'd caught on to what was happening, his determination had been to save her and the others. But he also knew that she would also do everything in her power as well, not just to save herself, but to save those who were around them in the same position.

She also knew why he was waiting.

Just as she hadn't known until the last several minutes who was involved and who might be innocent, he had to know, as well. And now . . .

Now it was time to do something.

And she had been able to blink. She'd even been able to smile and she knew as well that she'd be able to talk, give Wes exactly what he needed, though he might know everything already—two of their suspects were flat on the floor while the other three . . .

"They'll catch you! The only thing you'll ever rule is a jail cell!" she warned as loudly as she could, which was barely more than a whisper.

Okay, her voice was pathetic, but . . .

Broderick was by the disposal shaft. But Amelia and Celia were still standing halfway between their victims and Broderick's position by the hull as he studied the mechanism to achieve his desired goal.

"I screwed up!" Amelia snapped at Celia. "But you did a hell of a job with this one!"

"Hey, I did amazingly well! I got them all down here before they became deadweight!" Celia snapped back.

And that was it. Wes's chance to move.

He leaped up from the shadows, 3D-printed gun pointed at the two women.

"I'd say that you both screwed up," Wes informed them. "Drop your weapons, drop them now. I'm sure you have secreted a few knives on you and that you may even have a few 3D-printed weapons, as well."

Amelia swiftly drew her own weapon. "Celia, damn it! He can't shoot both of us!"

But by then, Chloe had discovered that she could roll, that she could move and her determination was so strong that she could reach her bag and draw her own weapon, aim it Celia and warn, "Don't do it!"

"We can take them!" Amelia cried, pointing her gun at Chloe.

Chloe didn't want to kill the woman. She wanted her put away; she wanted justice for those who had died and for a woman like Amelia, life without the possibility of parole would be hell on earth.

But Amelia was taking aim to shoot her. She and Wes fired at the same time; the gun went flying from Amelia's hand as she screamed and fell, her wrist blown to hell along with her left knee.

Celia evidently didn't want to die.

She was surrendering even as five of the ship's security officers came around the bins, ready to take her into custody.

But they heard a resounding curse and looked to the hull.

Broderick McClintock had maneuvered the disposal hatch.

And he was gone.

"Can he survive that?" one of the security officers murmured.

"Yeah, possibly," another answered him, glancing up as he set Celia Henderson's wrists into a pair of cuffs.

"A doctor! I need a doctor!" Amelia screamed.

"Too bad you knocked the ship's main doctor out," Wes told her, apparently feeling little sympathy.

He put his hand to an earbud in his ear and turned to Chloe. "The captain is talking to me—I left my phone on after I called him. He's sending Doc's second down to tend to Amelia and he's gathered the nurses to come look after those who are drugged, but they should be fine as soon as it wears off. All right, I'm going into the water after Broderick—"

"I'm coming with you!" Chloe told him.

"No! You've been drugged! You couldn't even move—"

"Because I believed I couldn't. Once I heard you, I could do things—"

"The ship's crew will be out in force, Chloe!"

"And I'm fine. Remember? I was only half dead, and now, every second, I'm realizing I did manage to avoid the real thrust!"

He shook his head, turning to walk toward the elevator. She followed.

"Don't make me have to save you!" he snapped.

"Wes, stop! I wouldn't go in if I couldn't, I swear. And if I see the bastard, I promise I'll yell and let you get him!"

The captain was out; the ship's crew, as Wes had said, were already in motion, setting lifeboats into the sea with a few of the lifeguards plunging right in.

Wes threw off his jacket, shirt and shoes, covering his 3D-printed gun with his clothing and nodding to one of the security guards who was standing on deck, watching the water.

Chloe threw her cover-up on the pile; her 3D-printed gun was already back in the bag, and she looked at Wes, concerned.

He paused, nodding to one of the security officers and indicating the pile.

The security officer nodded in turn.

"He'll watch our stuff. I'm in," Wes told her.

And as he said it, he plunged over the railing into the water.

Chloe followed suit.

The waves were rough that day. While the sun was out and beautifully shining, the breeze was swift and moving the ocean.

But Chloe loved the water.

She tried to reckon the time since she'd been stabbed with the needle. It had been more than twenty minutes now and the little she had gotten into her system was truly fading.

Helped by the slap of the cold water!

And yet that day . . .

She loved the force of the waves against her, the feel of the heavy breeze, cold on her wet flesh, the taste of the salt on her lips.

She loved it all. It was life; it was being. It was feeling.

The chute let on to the aft of the ship and that was where the lifeboats and crew, searching for the man, were centered.

Treading water by Wes, she shouted, "Could he have gotten a grip on the hull somewhere? Or is he back there, or was it so rough he might have drowned already?"

"Any of the above!" Wes shouted back. "My guess? He found something to hang on to . . . Let's follow the flow of the water."

They did so, quickly catching up with the several lifeboats and crew who were on the hunt.

That was when they saw the man.

Somehow, Broderick McClintock had managed to find a piece of wood floating in the sea, as if a broken desk had been discarded overboard. Chloe knew that the cruise line was adamant about their recycling, their treatment of any kind of water that was discharged, incineration of some waste, and their respect for the ocean and the seven seas.

But they were in the Caribbean where pleasure vessels of all kinds roamed about from a multitude of islands and countries.

Someone had tossed something broken overboard and Broderick McClintock had found it. He was kicking away, using his float, trying to veer to the starboard and aft of the ship as fast as he could.

As Chloe and Wes swam hard to catch up with the closest of the lifeboats, the lifeguard aboard it dove in after the man.

Broderick slammed him in the head with his makeshift wooden float.

Wes swore softly, hurrying forward with swift, fluid strokes to reach the injured man, to bring him to the second crew member in the lifeboat, there to retrieve his coworker and friend.

As they worked, Chloe moved on ahead.

Forewarned.

She didn't swim straight at the man. She dove deep and came up beneath his feet, grabbing his ankles and dragging him downward.

As she had hoped, he was unprepared, and he came down into the water, expelling a savage cough.

But he had fury in his eyes as he reached for her.

She kicked back, leaving him desperate for breath and flailing at the water.

And as he shot up to grab a mouthful of air, Wes shot past her, dragging him down again.

He wouldn't drown the man, Chloe knew.

He was just making him as weak and desperate as he could before grappling with the man in the water.

Wes let him up; Broderick inhaled on a shaking, ragged gasp.

He grabbed for his lost bit of wooden float; Wes threw it far away from him and stared at him.

The man lunged at Wes through the water.

It was then that Chloe saw that he was still bearing the knife he'd threated to stick into Edward Thompson's rib cage.

"Knife!" Chloe screamed, lunging forward herself, kicking as hard as she could and almost managing to leap from the water.

To her relief, she did get herself high enough to knock his arm.

And Wes was able to grab the man by the elbow, twist it hard and force him to drop the knife.

It went down . . .

Down to the far depths below.

"Let me go, you bastard!" Broderick raged.

There was, of course, no way in hell that Wes was letting him go. As the man continued to struggle, Wes told him, "You know, I really was a lifeguard, but keep it up and you're going to die!"

But he wasn't going to die.

Another of the lifeboats had reached them and two men were pulling Broderick out of the water, one of them prepared with cuffs and in no mood to take anything from the man. As Broderick tried to fight him and unbalance the lifeboat, the officer got the cuffs on him and gave him a hard shove that sent him flying to a back seat on his rear.

Another man on the boat had a chain that he attached to Broderick and the rail on the lifeboat as the first turned to help Chloe out of the water and then Wes.

"Thanks!" he said simply. He had a radio on the boat; he used it to tell the captain that they had their man and were headed back.

They couldn't hear what the captain was saying and the radio call was quickly ended.

"And thanks again!" the man said.

"Incredible faith in you guys," Wes assured him. "But I guess we had to see for ourselves that this man didn't get away!"

"Oh, trust me, he will not be getting away. Nor will the

others. We're headed straight back now—every passenger will be offered a future cruise with all perks. Still, we have a chopper coming for the prisoners. You know, I've worked ship's security for a long time. I've had more than a few petty thefts, a few unwanted sexual encounters, but . . . Ah, hell, nothing like this! Nothing like a trio trying to murder people!"

"Well, thankfully, I don't think it's a common occurrence," Wes told him.

The security officer looked at Chloe, smiling.

"And I heard you were among the drugged!"

"Nothing like a good swim to knock it all out," Chloe told him. "For real!" she added softly to Wes. "I don't feel at all drugged or paralyzed in any way; I feel invigorated!"

"Have a seat," the man said, smiling. "We'll get you back to the ship in no time. And, well, it will be one interesting day. I think that Mr. Thompson's lecture is going to need to be canceled and, of course . . . Well, the captain gets to explain it all. Thankfully, not me!"

He indicated that the two of them should take seats on the lifeboat for the short distance back to the ship.

They took seats as suggested.

"Well, Alonzo was right, that's for sure. They had planned something for the ship. And I believe that the man who was the most decent to them, Edward Thompson, was the main target, though I guess Celia was glad to get rid of her husband and maybe Broderick was supposed to get rid of his brother."

"I wonder if we'll ever know," Chloe murmured.

"You really are fine, aren't you?"

She smiled. "So weird, though! There were moments when I truly felt paralyzed."

He smiled, nodding at her. "I don't know how I knew, but I knew . . . I knew you would have figured out how to avoid most of it."

"We both knew how they were pulling it all off," Chloe said. "I mean, getting people to just sit there staring while they were being shot. But at first, when I felt the needle . . . I really didn't know! Wes, it was all so fast, and then . . . that knife. He had that knife held against Edward's ribs! That's how they moved us all—they were threatening to kill Edward then and there." She frowned suddenly, looking at him anxiously. "George—George and a security officer were down there when we got there. I don't know how Amelia—oh, no. Is Doctor Kilbride going to be all right?"

"Here's where we got lucky. I don't think that Daniel had any idea about what his brother had been up to. But once he'd drugged Daniel, he just—"

"Stretched him out on a lounge chair. I saw," Chloe told him.

"Who knows? Maybe when Amelia figured out that he hadn't killed his brother, she would have come back and figured out a way to finish the task herself. But I asked for help before leaving him and a doctor was onboard, so she headed down with him and security and they're all looking after Kilbride. Well, now they'll have Kilbride, George, the security officer, Edward, Sally and Jeff Henderson to look after, too."

"But our suspects will be off the ship!" Chloe said.

Wes nodded. "And we'll be heading back." He smiled at her. "We'll have . . ."

"Paperwork?" she asked.

He laughed. "Tonight! We'll probably get to port now—the Port of Miami—sometime in the wee hours. I don't think they'll wake people up to force them off the ship at two in the morning, but after this voyage, who knows!"

They heard a sudden clanking sound and turned. Broderick was seated at the back, wrenching as hard as he could at the chain holding him to the rail.

"I'll say this for the man, he doesn't give up!" Wes murmured.

Chloe shook her head. "They just wanted power! For that, they killed so many people."

"Greed has always been a major motive," Wes commented.

"They will be tried in a federal court," Chloe murmured.

"And maybe in state courts, too," Wes told her. "But our part is done. I know that Edward was angry enough, that he wouldn't have minded if one of us would have shot to kill when Amelia wouldn't drop her weapon, but . . ."

"We're not judges and we're not on the jury," Chloe said. "We've done all that we came to do, except . . ."

"You still can't figure out why anyone would go so far, right? Or how—looking at the hateful dynamic that even seems to go through the threesome—they managed what they managed."

They were drawing up to the ship and great chains and ladders were being cast down to them.

Wes didn't move. Chloe knew that he was waiting.

Broderick would try to escape again, even in chains.

And he did fight, but the ship's crew had the situation now. They got him back on the ship.

Chloe and Wes came up, as well. Captain Millbrook was waiting for them. George, looking a bit under the weather still, was with him.

He was upset.

"I failed you!" he told them.

"George, I got hit with one of those needles, too," Chloe told him quickly. "I'm just glad to see you up and—"

"I'm good and Kilbride is coming around, too. Like the security officer. They got the three of us, first . . . Man, I turned my back for two seconds! I was trying to figure out what the hell was going on and . . . forgive me!"

"George!" Wes assured him. "We're good; the trio has been taken down. And we weren't alone. We had security officers, and we wouldn't have known where we were going, what they were up to . . . It's all over. Take care of yourself!"

"Here's what's good. I don't need to be with Amelia and her poor, sick stomach anymore!" George told him. "Edward, great man. And this whole thing . . . Well, thank God it's over. Almost over."

The ship's security officers were having a bad time getting Broderick along the deck.

"The brig isn't that big," Chloe murmured.

"Oh, they deserve to be on top of each other, but it won't be that long," Captain Millbrook said, joining them. "The chopper will be here to get them soon. And personally, I can't wait. As soon as it gets them, I need to make a major announcement and . . . Well, along with law enforcement, the cruise line's lawyers have all been warned about what's been happening, too." He hesitated. "I can't thank you two enough," he told them.

"Sir, we were just doing our jobs," she assured him.

"Well, you did them to an amazing level!" Millbrook said. "And please believe that you are welcome on our ships anytime, gratis, of course, and that you should come on a cruise when you're not on duty."

"That would be great," Chloe assured him.

"After the paperwork, the court dates . . ." Wes reminded her.

"Of course," Chloe said. "And now—"

"When they've got Broderick McClintock duly locked up, chained and shackled, whatever, I want to talk to him," Wes said.

"Now would be the time," McClintock said. "I want him off the ship! In chains, of course. I'll call ahead and they'll have him in that little room where you spoke with Amelia previously."

"Thank you," Wes told him. He turned to Chloe. "You don't have to come with me. You can go and take a shower—"

"Oh, no. I'm happy to talk to him with you. Maybe . . . I don't know. Try to understand why anyone would do what they did, exactly who did what."

"We need to take the elevator back down to the security level—where you were forced before," he reminded her.

"And I'm fine with that!" she assured him.

She was. It was over; it had ended with them being alive and well.

She was quiet in the elevator, and she knew that Wes glanced at her, concerned.

"I'm fine, really, I swear!" she told him.

"And thankfully, we went to the right and not the left!" he said. "Strange, how coming to talk to Amelia—you know, having the captain give us a tour of the ship—turned out to work well for us today. I knew where I was going and how to hang back . . . Things do happen for a reason."

They reached the security offices and were gravely led in to speak with Broderick.

He stared at them with such hatred in his eyes that they seemed to burn.

"They should be here for you soon," Wes said, pulling out a chair for Chloe, letting her take a seat before he did so himself.

"So, what the hell do you want?" Broderick demanded.

"Well, I guess we just wanted to figure out how you did it all! I mean, really, an amazing plan. But Edward isn't the real power behind his company—" Wes began.

Broderick started to laugh. "You don't know anything. The man has been buying more and more stock. With his position there and what he owns . . . he's got the power, trust me!"

"But why the others?" Chloe asked him.

"It's a commercial world!" Broderick told them, as if they didn't grasp the truth of anything at all.

"Right. Of course. Eliminate all the competition? But is that even possible in today's world?" Wes asked.

"For me? It would have been. I just discovered too late that I was working with two idiots," Broderick said, shaking his head.

"So," Wes said. "Amelia was supposed to see to it that Sally died. That way, she could get closer to Edward?"

"She's an idiot. Couldn't do anything right," Broderick said wearily.

"And yet, hm. She messed up a little, but . . . you left your brother up on deck!" Chloe reminded him.

He groaned. "That was Celia's fault! She was supposed to hit him with enough not just to paralyze, but to kill. Drugs are tricky—she did all right most of the time. We had to get them pliant to get them down to where we needed them to be, so we had to see that it was slow-acting. Now, the great thing is that most people don't want to see another person—especially one they like—knifed through the heart." He smiled at Chloe. "That's why you were all so obedient! Still capable of walking until the drug really set in—but then out like lights to be disposed of like the trash you are!"

"Oh, yeah, your plans and the execution of them were brilliant," Wes told him. "Except, of course, that they failed in the end."

"I didn't fail!" Broderick thundered. "The idiots around me failed. If I could have done this by myself, it would have been done properly."

"Yeah, I guess that's what I really want to know," Wes

said. “All the people who died in different states—especially that large group in Broward. Did you do that by yourself, or did you have help—”

“Celia is my queen of drugs!” he told them. “Amelia . . . well, she was just clean up, to help with everything else that was needed, causing cameras to go down, that kind of thing. Her real challenge was here on the ship—and she screwed it all up!”

“So, you are the one who shot and killed all those people,” Wes said.

Broderick smiled. “And I came very close to killing you, too. I had you in the water! Except of course,” he added, giving Chloe a sneer, “girlie here managed to give you a hand.”

Chloe smiled and looked at Wes. “I’m so glad I was able to offer my assistance.”

“You never had her, you know,” Wes told Broderick. “She was just waiting. I mean, you did see that she blew Amelia’s wrist to shreds, making her drop her weapon.”

“At that point, sorry, I didn’t see a thing. I gave up on my hapless partners, knew that I had to save myself.”

“Yeah, but you kind of failed at that!” Wes told him. “Well, thank you. This conversation is going to help a lot when you get to trial.”

The man frowned. “What? What the hell do you have to do with that?”

“I guess we were never properly introduced!” Wes told him. “I’m a Fed. Special Agent Wesley Law. And this is FDLE Special Agent Chloe McMurray. We’ve been tailing you the whole time,” he said pleasantly. “And trust me, Mr. McClintock, we’ll be seeing you in court where this conversation, legally taped, will be very helpful.”

Chloe thought the man was going to rip his arm off, he'd become so enraged by Wes's words.

Wes just shrugged and opened the door so that he and Chloe could leave the room.

"Man, am I glad that they're coming for him!" Wes said. "He hid it so well—the man is an animal!"

"Scientifically, Wes, we're all animals!" Chloe told him.

They checked out with the security officers who were on duty and headed on out.

"A real beer?" Wes asked her.

She smiled. "Shower first. I think that somehow I'm feeling really dirty, and that's not from our dip in the ocean! Oh, and we need to get our stuff from where we dumped it on the deck."

"Good idea," he told her.

They headed to the open-deck area where they had left their things. The same security officer was there, and he nodded gravely to them.

"Thought you'd be coming back for this stuff," he told them. "Kept an eye on it for you!"

"Thanks," Wes told him. "Appreciate it!"

"Now, shower," Chloe said.

"Shower. And you know . . ."

"I know what?"

"We have time, we've done our duty . . ."

"Right?" she said, waiting.

"We could share a shower," he suggested.

She grinned. "We don't have to pretend to be a married couple anymore. We just told the main killer who we really are."

"I didn't want to shower with you as your fake husband. I wanted to shower with you as you, and me as me," he said quietly. "And, of course, I'm hoping that maybe you'd like to shower with me as me, because I need to wash off all this salt water—"

Chloe smiled. They hadn't met through classes, through friends . . . They hadn't even met online.

But she hadn't met anyone who attracted her as much, who made her laugh, feel comfortable—made her happy!—in forever and ever. And while they had met "at work," they didn't work for the same agency. There was no reason they couldn't enjoy one another.

As themselves. Except, of course, if they did wind up going separate ways, she would feel as if she had lost a part of herself.

The best "husband" ever.

"Well, as long as you don't take up too much room!" she told him, making him laugh.

They headed back to the cabin where she set her bag down. As she did so, she was surprised to see that it was open. And when she looked into it . . .

*No.* She dumped everything out. *It has to be a mistake . . .*

There wasn't.

"What's the matter?" Wes asked her.

"My 3D-printed gun! I had it when we ran up and dumped our clothes and all to jump in the water."

"The security guard said—"

"I know! But my weapon is gone, Wes!" Chloe told him in distress.

"All right. Okay. Amelia, Broderick and Celia are being held, about to head off to the mainland to be charged. It might have fallen out. We just need to find it. There are little kids on board this ship. Come on, we'll head back. The shower can wait."

She nodded.

But if it had fallen out, wouldn't someone have seen it, reported it? Wouldn't the security officer have been concerned . . .

Maybe he took it, afraid of it falling into the wrong hands, and forgot to tell them.

"Come on," Wes repeated.

She nodded and followed him out. They hurried to the deck where they'd dropped their things, but nothing was there. A different security officer was on duty.

Wes started to explain, but before he could begin, he saw that Captain Millbrook was coming toward them.

"The chopper from the Feds will be here in ten. I thought that maybe you'd want to see the people you apprehended gone for good," he told them.

"Not a bad idea," Wes said. "We've a problem, though. When we went after Broderick McClintock, someone took Chloe's weapon out of her bag."

"I'll get security on it immediately," Millbrook assured them. "It's a serious matter, of course. But first . . . come to the helipad with me, no work on your part. Just watch them go," Millbrook said. "Then we can get on finding your gun," he told Chloe. "3D-printed plastic, I believe."

Chloe nodded and thanked him.

"Come along, then!"

They headed to the yacht's small helipad and stood next to the captain. The man hadn't lied; they'd barely arrived before they could hear the helicopter and then, within minutes, it had set down.

Feds stepped out of the aircraft.

Amelia, Celia and Broderick were brought up, all cuffed, Broderick still screaming at anyone near him, calling them all idiot sheep.

Both women were shuffled into the helicopter.

And it was then that the sound of a shot exploded through the air. It was followed by a second sharp retort.

A bullet had slammed into the side of the helicopter, just missing Broderick McClintock.

Officers, the captain and half the people around them shouted, "Get down!"

Broderick was forced to his knees.

As everyone ran for cover, Feds, ship's security, the captain and Wes and Chloe all searched for the direction the shot had come from, searching for the shooter.

Because Chloe knew they had to find the person. Because she was certain she now knew what had happened to her gun.

But this time . . .

*It seems that someone is trying to kill the known killer!*

# EIGHTEEN

MANY PEOPLE ON board had already moved on from the chaos of the hospital being closed, crew running all over and lifeboats being set down to find a killer.

The average person on board didn't know about any of the events down in the garbage disposal area and the captain had yet to make his speech.

He wanted the prisoners off his ship before he spoke.

Most probably hadn't heard the shots.

The Feds taking the prisoners dragged Broderick McClintock onto the helicopter. One man, obviously the agent in charge, looked at Captain Millbrook.

"We have everything under control here. Go, find the shooter!"

In another minute, the helicopter was gone.

The shot had been aimed at the helicopter, Wes knew. Well, it had struck the copter, he thought.

But someone had wanted to kill Broderick.

*Who?*

Someone who had figured out just what the man had been guilty of doing. Someone who had figured out that Broderick had planned out all the murders?

After a moment, Captain Millbrook said exactly that.

"I don't think we need to be afraid anymore, but we sure as hell do need to find out who has that gun. Security was supposed to be watching your belongings, right?" he asked.

"An officer said that he would and he told us that he had, yes," Wes told him.

"How could I have been so careless," Chloe murmured, distressed.

Wes took her by the shoulders. "My weapon was there, too, Chloe, just covered up by the pocket of the jacket it was in. You're not at fault here. We went in to stop a killer and we did."

She nodded, but she was going to blame herself, he knew. Well, he was the one who had said that their things were safe where they'd left them. The security officers on this ship tended to be good, really good.

But this man had evidently either not paid attention as he had said he would or . . .

Or worse. He was somehow in on something.

"We need to find the officer on duty on the lower deck, find out if—" Wes started to tell Captain Millbrook.

But Millbrook interrupted him. "No! No, no, no, trust me! I've been sailing for well over twenty years, young man, and I am no man's fool! I research every man and woman who works on a vessel when I'm the captain—even if we do have an almost equal number of crew to passengers on this kind of a cruise." He narrowed his eyes for a minute. "Nathan Samuels, that's the young SSO who was on then. Come, his break started thirty minutes ago. He's probably grabbing food in the crew's mess—right behind the casual restaurant with the open deck seating!"

Wes glanced at Chloe, and she shrugged. Millbrook was already walking.

They followed him.

They headed through the outer portion of the restaurant and through the kitchen to the rear where tables were set up separately for the crew.

The security officer, Nathan Samuels, was seated at a table with a book, reading as he consumed his meal.

He either heard or sensed them coming and looked up as they approached his table. He offered them a smile.

He stood, nodding to the captain, saying, "Sir!" Then he turned to Chloe and Wes. "Hey. Good to see you and thank you, once again, for saving the day on the ship! We think of ourselves as competent, but you two were really on top of everything!"

"They're really agents, Nathan," Captain Millbrook told him. "Chloe McMurray is FDLE and Wes Law is with the Feds."

"Oh! Well, now it all makes sense!" Nathan said, nodding. "And you're even more impressive."

Chloe smiled and said, "Thank you for that, and now I have a question. Nathan, there was something missing from my bag. I thought you indicated that you'd watched our belongings the entire time we were in the water."

"I had my eye on them and made sure that no one made off with them. Why?" The young officer appeared to be truly disconcerted. "Was something missing?"

"Yes," Chloe told him.

"No! I'm so sorry, I saw people go by and I said please, just leave those things there where they are. I mean, I did see people walk around the pile . . . and brush by a bit, but there were clothes on top and . . ."

He stopped speaking, looking perplexed.

Unless Nathan had studied with the best of them, he wasn't lying and he was understandably distraught because he believed that he'd watched over their belongings.

"Oh! There was a gentleman who almost tripped over the pile. I saw him straighten it out before walking off," Nathan said.

"What did he look like?" Wes asked the man.

Nathan winced. "I can't tell you hair or eye color and I can't even describe his face. He was wearing a baseball cap pulled low and he had big sunglasses on. Yeah, I know, that could be half of the ship's passengers. But I estimate his height at about six-foot even. He was wearing Bermuda shorts and a short-sleeved cotton shirt, and um . . . someone called out to him. I don't know who, but it gave me the feeling that he wasn't traveling alone. And, yes, I spoke to people—there was a fair amount of concern among the passengers—but I did keep my eye on your things. That's the only incident I can think of when anyone might have gotten into a bag. What did they get?" he asked.

"A gun," Millbrook said flatly.

"A gun?"

"Made of 3D-printed plastic, carried by our agents. Keep your eyes open and do excuse me, I'm putting the private warning through to all security," Millbrook told him, stepping away.

"Oh, God, I am so ashamed and sorry!" Nathan told them.

Chloe shook her head. "No, no, please, you didn't know, and it sounds as if this man thought maybe there was something that he could find. Please, don't worry. You're not at fault. But if you see this man, stop him, chat with him, tell him that . . . that the captain is looking for him with some kind of an invitation and then inform us immediately!"

Wes dug deep into his pocket and found one of the cards that bore the number to his burner cell and the name Wesley Douglas.

"Please," he said, handing it to Nathan.

"Right, absolutely."

Millbrook had made his call to have security on the lookout for the man, warning those who didn't know already that a gun was missing.

"Thank you, Nathan," Chloe told him, and Wes nodded, as well.

"Where do we go from here?" Captain Millbrook asked Wes as they left the crew's dining quarters. "Other than that, as far as I go, I need to get back to the bridge and, as I've said, our security people are good. It's hard on a ship like this—you need people who are vigilant, tough and still capable of making the passengers feel safe and that they're there to give directions rather than police the place. But is all that going to be enough—"

"We'll find whoever has the gun," Wes assured him. He still wasn't sure how the hell they were going to do it, but they wouldn't give up. Of course, before they went any further with anything, he wanted to talk to Alonzo.

Millbrook gave them a nod and left them.

Wes called him back and reminded him, "Sir, not to tell you how to run things, but you need some of your best people—"

"With me, watching over the ship. Got it," Millbrook said.

"Take care, sir," Chloe added.

He gave them a nod and disappeared.

As he did so, they stepped out to the casual dining area on the deck. To his surprise, Wes saw that Edward, Sally and George were at one of the tables.

"Time flies when you make a wild leap into the ocean to try and stop a serial killer?" Chloe murmured.

He looked at her and grimaced. "Might as well make sure they're okay!"

"Well, we know none of them took the gun. They were laid out with medical help on the way down below," Chloe reminded him.

"True. We won't stay long—"

"Long enough for a hot dog, wings, a sandwich . . ."

"Yeah, we should grab some food. I'm surprised to see them—I had no idea that they could shake that drug in a matter of hours," Wes said. "Then again, I'm not a medical man. And now I'm wondering how the hell Amelia learned so much. If she'd had any formal training with medicine or drugs, our people would have caught it."

"I can only say this—if you're determined, you can learn almost anything on the internet. It used to be books, but these days . . . Hot dog! I'll get food, you check in with Edward and company."

He walked toward the table where the three of them stood quickly as he arrived, each giving him a fierce hug in return.

"Again!" Edward said. "You and Chloe . . . you're so amazing."

"Well, as you know by now, we were just doing our jobs," Wes told him. "Not that they aren't jobs that make you really happy when there's a good outcome for a man like you, Edward. But I'm so surprised! I thought you guys would be in your beds, sound asleep and getting over the stuff that was shot into you!"

"We were all in the hospital . . . Doc Kilbride and his people and a few medical folks who happened to be on the cruise were down there, helping, getting everyone all flushed out. I'm not speaking today or anymore on this voyage, but . . . well, we wanted to come out and feel how beautiful life is, how the sun can shine, how one can feel out on the water in the breeze!"

"We're just being grateful for life!" Sally echoed.

Wes smiled and took a seat. Chloe, bearing a tray with hot dogs, fries and a couple of sodas, joined them, only to go through the hugging and thanking phase again.

"Oh!" Sally said suddenly. "I heard that a shot was fired! Or, someone said, it must have just been an engine back-firing, or even a noise from another vessel. Do you know anything about that?" she asked them.

He looked at Chloe. She nodded.

"All right, I'm going to tell you the truth and despite the beauty of the day, I'm going to recommend you all head to a cabin and stay there. Yes, there was a shot," Wes told them. "You know that Chloe and I are agents with two different agencies—"

"They know about me, too," George said quietly. "I told them so that they didn't need to worry about being accosted again. I was armed and will be practicing my agent skills instead of my nursing skills for the rest of the trip."

"Still!" Chloe said, looking at Wes.

"Oh, God, no!" Edward said. "Someone was shooting at you—"

"No. Actually, someone was shooting at Broderick McClintock," Wes told him. "But there is a gun somewhere on the ship."

"My fault. When we dove in to get Broderick—"

"Not your fault. If someone was shooting at Broderick, they're not a danger to us. And it's really too bad that they missed!" Edward said.

"Edward!" Sally said softly, placing her hand on his arm.

Wes lowered his head, glad that Edward hadn't been there when Broderick had been talking all about Amelia's failure to murder Sally.

"George, if you guys want to make us happy—" Wes began.

"Gotcha. Edward, Sally, we're heading to your cabin. No hardship. He has a great suite," George said.

"All right," Wes said. He ate one last french fry. "Chloe—"

"Yep. We're going to wander around the decks and see what we can see and . . . if we can find the gun," she said.

"You'll find it when someone uses it to get a bullet into your chest!" Sally told them, worried.

"I don't think that whoever took the gun wants to hurt anyone else. I think that they were aiming at Broderick," Chloe assured them.

"George, you know how to reach us. Please, just lay low. We'll talk later, and who knows—maybe by tonight we can have a great dinner of appreciation for the fact that the truth is known and a strange and horrible manipulation has been ended," Wes said, rising.

They were about to head away from the table when they heard someone call softly, "Chloe, Wes, wait, please!"

Daniel McClintock was coming toward the table. He truly looked the worst for wear as he approached them, shaking his head, apologizing.

"I had no idea. I didn't know, I swear! I was aways hearing that I didn't work hard enough, that I didn't put in enough effort . . . I had no idea, and even now . . ."

He broke off. There were tears in his eyes. He looked over at Edward, Sally and George. "I'm sorry. I am so, so sorry!"

"Daniel, we know you weren't involved. Chloe saw what they did to you and I found you in the lounge chair," Wes reminded him. "You can't be held responsible."

"But I—I—Broderick is my brother. I should have known. And he . . . Was he going to kill me, too?"

He looked confused, but a moment later, Gina was behind him.

"Daniel! They don't blame you!" she said softly.

"We don't blame you, Daniel," Sally assured him. "We're just glad that you're all right, too!"

"I'm so sorry!" he repeated. He shook his head, as if he couldn't begin to comprehend everything that had happened. "I think . . . I don't know. I mean, I don't know what happened with me, but . . . Celia was in on it! She was married to Jeff, she supposedly loved him, and he . . . he was supposed to get flushed out to sea!"

Chloe rose and walked over to him, smiling at Gina who stood by his side, and set a hand on his free arm. "Daniel, you're going to need some serious therapy. There's no way you get over something like this easily."

"I'm so glad my parents are dead! I never thought I'd say that!" Daniel told them.

"It will take time," Gina said. "But, Daniel, we went through this together. I will be there with you. We will get through this together."

Daniel must have had a fairly heavy dose of the drug because he suddenly seemed to veer to the right and had to grip a chair, even though the waves had died down and the sea had gone calm. It was as if the ocean itself knew that a problem had been solved.

Well, almost solved. They had to find Chloe's 3D-printed weapon.

"I'm sorry—" Daniel began again.

"Daniel, if you're sorry, please, go lie down some more. Take care of yourself!" Wes told him.

"Right, sweetheart, please!" Gina said to him.

Daniel nodded. He tried to smile. "She is incredible, isn't she?" he asked the others. "And thank God! I lost a brother, but I might have gained the love of my life," he added softly, looking at Gina.

"Quite incredible!" Chloe agreed. "Gina—"

"We're going!" Gina said. "Come on."

"She forgave me already for what he did to her!" Daniel whispered.

Then they were gone.

"That poor guy," Edward murmured.

"Yeah," Chloe agreed. "Hardest for him—and Jeff Henderson, I suppose. Has anyone seen him—"

"He was still down in the hospital when we left," Edward said. "I guess she got him extra hard, too."

"Well, life won't be easy for either of them for a while," Wes said. "Chloe?"

"Ready!" Chloe said. "Hopefully, we'll see you at a late last cruise dinner!" she said, then she hooked her arm into Wes's and said, "Let's do this!"

Wes moved quickly, knowing that George would protest in worry again.

"Bottom to top," Chloe suggested.

And so they moved through the decks, looking for men wearing baseball caps.

"You know," Chloe said as they searched, "I thought that if it was one of the McClintocks, it might be Daniel. Angry for always being second fiddle. But . . . he just doesn't feel the need to rule the world."

Wes nodded. "And I was thinking at first that it might have been Jeff Henderson who took your gun—except that he couldn't have because he was on the floor with the rest of you, all ready for disposal."

Chloe shook her head. "This time, I think we need to think vice versa. It's someone Broderick hurt, really hurt. Someone who might be afraid that he won't really face the full force of the law for what he's done."

"I talked to Alonzo. He has every computer geek at our disposal trying to see who on this ship might have a connection to one of our would-be murderers," Wes told her.

She nodded.

They moved from deck to deck. In a way, it was surprising to see the amount of people lounging comfortably on the decks, playing the games, sitting at bars . . . all the things people might normally do on a cruise.

But soon after they'd left the table, Captain Millbrook had come on over the speaker. He started out apologizing profusely, then explaining that they'd discovered they had a trio of wanted people on board and that ship's security and federal and local forces had secured them and all was well. Should anyone need the hospital, it was open to serve their needs from anything they considered serious to a hangnail. He thanked everyone and explained that they were required to return to port, but that each and everyone on board would be offered a free trip in the future. He begged everyone to enjoy their last night at sea.

His speech had been good. Better than that, it had been sincere.

"I give up," Chloe murmured after they'd been walking a long, long time. "I think on this we're dead right—whoever took the gun wanted to kill Broderick. They very nearly did. I think I'd really, really like to clean up now!"

He nodded. They had looked, and looked and looked some more.

And she was right.

"Back to our cabin. And if you're worn out, please—"

She grinned at him. "I'm not that kind of worn out! Just the salt I'm wearing is starting to get itchy!"

"Got an itch, eh?" he teased.

She groaned softly.

They reached their cabin and headed in. Chloe walked to the bedroom to grab clean clothing. Wes dug into his own little closet to get something to wear; they would head back out. They'd go to dinner.

They—like George and every member of the ship's security team—would stay on the lookout for the missing gun until they reached port and could disembark.

He paused, frowning, hearing something like a shuffling sound against their door. He froze for a moment, listening.

Chloe emerged from the bedroom, frowning. She had heard whatever it was, too.

He gave her a nod, indicating she should go to the far side of the door as she opened it.

He pulled out his own 3D-printed weapon, aiming it straight at the door.

He gave her a slight nod. They were ready.

Chloe pushed the door open.

Bryan Jordan stood there. He was holding Chloe's weapon.

But he wasn't aiming it at them. He held it to the side.

"Dad, Dad, please!"

Darlene came running down the hall, throwing an arm around her father.

But Bryan was ready to explain himself.

"I just . . . I found this. I needed to give it back. I'm so sorry, I had no right . . . I just . . . There was something about Chloe today. I knew . . . I knew that she was involved because she said something exactly the way Jane would have said it and . . . something, something just tipped me off, or worried me, and . . . I saw it when I tripped over the bag. I picked it up. I never meant to use it except if she came after me, Darlene . . . or anyone! And then . . . Oh, God, I saw them about to take him away and I don't know what happened to me. I was afraid he'd get his expensive lawyers and get out of it, and Jane is never coming back, never coming back . . ."

The man, always so friendly and dignified, broke into tears.

Wes stepped forward and swiftly took the gun, nodding to Darlene and saying, "Come on in, please, come on in."

She ushered her father on in before her.

Bryan lurched, covering his face, and Chloe led him to the couch to take a seat.

Wes looked at Darlene, arching a brow.

Darlene let out a long breath, tears in her eyes, as well.

"He's talking about Jane, Jane Sewell. He always knew that she didn't kill anyone and commit suicide. She was my dad's adopted sister's daughter. Well, she was never legally adopted so they didn't have the same name, but then Jane's dad died when she was little and we weren't even in the same city, but my dad would make sure to see her, make sure she knew that she was loved and . . . I loved her, too! Please, please, I know he stole your gun, I know that he fired a shot, but . . . please, please don't punish him any worse than her death has punished him already!"

"You knew that something might be off on this cruise?" Wes asked her.

Darlene sighed. "We'd booked this cruise over a year ago. My mom is gone, too, and Dad wanted to do something special for me. And . . . well, now I think that he might have been watching everyone, seeing if anyone messed up and then . . . then you and Chloe went overboard to catch Broderick McClintock and he was backing away and . . . I didn't even realize he had taken it!" she finished desperately.

He was an officer of the law, sworn to justice, Wes knew. But . . .

So far . . .

The man had confessed. No, not really, not in the necessary words. He hadn't stolen the gun; he'd picked it up. It could have been lying on the deck.

And he hadn't said that he'd fired the gun.

Darlene had tried to explain, but that was really all hearsay. And while there were cameras on the ship, they'd already learned how easily they could be rendered worthless—especially by anyone as computer and mechanically savvy as those in this group.

Wes glanced at Chloe.

Justice. They were sworn to justice. But then again, it would be served.

"Bryan! Listen to me," he said strongly. He handed the man the gun back. "Put it down. Put it down in the hallway."

"What?" Bryan asked, his tears soaking his face, but his expression now one of confusion.

"Do what I say, please!"

"Dad!" Darlene implored.

And Bryan Jordan stood and walked to the hallway and set the gun down. Wes picked it up and handed it to Chloe.

She nodded.

"We found it. We found the missing gun in the hallway. All . . . all's well that ends well. And I don't think that you need to worry. Broderick McClintock went off the deep end when we interrogated him today and it's all on record. He will go to prison for life or, God knows, even get the death penalty. But for us, it's over. Do you understand?" he asked, looking from Bryan to Darlene.

"Oh, God! Thank you!"

Bryan Jordan was a big man. His unexpected hug almost sent Wes reeling backward.

He was still sobbing.

"Dad, Dad!" Darlene said softly.

He straightened and nodded.

"Go on, get some rest, and—" Chloe began.

"Therapy, I promise!" Darlene said, and she ushered her dad out of the room.

Wes looked at Chloe, pulling his phone out and putting through a call so that George could inform security they had found the gun, it had fallen in a hallway.

"Was I wrong? Did I just betray everything that we stand for?" he asked Chloe as he finished the call.

She shook her head. "Wes, you know me. If I objected, I would have said something. No, I . . . I think you did the right thing, and in this case, doing the *right* thing mattered most. And then, of course, it's all 'as you wish!'"

She made him smile. She was stunning, brilliant, sensual and . . .

Amazing.

"I'm turning the shower on."

"That's great! That's as I wish!" she told him, smiling.

Soon they were in the shower with the hot steamy water washing over them. And he cupped her face in his hands and he kissed her.

And they kissed. And kissed . . .

And suddenly, she was laughing.

"What?" Wes demanded.

"Ye olde *Princess Bride*," she told him. "Something about

how since the invention of the kiss, there have only been so many that were the most incredible, something like that! But my darling Wes, this one is maybe the most amazing ever!"

And he laughed, too.

But then the kisses began again, and the heat between them rivaled that of the water until they left it behind . . .

They never did make dinner that night.

★★★★★